Also by John Whitbourn from Earthlight

The Royal Changeling
Downs-Lord Dawn

DOWNS-LORD DAY

JOHN WHITBOURN

Panel Two of the Downs-Lord Triptych

SIMON & SCHUSTER
A VIACOM COMPANY

London . New York . Sydney . Tokyo . Singapore . Toronto

First published in Great Britain by Earthlight, 2000
An imprint of Simon & Schuster UK Ltd
A Viacom Company

Simon & Schuster UK Ltd
Africa House
64–78 Kingsway
London WC2B 6AH

Simon & Schuster Australia
Sydney

A CIP catalogue record for this book is available
from the British Library.

1 3 5 7 9 10 8 6 4 2

0-671-03301-8

Typeset in Goudy by SX Composing DTP, Rayleigh, Essex
Printed and bound in the UK by
Omnia Books Ltd, Glasgow

DEDICATION

To: Master Sergeant Ernest G.Bilko/Phil Silvers
(1911-1985)
Gentleman and gentle man and genius

And

John ('*Wilkes and Liberty!*') Wilkes
(1727-1797)
whose time has come again. . . .
'*Give me a grain of truth and I will mix it up with a great mass of
falsehood, so that no chemist shall ever be able to separate them*'

And

to the gorgeous, pouting, staff at Godalming Public Library,
for friendliness and efficiency, 'above and beyond'

'He cast upon them the fierceness of his anger, wrath and indignation, and trouble, by sending evil angels among them.'

Psalm 78. Verse 49.

Thomas Blades, a seventeenth-century curate, discovers a magical door to another world – or rather to an alternate Earth. But here, humanity is not the top of the food chain, as Blades finds when the poor, burrow-dwelling humans he stumbles over are hunted and eaten by the Null – mighty, ravening beasts whose intelligence and killing ability makes them top predator.

Returning to our own world for weapons, Blades fulfils his vow to become humanity's saviour on this new Earth and, over the years, builds an empire of which he becomes the first god-king. Power shifts between humanity and Null but, as the humans grow in sophistication, so comes treachery, jealousy and murder – and god-king Blades changes much from the timid cleric who first happened upon 'New-Wessex'.

Decades later, new enemies appear; worse and more unnatural than the Null, the merciless 'angels' usurp the realm. With faith in his creation already shaken, Blades goes into chastened exile back on Earth and there seeks solace in poverty and repentance.

However, life goes on and in New-Wessex the god-king is sorely missed. To his abandoned and oppressed children, the return of Blades 'Null-Bane' remains their only hope . . .

The Downs-Lord Triptych offers three connected scenes of a baroque Empire in the making, dovetailing to create a portrait of eventful centuries. Here is an exotic saga of transformation and a hymn to the exuberance of unfettered life.

THE PROLOGUE'S PROLOGUE
or
FOREWARNED IS FOREARMED

Theophilus Oglethorpe (1650-1702), soldier, cavalier, Jacobite, duellist, MP, coiner of that truism *'Dead men tell no tales'* and all-round English icon, lived and died in the circumstances described in my *The Royal Changeling* (*Earthlight* 1998). His misplaced – in every sense – memorial looks down upon the interior of St James's, Piccadilly, whilst the dust and bones that bore him were relocated by German high explosive in 1940 so that they gild, even if only at the molecular level, the very air we breathe. Doubtless, the real he is safely in Paradise, looking down upon us now. My mind's open as to whether he's laughing himself sick or just plain sick.

However, back on earth, his family tree marched on to great things; one sprig of it being his second son, confusingly also named Theophilus (1682-?). *His* march took him to Parliament (MP for Haslemere 1708-10) and then exile, to India and China and Sicily – and even stranger places . . .

Turn the page in that same intrepid spirit and you may follow him . . .

The current state of Man (and new Wessex) an assessement made in haste by IVY AMBASSADOR for the illumination and use of HIS IMPERIAL HOLINESS BLADES I (or, the state we are in after four centuries of his absence.

Alba situation unknown

Mannish Humans

Null York
southern limit of raised Null

Null City

New Blakenev Utopia Coastal enclave

Remnant enclaves

Snowdonia enclave

Andean Latifundia Alliance (still extant)

WILD AND WILD NULL

Plain form bastions

PORT

Brecon enclave

Freeport Cae-di

WILD AND WILD NULL

razed coast

London's Ruins

New Godalming

Freeport Dover

Lundy Freehold & Standish princess

Freeport Wadebridge

Freeport Hastings

Pevensey Assurian

WILD AND WILD NULL

The Leona Man (our emblem)

Freeport Teignmouth

Vectis, or the Isle of Wight (Wizards)

To Null France

Kenow enclave

Freeport Mousehole

To Vectis Jersey & Vectis Guernsey

To Sicily and gunpowder

'Pennies for a poor man, sir?'

'Get a job, damn y' eyes!'

And there Captain Theophilus Oglethorpe (jnr.) would have left it, their divergent life-paths intersecting never to cross again. But then he realised the beggar had spoken in English. In Capri, indeed in all eighteenth-century Italy, that was rare enough to command attention. The sparkling blue sea, the crumbling headlong path down to the *piazza* and dinner still beckoned but they could wait. He backtracked.

'Say again, sirrah.'

Joanna, his mistress of the moment, frowned unbecomingly. She did not understand her lover's moderation towards street-scum. A true native of seething Naples, she no longer even saw them.

Conversely, Oglethorpe deplored that lack of charity, waving her on with his swordstick. In his English-naive opinion, seventeen-year-olds should retain some of the innocence of youth. Fine legs and skilful lips wouldn't save her from displacement if she didn't sweeten soon. Her sister was poised, waiting in the wings. *Her* tongue could tie a knot in a cherry stalk: he'd seen her do it.

'Come, come, my man. I heard you plain. Speak English once more.'

The appalling figure considered the request. He was not as humble as a broken oldster by the wayside ought to be. His grime and rags and wrinkles should have engendered servility. Finally, the toothless mouth cracked.

'Very well. How do you do, sir? Could you possibly spare a coin or two?'

1

Theophilus was so amazed that a hand was on its way to his pocketbook before he knew it. Just to hear the exquisite mother tongue spoken so far from home deserved reward alone – but to encounter its cultured version was veritable rain in the desert.

'Here.' He showered *piastres* and pennies mixed, down into the proffered hat. Thanks were nodded but not spoken.

Oglethorpe stirred the dust with his stick. Motes rose briefly, glorified to significance by the Caprisi sun.

'And so, my man, how came you here – and why?'

It was the least of requests. He was willing to waste a minute or two – and tighten the pout on Joanna's face. There might be a story therein to sprinkle zest on the waiting flagons of wine. It didn't arrive.

'I might ask you the same question,' came the sole reply.

Back home, the Oglethorpes were renowned for their tempers, for duels and falls from grace. It was through just such, and Jacobite opinions spoken boldly without thought for cost, that Theophilus now trod the path of exile, from Surrey home to France and then China and Sicily – and finally sybarite Capri. The easy south had relaxed him somewhat. He'd acquired a patina of the Mediterranean life-cycle outlook, learnt the easy-going resigned shrug, and draped both over the sharp *get-things-done* angles of an Anglo-Saxon upbringing. People liked him better, even as they became wary of his new charm. To themselves the locals recalled a medieval proverb: *'Inglese Italianato è un Diavolo incarnato'* – *'An Italianised Englishman is a Devil incarnate'*.

Now, his native nature reasserted itself, a unsuspected sea-monster rearing from the suave waters. Oglethorpe's whole universe telescoped down until it was exclusively outrage.

Joanna came hurtling back, a silk centre to a dust storm. She didn't want to lose this fountain of generosity just yet. Murder was still murder – even on Capri.

Her shapely boot connected with the beggar.

'Speak, dog. Answer the *Inglese* Lord!'

That did the trick, proving her tough wisdom nicely. The

2

old man was broken: abject. He'd learnt *her* language right enough.

He looked up into Oglethorpe's face, silently surrendering his story. He was read: he was understood. His eyes held all the sadness there ever was.

Theophilus had seen the like before. In Canton he'd observed a forger boiled alive. Before the cauldron even grew tepid the felon had peered out upon the world like that. The Englishman had hoped to reach life's end without witnessing it again.

'Actually, I'm not sure I want to h . . .' Oglethorpe's words were involuntary, instinct overridden and foreign to his nature. Accordingly, Joanna didn't recognise or acknowledge his fear. She booted again – and the deed was done. Speech poured forth: there was no point in protest, no lid to fit the box.

The consoling fragrance of the wayside flowers was lost: overshadowed; the sun shone less bright. Theophilus steeled himself.

'I have fallen far,' said the beggar, humbly; fearful of another blow – from any direction. 'I am the first of a long line of kings . . .'

Oglethorpe frowned – thinking he might as well get in that mode.

'The *last* in the line, surely?' he corrected.

For an instant there was backbone in the beggar, but it was fleeting, like a stillbirth's soul. Whilst it still lived he spoke.

'What I have *said*, I have *said*,' he told them firmly.

Hunter found God in the woods.

God was strolling in the cool of the day – which clinched the matter. Hunter knew the Almighty was partial to that habit – he recalled it from sabbaths in the stockade, when the elders read from the *Blades-Bible*.

Anything else in the thought line came later. At the time, all Hunter's powers were devoted to not fainting away. Here was an irony of ironies. He'd abandoned 'civilisation' to search for God – and now baulked at being crowned with success. Self-limited and desiccated down to the merely spiritual, his ambitions had never included an encounter face to face!

Afterwards, recalling that first reaction, Hunter would go pale and his weathered brow stud with sweat. He'd judged the chance-found figure just another bit of *Wild*-life and, of course, drew aim upon it. Afterwards, elders of the tribe assured him that was natural and that pardon was assured. After all, human-shapes met in the Wild were often only *seeming*-men and actually monsters in disguise – or else Imperials out for some purpose of their own. It was easier to just loose your bow and make identification after. So long as it wasn't Free-kin that was all right, even for staunch believers and non-harmers; even for Christians. In the Wild there was special dispensation. Turn the other cheek if you must, but first ensure you kept a cheek – and face and guts – to turn with.

In his head Hunter knew they spoke true but his heart walked a rockier way. In nights to come, memory had the power to wake him in the early hours, bolt-upright and silent-screaming.

Hunter had drawn aim with the arrowhead he'd intended for the first deer to cross his path, the *great-barb* that sundered tough hide and ruined resilient beast muscle. Deployed against human heads it would hit like a rockfall, exploding a skull as though it were a rotten apple. No wounds or cries: a perfect Wild kill.

It was the sheer thought. The possibility. He'd drawn a bead on the carefree stroller, had rested his arm on a bough, lining up a clear path to the unsuspecting victim. Of course, in reality, *He* must have known full well; *He* was never in any real danger – but that was poor excuse.

Then, just at the last and right moment (also naturally, because *He* was God), the visitor turned and looked at Hunter and knew all there was to know about him. That bag of sorrows saddened the divine face but sponsored no other reaction. *He* understood all – and thus forgave all.

Then the figure turned and walked on, displaying a complete trust that piled burning coals on Hunter's head. He was shamed into awe. A back was offered to the unmissable shot. From that range Hunter had pinned men deep into trees.

A tear tracked down Hunter's face, coursing over gullies and dead riverbeds worn by his history. He was riven by his unworthiness for such trust. In truth it wasn't *his* faith that had brought him out here beyond everything, but his wives' creed: that and the stubborn refusal to surrender them to an Imperial cross. He just wasn't a good enough man to merit any of this.

Hunter had fallen to his knees, without intending, without awareness of it. Only fear of losing God a second time brought him back to reality and his feet. The vision was moving away, unhurried but still fleeting. Suddenly, Hunter was galvanised with energy. By birth he'd partaken in a bitter communion, the unhealing wound that was mankind's loss of the divine amongst them. That separation had lasted four agonising centuries. Hunter wasn't going to let any chance of reunion slip away.

So he tracked him, as only he could, without a sound to further trouble that head or cause it to turn. As he went, threading his way over, round and through the twisted trees, he phrased simple but heartfelt thanks that he, he of *all* men, should be blessed with this window of opportunity.

Then God came to his own window. With one last wistful look back, he entered in and was gone. God-king Blades had left through the shimmering gate back home to Paradise.

Hunter howled at the leaf canopy, for the first time in his life careless of what hungry Wild-life the noise might summon. He would have broken the sacrilegious bow over his knee, were it not defender-feeder of the tribe as well as himself.

He was blessed only to be cursed. Life was cruel and taunting when it imposed not only loss but repeated loss, a wound opened in the same place time and again.

But then he realised they were not left totally forlorn. Unnatural light still shone in the deserted clearing. He raised his eyes to it, half-fearful, half-rejoicing. Experience led him to expect it would burst like the bubble of his hope – but it did not. It remained solid looking, a stable edifice opening into. . . . somewhere else.

Then he realised. As before, as ever, god-king Blades was showing them the way. That 'window of opportunity' was left open.

There was general disbelief till others went to the scene. The visitation was repeated for their benefit. Blades once again allowed his visage to shine upon them, before departing a second time. They watched it on their knees, cavern-mouthed, oblivious. A family of red deer ambled by without coming to harm, a feast rendered invisible by even greater joys.

In the stockade the elders listened and learnt and authorised opening of the *Book*. It was brought forth with ceremony, cradled in the trophy ribcage of a giant Wild monstrosity. Then the headman was doused in pure rainwater and repented his sins in front of the assembled people before he dared so much as to lift the cover. Gauntlets of flayed Null-skin stood between him and contamination of any page; a bone from his worst enemy served as pointer to the words he sought.

The lesser matter first. It was hardly in doubt but worth making the point that all was foretold. A valuable lesson for later.

'From the book of Genesis,' he read to them, 'chapter 3, verse 8: "*And they heard the voice of the Lord God walking in the garden in the cool of the day*".'

So there it was. The Deity had done it before. *That* day he had come to reprove and punish, the day that Adam fell short. Now, just perhaps, He arrived to lift the curse and reopen Eden.

Then the final hurdle. The age they lived in birthed black miracles as well as the more normal sort. There was need for verification.

The headman turned to the frontispiece and the engraved plate facing it. Every Blades-Bible contained the image of its creator.

Hunter stepped up as bidden, his first time upon the dais, and when he looked his face was all the answer any needed. That was as well, for words would not come. Hunter's throat was choked along with his soul. He'd always *believed*, after a fashion, when not distracted or embittered by the trouble and misfortunes of this world, but never in his wildest dreams had he thought to encounter fully answered prayers or the promised *return*. He had to be led away to rest and consider.

Then the others who'd seen came up and one by one confirmed it. What they'd seen was *He*.

The headman raised skinny arms to the sky and what lay beyond it. As soon as he'd become too old to hunt or fight he'd been inspired to make himself useful by memorising great stretches of the Holy Book. Now he saw why. An appropriate passage hurtled through his mind.

' "*Lord, now lettest thou thy servant depart in peace, according to thy word;*

For mine eyes have seen thy salvation . . ." '

As chance – or something – would have it, he died the next day, barely troubling himself with further words, slipping into final sleep, happy and easy as a child. Those who remained saw yet another sign.

The one thing he did say before he went was that they

should end their long silence, the sullen separation from the rest of man. *Babylon* must be told, the seed sown – and cast promiscuously. Some pearls might land before swine, true, but surely there was still fertile soil out there. It had to be done. Here was news so good that it needed shouting from the rooftops.

The only difficulty lay in getting on to the relevant roof alive.

They decided to send six delegates (though they could ill-afford to spare them), six separate ways through the *Wild*. Such generosity ought to ensure at least one would make it.

The stockade looked sparse when they were gone, the loss of so many young warriors a dangerous depletion given the hunger that existed just outside the stockade, ravenous to come in and feed. Yet, in another sense, the tiny human enclave was reinforced, even after the party was gone, slipping over the defences at first light when the worst of the Wild slunk home to sleep it off. Hope now filled out their thinned ranks, making a few seem like many. Good news has that sorcerous power.

Solomon-Weaver and Cromwell-the-Spear were eaten by Null before they went ten miles. Salome-Soldier was sucked to a husk by a spider the size of a sheep, snugly web-wrapped during the leisurely process. Thus ended the first day of journeying.

The survivors lasted a little longer, for a yet further bout of travelling. The Wild had began – just perceptibly – to thin when Shakespeare-Deflowerer tumbled into a pitfall dug by another tribe of misfits, and died on the cack-smeared spears within – eventually – after calling out for hours for anyone, '*in the name of a merciful God*', to help him. No one save salivating scavengers heard. That concluded day two.

By dawn of the third, only Grimes-Flintknapper and Hunter were left to win through the Wild. The former could even be said to have made it. He emerged, clad in sweat and rags, by the far bank at New-Kingston-upon-Thames. Falling at the feet of the bridge guards, he babbled out the vital message. However, they'd never known anything good come from the Wild and so shot him without listening.

Only Hunter, seemingly the chosen one, penetrated the green fields and normality of New-Wessex. Whereas Grimes-Flintknapper was Wild-born, Hunter had arrived there fully formed. He'd already suffered at the hands of the orthodox and so trusted less, and this saved his life from intolerant border folk. Patiently waiting for dusk, he slipped by the guardians of Epsom Downs, infiltrating through the fortified yards where horses, more valuable than thousands such as he, lived pampered lives.

Past there he scampered down the green slopes and into the heartlands, sleeping by day in huts and isolated dwellings he found empty. At night, where, in the Wild, wide-eyed vigilance was the bare requirement of survival, he travelled on quite unhindered, stopping to take what he needed. It was not in his nature to filch from working-men's larders, but he was under a dispensation. The elders had said he was upon a crusade for all and had *all* but known it they would have freely thrust largesse upon him. It was therefore no sin to harvest a little advance gratitude. Hunter understood the principle and sang it as a lullaby to his conscience. At the same time, he doubted it would be legal tender in New-Wessex just yet and so kept out of sight. A few tethered field-slaves saw him go but they were not likely to report anything to their masters. They watched, dulled eyed and envious, and failed to raise the alarm.

Truly, this was a *fat* place, Hunter reflected, as he feasted on loving-wife-packed rations liberated from a peddler who'd wake from his nap refreshed but lunchless. Here was ample eating and the chance to do things two-handed, without a weapon perpetually gripped. Here, the Wild only intruded as aberration. With the filter of the Fruntierfolke and rougher sorts at the fringes, Hunter would have bet his bow this deep interior was barely troubled at all. How marvellous, he thought – and yet at the same time sedating – that must be. Hunter didn't know whether to envy or pity them their poor grasp of reality. What a shame it was that good men could only live outside of here. Now, *there* was a quandary and choice to leech joy out of everything. Freedom and a short Wild-life, or else plenty in servitude? Why did it always have to be either/or?

Then Hunter remembered the contents of his head and how extra precious it now was for holding the wonderful tidings. When others knew, or others bar a mere select band in the Wild, then just maybe it would change cases. Humanity deserved a new deal – or even the old one, if fairly applied.

God had returned to them, showing He had no favourites after all, and that there was no one He cursed without end. His foot was coming off their necks and mankind would rise again when He did. Just the notion put a spring in Hunter's steps.

He only broke cover when in plain sight of the Castle. The high walls and red roofs of New-Godalming were vast and lovely in the light of a new day, but rising above them all was his objective – which was a metaphor, when you thought about it, if you chose to see.

Once upon a time everywhere was like this: fair cities surrounded by civilisation. Those of good intent had no need to approach them in fear and trembling, by night and on their bellies. Now, in present decadence, although the bearer of great gifts, Hunter had to sneak in courtesy of an unknowing accomplice. The haywain's driver interpreted Hunter's boarding as an encounter with a rut; an all too plausible explanation, saving him the trouble of looking round. Since of late there was less motivation to go round repairing or do anything energetic, the roads of Humandom teemed with pits and sloughs even here, right at the heart of things.

Hunter waited until the 'third circle' and the noble abodes to jump ship, ignoring the carter's surprised cries and the passive gaze of the citizenry. He need not have worried overmuch, even as he hared away like a hound on fire. An age of everyday miracles had made them incurious. It was unlikely anyone would give chase in pursuit of novelty. He wasn't Null or monstrous and that low minimum now sufficed.

The Castle gate-men had more exacting standards. Hunter was stopped, stunned and bound before more than a few words could pour out of him.

"'*Resurgam!*'" he told them, until a descending mace brought peace. 'It's the truth!'

The servants of the god-king had a high regard for truth – more than wages it was the reason they served and believed. They also recognised the promise at the very end of the Blades-Bible. Clearly under divine guidance, Hunter had said just the right words not to earn short shrift and a stiletto to his sleeping form. He'd raised a crop of curiosity.

So, he was taken away for harvesting and questioning – under torture, naturally; just to be sure.

It's only natural to protest when being eaten. Yet the slave tried to stifle his screams as long as he might. Only silent tears met the first few mouthfuls.

Guy Ambassador itched to intervene.

'Now, now . . .' said the angel.

He, she or it smiled at the Ambassador, warning him. Such sights were something humanity should be used to by now. It was four centuries since success deserted them: four centuries of humiliation offering ample opportunity to adapt. That particular nerve ending ought to have long since gone dead.

Till then the Ambassador thought his had. Or perhaps a protective scab had worked loose because he was leaving. He re-commanded his face to its normal mask.

'Be friends . . .' It was both angelic instruction and warning: a spoilt child imposing peace upon pet cat and dog.

Obedient, the Ambassador drew near the Null-King, feigning sadness at imminent parting. He had to transcend the feast, that obvious show for his benefit. Normally, the Null dined in far more wild style.

His shoes splattered through discarded pieces. He imagined a stick jammed across his mouth to fabricate a smile. He told himself he never, ever, stuttered.

No one was deceived. The monster extended his ham-like arm, languidly pointing one talon in the Ambassador's direction. What he really wished to do was use it, as the Creator had intended it to be used; to slash human flesh, to strip off succulent slices. His barbed cock rose like a pennon in daydreaming of it. Yet he too was under command. He dared not follow his true nature whilst under angelic supervision.

The Ambassador applied shrinking lips to the claw in homage. It tasted of blood and cloves.

'I must leave now, exalted one: under p-p-protest, answering only the sternest of homecoming commands. Rest assured, majesty, I shall pine for your presence all the while, and hunger and thirst for the d-day of my return to your delicious Empire of Feeding.'

Null declined to learn man-speech on grounds of dignity and taste. Instead, the words were conveyed into Null by one of the throng of human interpreters: semi-naked wretches shamingly eager for the ear of their master. A babble of silky, chiming tones that mangled a human throat, try as they might. Too octave-ascending, too . . . ravenous for true rendering.

The Null could not be bothered to conceal their hatred and hunger conjoined, not from lowest Null cub to this King of Mothers himself. His yellow, almond-eyes glowed only the fiercer for the honeyed words, simply nodding a sleek purple head in acknowledgement. Any deeper intercourse with humanity was demeaning.

Yet the angels stipulated courtliness between them, when there was not – staged – war. And what they wanted they got and had done for centuries past.

'So, sublimity, I must take my leave: until we meet again for the better understanding of our brethren races.'

Unscripted, unlike the last consumption, one of the great, prone, Null mothers on whom the King reposed, began to toy with an interpreter, a spectre of appetite rousing her from customary indolence. Normally they remained secluded, objects of veneration and mystery. Yet today was a special day and a batch litter-borne here in the Ambassador's honour. He tried – and failed – to bear that in mind.

Her vestigial arms kneaded the interpreter's legs; she slithered her great bulk forward slightly to apply bulbous lips. He too was Null-bred to unquestioning servility but at this stage nature took over. He wailed his fear and protest against consumption.

The King heard and saw. If there was one thing consistent in their behaviour it was tender solicitude to the mother class. Straightaway, he ordered other Null to assist her inadequate maw.

Guy noted that the man stood to await doom, even as his

face dissolved into rebellion. There had to be lessons learnt, advantages to be wrung, even from such excesses, or else it was waste. Guy obliged himself to observe. And besides, the monster King had not dismissed him yet.

Claws arced to die in juddering halt; white teeth joined, heaving resistant sinew away. Here was expert butchery, fruit of practise since dawn-time. The shrieking meal was soon silenced and passed, morsel by morsel, to the blubber mound on the floor. She dined noisily.

The angel's eyes were wide, her mouth likewise. From far away laughter emerged – perhaps her own, strangely distanced, or maybe from remote viewers of her kind. One was the same as all amongst that breed as far as mankind knew.

A blood spray flew the Ambassador's way. He dutifully forbore to notice it or any other private Null arrangement. What they did with their slaves-cum-larder was their own business: he told himself that a hundred times a day. If the remaining Null-humans could overlook then so should he, emulating their example in that if nothing else.

The great purple King snapped back to his official visitor in the fluid manner of his race which was so alarming. Everything they did had their entire focus until the next thing – with barely an intervening second.

The royal arm was again flicked in his direction. He was free to go, to cease polluting the throne cavity.

Guy Ambassador bowed low, first to the King, then to each of the mothers whose face was visible amidst the pile. Then he left that den and perpetual abode, walking backwards. A door curtain – quilted human skin – was parted for him. The obliging Null warrior exuded warmth and scorn as he was passed.

Guy's last view was of the angel in conversation. She slid her perfect feet in human gore whilst whispering in the King's ear.

Every ramp and passage out to the light was a well-packed womb of Null, sprawled lazily in grooming or half-hearted sodomy. They crowded close as could be to the mothers, just as in the sleep piles of the former days – before the angels put notions in their heads. The old urge still persisted.

Like an intruder into a dry orifice, the passage clear was not made easy. Grudgingly, they made way for the one wild human tolerated in Paris but were free and expressive with their feelings. By the time Guy gained the day and air, he was adorned with drool.

'We go!'

Bathie clapped her hands and a rare smile applied a flame to beauty that normally slumbered. His wife had been waiting for him, a dark head at one of the apertures in their crazed dwelling; already and easily packed. She'd few enough possessions save her hereditary crimson gowns. Guy Ambassador was likewise built for speed. He'd brought little to Null-France and was departing with less. Shed illusions outweighed gained experience. It was the work of mere moments to throw a few things into a trunk and then be poised, ready to ascend out of nightmare.

Nothing was straight here, no angle true. Every room, walkway and larder in the Null city offended the regularising eye. They built like their thoughts, full of abrupt changes of direction, sharp and cutting as a fang but without guiding reason.

The human dwellings had been tacked onto the main thrust of Null-Paris, another lunatic protrusion high above the ground with no support but hope, a growth upon the body sicked up under protest. They saw fit that its rooms should be wormed into only after a weariness of narrow, knife-edge passages, penetrating a zone of enigmatic spaces, barred ways and dead-ends. There were larders there also, pre-existing or rapidly relocated, and thus screams at unpredictable hours.

Bathie took it better than he, though she spent longer in the fetid burrow. Whilst he was out on his business – wretched though that could be – it was she who was there to hear the scratchings behind the walls, to hear the lightning strikes of agony and despair from just rooms away. Her world was just the twists and turns of that tiny reservation; up to there the Null guard assured immunity – but no further. Guy hardly wondered at the increment in her strangeness when he returned from his days of abasement. Whilst he endlessly shuffled a pack of cards and purged his memories away, she sat and stared at the un-true partitions, as though seeking to pierce them with just a burning gaze. Just beyond there might be serried Null youth, scenting, salivating, at the aroma of meat seeping through, or maybe, meat-to-be, patient, bred to silence, pinned to the wall with Judas-manacles imported from home.

They never discovered. It was never revealed. All she had was the noises and her imaginings. People said the last was worse than reality – but not in Null-land. Mere imagination was unequal to the full horror, was merciful ignorance. There was that small comfort. Left on her own she had nothing to do but picture it: herself the one clean cell set amidst a cancer – long and bad days for a seventeen-year-old girl. Snaky outside darkness entered into Bathie's thoughts to mate with her own native variant. Guy stamped on the ensuing offspring at birth, successfully so far, but knew it was a matter of time. One day a monster-birth would escape and grow to adulthood and he feared that more than their surroundings.

Null-human servants were provided them, ever changing but all the same. In their averted eyes and nakedness they tended to a muchness. One told them apart by their missing limbs and mutilations – fingers missing here, an eye gone there: either punishments or snacks taken on the hoof. Sight of them sprinkled anti-savour on the food and fresh laundry they carried.

On this final day, the survivor of a scalping had brought a piping hot-pot and proper metal spoons – an unusual, signal honour. The couple were hungry but looked askance at the mystery-meat amidst the bobbing vegetables. It might have been pork; it might not. The Null had a sense of humour and no carnivore meal from them could be trusted. Not for the first time, stomachs had to be deceived with slave-baked bread – and Guy wouldn't put it past them to grate human even into that.

Belatedly discovering the betrayal, their guts growled discontent all the way to the English Channel.

Under angelic prompting, the Null could be considerate hosts. From somewhere they'd obtained a coach and four, plus a clothed slave-chauffeur to drive. That job presumably represented thirty pieces of silver for one of their luckiest trusty-humans, a marvellous exemption granted until he got frail or was ousted by someone even more shameless. Then it was the larders for him. No more going dry-shod or covering his parts with a loincloth on that day. Guy Ambassador had no sympathy.

Guy had been excluded from the company of the worst collaborators; those favoured few allowed to dress and command. If he sought them then 'his safety could not be guaranteed', as their mouthpieces repeated like mindless birdsong, and so he'd had to forgo the pleasure. Given that even his allotted Null bodyguards dribbled on him, when hunger pangs struck or their streamlined minds wandered, Guy was wise to stay within bounds. Stripped of regal protection amongst the Null crowd-like orgies that packed Paris, he would be jointed redness within minutes.

That suited the King-of-Mothers well. Intelligence reigned sufficiently in that head to see the danger of Guy mixing promiscuously, spreading new notions and subversion amongst previously compliant *meat*. Therefore their higher lickspittles were kept well away from him and he from them. And so that was another aspect of the Ambassador's brief from New-Wessex thwarted.

The other coachmen were the more usual sort: mute, de-tongued probably, as a lesson or to give some monster a titbit;

17

naked and frightened since birth. Even the horses were fixedly-skittish. A keen appraiser of horse-flesh, albeit purely for racing purposes, Guy saw the healed claw-rakes down their flanks, the signs of slices taken and then regrown. No gallops for these creatures, no glad morning runs or Derby triumphs. They trembled when it was not cold; their spirits were broken.

It was vital to recall that, city or no, the Null were as much animals as the beasts hauling this conveyance, he reminded himself. They were slaves of the impulse, reluctant postponers or investors-in-patience. A horse was not servant or contrivance to them but mere severe temptation. The Ambassador was determined to learn right up till he spat goodbye to here forever.

Their protectors maintained a corridor of almost-safety for them. The low throat-growl that everywhere accompanied him sang them to their carriage. Their appointed guards were larger than the normal variety of the breed, and perhaps captains amongst them, a foot above their lesser brethren, two above their charges.

Even so, the throng pressed close, to see and scent and express disapproval. The scent of cloves and desire became overwhelming. Bathie sneezed repeatedly and the outer Null chimed joy. They did not understand human responses but embraced anything that might be distress. Beyond the age-old hunger, the great hatred ran deeper still. It had worn a chasm, a rut that would hold the wheel of relations between them for ever and ever.

'Where are our brothers?' they were asking. 'Where the companions of the sleeping pile? Where the mothers across the water? What, why, where? What have you done with them?'

They hadn't the words, or inclination to acquire them, but Guy the Ambassador read it all the same in those flat, purple faces. Leper-yellow eyes, all aglow, expressed it as good as English.

The carriage seats had bloodstains on the upholstery. Old but not that old. Shift your backside as you would there was no avoiding them. Or the backsides of the coachmen in front.

18

They confronted the jostled, stricken couple like a final message. You might put on airs and graces and clothes they implied, but, underneath, all you are is pink *meat*.

A whip was cracked, over horse-flesh for once, and they were away, abandoning the crumpled pyramid that was Paris. Neither Guy or Bathie looked back, even though the alternative was Null or hairy arse. They took no happy memories with them, no pleasures tied to what the god-kings assured them was once Paris, 'the City of Light'. Doubtless, the Null had their own name for it but no one had troubled to divulge it. It was unlikely human vocal chords were equal to recognisable translation in any case. Guy preferred the good old New-Wessex naming, symbol of what had been and might be again.

Null guardians kept pace to either side, easily the match of cantering horses, a fluid lope that ate up miles without sweat or effort. The pursuing mob were thus kept from closing in to dine. If they had, maybe an angel would have intervened, maybe not. They were capricious and, to be fair, distracted masters. They couldn't be everywhere at once – which was another consoling thing Guy Ambassador had learnt. All the same, the possibility couldn't be ruled out. Soon enough Null-Paris would be out of sight and the great Null-King's protection distant: maybe even withdrawn.

If things did turn that way then Guy had his plans already laid. The forbidden revolver was an extra virile member in his crutch. Four shells for the monsters, then one apiece for him and Bathie. Likewise the flimsy but wondrous letter from home, source of a sparkling star of hope amidst this Null-night. It would be eaten before he was.

There was nothing much to see in Null-France, and nothing at all of cheer. Scripture described a great human culture there once – they had it from the mouth of the first god-king himself, Blades the Progenitor, *Null-bane* – but the text was

19

obscure, possibly referring to this world, possibly his own. Sometimes he'd admixed the two, for reasons best known to himself; reasons Guy would rather die than doubt.

Yet, all the way there and, now, all the way back, the Ambassador looked most attentively for any signs of 'Le Roi Soleil' and his works, but there were none, not that he could discern. Wayside lumps and bumps that might have been remnants of human achievement, or leaning ivy-strangled might-be trees or towers, would require an antiquarian to interpret and, given there was only a heart-breaking tale to tell, that profession was thin on the ground in modern New-Wessex. The matter remained obscure but Guy did not repine. Whatever might have been was now long gone and didn't bear thinking about. Scattered summer wild-flowers were taken instead as some small consolation. They allowed Guy to argue that Mother Nature set her face against *total* horror.

All the same, the principal landscape features were waste-land and fire-cleared hunting grounds; the only higher life in it potential Null food or its slave shepherds, plus the occasional late unfurling Null sleep-pile. These unravelled like maggots at the sound of the carriage and came over to inspect the novelty breakfast.

Each time the would-be predators were warned off by their guardians, meeting dismissive chimes that brooked no dissent. Happily, the unincorporated and traditionalist Null seemed predisposed to defer to their evolved brethren, one tendency defecting in trickles to the other but not the converse. The city-breed had angelic prestige and received whispers in their pointed ears. Pragmatic as ever, Nature-compliant, the old made way for the new.

The sole free humans in Null-France were glad of it and dulled their eyes. Bathie was already gone, her black painted claws clenched in a merciful doze, saturnine face relaxed back to the frontier of childhood. Guy forced himself to stay awake, ever observant even as he screened out the worst of repetition. Those two things most precious to him in all the world, love

20

and faith, were nearby, meriting every vigilance. Guy the Ambassador hugged both Bathie and the letter to himself, all the way to the coast.

'Sir Guy Ambassador,' announced the huscarl, at the tower door. 'Lady Bathesheba Fruntierfolke.'

Out here, beyond everything, New-Wessex put on a show for no one, making the heartache of being there all the worse. The very best of Imperial etiquette was strictly enforced. Alighting from the carriage, the couple had to pretend they were not observed or recognised by their host until formally introduced. Nor might they be addressed over the gargoyles from atop the ornate walls. Only now could he hasten to them.

'Thank Blades. Thank Blades!'

Sir Samuel Musket, Castellan of Dieppe, embraced the two. Bathie shook free of it and him and shot a sulky glance. Her husband understood full well. The two had history. At the honour banquet on their way out, enraged by ale and loneliness, hands had lingered overlong on the scarlet cloth; employing a modicum of lift and grip. Guy forgave, had almost forgotten. It wasn't a duelling matter. For his wife, however, it touched on more delicate areas than just her behind. It was partly his fault. Guy understood that too.

At least Musket had the decency to be embarrassed. He withdrew, red-faced as her gown.

'Yes, well, anyway, welcome, welcome . . .'

And they were. The Dieppe citadel, New-Wessex's permitted toehold back in its old Empire, saw precious few visitors, and almost all those from the seaward side: supply ships and relief garrisons. Save for today, only evil came from the south. Other than for angelic whim they wouldn't be there at all. For their own reasons, they required diplomacy between former predator and rebellious preyed-upon. Its accoutrements therefore had their protection, but that was all. Even they couldn't enforce cordiality.

21

Thus, though the 'Long Man' pennons flew brave over its garish turrets and brass cannon protruded below, they weren't fooling anyone. Two-leg pink *meat* set foot here on sufferance and oughtn't to forget it. Sometimes the Null brought their still shuddering meals right up to the walls to make the point.

Today, the Parisian escort lingered in insolence, studying this tiny canker of vermin down their snub noses. Then some took each other, in full view and chiming joy, whilst another strode up and pissed luxuriantly, a high arc reflecting bright sunshine, against the painted stone. An insult of no particular occasion or cause – just a regular marking of cards.

Inured, the sentinels didn't even heft their guns. It was business as usual; spectators not soldiers. The Castellan drew his guests and everyone away out of sight.

Show over, the Null withdrew, from the scene and from each other. The carriage was set on its way with a deep raking claw down one horse's flank. It rocketed away from consumption, drawing all after it, the coachmen wrestling for control, a fizz of red in its wake.

The presiding Null licked its hand clean of horse juice and waved farewell to the human nest. No one acknowledged him but he knew humans, knew the way and taste of them. He was seen all right.

By synchronous and collective decision they turned and were away. But they would be back – when they wanted – and no one could object.

Dinner in the Great Hall of Dieppe: an echoing vault under-utilised by three diners plus guards. No matter how hard flunkies stoked the log blaze its comfort faltered short of the far walls. Murals on them showing the greatest triumphs of humanity tried to cooperate, combating the cold by their warmth of colour, alas with less success than in the scenes depicted. One in particular, of Emperor Blades (his face left a pious void according to the iconoclastic dogma of a previous age) at that first and sweetest of victories, the 'Battle of the Barrow-of-Those-Before', was positively aglow with violent greens and reds. It was a rare surviving work of the incomparable Earl Kevo Palette-Jenkins, court painter to three early god-kings, and thus prized evidence of pre-angel achievement. Guy's eyes focused on it in adoration before his wandering attention was dragged away. Sir Samuel had said something.

'The Levellers censor our post, I'm convinced of it. We hear only what they choose.'

It was a reasonable supposition. New-Wessex's only life-line to the sea lay through those ancestral enemies who could be relied upon to take advantage. Imperials wrestled with Levellers – it was the way of things, two chalk-and-cheese world views; nothing to remark upon or be surprised about. Given his abode, Musket oughtn't to have lacked for more serious sources of outrage. The struggle had gone on for centuries, sometimes hot, sometimes not. Resolution – and then revenge – would come one day, when the divine will willed. Ever obedient to it, Guy was happy to wait. His letter had got through at any rate and that was all that mattered for the moment.

He corrected himself. The other thing that mattered sat across the broad table from him. He checked she was all right. It was difficult to tell with Bathie: she was intense about all, good or ill.

What a relief it was to bite into meat without reservation. Bathie's full lips were parting wide to apply pearly white to the grilled chops. Guy looked and was stirred, despite himself. He'd have thought a season with the Null would finish her with flesh-eating for good, but no. Stripping away each band of crisped fat, she wiggled her head to wrestle it free and then gobbled all down like a bird with a worm. Her black mass of hair tossed back with each swallow, emphasising the abandonment. He did not mind. Guy the Ambassador felt sure his relish was equally plain to any observer.

He smiled at her and above her meal Bathie's opal eyes

23

flashed at his. No message there, other than devotion, subtracted from by unassailable reserve. Their gazes disengaged, abashed. The temporary, arms-raised, body-arched, tightness of her liquefying gown was suddenly matched by his own constriction, lower located; a stiffening fighting for space against gun and missive. It was no shame, just another skirmish in an old battle. He slapped the inappropriate response down. Chat would help, any distraction that could come swiftly.

'Levellers? Censorship? I don't doubt it, Musket. But this is a different case. They'd not withhold anything vital. We're all humans together, when all's said and done. In this age believers ally with atheists, each party holding their nose. Even Levellers hate Null and angels . . .'

Sir Samuel looked round in unease, the massed candlelight from luxuriant iron trees caressing his swivelling head.

'Ambassador!'

Guy's long fingers mimicked an imaginary calming spell over the Castellan's distress.

'We're alone,' he reassured Musket, in the same melted-honey tones as he had poured over the Null-King's growls, 'never fear.'

Nevertheless, the Castellan checked again. Over their heads the decorative banners of myriad clans and noble houses of humanity, each protruding from a brass monster visage, moved with nothing more than the breath of the blazing fire. They were alone save for the statue-like huscarls.

Guy excused and sympathised with the poor, frazzled, randy man. Especially the last. He saw the evidence of his war against pointlessness in the new outer earthworks slowly taking shape round the castle. Doubtless, they were the cynosure of modern military science, but at the same time empty efforts. Here all labour was in vain, except insofar as distraction might stop them cutting each other's throats. Angels permitting, the Null could take Dieppe any time they liked and everyone knew it. That being so, there was little of real merit to do in this cursed posting and every temptation to seek invisible enemies in the aether. The real ones were all too plain in your face, before the walls, in range but inviolate.

Yet Guy knew angelic omnipotence was overrated. Back when life held little appeal he'd risked all to prove it. Private blasphemies shouted in his chamber had brought no response, neither punishment nor amused indifference. They'd simply not heard. The younger Guy had arisen from his divan, experiment over, hope revived, and gone on into the years ahead.

He did so again, crossing to refill Bathie's wine cup. The garrison here was skeletal, sufficient for a show, insufficient for proper menials. Musket's apology was graciously brushed aside.

'No matter. I could do with stretching my legs. Null-Paris was a confinement of the body as well as spirit.'

Sir Samuel didn't like to think of it or there.

'I dare say, Ambassador . . .' Plainly, he'd sooner speak of piles.

'Hmmm . . .' Guy studied him over the rim of his goblet. He wanted to put the man at ease. He felt sorry for him stuck out here, shredding himself in days of worry and uselessness. 'Don't suppose you get the results sent over, do you?'

Musket was murdering his meal, pursuing it round the platter but not enjoying it. A forkful of cutlet was left, poised halfway to death.

'Results of what?'

That meant no. Guy's generally gossamer spirits fell slightly. The Null didn't follow the horses either – except to eat them. Just when he thought himself almost back, he found civilisation still some way off.

'Doesn't matter.'

Yet he remained a sunny optimist; try as he might to suppress it. Hope kept bubbling up through every obstacle; a sturdy weed penetrating whatever pavement was laid over it.

'Though you might just have caught the name, I suppose . . . *Frisky Liz*, heard of her?'

Musket considered, reeling in the years.

'I've known a few so called,' he said, trying to be helpful, 'and some that answer that description . . .'

'A horse, dear Sir Samuel. A thoroughbred: flanks like stuffed satin. She was to run in the Blades Gold Cup. Didn't hear, did you . . .?'

Musket looked perplexed, screwing up his face in search of some code that wasn't there.

'No. I . . . er, no.'

'A pity.'

'Yes.'

Sir Samuel suddenly brightened.

'Though I did hear something about horses. The Levellers thought it fit for my attention.'

Guy was all ears. He set down his glass, postponing the vital task of anaesthetising himself to sleep.

'Do tell.'

'The angels permitted a summer incursion. Wild Null plus some fungoid creations we've not seen before. Oh, and those eel-men hybrids, too. It got quite torrid till the Huscarls and some cataphracti worked round the back, edging down the Mole Valley. Then we got to grips with it and . . .'

Guy would never normally have interrupted but he'd felt a shadow fall over some vital interests.

'Forgive me, Musket, but I can't quite grasp the equine connection. D'you see? Sorry.'

Sir Samuel didn't mind. Any conversation was good conversation. Stuck in the company of soldiers with fairly basic tastes, he realised he could do with some point-sticking practise.

'Well, they overran Epsom, you see; early on, at the start. Got amongst the training stables.'

Guy kept his gasp to himself but Bathie knew. She stared at him, concerned.

'D-did they indeed?' The strangulated tone was barely perceptible.

'Oh yes, quite a feast, apparently. Worked to our advantage, though. A lot lingered on the banquet. Blunted their advance,

26

else they'd have been through to the capital.'

'S-s-stroke of luck then' said Guy – only it wasn't really him.

Musket drank to it but drank alone.

'Suppose so. Though not for the thoroughbreds. Wasn't always quick either. I got a briefing about the fungoids. Seems that they slow-feed and drape themselves over the beasts. Then they sort of meld with the still living creat . . .'

Guy let fall his fork. It clattered against the pewter, disrupting discourse. An indulgent but, he hoped, forgivable ploy.

'Gracious,' he said lightly, resurrecting the smile he used at the Null court, 'isn't nature inventive? That must have put a dent in the Derby!'

'If there was one,' agreed the Castellan, uninvolved.

And then, though he went through the motions, Guy found all appetite gone. He lingered the minimum permissible time till the scraping back of a chair wouldn't seem actively offensive. 'An early start. Draining duties . . .' – and so on. Bathie followed the cue, grabbing fruits and pastries to take with her.

Their allotted quarters were in the seaward wall. With the eye of faith, the lights of land, albeit Leveller land, could be seen across the inky water. A balm of summer spice rode on the breeze that entered their open window, only slightly abated by the arm-thick iron grille against the sea-Null. It visited them from Humandom, not the tainted southward realms – or so he chose to believe. That sufficed to make it beautiful.

Scenting it, Guy's buoyant spirits rose again. There would be new racing bloodlines, some survivors to carry on. An influx of fresh yearlings would bring welcome novelty to the sport. If you did but enquire there was always something to look forward to.

At that precise moment, it was watching his wife undress – though that was also bitter-sweet pleasure. Her eyes, unreadable, never left his.

27

Naked, they embraced warmly – and then retreated to cold, sad, separate, beds.

For consolation, when the worst of frustration had abated, he consulted the letter, sneaking it out from beside his pounding heart. Back turned to her – for not even Bathie could know or be endangered by the knowledge – he read by silvery moonlight.

The handwriting of a god-king: unprecedented. Unprecedented honour, unprecedented hope and fear.

"'*Resurgam! I will rise again! The Promise is fulfilled. Return. Resurgam!*'"

Bathie and the sea: twin sisters, both thinking up a storm.

All through the Null posting she'd been restrained, by the monsters' indifference and her husband's mission. In courting the Null-King the ambassador of Humanity required an entire absence of distraction. Therefore, like a good wife, she'd driven the inner demons over some private frontier, so far away their voices could not be heard. Either that or a pillow had been applied to their yammering faces, stifling the constant chatter. But my, *how* they'd struggled under the smothering. How they'd protested their exile. Now the moment was gone and her temporary strength with it. They invaded again, with renewed vigour. They slipped out from under the pillow, not even winded. Bathie sat at the ship's dragon prow waging war in her head.

Guy recognised the signs of approaching tempest in both places – and could do nothing about either. Both baroque vessels were being tossed by weather there was no controlling. He sympathised but, unable to assist, settled for polite disinterest. The captain was driving the *Wessex Wyvern* before the iron clouds with every effort and inch of sail. The slave rowers below had been threatened up to maximum assistance. Guy could do no more. Bathie would attempt what she could or, at the very least, apologise after. As both passenger and husband Guy was reconciled, if not content. To pass the time, he set and solved puzzles upon his backgammon board, one of the mainstays of his sanity in Null-Paris, till the motion of the ship aborted even that distraction.

There was thunder down below as the slaves shipped oars, for fear they be sea-seized. Already bones had been broken, pinned and tested to shattering against the row-benches by storm-commandeered wood. Occasional stifled sobs to evidence it wafted up to spoil lulls in the wind.

For memory and comparison's sake, Guy looked over the side at the moment-by-moment increasing waves, but thereafter spurned the wild excesses of nature with aristocratic disdain. He rather disapproved of water in large quantities – even the Null behaved with more decorum. The Ambassador turned to shuffling his favourite pack of cards, just to keep his hand in.

Soon Bathie had to retreat, soaked, from her forward position. Guy sensibly averted his eyes from the wet dress moulded to her form – and was glad to see even the rough seamen do likewise. That was proof of their closing with civilisation and real New-Wessex style respect. They drew nearer to it with every crack of the sails and each protest from the mast – if only providence would permit a homecoming.

Guy arose, stowing away the hand-drawn picture-book, recalling his responsibilities. He was of the blood. He had . . . contacts and the responsibilities to go with them.

'Ahem!' Even above the blow he had their attention, because of who he was. Standing directly above the hold, so that even the oarsmen might see or hear, Guy raised his arms in the beseeching attitude of prayer.

'Though storm rises o'er us, we are not of it. We are of firmer assurance. We are human. And in us a light shines!'

A roll of the ship put him comically on to one long leg, along with, it must be said, almost everyone else, and he allowed fitting dignity to return before continuing.

'Therefore, may Blades, who is with us always, together with all his descendants in whom the divine spark sparkles, smile upon us; his favoured children in his image. May he and they hear us now and bring us to safe harbour, in this world and the next.'

Guy was disappointed to note a few sailors not participating, and one or two even sporting curled lips of distaste. The *Wessex Wyvern* was an Imperial ship, for all it docked at Freeport-Hastings. It wasn't fitting that she should carry Leveller-atheist recruits. Though it was hardly the moment, Guy resolved to raise the matter, to the point of speaking sternly, if and when they made port.

A wave caught him at an equally inopportune time. The final blessing was drowned in cold and green and wet.

'Mighty Blades, Creator of stars and stones alike, we thank you for keeping us alive, for preserving us, and . . .'

They all knew anyway and those not underwater completed it for him.

'. . . bringing us to this moment.'

Some of the mariners crossed themselves, which was a further shock, akin to but more chilling than the recent refreshing wave. He'd had no idea. There'd been the blithe assumption that Christianity was a purely Wessex problem, a stubborn legacy from less enlightened times. Guy didn't know whether to be sad or glad to find it further afield. Leveller-land played with the title, just to spite the Imperials, and so it only served them right to be infested with the commoner-corrupting full-blown version. Also, there was a crumb of comfort in finding nowhere immune. The swines got everywhere, like vermin and bed-bugs. The most dignified, most Ambassadorial, course was to ignore them. Guy ushered his thoughts on.

In one or other of the Apocrypha, those numberless volumes of anecdotes of Blades written by his servants and apostles after his ascension, Guy recalled mention of something called *Fimbulwinter*. One evening in his favourite pleasure villa at New-Lulworth with cup in hand, the god-king Blades had mentioned the wolf-head, horizon to horizon, storm that would presage the end of the world. *Scop*-poets, hanging on his every word, had instantly noted the throwaway scrap from his omniscience, and later theologians expounded upon it. Essentially they were none the wiser, but as in all things from *those* lips, they took it on faith.

Guy recalled the para-scripture now, as he raised his head from prayer to query the sudden lack of light. It was almost overhead, angry and slate coloured, its lips overhung like the predicted lupine maw. A tiny, deluding margin of peace was pushed before it. They lay in that false penumbra now.

Guy proved not alone in his piety and erudition. Sailors mouthed 'the wolf' to each other and hastened at what they could. The very antithesis of a seaman, Guy nevertheless found in the captain's worried face all he needed to know. What was formerly weathered-brown and at home, was now paper-hue and lost. Unfortunates were ordered aloft to reduce sail. The gamble was lost: they wouldn't be making it under their own power.

Bathie crossed the desk and wrapped herself around Guy – for all their earlier agreement that undue embraces were unwise. He draped a fibbing-confident arm about her hunched shoulders.

'We have done what we can,' he told her, above the now soaring noise. 'Who could do more?'

Her troubled eyes returned to no worse than normal state. Alone of all creation, she trusted him.

To avoid her flying frizzles, a spidery screen of black, he had to turn his head – and then deeply wished he hadn't. Between them and the already visible Sussex shore, a water-spout was on the point of birth.

'Oh, Lord . . .' It never rains but it pours.

As if on cue and to Guy's prompting, the rain came down: vertical curtain rods, driving into any exposed skin. At the same a wyrm arose from the maelstrom its rocketing ascent had made.

The thing was grey-green and penile, an obscene expansion of its tiny soil-dwelling-cousin. This more ambitious branch of the family could loom over ships and take them. It proceeded to the first preparatory to the second.

31

Water cascaded from it and on to them, a second downpour adding to the sweeter and more natural torrent. The creature reeked of obscure depths and made them retch. For want of anything more meaningful to do, Guy wondered at the vestigial eyes and derisory fins about its segmented neck. These features had not been noted before in New-Wessex's bestiaries – and now, most probably, never would.

From below, and most commendably, a cannon spoke. Predictably, in such a rolling sea and so ill-prepared, it missed; but the thought was there – a last gesture of species bravado. The sound also proved to be solo. All the other gun ports had been close-battened against the waves.

As the now-sidelined storm broke full blast, the wyrm rose and rose in its peculiar spinning motion, threshing its particular patch of water to extra fury. The green dragon prow where Bathie had sat was now lost in perpetual spray.

Men ran hither and thither, to no especial purpose or effect. Someone, perhaps the captain, although it was hard to tell, emptied a revolver into the beast. A marksman's ring of pink love-bites appeared in the ever nearing – neck and could have been the real thing for all their stopping power.

Guy stooped to say farewell but Bathie was not there. What he'd thought was her continued embrace was the sea's questing, curling arm. Already torn from him, she was at the ship's rail, seconds from the gaping ring-jaw's descent. A scarlet and black figure she stood alone, slim legs astride, and cast her all at it.

Bathie's power was intermittent, its thwarted straining for realisation the probable root of all her problems. In some, a few of the few, the blessing required special urging to take up its bed and walk.

The wyrm was it. Bathie's word alone cracked wicked painted splinters off the rail and then drove them, one by one, deep into the pulpy hide. When that did no good, her unleashed will drove them still further in, to vanishing point. It might have been imagination – though that faculty was at low ebb just then – but Guy thought he detected an at-the-edge-of-hearing whistle of distress. If so it was a pleasing final word, the petty comfort that a meal was spoiled.

But not delayed. Appetite remained unabated. The watery, crashing descent continued.

No sense, no feeling, thought Guy – and then realised it was a poor one to have as his last.

There was no time to compose a better. The wyrm was amongst them and slipped its pink mouth over a mariner, stopping him in his tracks, thrusting down till he vanished within. Inappropriate sexual parallels were inescapable, even at this gate of death, requiring some shaking off. It was more serious than that. One moment he had been as they were, and then a practised lover had sucked him up. The wyrm withdrew, rearing up to swallow, its orifice skywards, taking in the cascade to lubricate reception. When they could tear their eyes away they had to concede the empty space and admit the appalling absence. The sailor was gone to a new and warmly welcoming home.

Guy drew his pistol and, dropping to one knee on the bucking deck, took aim to score some token consolation. An inner decision also arrived, unbidden. If it selected Bathie he would make sure of her first.

He needn't have got his breeches wet – or wetter. A golden figure appeared atop the cabin roof. She, he or it could afford to ignore both wyrm and storm.

'Pro-*tected*!' she decreed, icy, high-handed tones sounding in every ear, perhaps even the wyrm's – if it had them. The tempest was stilled.

A little way off the deluge continued, but for the moment they didn't care about *way off*. Their own little bubble of immediate calm sufficed. It travelled with them, coastwards. They might make home.

The stupid wyrm did not know that circumstances were changed. It returned to the attack, unaware. The angel disapproved.

She struck out with one milk-white hand. A portion of her intrinsic gold travelled along it, a bright pointer against the leaden sky, all the worse for the utter silence of its energy.

Its arc met the wyrm's neck, bit, and then carried on, traversing through. The monster hesitated – on the brink between this and whatever lays beyond. Then it fell, like a plumb-weight, into the depths, the severed head taking a separate, independent, route.

Guy could not avert his eyes from the wyrm's tortured majority. Unnaturally truncated, it writhed as it sank, spewing grey life-liquor. Here was neither the time or the moment, but Guy wasn't entire master of his thoughts for once. He was sure he'd read somewhere that the creatures could regenerate even from such grievous loss.

The head landed with a wet smack athwart the forward deck, testing its timbers, briefly tilting the stern free of the sea. Those glassy eyes had probably been the same in life but to observe their lack of animation was endless pleasure. Then they observed that something of the sailor was still within the gullet and they looked no more.

The angel greeted them from her vantage point with one of the over-extended smiles that so disconcerted lesser breeds. Subject humanity had learnt – at cost – they could not be taken at face-value.

'Pro-*tected*!' she said again, and left.

A golden afterglow remained, slowly ebbing towards the prow. There it stayed, lighting and calming their way; a minor residue of her tender care lingering to see them safe.

Likewise, she left behind a cloud of uncertainty. Were they actively watched over, or had their saviour just chanced by, treading whatever unseen paths her kind took? Either way, Guy was – ungratefully – displeased. Obligation tasted no more sweet whether it arrived through fluke or lapdog status. Ambassadors were cosseted, true, and Guy Ambassador might benefit – but he would *not* give thanks. He knew full well the angels ordained envoys between the races not to advance understanding, but for their own amusement. They expended equal care over bloodshed deliberately staged. Guy's world was a sandpit to them and Null and Human alike the toys they set to play within. He would not be deceived. He carefully

34

expressed all his gratitude to the correct Deity.

Not everyone was so enlightened. They had contrary indications: just now and still before their faces. Some bowed to the haloed prow and the evidence of their own eyes.

Even the Levellers and Christians, Guy had noted – notoriously impious beasts – had the sense and weakness to look lost. The angels' instruction that they should not be worshipped was a flimsy dam holding back an ocean of potential converts. It wouldn't hold for many more centuries.

For a second – and only a second – Guy suffered waves of melancholy worse and wetter than those Neptune had thrown at him. Surely he only struggled and strived in vain. Mankind's entry in this vital race was a twenty-stone jockey on a donkey. How could a war be won when one side refused to recognise the enemy?

Then he recalled the *letter*, secure in a waterproof pouch against his breast. And Bathie rejoined him, at speed, desolate amidst the aftermath of sorcery, briefly grasped but now lost again. Usually, magecraft acted as a purgative for her, flash-cleansing the stables of stockpiled thought; but not today. She was drained and mourning her loss.

In her encompassing arms, in her need, Guy recalled his true self and was strong – and – cheerful – again. He shooed despair away. Over Sussex the summer sun was prevailing over the gloom and lighting up the verdant Downs. They were heading the right way, away from the past.

Singled out for storm-immunity, a pocket of peace amidst a sulky sea, the *Wessex Wyvern* made for harbour bearing the mother of all fishing trophies.

Only much later was it recalled: the same era but later. The angel recollected to a brother/sister as they made love.

There'd been *infringement*: some lead-witted act of trespass. In passing that globule of atoms the angel had decided to protest. It adjusted and revealed itself to the native fauna.

One – the larger, unified conglomeration of life – wished to imbibe the smaller, separate sparks. They did not wish it. Far more importantly, they – or maybe just one of them – bore a marker. Some predecessor had attached significance to their continued survival as discrete entities.

The angel refused to spend even one thought discovering why. It would have been far too tedious. All the while, a new discovered dimension was awaiting serious ravishment: positively gagging for it in its virgin un-discoveredness. She/he/it remembered wanting to be amongst the first there.

The less sparkling, larger, growth wouldn't obey a simple command. The angel had sent it back to the realm of potentiality, there to decay and then regroup into alternate being.

The favourites were also troubled by some localised air disturbance. It had graciously taken the time to calm it for them, smoothing the currents away elsewhere to inconvenience and kill other, expendable, vitalities.

The angel recalled straining, as though through a swirling, multi-coloured film of oil, to perceive the insects as individuals. It took great concentration to close down enough faculties to see such limited forms truly.

There seemed to be inequality of gratitude between them and it had crossed the angel's mind to breach their wooden bark and immerse the lot – but that would make the detour even more of a nonsense. Still, it was a close run thing. The angels did not want worship – most definitely not – but abasement, yes: certainly. Here it smelt remnant rebellious particles of restraint – but at the same time couldn't really be bothered to draw the sword. Mosquitoes didn't merit cannon fire.

So it relented and went and forgot – and now, along with all its species, wished it hadn't.

Their coitus ceased abruptly as both now rushed to amend the mistake.

'Arise, arise'

Guy gently assisted the dockers to their feet. Some grasped and kissed the hand that helped them.

'The poorest are always the most pious,' said Bathie to him, not troubling if she was heard more widely. He still did not know with her: whether it was cynicism or reverent reflection. The former probably. Sometimes all the contradictions boiled over and she lashed out – meaning nothing bad by it. Guy was sure the further she drew away from a wild and spoilt childhood the less it would occur. He could wait and be patient.

'It is they who stand in greatest need of consolation, my dear. Let's not deprive them of it.'

As the *Wessex Wyvern* made secure, he moved amongst the swarming day-wage dock workers, Freeport-Hastings's lowest of the low, dispensing encouragement and blessings. They bowed their heads and were grateful: some tearfully so. It was rare enough for them to see any of the divine blood, let alone one that would take notice of them.

Guy sympathised and moved on, Bathie and escort in his wake, showering back a rain of coin. Their's was a sad plight: Imperialist slaves or prisoners of war bought or traded by the Levellers, then freed through their prejudices but left with no means of livelihood. Hand to mouth labouring was their only hope, disdain from freeborn Levellers their daily bread. No wonder they turned with zeal to the faith of their fathers.

To Guy's mind they would have been better off taking their chances with the Wild zone and an uncertain welcome back home. Evidently they didn't dare. It struck Guy as odd. Better one day standing upright than a long lifetime on your knees: that's what he'd been taught. Maybe the lower orders received different instruction. Either way, he didn't like to be judgmental. These poor wretches had enough problems without exhortations from him.

The angel light had faded before they docked at Freeport-Hastings. The sailors – Leveller hard-heads and all – groaned to see it go, and in that Guy saw the seeds of growing dependence. A few more generations and bondage would be ingested along with their mother's milk and what was bred in the bone would out in the meat: an inbred pre-emptive cringe. They would be back as they were under the Null, before Blades the great came to raise them – just as Guy, his direct descendant, had raised the dockmen. Humanity would be returning to their beginnings – raw meals eaten in burrows – unless that happened not to suit the usurpers. Everything good had become contingent, not one inch of progress safe. Guy felt an unfamiliar bat-squeak of panic amidst his predictive faculties.

There was no time to lose. The thought of it sped his feet up Hastings quay into the shadow of its ramshackle – and distressingly plain – walls. Not an eye-refreshing gargoyle or splash of any colour in sight – bar dun.

'Money!'

To Guy's mind, all Levellers were scruffy and brusque; a function of their solipsist ideas. The easy, sleazy, notion of *it'll do* . . . presided in all their heads. Amongst their functionaries the problem was thrice compounded.

'Exempt!' He could be terse too, though it didn't come naturally. Amongst the Ambassador clan that temptation was knocked out early on.

The Customs Master sat up straight. His flunkies hastened over to him. Every time the same old story . . .

'Lilburne's law number twenty-five. "*All men is equal* . . ."'

' "*Are* equal",' Guy corrected him. 'I happen to have read the statute. I know I'm right.'

The officer debated within and then proffered the customs box towards him, gaping mouth outwards. There was less fun in baiting an Imperial who knew all the rules.

Guy deposited a token *gold Tom*: acceptance of the principal of debt but not the full payment. It was accepted and the box lid snapped shut. Honour was satisfied with a nod to

38

either extremist position. Wars had been fought over this and related issues, till the coming of the angels showered common sense and forced understanding. The Levellers would grant access to the sea, so long as it was acknowledged as a free concession; not extorted by threat or deference. The Imperialists graciously agreed to overlook the slight to their claims to overlordship of Mankind.

'Atheist!' snapped Bathie at the Customs man as she passed, and the hard-faced officer smilingly crossed himself to confirm the charge. Many Levellers adopted or feigned Christianity just to prove a point and accentuate their deviancy. In effect, Mrs Ambassador was still right. The two things amounted to the same. A god who was so ubiquitous, so *every*where, was actually *no*where. By contrast, Guy and Bathie knew where their God was. They could and would go to him. He, like all his precursors, lived a few days away in a city-sized Castle called New-Godalming – hence, presumably, the name.

Before the sea-gate was a 'ranting corner' and Guy hated them worst of all. Every entrance to every Freeport had one, the home of every opinion, protected by law. Simple fishermen and soldiers could pause to hear the vilest of things spoken plainly, inviting license into their heads. The Imperialists and other religions sent their own orators, assured at least of a hearing, but the sheer chaos of it still disgusted all right-thinkers. You might as well spike half of mankind's guns and invite the Null in. The heroes of early days, Bladian days: Lord Firstmet Null-ear, Count Sennacherib and Arthur Kent-Camelot, *they* wouldn't have stood for gaps in the shieldwall and disunity.

To Guy it smelt of discarded fish and danger and he and his hurried by, a passing rattle of disapproval and brandished rifles, across the now-disused sidings and stockyard. It offended him that Bathie should have to hear shouted words about 'change'.

Those feelings weren't all one way. From the moment of entering Freeport water and the predictable attack of sea-

Null, everything had been grudging and slow. Though they gathered outside every Human port, waiting to waylay boats and feed on waste, today their presence seemed a surprise. The harbour-master's boats had come forth to dislodge the beasts with shot and flame – but like dogs to a bath. Long after each successive wet clump of the beasts' arrival, they had been allowed to adhere, grinding hard at the *Wyvern*'s wood to get at the meat scented inside. Hastings's guardians were obviously in no rush to do their duty or risk themselves for Emperor worshippers.

Eventually though, the purple, plate-like, creatures, distant cousins perhaps of the land variety, were prised away by death or encouragement, and the *Wyvern* was given permission to proceed. She edged in to a tepid welcome.

Guy could have stood disdain or hatred but pity he found hard to bear. Bred to it, even the most wretched of Levellers – wiry women gutting fish upon the *Stade* or prematurely aged men mending nets before their tall drying huts – looked on him as if afflicted. The *Wyvern*'s marines put on a show, marching briskly, sloping shiny rifles, but failed to impress. The Freeports had weapons of their own – some said better – and though little used since the angels came, they still mostly pointed north, Imperium-wards. The rank and file broadly felt they had nothing to worry about.

That same opinion was written on the face of the *Lilburne*. He graciously came to the gate of Hastings Castle to meet the arrivals after their long puff up the cliff-steps – which was more than his predecessor had done. That Lilburne had obliged Guy to knock on the gate until his knuckles were sore.

He wore a sea-green sash of office but nothing else to distinguish him from the generality. After a year of service as chief magistrate he would go back to whatever low trade he pursued and resume his real name. For this twelve-month though, he was just *Lilburne* and he had some – temporary – power. For an Ambassador there was no way round him.

If there had been Guy would have trod it, though the detour might be long: this Lilburne was grossly fat. A butcher?

A publican? A humiliation at any rate, but at least a jolly one.

He'd offered his hand; another improvement on before. Guy slipped two long fingers into it and had them crushed.

'Congratulations,' said the Lilburne.

'Thank you. What for?'

'For not being munched. There's not much meat on you, mind. Seen more fat on a slaughterman's pencil. You and the girl should dine better. And a bit cruel taking your daughter to Nulldom, I should have thought. She'd see bad things – put years on her.'

'May I introduce my *wife*, the Lady Bathesheba Fruntier-folke . . .'

A dutiful diplomatic partner, she stepped forward to be surveyed. The Lilburne executed a surprisingly graceful bow: a kindness to her, contrary to local custom.

'Oh, right . . . So mebbe she could do with those years after all. A pleasure to meet you, mistress. Come and eat with me, Mr and Mrs Skinnyribs.'

Guy could transcend. He aimed to imitate his Maker in understanding and thus forgiving all. At the same time, he could hear Bathie grinding her teeth. She dropped back, a scarlet length of anger, to avoid being first behind the monster backside now leading the way.

Where a normal castle of normal humans would have the bustle and conviviality of a courtyard, here was only a bare and lifeless place kept for their ceaseless 'moots' in which to jaw and parade their indecision – that and a chapel Guy knew would be absurdly bare, stripped of every inspiration for the senses. This was no one's home, save some here-this-year, gone-the-next elected shiremasters. And what no one owned, no one loved, not as people did in Castle Blades and the other high points of the Imperium. It showed in every direction Guy averted his eyes. Chaos and 'it'll do' was everywhere offending him.

'So how's tricks in Yokedom, then?' A query directed back over a podgy shoulder.

Guy smiled, quite genuinely. Employed too often that gibe had killed the nerve it sought to rub.

41

'Actually, I was rather hoping you'd tell me, given I've been representing it – and you – to the enemies of Mankind.'

That was another trouble with the more ideological Levellers. All the debating entered their soul and made them annoyingly reasonable.

'Good point,' the Lilburne wheezed. 'Sorry. I'll see what I can dredge up from memory.'

'And intercepted letters.'

'And them, too.' The easy-going admission was disarming. Also Guy hadn't much room for outrage. Most of what passed between Freeport Hastings and Freeports Dover, Teignmouth and Mousehole and all the disgraceful rest, was an open – forcibly prised apart – book to New-Wessex. This emissary of the kettle couldn't shriek 'black!' to the pot too loud, and both knew it. For once, Guy didn't care. The letter of *all* letters, the scorching hope against his breast, had gotten through, unmolested. Bathie's magecraft had risen from its coma to positively confirm that. Between leaving the god-king of all humanity and his own ecstatic reading, the missive had remained faithful, its lead sealed virginity intact. This overweight peoples' potentate had not read it.

Quite aside from a fragment of the divine spark sanctifying his veins, Guy also had that over him. The man could keep his sturdy independence. Guy knew better.

'Follow I, we'll find a place to talk.'

Three floors high up in the Keep, winding there via a spiral stair in the thickness of the wall, was the civic dining hall; complete with the remains of some previous meal. The Lilburne puffed over and swept a portion aside to clear space. With audible relief he sat himself behind it.

'Care to join me?'

'We've eaten, thank you all the same.'

Guy knew it would be bread and beer, the same old *we're plain frugal folk, us* protestation against any visitor from 'Yokedom'. Livelier stuff lurked in their larders – you only had to look at this Lilburne to see that – but Guy wouldn't give them the little pleasure. And besides, Bathie, a unreflective true-believer, would never break bread or anything else with 'traitors'. She sat, less than lady-like, gown hitched thigh high, astride a bench end and picked her nails, fully, childishly absorbed in the painful pleasures.

Their marines retreated to the poster festooned walls, each matched and marked by a Leveller *fyrdman*, to eye each other with expected contempt. In each it was mitigated by guilty curiosity about freedom, and by curiosity about faith. One side lived by the sea, were wide open to it, the other had dared breathe the air of Nulldom. Their mutual scorn could never be total.

Also, they were all human, in a world not the least obliging to the breed. Even the wars between them were half-hearted and full of mercy. The angels hated that.

'Do'y mind if I do?' Yet the Lilburne had signalled for breakfast or whatever it was before that politeness had finished falling out his lips. One of the fyrdmen tugged a turquoise cord. In time a tankard and platter arrived. Graceless in every sense, the Lilburne engaged with each.

'I recall one thing,' he said at length, red face emerging from a dying loaf. 'Two month back. There was a bad incursion. Wild Null and new things. You threw them back, I hear, but lost a lot. New-Epsom caught it bad.'

'So one hears.'

'Funny thing, but my family came from round there.'

'Really?'

'Till great-great grandfather struck out for freedom.'

'Fascinating.'

'He was a jockey: in one of the Imperial stables on the Downs.'

That genuinely did sink a hook in Guy's interest. He knew he shouldn't but couldn't resist. The Lilburne observed, and without malice reeled him in. The Ambassador writhed against it.

'You do surprise me . . .' He meant the horse-breaking bulk before him. The ensuing generations must have given appetite its head.

43

The Lilburne caught on and laughed, cupping sausage fingers to belly.

'Oh, aye: life here agrees with us.'

Guy realised that temptation would win but went along protesting, heels scraping, clawing the walls, for form's sake.

'And, um . . . do you still keep an interest . . .'

'They still ran the Derby,' beamed the Lilburne. 'As soon as the incursion was killed, some horses were scraped from odd places; even a few from here.'

Guy couldn't hold back, it was too inviting. Life owed him a little latitude.

'And? And?'

'*Cromwell's Nose*. Six lengths. Eleven to one.'

Guy's clenched fist hit the table, cups lifted and soldiers awoke, fingers hastily wiggling into trigger guards. Even Bathie looked up, still miles and centuries away but hurrying back with ill-grace.

'I had money on that!'

Without asking, the Lilburne poured beer into a second leather container and passed it over.

'Me too. Bottoms up!'

They crashed tankards and, though he knew it would get back to New-Wessex and others would frown, Guy could not forbear to toast this fellow human being.

It was not the news or winnings, though they were nice enough; nor even the upcoming high-life and loins and charity they'd allow. The truth was he'd had a vision, had been assured. A disbelieving Leveller and faithful descendant of a god-king had made contact, if only for a fleeting moment. And in that fleeting moment Guy saw that neither Null nor angels would prevail.

The hope he carried against his heart burned brighter.

A richer man in every way, Guy moved on.

Typically light on rhyme or reason, the angel-dictated

44

route wound west from Leveller land to Pevensey-Assyria, ignoring dead-straight golden-age roads or rail, and only then shooting arrow-like north to New-Wessex after brushing that loyal enclave. What should have been a half day march or less as the crow flies, was turned into full day's adventure, courtesy of angelic caprice. Forces of the two sovereign states met warily at the frontier to pass Guy between them like a ticking parcel.

En route, the *Wild* sometimes pressed in on the path of normality, reducing it to a ribbon, requiring single file travel. Elsewhere, it broadened to a great swathe of countryside where rules applied and only the ordinary dangers of life were found. There, with just roving Null and similar threats to worry about, the Leveller escort visibly relaxed.

They hardly needed the rag-clad and strange-eyed guides to discern where their world ended and weird began. You could see it in additional vigour and exuberant growth. One patch of grass was as it should be and serviceable; whereas its neighbour looked additionally vivid and fit to grab an ankle or maybe sink beneath it into unknown depths. To a man they tried not to see, but trees that beckoned and flesh-mockeries that sang, *commanded* eye and ear their way.

Guy saw a man made of flowers and ivy who returned his gaze and called to him from its hilltop; so close and yet also a universe away. The knoll which rang with its ululation was ringed with whitened bones and the Ambassador felt at liberty to decline.

His nearer, more welcome, company were a typical Leveller *fyrd*-militia miscellany, bearing everything from rifles to the great axe. Guy noted a few latest – and now last – pattern Martini-Henries amongst the firearms and was duly honoured – if not impressed. New-Wessex had given the Levellers those – via the *Professor* – may his name be blotted out whilst he roasted in Hell . . .

Guy deplored their flock-of-sheep formation, their lack of drill, even as he was aware of the reasons for the decline in discipline. Secure behind angel-decreed frontiers, the

Freeport civilisation no longer dwelt upon land war. Doubtless this shambling armed mob could throw a boat about, weather storms, fetch gunpowder from Sicily and board vessels to spread their social contagion. Doubtless they thought that that sufficed. Turning their backs on the uncongenial, slow-profit soil, they claimed sea-salt in their blood and the sea as their – metaphoric – mistress. That was world enough for them.

Alas, and as all too often, Guy entertained mixed feelings. As a perfidious Ambassador and New-Wessex patriot, he should approve. This proving time, these trial centuries, would not last forever. Heavenly deliverance would arrive and proper order be restored. And on that day the scarlet Wessex legions would roll back all rebellion and sweep the stables clean. A rabble of pirates wouldn't last two minutes against that tide. It was one wave they couldn't ride out.

Yet, from the purely human perspective, here was another weakening of joint defences, another malign consequence of slavery. The angels had struck again. They were everywhere you went – and Guy went far afield.

Guiltily, he looked around, recalling the escort were still men as he was; living creatures with mothers and mates and children. He repented of his calling down destruction upon them and his exulting harshness, even as he acknowledged its sad necessity. It might be that Blades would be merciful to him, as he had been to Moses, permitting a glimpse of the Promised Land, the 'Glorious Day', and then call him to Paradise before its uglier consequences were enacted. It was a weak wish, he knew, but in character; an emotion in accordance with his destiny, his *wyrd*. The Lord of All had already torrented kindness down on him by arranging birth into the Ambassadorial caste. Heaven only knew what he would have endured in, say, a frontier berserker-clan . . .

He recalled himself to the strictly present-and-material. There was comfort, as every soldier sooner or later discovered, in mindless marching. In time, without incident, the dour Levels came into sight, guaranteed human land, privileged with only, merely, the mundane law of nature. There was a border post at Pevensey Sluice.

The Neo-Assyrians had come to meet Guy there in full ceremonial iron, glinting in the light like signallers. Advancements in firearms had rendered their beloved armour obsolete and present straits meant there could be no more of it, but on high and holy days they fetched it forth and weighed themselves down in emulation of Assyria the Great: dimly remembered, increasingly misunderstood. Their black and gold 'Impaled Enemy' banners were visible on the flat marshes long before they were.

This was a proud and stiff-necked race, amongst the first to rise from burrowdom and farming by the Null. Also, their founder, Sennacherib, had been the second god-king, successor to Almighty Blades. Alas, there was history between them and the Levellers, some early period of alliance now deemed shameful, compensated for over the succeeding centuries by exaggerated hostility. Pevensey would not trade with Hastings, though they were neighbours, though they might both go hungry. What they could not wring out of the Pevensey Levels and South Downs had to come down the corridor from New-Wessex. Any Leveller-believer who strayed over their border was sat on a stake till it showed through his mouth. In this way they atoned and proved their piety.

Guy approved the end even as his kind heart deplored the means. It was long accepted that Pevensey-Assyria just had a harder edge than New-Wessex proper, perhaps a function of its chosen model – itself known only from the Blades-Bible and Blades's tales. Or perhaps the abrasive life of the untamed Levels: the mud-Null and lizard steeds that haunted those wetlands, bred iron in the soul to match their bodies' favourite covering. Guy chose not to chase the explanation to its lair. What could he do even if he cornered it?

'Cheerio!'

The Leveller colonel just stopped in his tracks, well short of the nominal limit of his domains. He knew that if they came

47

too close the Pevensey men would feel piously obliged to stage an 'incident' and, secure in Leveller values, he wouldn't give them – or the Null for that matter – the satisfaction. He ordered his troops around and they shambled about at their own speed, chatting. A distant jeer reached them from across the line but was ignored.

'You're on your own,' the colonel told Guy and Bathie.

Indeed they were. Guy's guardian marines belonged to the *Wessex Wyvern* and had remained behind. Out here and cheek by jowl with the Wild they had only their own resources and whatever protection others graciously cared to provide. A chastening thought in a hazardous world.

The angelic corridor wound on, green and under-trampled underfoot. Weeds and wild-flowers now predominated over paving. Neither side troubled it much or claimed exclusive rights – though not through humility but fear of pointless war. There was already enough of that at the new masters' prompting.

For a instant Guy was sad, as the scene shoved his face right up against reality. Humanity was fragmenting. The Freeports looked to the sea, Pevensey-Assyria strived to be more than Wessex than Wessex itself and failed. Here was another fault-line, a no man's land – though no man truly owned anything anymore. Its fecund beauty was illusory, the prevailing scent that of decay. His present guardians cherished their heterogeneous weaponry because they knew in their hearts that soon there would be no more to come. All the scene before him was nothing but setting for the last act of a old and honourable story he didn't want to end.

Then Guy overdrew on his Ambassador inheritance to transcend the slough and fill the pit in his stomach with duty.

He bowed his thanks to the Leveller captain of the escort who, in turn and as a special concession of respect, inclined his *lobster*-helmeted head to the Ambassador. A thunder of boots and clinking weapons and then Guy and Bathie were alone, now in fact as always in spirit. Husband and wife did not look back but set off together; just they and the Sussex sun overhead like the eye of Blades, little figures treading between two ways of seeing things.

The sea was now close, tide drawing in and crashing on a pebble beach immediately to their left. On the right the sombre marsh and reclaimed fields spread far away for miles. Striking contrasts set amongst them screamed out for attention, to be interpreted as sad, subsided, buildings from the gone-before, noon-day, times; now gaping and ivy-covered. Whether they had once been dwellings or no it would take a antiquary some time and investigation to say. Guy declined to speculate. It lowered him to think there might have been merriment and family festivity within the green ruins.

To distract himself, and appear leisurely before the watching Pevensey-Assyrians, he consulted his scroll way-map and read that here had been *New-Northeye*: yet another place snuffed out by 'The Great Contraction'; squeezed free of people like some unwanted spot. There could be no consolation drawn from the place, not even reconciling philosophy or perspective. Even if there had been local survivors from that day of wrath they would all be gone now, and their great-great-grandchildren teetering on the brink of departure themselves. New-Northeye was no more, not even in memory.

The dead place threatened him with renewed discontent and so he hurried on. That increase in pace was translated along his hand to Bathie and she was pulled along more smartly in its wake. She did not protest but stretched her gamine legs longer to comply. There existed implicit trust between them which saved so much time on mundane question and answer.

As a youth he had queried why everything was 'New-' this and 'New-' that; even *New-Wessex* and its capital *New-Godalming*; and he received the orthodox – and definitive – answer that Blades had made the world anew. Out of the goodness of his heart he had come and reconstructed all after the perfect images held in his divine head. It was prying and ungracious to enquire where precisely those originals might be. Gift-horse-in-the-mouth attitudes like that were why they were now bereft and alone, the playthings of arrogant invaders.

Imperial theologians speculated that ingratitude was one of the factors leading to Lord Blades's ascension to his home beyond, there to watch what his children made of the world he had so painstakingly constructed. And unless they mended their ways, there he would remain until they were fit company again. Curiosity about tracking him down, like some fox to its earth, was precisely the kind of wrong-thought which postponed that day.

With adulthood had come the calming acceptance of unknowing. Indeed, it now lifted Guy's prone-to-be-buoyant spirits every time he framed the name of his native land. If New-Wessex was good, if New-Godalming the protective mother of risen mankind, then how much better must be the unsullied archetypes beyond the veil? There Blades would permit no imperfection, no shabbiness. In that city there would be no need for impaling stakes and high walls and rifles. Guy lived in modest hopes of one day beholding it, of acquiring citizenship of the original Wessex, where tears were unknown and he would abide with Blades forever.

Then, bolting up on the outside like a long-shot bet came a saucy, unsolicited, inquiry. Was every wager a winner in Blades's world? Did every fancy romp home? And, come to that, was every marriage bed there a riotously happy one?

Guy whipped and kicked the impudent curiosities aside before they could be answered and gate-crash into a prayer. He might well have been given a frivolous soul but there was no need for his faith to conform to it.

The Pevensey men would not come over lest they be accused of provocation, although it wasn't Leveller steel they feared but angelic retribution. Once, an unsanctioned barge-borne invasion of Freeport Harwich by headstrong young Assyrians had been on the point of victory when they were smashed to splinters daubed with red. An avenging angel had swept the survivors home under her wing and made example of them. When she'd done they were just puddles of fat in a smoking, fresh-minted saucer depression. It still stood – or lay – right outside Pevensey-Nineveh's walls, a monument both noticed and ignored at the same time, and a by-chance effective dew pond that no farmer ever utilised.

The Assyrians come to meet Guy remembered it: they had passed the cursed place on their way and recollection now helped them stand their ground – or all save one amongst them. He evidently felt free to advance and greet the esteemed visitors.

Bathie had long-sight and even longer memory.

'Cousin,' her voice echoed dully in the salt air, though she could only have seen him once previously, and even then ought to have much distracted by her wedding day.

Though profoundly unimpressed, as befitted the twig of a warrior tree, she kept perfect recall of all Guy's widespread brethren. Ambassadors were to be encountered everywhere New-Wessex required representation – and some had grown in stature during long years residence beyond civilisation, a few almost to the point of worthiness.

Not this one, though. Guy observed Bathie retire back into her sense of self, the smoky sullenness floating once more in her eyes. She was now out of this, he knew, and beyond his command. He might as well accept it with good grace, coating her mood with unsolicited permission.

'Ambassador.'

'Ambassador.'

The two met and embraced stiffly.

Guy was still young in his subtle art and retained feelings of his own. This one, though, he'd been so long adjusting his notions to others that he had precious few left of his own. Not that Guy disapproved: it was paramount that this man be good at what he did, regardless of selfish considerations.

Still, there were all the signs recalled from childhood memories of old aunts and uncles retired home: they too were all charm, all glittering polish and kindness – and if they'd had

51

to kill him they would have, without a blush. The grasp on his extended hand was precisely as firm – not one iota more or less – than he required it to be. It signified nothing.

'Welcome to Pevensey-Assyria.'

'And you are welcome also, cousin.'

'The famous Guy, first Null Ambassador. I defer . . .'

The older man stepped back and made a low sweep of arms and shoulders in fluid concert. His ringleted wig brushed the ground.

'No, Genghiz Ambassador,' countered Guy Ambassador, 'long-server, Pevensey-speaker, I defer to *you*.'

Guy was by far the taller of the two, and the lithest by dint of years and unspent enthusiasm. He bowed even lower. 'I insist!'

Bathie had seen it all before, even if she couldn't grasp the nuances – for that you had to be born in and generations into an Ambassadorial line. She appreciated that somewhere in the successive ceding of precedence there was a struggle going on, as open as the clashing of two bucks in her father's deer park. Yet, concealed amidst a cloud of etiquette, the finer points of combat weren't her's to see.

'Cousin, there was *bravery* in stepping forth,' said Guy. 'We were impressed – and gratified. As Ambassador to Pevensey-Assyria, incursion into the Leveller-Libertas domain might not have been . . . understood.'

The long-wigged relative declined the praise. He spread wide his open palms, extending out the embroidered flaps of his brocade and silver coat.

'No. You do me the honour in merely passing on your way. And, having an urgent dispatch for you, I would have been remiss not to take the chance to deliver it unsullied by snooping gaze.' A twitch of the head and raised painted eyes indicated the clot of Pevensey men behind. 'The risk, if such there be, was purely personal and therefore nothing. What am I compared to the good of our New-Wessex home? Sudden incineration would be a price willingly paid . . .'

'Except by the message itself,' said Guy, smiling. 'And your

52

courtesy outweighs that minor cavil . . .'

There, Bathie saw it, pleased despite herself. Then and there her husband had felled his family-foe. She saw it in just the tiniest shoulder-slump, the most minute stagger back.

'Just so,' said Genghiz, and once again extended his lace-bedevilled hand, accepting the role of underdog. Guy took it on that understanding.

All Ambassadors were taught the sleight of hand in childhood. Depending on how well they learnt, they received either their rations or a ruler or razor swipe from the offering arm, according to age. Therefore, all Ambassadors perforce became accomplished finger-smiths – or else grew disfiguring bands of scar tissue (and skinny to boot). The swift, nigh invisible, transfer of objects from palm to palm became second nature to them, inspired by memory of nights without supper. No one liked to play them at cards.

Both Guy's and Genghiz's hands were lily-white and pristine. Guy scarcely noticed the letter palmed curving up his wide sleeve. He discerned a seal, a heavy one. Heightened senses could almost read it: the pattern felt familiar – and Imperial.

The two relative-Ambassadors walked across the Pevensey frontier arm in arm, chatting of inconsequences. Bathie followed behind, the aristocratic, not forgotten but self-isolated, wife. She was aware of what went on. She would rather die than give away any sign of it.

Not one waiting Assyrian saw or even suspected. Guy's speed was a credit to his instructors and long, painful, training. The seal was cracked against his hip; a bump, a slight lapse in gait and it died. The letter was unfurled and scanned, all in the space of an adjustment of his sleeve.

He saw nothing of the formalities, heard nothing of his cousin's courtly explanations. He was sleep-walking but Genghiz covered for him as though by telepathy.

In betrayal of his upbringing but true to his humanity, Guy's pulse was frantic. Every vestige of his attention, the full entirety of his focus, lay upon the update and its words of flame were recorded, concealed behind his eyes.

'Return. With speed. It is sure. He is found. Resurgam!'

The seal was glorious red, more scarlet than Bathie's flowing dress, protecting contents almost as sacred to him. It depicted a Leviathan, stylised god-king with sword and pistol in hand, glorified by the rising sun and bestriding the Downs, driving tiny Null before him into death and into the sea. Normally, Guy never tired of studying it, for all history and theology and everything needful was there.

Today, though, he had to restrain his gratitude and piety and steel himself to nigh sacrilege. His skilful fingers must first shatter the seal into the tiniest of portions and then pass each to Bathie for grinding into paste. She laboured zealously with mortar and pestle to that end, driving the marble weapon into the bowl held positioned over one hip. He hadn't volunteered the need or its urgency, nor had Bathie enquired, so there was *some*thing gained from the loss. They were a perfect team. Time and again, in all – or almost all – their interactions he found wonderful confirmation of his choice for life.

Nothing must remain save anonymous red dust, no sign that the divine will had been read here. The residue would go into the moat which, since Pevensey-Assyria drowned its lowest felons there, could do with the sanctification. The two letters had already gone, shredded and burnt and then liberated to the sky as ashes during a storm. Guy now reddened at remembrance of retaining the first missive for re-reading and comfort's sake during lonely nights: a shocking indulgence. The pressures of Null-Paris had obviously affected his judgement. What if? What price a Leveller pick-pocket or interfering angel? He forced himself to think of what corner of perdition he might have merited for that.

'First flushed, then pale,' said Bathie. 'Why?'

She'd caught him envisaging a pit of his own filth, and himself sealed within forever with the *Professor* and a Null for company. Gladly he pushed the scene away.

'Making amends,' he explained, and she understood.

'No harm done. All finished now.'

So saying she put the last of the seal-remnant down the closet-of-ease, a simple chute through the walls positioned conveniently above the water. Guy was at the window to ensure no intervening party intercepted. He remained until the red shower dabbled the water and then was gone, poor competition even to the ripples caused by water-beetles and the wind-stirred reeds.

Task over, objective achieved, they could relax to their theoretical maximum of ninety-nine percent when alone together. Guy poured the mead provided to them into a wooden cup for Bathie, then watered it as he knew she liked.

She accepted it with fingertips still tinged Imperial-red, and drank thirstily, regarding him with wicked black eyes over the rim – as she knew he liked.

Prodded into it by her look, he could now mock-reproach himself for his excessive concern. There'd been no real need for the window vigil. During daylight hours Pevensey-Assyria had better things to do than gawk at other people's business or tempt fate below a privy. Time was short and their tasks many. At nightfall all bar its very centre was ceded to new nocturnal masters and mankind stayed indoors, muskets close to hand.

On his way through there to Null-France Guy had wondered aloud at the number and thickness of window and door bars on all the external dwellings. The culverted streams would have been called fortified bastions in the green Downslands he was bred to, but not so in the darker, more aquamarine landscape raised just above the *Levels*. There the most robust of precautions were just termed *necessaries*.

Guy and Bathie had found out why on their first night of residence. Though exhausted by their journey, they were kept from sleep by continual chitterings and scratching from outside. Larger creatures rent the night with single cries, and their victims with prolonged – then truncated – protests. The terrifying opera even led them to share a bed – which naturally led to another unhappy experiment to compound their sorrows. They got no rest, no respite of any sort and awoke drained and tired of life.

The Levels had always been contested land, even at the zenith of the Noon-days, but the angels coming both restocked them with rivals and bred new twisted life to argue the toss. When the sun sank and the curfew bell tolled over the sound of the tide, Pevensey-Nineveh was a city under siege.

And so, in a sense, was Guy. Ancient family tradition said that no land should have more than one Ambassador – lest diplomacy speak with multiple tongues, giving monstrous birth to rivalry and plots, twin occupational hazards of the trade. Accordingly, Guy could neither speak or be spoken to, nor greet or be greeted save with his own kind, and this polite fiction was rigidly adhered to. Genghiz Ambassador might find his rations miraculously tripled, his allotted quarters expanded two-fold, but it could not be through any formal request.

Their nominal host, Shalmaneser-Sennacherib III, would certainly not be seeing them, unless it were by unacknowledged telescope peeping. From the day of his accession, tradition decreed he live and die alone, in a needle-like minaret of exquisite beauty high above the silly bustle of the sea and Levels. There, he pondered the eternal verities on behalf of his subjects and conveyed his conclusions to them in proclamations and dreams and answered prayers. And, as in everything else in that realm, he set the tone. Even the iron guards who'd met them at the border had averted their faces, forming a hollow square round unseen guests. Guy and Bathie were invisible, ghostly, visitors; welcome but not in any way to be acknowledged.

In one sense that was as well. Genghiz had been in post many years and knew their ways. Guy's knowledge was book-learnt and he saw numberless pitfalls even for the Ambassador-subtle. The numberless, inanimate, Sennacheribs for instance . . .

One of the stubbornest prejudices against mages was that

they could read minds. No amount of denials from even the most trusted of them could erode it. '*It might be true of you,*' would come the unanswerable response, '*but how can you guarantee that maybe some . . .*'

For a unworthy instant Guy thought of that when Bathie asked:

'Why all the little figurines . . . ?'

But then he accepted love and marriage as far more likely explanation, and no longer worried. Let her read him if she wished, or wander within his inner library as much as she liked. He had nothing to hide

'A very good question, Bathesheba . . .' – and by his use of her given name he warned her he was in earnest and on duty. 'I presume you refer to the images of Sennacherib, second god-king and founder of this realm. They are accorded the very highest respect . . .'

Bathie was already fluent in Ambassador-speak – or at least the outer layers of that onion skin. She caught on that the conversational rope bridge was fraying and a chasm yawned below. The Assyrians might not be talking to them but there was every chance they were listening.

'And *deservedly* so,' said Bathie, in ringing and soldier-stiff tones. 'I detected that esteem in the flower-chains and offerings with which many are laden.'

'Indeed,' *agreed* Guy, and winked at her.

'I was so impressed as to be tempted to add my own.'

Her husband's face tumbled into distress before hasty rearrangement.

'Were you?'

'Or possibly not . . .'

She'd walked with him this far but suddenly, according to her way, tired of the scenery and strange native customs.

'Or whatever . . . !' she flared, tired of all the caution and code words and walking on eggshells.

In a flourish of leg-show scarlet she flounced to their bed – an unrequested and invitingly, voluptuously plump double one, and so another source of not-to-be-spoken tension between them. Seconds after hurling herself athwart it, she was almost asleep, breaths lengthening, long black eyelashes flickering slowly down to shut up shop.

Easy sleep: how he envied her and all youthful, unburdened, minds that luxury.

Guy dared not look; it would be too painful – and that choice mischoice of words reinforced discomfort in endless loop. He didn't want to think of pain right then. Commanding himself to both that and blinkers was difficult enough but the unbroken beast, imagination, would not be put into a corral. It supplied a picture of what he was missing: the abandoned pose: growing less *held*, more languid, by the moment; too possibility-rich to be borne.

Guy rose whilst he still could, whilst there was still fair chance of his ship answering the helm, and made hastily for the door.

Outside there was a low-grade, doubtless diversionary, eavesdropper to be shooed away: a swarthy, nimble boy who shifted even speedier aided by a Wessex boot. If his curious masters thought that Guy would be lulled by *him*, then they'd sadly underrated Ambassadorial awareness. Whilst they were in foreign accommodation not a word would pass between husband and wife that could enlighten anyone, be they friend or foe, not privy to their personal dialect. More like a forty-year married couple rather than a two-summer partnership, they spoke their own code, special to them alone. Shared dark secrets and pre-nuptial training ensured it.

Outside their borrowed Castle residence and venturing into the boggy, black, little capital that clustered round its walls, his unhappy enticement eased. The sea air was effervescent on Guy's angular face, reviving him, but internal peace proved more elusive. In the fortress-city it was *clattering time*, that period between light and dark when the more organised were already battening up for the night. All around him as he wandered, outwardly ignored, householders and flunkies were crashing great wooden shutters over their domestic strong-holds. They made no allowance for strollers, even invisible ones, and several times he came close to being brained by speedy security precautions.

He wanted to walk it off, though unwilling to define what 'it' was. Generally he found a mile or two in uninspiring surroundings did the trick. Afterwards he could return home untroubled and sleep the sleep of the just. Lack of thought – that was the key – that and not pestering life to be neat. The whole basis of the Ambassadorial role was accommodation to the ragged edges of others and so it ought to be child's play to extend the same courtesy to himself. He toyed with that should-be-easy-to-swallow medicine all through the first circuit.

The layout of Pevensey-Nineveh was ideal for his purpose. Beyond the hedgehog of angular bastions and quays and landing stages, the high walls were pierced by four gates (and numberless, some forgotten, postern and secret entrances) which opened on to a paved spiral winding inexorably – though at its own pace – to the Castle at the heart of the labyrinth. Each circle delineated a certain caste or occupation, the more exalted as it closed upon the centre; the amount of swirling turquoise-blue exterior decoration increasing in direct proportion to proximity to that focal point.

Conversely, black-tarred house fronts and homely-carved warding sea-demons did not start till half way out, but then fast-bred to ubiquity. It was a crowded-in, baroque, jagged jumble, inclined to ferment claustrophobia and madness in those not bred to it. Guy's headache failed to improve.

He'd strolled out from the serpent's head, the home of the Divine Vicegerent, and his Iron Nobles and their most exalted guests. It suited him to wind outward, away from the flint-pebble Castle walls, out to the less decorous bustle and sound of the sea. There were pathways between the circuits: *twittens* in the local dialect, supposedly a word dictated by Blades himself and thus sacrosanct, not fit to be pondered or examined. Nevertheless, Guy rejected their proffered short cuts just as he declined to query the divine vocabulary. Many were gated off or blocked in any case, through private purchase or ancient custom, transforming the former clarity of the City's disc into a maddening maze. Guy felt the need to stride the long way, rather than peer here and there, looking to see if there might be a way through. The sea and the walls from which to observe it weren't going anywhere and would patiently await his arrival, however leisurely.

He concluded Pevensey was built of three P's (four if you counted the name itself): precautions, pride and piety – and sometimes all three combined. It was a notion thrust upon you and then verified everywhere you stepped or settled your gaze. Everything was aggrandised and defensible, each structure down to humble coal sheds the ideal, ornate, venue for a last stand. God-figures filled most nooks and alcoves devoid of military value or presided on high over more vital zones. Even the sky was not exempted and each roof bristled with wicked, black-tarred, stakes to combat the enemies that flew by air. Not one opportunity of architecture was allowed to shirk its addition to the chorus: that Pevensey-Assyria was great, if embattled, and the recipient of divine favours.

Guy paused and studied one narrow view of the sky above, curtailed by looming tenements to either side and their crowning hairbrush of spikes. In his head he knew they were protection against the leathery 'Parliaments' (another Bladian christening) that swooped on infants and the unwary, or other rarer air-mobile inhabitants of sea and fen, but in his heart he wished them a symbol against worse enemies. In a vision, as necessarily swift as it was pleasing, he imagined every last one adorned with a writhing, dying angel.

Such thoughts were dangerous and he flushed them away. It was said – and who was he to deny it? – that the occupiers could detect hostility and might capriciously home in on it to ask probing questions. Rationally, Guy found grounds to doubt that – elseways he and his circle would be permanently in angelic company – but right now there was no call to run even the slightest additional risk. For once his head held grounds for hope and he did not wish to invite the great enemy to a tour of inspection.

He sought for swift, purgative distraction – and found it in thoughts of the oncoming night and sleep upon the cold floor. Then, when that was too savage a potion he retired to the comparative anathema of the *Sennacheribs*. Two flanked him at that very moment, at the opening to a very ordinary twitten leading to an arbour of pampered roses: some prospering Assyrian's garden, a place when he or she sat to contemplate their next move or recuperate from the fray. Nothing special but still worthy of a double god in brass.

Guy moved away as from error, taking with him ample smoke-screen food for thought. The Pevenseymen worried him. They said they were orthodox, that they worshipped the ONEGOD and his successive projections on earth, but Guy didn't need to be a trained inquisitor to suspect the excessive honours paid their founder. Sennacherib might well be in the recognised king list; doubtless he *did* found Pevensey-Assyria and thus was due his fair share of remembrance and worship – but so were the dozens of his successors: equally worthy intercessors that Guy saw none of here.

It wasn't just swirling suspicion or prejudice. Trained to at least entertain the notion that all men intended well – as they conceived it – Guy required firmer foundations for distaste. Yet, being an educated man, descended from an old-style second circle family – a Blades-touched line no less – he was aware of the dark legends and could not discount them. They said that before Sennacherib had ascended to the throne and divinity, he'd had lapses and a rebellious soul. Blades had had to forgive him thrice. It was not a bar to godhead, true, but ought to put a break on full-blown adulation. There were others more worthy of worship: he could think of a number without effort. There was *Joseph 3 Purple*, for instance, slayer of the last native Wessex Null – or the martyr god-king, *Sherden Weshwesh*, who'd given battle (the mere notion both inspiration and ice-shower admixed) when the angels arrived and settled the theological poser about whether a deity could die. In fact, the invaders had answered that one with excessive clarity, over a period of shrieking weeks.

So there *were* alternatives; exalted beings, as much or more worthy of worship than the first Iron King, but Guy had seen no trace of them – and knew that even if he lingered a month he would still search in vain.

The Christians had their Trinity which was cause for laughter enough (when it didn't require suppression), but that was just slave and Leveller philosophy and so not expected to make sense. The whispers Guy had heard of the Assyrian's secret *Binity* concerned him far more. If the decent and refined portions of risen humanity could not agree on absolutely vital truths, then they deserved conquest by others more convinced. The angels decried all worship, even of themselves – a strong temptation to weaker brethren – and so far had done very well, thank you, on such damnable doctrines.

The priests told Guy that present troubles might be Blades's punishment for heresy and he could see the logic of that. If the first god-king had not come through to communicate the truth then what else *had* he come for? And then, if after all that, after all his labours and sufferings and ceaseless toil, men chose to bow down to a variety of imperfect idols, was it any wonder he withheld his smile from them?

Left to himself Guy was no theologian and saw the wonders of God more in horse and female flesh, or views across the Downs, than the cerebral beauty of doctrine, but thus far he could follow. It made sense.

It likewise made sense to let the Assyrians harbour (sic) their little bi-polar heresies for the while, solely in the interests of desperately needed unity; but a time would come when clarity was all. They're seen off a Trinity with fire and sword and firm persuasion, so a Binity ought to be one-third easier.

He strolled on, leaving the gods behind, confident he was surrounded by the sole and true one, till the city opened like a whore before him. Space was at a premium upon Pevensey's narrow isthmus; once upon a time three sides had been surrounded by the sea. Now the tide had receded and the ocean trade and piracy (or mixtures of the two) was perforce ceded to the Levellers. Even the former lifeblood *Salthaven* which penetrated the walls was now silted up beyond accepting all but the shallowest craft. Where once stately galleons had issued on to the sea-lanes, now only fishermen and pike-like galleys darted in and out to raid or trade with the successor Freeports that dotted the littoral. Lines of once-proud warships subsided slowly into mud, dying for lack of water and anywhere to go, now poor-men's firewood.

With that excuse and incited by greed and need, the Assyrians had seized upon the under-used harbour and warehouses, easing new mundane activities and livelihoods into them. Yet, revealingly, that wasn't so with the abandoned station and silent marshalling yards. *Their* Sennacheribs in metal and stone still held their perimeter inviolate against the day when trains would run again and each engine would need its god-king figurehead. All was forlorn now where once passengers waited to be sped to Wessex by steam, but the ideal was not abandoned altogether. Guy could see the locomotives peeking from their shed, intact, unravished despite the desperate need for metal. The dignity of the realm and its founding deity would not admit to them being stripped down and a final admission of defeat. If there was one place that conveyed the best of the Pevensey-Assyrian spirit and its indomitable ambitions then it was here.

Guy looked around the silent grounds and almost forgave them their heresies. If you focused your scrutiny to a tight beam, then Pevensey men were also the best of humanity. Wessex had scrapped its locos long ago.

He took that spirit of reconciliation with him across the platforms and rails. It lasted all the way to the walls and the view over the darkening Levels and the shingle bank now between the city and the sea. Then he saw the tightly-clustered lights a little way off.

Pevensey-Assyria might say they were true-Wessex but it had its limits. No *foreign* troops might come within the walls. Guy's waiting escort back to the homeland had to camp outside and take its chances with the lively night.

63

He gripped the old pebble and mortar of the many-times renewed ramparts and shuddered as he heard the myriad sounds of the Wild, awakening full of energy and appetite, and eager for the night ahead.

They rose again, as did Guy's spirits which had dipped for a minute. The thought had occurred to him that *they* were hungry for the future, but was he? In truth, was any of his species?

Answer came from the precious cargo concealed in his memory. The night devourers could rise again as they had done every night since the beginning, but tonight they were not alone. Others were rising with them.

'*Resurgam!*'

The Assyrians saw fit to place the exposure tables right outside their city. There the dead waited with all the patience of that condition for nature to strip their bones. Only then were they ready for their funeral: pale and clean and collected, baled like hay with black ribbon.

In New-Wessex proper such places were always sited atop the highest Downs, which speeded the process and granted the gone some privacy. Likewise with the long barrows in which the more memory-worthy or richer Wessex-folk awaited Doomsday in company. They graced far hills, greenly merging in with them, and were numinous places of pilgrimage. Here red-terracotta beehive ossuaries, many conspicuously overstuffed, nestled right up to the tables.

Again, the Pevensey men saw things differently. Having the 'Field of Dead' circling around the *Way*'s end conveniently robbed it of the slightest shred of welcome, draping a sombre air over the jolliest of visitors. In short, Pevensey-Assyria approached the world and life seriously, and preferred that visitors approach them in the same way.

Guy was going the other way but still got the message. It frowned upon his ever buoyant smile.

64

'Fare ye well, cousin,' said Genghiz.

'Likewise, cousin.'

Ambassadors were permitted one moment of indulgence per exchange, according to the ancient wisdom of the clan. The dangers of repressed sentiment had long ago been recognised and allowed a little controlled venting.

Guy and Genghiz shook hands, their well-wishing genuine. Now precedence was established between them they could appreciate each other for what they really were, not what their birth demanded. Also, the golden light of Guy's hope bathed all, showing even the meanest things in favourable colour. So, he now found much to be said for Genghiz: like that long hours toiling in the statecraft vineyard had really worn all his edges away. He could have walked into the lowest trooper tavern and exuded an air of peace over proceedings. The man was so *nice* that, all other things being equal, you found yourself wanting to please him.

Suddenly the mood changed.

'What is it that you *know*?' Genghiz was hissing into Guy's ear: fervent, unrestrained, as they embraced in farewell. Guy pulled back but the fraternal arms adhered like a burr.

Naturally, he retained control of his face – the reflex nerves between feelings and features were ages ago snipped – but there was danger that the horror he felt would leak to the surface in some confirming manifestation. Somehow he had betrayed himself. The hope of deliverance had shone through all his best shielding.

Genghiz must have been ravenous for hope himself, starved beyond all control, to make such an un-ambassadorial scene. Bathie noticed, the Pevensey gatemen noticed. They looked on, shocked, without understanding.

Guy's years and height prevailed and he disengaged himself. Genghiz Ambassador stepped back abashed, as though caught in furtive self-abuse. Perhaps for the first time in a long and distinguished career, he had weakened.

'I'm so . . . sorry. My mistake . . .'

Guy knew his gaze was being sought but averted his eyes

65

from the unhappy event. There was no reply he could give. Instead, he seized Bathie's hand and walked away, never looking back: the only merciful option really. The Ambassador elders would not hear of it from him but he confidently expected a resignation would follow in his wake. '*An emotional Ambassador,*' said the thirteenth clan precept, '*is no Ambassador*' – and it was interpreted literally. A career had withered to death in an instant and Guy could not be so ghoulish as to stay and study the corpse.

The New-Wessex soldiers were waiting for them as close as allowed; almost in sight of the embarrassment before Pevensey-Nineveh's walls but thankfully not so near as to perceive it. The couple joined them with relief.

'My Lord Ambassador. My Lady.'

Their officer was all wig and scarlet, top and tailing a white-flashing, saucy, smile. Treading the Wild and Demi-Wild had poured temporary promotion over him, garnished with '*nothing matters, for tomorrow we die*'. In his own mind he was a general at least. If he survived escort command a few years he would be.

'Captain.'

Whilst the couple's scant luggage was taken and loaded on the communal handcart, their two-score new friends took stock of them. Some of the more devout amongst them went on one knee at first sight. Others, mostly the younger, Guy noted, didn't flinch beyond a courteous nod of the head. Alas, rationalism, atheism and their sister, Christianity, respected no borders, even seeping in from abroad to infect the land of the living God. It was a constant battle to repair the sea walls of Truth.

'How was your night?' asked Guy.

'Lively, Ambassador; but without loss, Blades be praised.'

'Praise him, indeed.'

By way of a message, the Pevensey-Assyrians placed the outlanders' holding-corral right at the edge of the Wild and so it was rarely without after-dark visitors. The place was fortified but defence of it was up to the guests and above the stockade

66

gate were burnt the words: 'Stranger – you are welcome but not safe' – which fairly told entrants all they need know. New-Nineveh valued its humanity but prized its distinctiveness even more.

A token number of Assyrian axe-bearers still ringed them, again to make a point, but remained behind once the foreigners set off in the right direction. They lingered long enough to see them safely on the railway track and then dispersed.

Guy paused. In common with almost all the party, he bowed his head in prayer.

'Omnipotent Blades, we thank you for keeping us alive, for preserving us, and bringing us to this moment. May you stand between us and harm in all the godless places we must walk.'

It was the standard waking and Way acknowledgements combined. Most of the mouths there echoed '*amen*' – and almost as many hearts affirmed.

A moment of reflection before any journey was considered both healthy and sign of refinement in New-Wessex. True, they were beyond its borders, but the company was of it and the path there clear. Also, the preservation of standards was all the more vital when in a strange land – and land hardly came any stranger than that before them now.

A green lane, dead straight and lined with rusting iron, stretched into perspective infinity, loving the Levels, transcending quagmires, ignoring and boring into the Downs. A blind man could not have got lost.

Sometimes, duties in the Wild and its corridors eroded faith (a consequence which part reconciled authority to the high casualty rate) but the escort commander seemed unafflicted. He waved one wide cuff of scarlet and lace at the beeline before them.

'Our path is straight,' he said, in all – it seemed, rare – solemnity. 'For which we *thank* the god-kings.'

Being an educated and religious man, Guy could both confirm and refine it. Their proper gratitude was owed to one particular spark off the divine.

Thinking of him, Guy Ambassador led the way.

When loco boilers die they aren't reticent about letting the world know. The silver and gold body shredded itself into a sunflower of jagged metal, spraying a lethal soup of boiling water croutoned with glowing coals.

They had been given a shred of warning and so many of the passengers survived at the expense of dignity. The slower and more considerate, who declined to trample others, were caught at the tidal wave's edge and melted.

Quite properly, god-king Malfosse I was not numbered amongst the meek and thus dead. His huscarls had him off the train and clambering over people at the first syllable of angelic command. It wasn't fitting that he jump to it and scramble for survival himself, but that others do it for him was borderline acceptable. He was lifted and bundled like a parcel up the steep cutting and he felt some of his bearers take the force of the loco's rage on their armoured backs. When they fell he went with them.

In fact, though it broke his heart, the combustion of his beloved personal train also saved his life. The aftermath of its nova flung him to earth: a suitable position in which to abase yourself and beg for mercy. Standing would have equalled defiance and thus some inventive death. That lucky prostration also enabled him to do some good for others, as yet unborn, as well.

The angel knew this was a high caste insect by the deference shown it and the wrappings worn: gold and frothy lace seemed essential camouflage for the higher end of their hilarious hierarchies. They were useful insofar that a message to one served as speech to all: a delicious saving on effort. It also seemed conveniently humble: no lesson to teach there then.

She/it appeared to Malfosse in a guise of wrath. One frost-white arm indicated the burning train, the other pinned the god-king writhing to the ground.

'Arrogance!' she said. 'Forbidden!'

Stretches of the track peeled up and back to amplify the point.

'Nevermore!'

So that was that for steam-power and swift travel: another advance taken away from them. The angels required only horseback or 'shank's pony', and leisured, laboured, communication. And having spoken once they expected no appeal.

It was not that long after their arrival, post the days of the martyr god-kings but before total capitulation. Humandom was shrinking, the Wild burgeoning at angelic behest, provinces becoming enclaves and the centre an embattled bastion. That novel claustrophobia was probably the inspiration for what was left of resistance, or at least protest – even successful protest on occasion.

'Leave us the lines,' asked Malfosse, flat on his face, eyes wide at his own temerity. 'Please let us still walk the beautiful straight lines . . .'

At that moment, after the whimsical but iron decree, it looked as though the squeezing would go on to leave only islands: discrete pockets of mankind separated by Wild. Intercourse between them would be left to the tired of life who cared to dash through Mother Nature turned mad and bad. Since that wouldn't constitute contact, what was left would grow isolated and set in their ways, then bored, then strange.

God-king Malfosse, an intelligent man, saw the future in an instant. He'd seen what happened to the inbred and so dared to plead for loopholes. If he couldn't have his gleaming train, then at least let there be *novelty*.

'Leave corridors . . .' he requested, pinned like a glorious butterfly, perfectly manicured hands feebly accentuating the words. And then a plea from the heart. 'Leave us room to breathe . . .'

His courtiers and huscarls had already said private farewells to him, anticipating another martyr monarch and yet one more embarrassing king-contest. No one would admit it but the hunt was on for humble and pliant candidates; men with pre-broken spirits to grovel before the angelic host. Standards were declining in everything: pre-birth sadness forcing its way into the collective human soul.

Then, though its mind was already plainly far away, the angel actually *agreed*.

'Very well,' she/it said, maybe seeing what the god-king saw and a brake on their entertainment. The train-fire was quelled with a sudden deluge of hard rain that stung. 'Corset, yes. Strangle, no.'

And then she left them to their victory – or so the legend said.

Centuries later, there was still a way through from Pevensey to New-Wessex, as straight – if only as broad – as the old cutting it followed. For as long as it remained Assyria proper, even the iron tracks remained, though beyond and in less pious lands they had long since been wrenched up and recycled, and the hard-wood sleepers likewise. Under the new dispensation nostalgia wasn't enough to save the underemployed. All the same, the way, or *Way*, was still plain and clear. Travellers were granted corridors of merely 'demi-Wild' which were traversable – with courage and caution.

All along the Way, at intervals of a mile or two, there were altars to the Way-lord, *Malfosse-of-the-Concession*. Invaders from the true Wild had gnawed or disfigured some but most remained, decked with offerings and honours. Guy and his party did not neglect to pay their respects to each.

So their way and Way was straight, a sunken, deceptive ribbon of peace threading the Wild, often cut deep enough to seem a world of its own, blinkered against the disturbing sights beyond. Only occasionally, when the Downs rose high to one or other side, was their predicament brought home to them. Day-haunting Wild-life strode long-legged across the slopes and their chittering calls crept over the cutting's edge.

At those times Guy was reconciled to tired feet and having to walk it, since, mounted, he would only have gained an improved, grandstand, view of the gut-churning perversities beyond. Either way, for better or worse, the angels barred horse-flesh from the Ways. Any defiance of that was to risk incineration at best.

Guy reckoned he could discern their motive for once: a tolerance of intercourse between the remaining enclaves just to vary and spice things up for themselves, but nothing speedy or efficient – or threatening. It only made him all the more determined to find a crumb of comfort in the ban.

And so, since progress was slow, conversation became even more of a boon than normal; a comfort to fill the plodding hours and filter out roars and cries from beyond. Also, it was a plausible excuse to just stare straight ahead.

That rather depended on the conversation, though. Escort-Captain had the bit between his teeth and was setting Guy's on edge . . .

'Nothing *but*. Dead men; dead slaves each way you looked: barely an oar stirring. Still, the tide was carrying us in so we went with it. Well . . . it beached us within rifle range and we set to for an hour till the town walls were like a poxed face. Then a wizard came under truce and stood on the sands to offer terms. Don't judge – there was nothing else for it. You could see the infantry massing in St James's churchyard ready to rush in with the dusk and the rest of the fleet had given us up for dead. Oh yes; we'd seen the flag of farewell hoisted. That brings a lump to y'throat I can tell you: that and knowledge of what wizards do to prisoners.'

'Indeed,' said Guy, wishing the subject would pass by swiftly whilst in Bathie's hearing. Her taste for the macabre already fanned, she'd ceased mouthing her own, private, story and was all ears, even signalling it by drawing back one side-thicket of black tangle.

'By then, of course, there were angels in the air; more and more arriving to spectate – a picnic in the sky. I think that's what saved us in the end – that and our abundant

71

ammunition. Neither side wanted to prolong the show for *their* amusement. So we accepted the terms and swam for it: no pursuing black-spells or mind tendrils, not even a pistol shot. I'm a strong swimmer: unlike some. I made it back to an Imperial who hadn't yet turned for home. So that's *that* one.'

Escort-Captain let go the brilliant starburst, elder brother of the gaudy family that sat on his thin breast. At no one's request he was going through the earning of each decoration, all the little colonial campaigns of diminished Wessex.

He seemed to actually fear silence, blanking out the miles of their route from Pevensey with tales of themeless post-imperial scuffles and five-score-a-side wars amidst the fields and Downs. The last, a breathless account of the latest attempt to reincorporate rebellious Wight, all about Wessex infantry aboard borrowed Pevensey 'pike' galleys, had occupied them from New Polegate almost to lost Wilmington. Alone amongst the martial torrent, Guy hadn't tuned that one out. Here was a rare chance to learn the truth of a very opaque matter – for there were few enough surviving eye-witnesses who'd got close enough to shoot at Yarmouth. The wizards' island citadel remained mysterious and independant.

Guy was intrigued, despite himself. In his library at home was a pamphlet written by a slave who'd escaped the great sacrifice ceremonies at Mottistone: a rip-roaring account of dawn holocausts to a savage Island god. There was cause to both interrupt and mine the monologue.

'What did he look like?'

The soldier had expected, didn't like, his therapeutic outpouring interrupted. 'Who?' he barked, frazzled by some inner, interrupted, coition. 'Who?'

'The Yarmouth wizard.'

That apparently interested him and he was mollified. He considered the captured memory, forgetting even to walk on. His warriors gathered round him as they caught up.

'He was tall,' he said eventually, recounting each snippet fresh as it was received, 'and his gown was star-painted . . .'

Guy liked that image: he could see it himself: the magician

on the muddy estuary, sole seen exemplar of the academy town behind. The stranded galley, the survivors amongst all the dead men, a box of cartridges beside each, waiting to sell their remaining minutes on earth.

'. . . painted in blood.'

Suddenly the picture shrivelled, its appeal bled away into the still beheld sand.

'His eyes had seen too much.'

The soldier looked straight into Guy's face and revealed he had imbibed some of that same misfortune. Having long wavered on the edge of abyss he was now half in love with the view. The Ambassador declined to be tempted and drew back from the brink, breaking the mutual gaze.

' "First-rest" is here.' he announced, re-establishing rank and propriety 'We have walked far enough.' Guy was content to let it seem like a whim and thus a test of their pliability. The image he cultivated did not go with nice calculations of time and pace.

Whereas others might have protested, Escort-Captain's well-concealed madness allowed him to ride that particular tiger. What was a little – or even a lot – more risk to a life he didn't especially esteem?

'Very well. Halt. Fortify. Feed. Sleep.'

The surprise was relayed down the line by his lieutenants. Some soldiers gaped and looked about but nothing was said. Their commander might seem a world away but they knew he heard all and forgave nothing.

Guy was barging against good sense and tradition. Paradoxically, it was beside the Way that the Wild, even this demi-Wild, was most voracious; its inhabitants both sustained and attracted by such a replete artery of food. Further out, star-clothed nights might, with luck, be survived but here stout walls standing between succulent flesh and harm were an absolute requirement. Customary 'first-rest' on the Assyria-Wessex trail was either New-Glynde, or else New-Polegate for the really leaden-paced: secure night stockades constructed around the former stations. However, borne along on Escort-

Captain's word-waves, they'd sailed past the one and were short of the other. Innovation was now called for, improvisation required: qualities ever more atrophied in browbeaten New-Wessex.

Still, even high effort came easier than questioning a birth-line touched, albeit centuries back, by Divine sperm. Keeping their fears and grumbles to themselves, they shifted about looking for night safety.

Guy could have told them: he knew, had never ceased to. Whilst they'd walked and been distracted, he had counted the paces and noted the world beyond their green and tranquil gouge. People continually mistook his diffident exterior for the entirety and an occasional stutter was the seal on their error. However, behind the pleasantries and all-too-evident willingness to please, cold calculation had been inserted at birth: the mark of the Ambassadors, as lasting as circumcision. Guy never ceased to be aware of time and place and score. The effort would fray years off his life but that covenant had been made long before his birth. He couldn't be without it now.

New-Wilmington was a minor hallowing on one of the obscurer pilgrim-ways. Blades had rested there the day before the Professor – '*may his name be blotted out*' – first appeared on the scene. He had been happy there, attaching some special significance to it, naturally not fully vouchsafed to them in this world but heavily – say eight months – pregnant with meaning even to the shallow. Two – possibly three – attributed sayings had been uttered on the spot – and, most importantly, *there* he had blessed and left them with his own lasting image. Until he should come again it was all they had left of him, their best and closest view. Here you could practically kiss the lips of God – or leastways glimpse them at a distance. Guy could no more pass it without a word than he would – or could – his father.

There was no doubt or argument within him. When the sharp shoulder of Firle Beacon was clear, and Mount Caburn almost but not quite visible round its corner, then it was time for the pious to pause and turn aside to greet the *Long Man*.

For His feet had trodden there.

Guy's lips were still stumbling over words of praise as last-light
retreated from Windover Hill. He hadn't finished thanking
Blades for taking the trouble to assemble the world's
constituent parts when Escort-Captain decided their day was
done. The night, beyond any dispute, belonged to others.

Paradoxically, it was the time when the great hill-figure was
most manifest. In the present decadence and humiliation he
had declined into a 'green-man', an elusive hint and
suggestion now that none dared the annual scouring of turf
down to the gleaming chalk below. It had become necessary
that he be known beforehand, his whereabouts and shape
familiar, for him to grant audience. Even then, he was only
seen when it suited, when light and shade were right and the
eye of faith deployed. Only then, or else under snow or in
times of drought, could long shadows throw his lines into
relief, revealing the huge but graceful being, enigmatic but
benign, hurling open the doors to another world.

Here was a holy place, requiring a key to enter. Guy had it.

He reluctantly turned his cupped hands to earth. They had
held wisdom harvested in the course of prayer, for all that he
couldn't weigh or feel it. Now it was returned whence it came
for others to benefit from. He had added his tiny increment to
sanctify the site and by his living the Long Man was a speck
more holy than before. Pilgrims who came after would reap
the benefit. Whatever else might befall him as a man, a
transient mote traversing the eyeball of the Almighty, he,
Guy Ambassador, A.B.430 to ?, had not lived in vain.

In the interests of his surviving at least five minutes more,
the soldiers hustled him away. It wasn't that they believed any
less than he, but they did fear punishment in this life and the
next for losing him.

There was a church in New-Wilmington which would be
their salvation. When the sun failed then the Wild-life felt

free to invade the angelic greenways. Once the warmth was out of the turf even there would be crawling with them: a streamlined meritocracy of meat-eaters and human-haters. Their gambolling and chomping were not fit sights to behold, let alone encounter. Survival required solid walls and sharpness of metal and mind.

New-Glynde Station, now an impossible dream, was a lovely hedgehog of wicked spikes and swivel-guns. Braziers of tar and sea-coal lined its walls and did the trick worth a hundred muskets, since, for the most part, the new-life had surrendered understanding in return for existence. The slithering, snapping, things were more easily deterred than killed.

The Church at Wilmington had been built for other purposes, was frozen in the transition between the Christian delusion and true worship. A Wessex god-king's crown surmounted, but had never replaced, the spire pointing direct at the old Father-god. Within, you could still see where the altar had sat at the eastern extremity. Since, for reasons best known to himself, Blades had withheld the hand of transformation from the place, it was not for anyone to question the resulting unhappy mix. Yet Guy couldn't help but notice that the Unconquered Sun, the inimitable Imperial starburst, sat ill on walls dishonoured by saints and crucifixes.

'You, know,' he'd told Bathie, 'it was here, right here, that he said: *"Everything has a beginning . . ."*'

She'd shrugged bird-like shoulders, a gesture typical of her kin, not dismissive but not awestruck either, and continued single-mindedly with the washing of her dust- and travel-irritated feet. That was both the strength and bane of the breed. You could take the Fruntierfolke out of the frontier, but not the reverse. They brought it along with them in their head and on their back. It was needful on occasion – like an axe – but still a bit daunting elsewhen.

Also, both he and she knew that soldiers were drinking their fill of the sight of long, white, aristocratic legs. A scarlet gown gathered round the waist and vigorous ablutions left

76

little unrevealed. Of course, Bathie didn't mind – being bred to that brazenness too. '*Let the dogs see the hare,*' her father had often said, '*and they'll run all the harder.*' Then he'd laugh and slap someone's back. He'd done it to Guy once until Guy let the eye-flash be seen. Fruntierfolke weren't the only ones who could dole out selective lessons. He now recalled that rare indulgence and, jealous of others' freedom, relived the emotion.

Yet, come to that, he was staring no less than they, so hadn't grounds for too much anger. It seemed ungracious to monopolise a view, especially one so lovely. So let them look, so long as they didn't dream of trespass. Confident of that bare minimum, he used up his excess energy in prowling instead.

In one corner there an organ, abandoned to dust and rot, its cunning wood-carvings now shrouded by spiders' – just as skilful – constructs. Guy looked at its soaring pipes and toyed with the idea of having the bellows pumped, just to see what vestigial sounds would emerge. Tortured shrieks, most probably, not something they required reminding of right now. Still, it was tempting . . .

His fingers brushed over the stops and keys, the first to disturb their quiet accumulation for decades. Yet, beneath the dust, the leather of the seat was still red and glossy; intriguingly cracked and gaping. In his mind's eye . . .

Bathie's actual eye caught his. She knew his idiosyncrasies and could gate-crash his fantasies. *Time and place*, that look told him, more amused than reproving: *time and place* . . .

The music in his head stopped even though it was thought of her that had started it. He smiled and shrugged and moved on.

Escort-Captain was making the rounds whilst those allocated the chance of sleep settled down to attempt it. Guy joined him just as the oak door was barred and thrice fastened with iron-hooped beams. Riflemen were ordered aloft before every window. Where once was stained-glass now sat spiked grills and ominously punctured mesh. Ample lanterns made everything painfully clear.

77

Soon enough, all was readiness. The 'Ancient of Days' yew tree abutting the building, honoured recipient of recorded comment from Blades himself, creaked and troubled against one wall and its various piercings, making shadow-play inside. Otherwise, Guy and Captain were the only mobile part of a tense and anticipant scene.

Even before day failed, Escort-Captain had pointed out the Church's successive fittings for sundered door bars, but by then the die was cast and there was no better place to run to. The latest replacements appeared the most robust, the most iron-blessed, and so they made light of their predecessors.

'Practise makes perfect,' the soldier had said and Guy smiled – even though he'd noticed the old wall-wounds and gouges all around. You had to be *reconciled*, he told himself at frequent intervals, otherwise you'd not get out of bed, not in the new New-Wessex. No act of virtue, no act at all, was without risk equal to its value. Life without risk was life without virtue: without it you might as well stay at home and put a frock on. The thirtieth precept, as Guy now recalled, of Hobbes Leviathan Ambassador (A.B.299 – 340)

The thing with Wild-life was that, aside from rare 'king-beasts', they were cowardly for all their strength and madness and hunger. They tended towards flock action, despite rampant individualism. Thus the first probe was a long time in coming and very cautious even then. The foremost, presumably egged on by the drooling many behind, took a while to pluck up courage.

It started with a polite knock at the door. Something had a hand and knuckles to rap with but no words whereby to make its wishes known.

Receiving no answer, it persisted. All within were deathly quiet.

'Sorry' said Escort-Captain, smirking through the door. 'But no one's *home* today . . .'

The knocking ceased and confident footsteps receded. They were left in peace.

Then something flew through a window, through its razor

grille, through its guardian soldier. It landed, shredded but still alive, a flapping mess of wings and red and long legs. Two revolver-fulls stilled it. Replacement shutters, alas only oak, were hurried aloft.

Guy drew Bathie close to him even as he reloaded. In death, as in life, they would go together if need be – a package; take both or none but not either.

Through her thin gown and his own thick buff-coat, he felt more than body heat. The fickle sparkle of sorcery was upon her and thus they both crackled, enlivening the soup-like air when they moved.

The knock returned to the door, along with a soft sound that might have been

'*pleaseeeeeee . . .*'

It was a long night, doubtless rich in grace but sleep-poor, with little time for prayer or thankfulness.

Day came like the ending of unwanted celibacy. There were indigestible pieces of things piled in front of the Church and someone's blood all up the door. A message, perhaps, or maybe that was reading too much into leftovers from an easier meal than the building's prickly contents.

An earlier mist lingered at lower levels but promising sunshine soon scorched it away elsewhere. The Downs were emerald with light and the Long Man looked down on all, not in the least shocked into passion by what he had witnessed the night before – and probably every night. There was peace, but they were ungrateful. It now seemed false to them.

When all was declared safe by expendable scouts, they regrouped on the Way, rifle and musket men both fore and aft, then a pincushion of pikes and swordsmen at the middle for them to retreat to. Escort-Captain put his valuable charges into the centre of all, and only then decreed that *it was good*. After a theatrical wave of his tasselled sword they set off.

By Lewes there was a wicker-angel, thrice man-sized,

laughable rather than imposing in all save its size. Wooden wings, already weather-dappled, spread across their perspective of the ruined town. It might signify anything and they wouldn't draw close to narrow their speculations, but Bathie's keen eyes picked out a tiny gate in the structure's breast.

It could indicate either worship or something worse. Did someone climb within and act the angel, awing whatever scraps of humanity hung on in the lost town? Or was the entrance one-way, the mouth for sacrifice?

Either way, it was a cursed thing, a prayer for retribution from someone or other. Angels sometimes went rabid at any worship of themselves, dousing the weak and apostate in spectacular disapproval. It was another of their inexplicable foibles: first they counterfeited arbitrary, unanswerable, and thus godlike behaviour and then disavowed the consequences. No wonder humanity wobbled giddily on the edge of a complete loss of morale.

Guy thrust the thought aside. He'd never been tempted to transfer loyalties himself, nor had any of the steadfast he chose for his friends, but he could, at the very edge of hearing, still detect the siren call. You just had to hope you'd get through life – as presently formulated – without capitulation. Heaven knew, there were enticements to stray every minute of the day. Like now. Again the grotesque, hollow, angel caught his eye. Decadence – decadence all around and everywhere you rested your gaze.

To prove it Guy turned his head – and sure enough there was no respite. Lewes had been a fair town once, the direct initiative of Blades himself. Now its castle was falling to meet the steep main street and the Ouse was seeping in to overcome the suburb of Cliffe, ambitious of licking away its walls. Sun brought pseudo-life to the gap-tiled roofs of Lewes but Guy knew they sheltered no one he would care to meet. So depressing, so dispiriting . . .

To punish it for spawning such unnatural thoughts, Guy was minded to burn the angel himself, depriving the real variety of the pleasure. But to do that would be to display his discontent far and wide. A consequence might be meeting its creators, the neo-Lewesians he didn't wish to know. So, he let sleeping dogs lie and fate take its course.

Within half an hour he had quite forgotten the day's poor start, even before Southerham and Lewes were lost to sight or New-Falmer hoved into view. Soon, Guy was happily lost in contemplating Bathie's callipygous back and the race-card he could imagine for Epsom that day.

Only Escort-Captain lingered to note the activity they left behind. Matchstick-men ebbed out of ruined Lewes; darting dark heads enlivened the Downs. He informed the rearguard that maybe, just maybe, their day had come, but otherwise said nothing. Then, suppressing his shoulders' wish to clench, he pressed to the front of the narrow column to become vanguard treader of the dewy, virgin, turf. His face was a silent and undisturbed pool. Few even noticed he set them an increased pace.

Bathie had the *eye*. She saw them first.

Her debut defence of Castle Fruntierfolke had occurred at the age of five. She'd been given weighted darts to drop through *murder-holes* in the gate-house, should the besiegers ever penetrate that far. They didn't that day but not for want of her wishing: the requisite steel and spine had been there. All the tumult and excitement, the truly being alive and cares being only minute-to-minute had entered her like Guy presently couldn't, touching her deep inside.

Aged twelve she'd played the fullest possible role in defending an aunt's bunker against Christians and fungoids mixed. Afterwards, her father had even *smiled* at her and followed that with occasional episodes of recognition. Her life – and lifestyle – improved immeasurably and, given that affection was in famine-rations at Castle Fruntierfolke, the impressionable proto-Bathie gladly accepted approval in its stead. Formed by such incentives from earliest days she thus never ceased to scan the Wild with serious intent. So now she had the eye.

It presently beheld fleeting figures, hints of people taking advantage of mist on the Downs. They flickered from tree to tree and bush to bush through the distant Way-side growth: expert but pressed for time. There was the uncompromising line of a weapon here, a non-Downs hue there. Unmistakable: informative. She tried counting numbers but soon gave up. There were . . . sufficient.

Bathie hoicked up her skirts to run and mount the opposite side of their confining furrow. Sure enough, they were both sides, keeping pace through signals not vouchsafed to their prey.

Returning, an arms-outstretched charge of flying crimson and black and white against a backdrop of turf-green, she first told Guy, then Escort-Captain. Of course, he already knew.

'They may be just *flotsam*,' he said, seeming assured enough, 'cemented together by hunger. It's easily tested.'

'*Flotsam*' were the flakes off Wessex civilisation: escapees and rejects, not even good enough for the heretics who banded together beyond the family of mankind. Atomised, without fangs or claws or natural armour, they were stunningly short-lived in the Wild. The good-hearted sometimes threw bread to them from the walls of frontier fortresses – and then noted they rarely came back for more. A night or two's life expectancy, a week at the outside, was the conventional wisdom, and thus far you could have sympathy. But when collections of them bumped into each other and dared to impinge on legitimate human life . . .

'Elias,' ordered Escort-Captain, 'go give them our blessing.'

A musketeer – not a rifleman, Guy noticed – went aloft. Feet planted firmly on the slippery bank, he took his time to select a target and then obscured it all the more with a cloud of powder smoke.

He did well, a cry heralding his success. It came from a man's throat, sounding like a last sound; two facts which were heartening. It was followed by anger and shared fury from a choir not exclusively human – which was not heartening at all. Rumour said that the out-people mated with monsters, revelling with the 'new-life' by the light of the campfire. Allegedly, some of their orgy-offspring survived and grew up to combine the worst of both ancestries.

Adding – lead – weight to the overall gloomy verdict, there came return fire, both musket and rifle, distinctive to the attuned Wessex ear. They still liked to think of themselves as a rifle-armed civilisation, but under the new constraints the proportion of old guns brought back into service rose year by year. It was just another humiliation, universally recognised but never mentioned. Regression back down to arquebus, then slingshot, would probably be treated the same way.

Flotsam didn't have guns of any sort. They fought, if they had to, with hunger-enfeebled hands and branch-spears. A show of force was invariably enough to convince them back into the Wild to be eaten.

Not so here, not so today. The convoy's *wyrd* proved to have a fray – and affray – in it: some strands were likely to fall off.

The musketeer's hat did. A shot took it right across the Way, showering them with a rain of murdered feathers. Embarrassed by his luck, Elias followed it almost as fast.

'Hmmmm,' said Escort-Captain, poised comically, one extended finger to mouth. He was smiling. 'I wonder. Let's stay here a moment.'

And so they did, obedient to him, fully to arms but with nothing to do. Employing useless sympathetic magic everyone looked up, as though their concern could transcend the lines of sight. Unseen, their assailants continued to shoot.

Guy prayed against his stutter, now of all times. It favoured him by staying in its remote cave. Sword and revolver to hand he appeared quite the part, unable to be any more useful for the moment.

Along the Way's edge, patches of turf lifted in brief life, exalted by a passing shot. They were trying to angle ricochets down amongst them.

That settled it for Escort-Captain: he had the information he required. Wessex etiquette then dictated he pass on at least a summary of it to Guy.

He leaned close with a broad, mad, smile that was wholly inappropriate.

'Good and bad, Ambassador, good and bad. I count half a dozen guns and smell enough cunning to husband all the rest. Likewise, I hear full ammunition pouches if they're willing to try indirect fire. No, honoured sir, this is a bad place for us, becoming worse. They have their chosen position, otherwise they'd not try it. There'll be firing pits and boughs to aim along: plashwork barricades; all prepared. I suppose we've a good firing station too: we could try exchanging rounds and an occasional fluke death . . .'

'But night's coming,' said Guy, stealing his words.

'In due course. They may have some bolt-hole to hide in but we'll be out in the open.'

'And someone's supper.'

Escort-Captain raised his revolver to his head and grinned even further.

'I'll not be a live-meal, me. The last shell's reserved.' Suddenly all the verve and lustiness seeped away. He'd just received a disappointing revelation and *doubted*. It was a dull-dog thing to discover you'd cling to something not valued, even something pleasure-free, rather than embrace honest oblivion.

'The end will be the same,' said Guy, further crushing him. 'I suggest we press on.'

Just as swiftly, Escort-Captain was his cheerful, past-caring self again.

'I agree – though they'll have people fore and aft. We'll be obliged to clear the way.'

'And *Way*: ho ho!'

Escort-Captain laughed back – but too long and loud.

Guy had never doubted their dilemma. The Wild, even the demi-Wild, didn't deal in minor crises. Also, the careful planning of the hungry ones failed to surprise him.

84

Ambassadors couldn't go through modern life without a modicum of military awareness – not that they should even hope to.

Guy scented the air – as though that would or could tell him anything. All he found was the memory-sweet scent of his cologne, admixed with Bathie's freshness from a recent embrace. The two were all he could wish for but he persevered with the masquerade of decision.

'Ahh . . .' said a soldier, as though in gentle reflection, and laid down first his rifle and then his life. A bullet had flicked down from the green parapet and found him waiting. His assassins would not be aware yet since he was so discreet about it but they were probably calculating on a certain rate of joy per period of fire. Somewhen fairly soon, their presumptions would add up to justification for attack.

A pikeman stepped sprightly to take up his former colleague's gun, for even the armour-clad aspired in their hearts to a rifle. Spectral belief in their own higher status came from a previous era, of slow firing muskets requiring spear-protection by selected, beefier, comrades. Along with every noble notion, it failed at the first test with reality. The man's old armament was covertly set aside: the same as its supporting ethos.

Guy and Escort-Captain looked at the corpse, as if he might oblige by rising again to offer advice.

'It's a thought . . .' agreed Bathie, somehow interpreting correctly. 'From up in the clouds he'd have better perspective . . .'

Escort-Captain was appalled and shrank from her as he would a witch.

'Madame!'

Again, it was that perennial *do they or don't they?* business, never to be resolved and not helped by comments like that. Guy assumed Bathie had followed their thoughts, not read them, but the darling, daring, girl really must learn. She shouldn't assume the whole world would be charitable or know how Fruntierfolke were. Out here in this narrow trench of normality, Escort-Captain's opinions carried enhanced weight; his goodwill a passport to survival.

'My Lady!' said Guy and theatrically wagged his finger. He preferred to ration his reproofs, not only through indulgent affection but for the price they bore in sullen days and spurned affections. Human life was so short, especially now, that it seemed a sin to wilfully spoil even one moment.

Bathie glared and bit her lip, eyes slanting up from under the black frizz, knowing she'd overstepped but not repenting.

'Guesswork,' she assured Escort-Captain, but it was a conscript word, dragged out of her. Guy felt the kiss of charged air that was the sign of her powers rising. It both was and wasn't an auspicious time.

Another missile split the distance between them, at least severing the tricky moment. They actually saw its deep burial in the cutting's side and had imagination enough, even if for only a moment, to imagine that soft turf as their own flesh.

'So we can't stay,' said Escort-Captain, pointing down to the dead soldier, as casual as you like, the past forgotten, and again drawing in the deceased to their calculations. 'Therefore, it's on or back. I place the menu before you: what d'you fancy?'

Bathie turned back from studying the corpse. She liked the sight of death first-hand: it reminded her of a happy childhood.

'You forgot *over and at 'em*,' she reminded. 'We could carry the day!'

Guy liked Escort-Captain. He didn't bear yesterday round with him like baggage. When he looked down on Bathie he did so at a mouthy girl rather than resented witch.

'And *you* forgot the fields of fire,' was his response.

She had – and silently retracted. Glory yes, but suicide no – except in special cases.

Either side of every Way the trees and undergrowth were cleared for two pistol-shots distance. It wasn't human work, though it served their purpose, but some blight the angels bestowed as part of their agreement. In that span nothing grew straight or higher than moss. Without it these last arteries of communication would have been useless, too dangerous for even the desperate to venture on. The Wild proper held flowers that could reach over and select dinner from a roadway and mere flotsam would try their luck if a decent ambush were possible. Ravenous ambitions had to be curtailed if the angels' gift was to work.

Cosy in the furrow's depth, she'd lost sight. A charge would be satisfying but futile, a one-way scamper across flat green to perdition.

'An attack's *right out*!' said Escort-Captain, hammering home a point already well embedded.

It was neither the time or place but Guy was charmed anew by Bathie's blush.

'I say forward,' he said, to cover for her. 'If we return it will mean an embarrassing welcome from Pevensey. "*Again? So soon?*"'

He'd caught the Assyrian accent spot on, the blend of country burr edged with *you did your – poor – best* condescension.

'You're right,' said the soldier. 'Lead on.'

Actually, that was Escort-Captain's own right and privilege, but he'd meant it metaphorically: a token of restored respect. Magnificently dashing and quite properly, he led the way.

They fled without flourish, leaving some pikes and a few of the rustier guns propped up against the edge to mimic stasis. Guy graciously suggested they lose his luggage and was surprised to have the offer declined.

'Not yet,' was the mysterious reply – and Bathie, who loved all her scarlet gowns and jade jewellery, hissed a sound of relief.

Crouched low, the party moved at pace, careering baggage-cart and all. Every few hundred yards, as counted under his breath, Escort-Captain would order riflemen to linger behind, hopeful of catching the enemy when curiosity got the better of them. Then, at reasonable intervals, the main body slowed to take wind and let the stay-backs catch up.

It all went rather swimmingly. They managed to advance that way almost a mile before, obscured from sight by a subtle curve in the Way, the rear erupted in noise. Guy stopped to listen even as he urged the others on, detecting the crackle of small-arms dancing above deeper notes. There were voices also but very much the junior, protesting, partners in the composition: scaling high and sudden, then departing the same way. The rearguard didn't sound to be doing well.

'Shall we wait?' asked Escort-Captain, in an excess of consideration. Only the starchiest of New-Wessex diehards would insist that Guy took precedence at every juncture. Even back home, time and events were fast dissolving those old certainties.

The whole essence of diplomacy, Guy's second religion, was the exercise of managed betrayal. People, places and causes must all, if need be, lay down to be squashed by the juggernaut of higher calls. Therefore, an Ambassador had to acquire the art of betrayal, steering a middle course between relish and self-disgust. In that respect, Guy played with four aces.

'No', he decided with ease. 'Let them serve their purpose.'

People expected little less from Ambassadors but, to his credit, he kept his voice low, to spare less clear-minded folk pain. Only Escort-Captain heard and he understood.

'We go!' He relayed Guy's resolve in soldierly terms. 'No, leave that – but spill it first.'

The couple's trunks were wrenched open and their contents tipped to the floor. Bathie's colourful stuff lay there mixed with cracked-open books and Ambassadorial stilettos. Then the soldiers' humbler belongings and supplies joined them, followed by the handcart itself. Some cast wistful looks but Guy said farewell to all without regret, for detachment had also figured in his early lessons. He believed a man's only true possessions were those portable in the head.

Also, he now saw treachery wasn't his exclusive tool alone. Their possessions had been betrayed to buy moments. Pursuers might pause to pick through. There was no question of protest: time for objects was a worthwhile exchange.

88

They moved on even faster, leaving the rearguard to absorb all they could before death or own-initiative escape. Very plainly, Escort-Captain had trodden this path before, in every sense. For a certain while he remained the soul of ease, moving a little swifter than strict dignity might dictate, but not particularly involved. Then his experience told him a line was crossed and different, efficient, he arose from slumber.

He moved up and down the hurrying line, shifting some forward and others back. Guy and Bathie he ignored. The fugitives began to take the shape of a moving fortress, bristling with guns. The leading double rank of riflemen sheltered under a hedgehog of pikes over their heads. Behind rolled the main body, a spiky mass loping in step. Musketeers and miscellaneous soldiers straggled back a bit as ordered, eyes and implements on the empty ramparts to either side.

'Soon!' he told the formation when it was constructed to his satisfaction, and they seemed to know what he meant. Isolated in their midst the aristocratic couple allowed themselves to be borne along.

Then they rounded the rare curve and saw their future. A square of coarse wicker, doubtless backed by something more substantial, blocked the Way. It was still some distance away but unavoidable as death and disillusion. Heads appeared over the barricade and mocked in confident voices.

In his mind's eye, Guy saw it all; how *he* would arrange things were their positions transposed. The rearguard he'd soon see for what it was, a sacrificial lamb to be dined on later. The lion's (whatever *they* might be – but Blades attested to them) share of effort would be in making haste to catch up with the fugitives, ignoring all distractions, streaming along the fields of fire, careless out of haste.

Guy couldn't view the scene and so imagined it all the more vividly. Men and monsters, allies of the Wild, were keeping pace to either side, waiting to converge at the point of stoppage right ahead. They were surrounded and without any hope save speed. If only that could carry them round or through or over the barricade then there was no stopping them. But if they *were* stopped they stopped for good, maybe postponing the moment heroically, but unseen by any to make a song of them, as more and more vileness flooded over the edges of the Way.

'*Fire first and often*' was the motto of the rifle age. Reloading had lost all the foreplay of musket-times past; hope of a lucky hit and thus one enemy who'd never reply, outweighing all else. A cannonball in human form themselves, they rolled down the chute of green, spitting venom as they went.

The wicker barrier was soon shredded, the seventh veil being torn away to reveal uncompromising wood. From somewhere the now visible enemy had gotten a buggy and trundled it down to bar all progress. Where once a farmer and family had sat, there now lay their murderers, flat on their bellies and taking aim.

'It will be hot . . .' Escort-Captain confirmed to those round him, somehow making it mimic reassurance. Fate then either mocked or assisted him by illustrating his thesis.

The side of the cart vanished into powder smoke at one command. Escort-Captain's closest companions were stripped away from him, flung back as exploding rags. Their rush had become gap-toothed and, even more than the glow-bath of mere survival, it pleased him how others promptly stepped into the breach. He hadn't even to ask.

Guy looked for Bathie. Finding her still there and moving he edged in front, covering her litheness with his own skinny frame. Since they were still beyond pistol shot there was no other way to be useful.

Volley fire was another hangover from a lost era of warfare. Once that nicety was observed and over, the bullets came in when it suited their former owners. The New-Wessex advance was steadily chipped away, a grunt and gap here, a spinning away wounded there. It became a question of momentum versus morale.

'We've nowhere else to go, lads!' shouted Escort-Captain, above the thunder and roars, adding his own feather weight to the balance.

Indeed not. The original rearguard was gone now, trodden, shot and eaten probably. Its successor was now engaged as pursuers rounded the leisurely curve behind them. Hot fire: every way they turned and also, best-not-thought-of, out of sight, to either side. All the options shouted down self-preservation as it tried to influence their feet. They still sped on as a unified, if diminished, whole.

At last, Guy could do something. Surprisingly strong in chest and upper arm when occasion demanded, he'd had his eye on a scrawny musketeer just in front. When a bullet found him out, Guy scooped the dying man up and held him aloft as shield for himself and Bathie. It wasn't long before straining muscles felt the dull, proxy, cricket-bat thud of a cheated impact.

'Thank you Blades,' he whispered. 'And thank you'. This last to the now definitively dead man as he was allowed to fall.

What a joy it was to cross the final yards when nothing could stop them, and see the look of enemy alarm as the pikes crashed into anything going.

Up till then they'd just been anonymous faces: wood-craft clad figures in his way. But now Guy saw clearly and spat. They were all types: men-of-Wessex and Assyrians and Sicilians, mixed but united in disgusting beliefs. Only atheists and Christians would choose to live in the Wild and prey on proper human travellers. He saw the twig or stone crosses dangling round each neck and they told him all he needed or could stomach to know.

Sliding across the buggy's flat back, a row of iron-shod pikeheads shoved it clear of life. Nimbler types shimmied underneath to deal with the blockage beneath. There was a respite of shock. The survivors took a minute to regard each other.

The temptation was to try and scramble over, every man for himself, but that was an inefficient way to pass and each knew it. Escort-Captain's seed of sense fell on fertile ground.

'Five paces back. Level pikes. Forward. Heave!'

The red repainted spearheads engaged with the buggy's

side, bit and, as they transferred their owners' energies from fifteen feet back, methodically pitched the obstacle over, out of the way.

A revolver was a comparative rarity nowadays, for colonels and third-circles and above. Blessed out of turn with his own, Guy felt under obligation, if for no other reason, to go and make use of it. He left Bathie behind, trailing farewell fingers over her thin shoulder, and trod out into open space that felt strange after the recent camaraderie.

As it happened there were six foemen left, all furiously reloading, or making debate between an empty gun and still scabbarded sword.

Guy had all the time he required – which wasn't much – to drop them one by one. Standing atop the now colandered and trampled wicker-wall, he felled them all. Abandoning hope of response, they looked at him, also one by one, as their turn approached.

'Thank you, Ambassador,' said Escort-Captain hurrying past, and what was left of his command streamed with him, a smaller but still compact missile once again. Guy and Bathie were left to tag on behind.

Another rearguard had been lost. Guy saw the final seconds of hacking blows and appeals for mercy from the ground as it was overwhelmed. That sight lent wings to his heels and catching Bathie by the elbows he practically carried her along.

They hadn't hung about, and had cleared the stoppered Way like practised wall-stormers, but those who chased alongside were even less hindered. Calls from behind alerted them to the danger that the prize might flee. Unseen but well heard they closed in from left and right.

Guy tried to reload as he raced but, butter-fingered, shells went to the floor and anywhere but their proper home. He'd only charged two chambers by the time he gave up. Which seemed to be the case with everybody.

Non-believers started to appear on the skyline, only to be shot or prodded back over it. The wiser amongst them must have then increased their pace so as to appear further down, beyond immediate dismissal. The path ahead was clogging up again. Worse still, some of their grosser allies were at last lumbering in. Horns and sinewy stick limbs were seen amongst those who peeped over the edge. Every sighting brought a groan from one or more witnesses – for when man plunged down so far as to ally himself with the Wild what real grounds for hope were there: either now or in a thousand years?

True, a bullet – sometimes two – killed them the same as anyone else, but there was deep treason in seeing the two breeds together. Guy saw; he saw and was sad, renouncing all mercy for them.

Skirmishing continued for half a league: a lifetime when lived moment to moment. Shots and spears from the sides brought them down in increments, a retreat mutating, quantitative converting to qualitative change, into a rout. Defying all the odds by survival, Escort-Captain still led the way but soon he would be merely furthest forward rather than a vanguard.

But they must have looked to be doing well to frightened, outside, eyes. It can only have been that false impression that made them deploy a terrible weapon.

Over one green bank swarmed a mass of limbs, twice man-sized and raw brick-red, writhing faster than any human could, more assured than an army. It took the slope down as though reclining on a divan and then stood erect in their path. They could not see past: it: the thing raised its many arms to make sure of that.

There were still pikemen to the fore and they retained spirit. Spiked iron was thrust at the brazen offered chest – and crumpled like paper. The nightmare drew one man to him, reeling him in, grip over grip, by the spear-haft till in range of the luxuriant tusks that spilled from its mouth. Then, again and again it put its face to his, a parody of a loving couple, till the bubbling screams stopped.

The party hesitated and thus courted defeat. Another few seconds of pause and they would not find the will to stir forwards. The creature saw it and roared delight, even stopping off its feeding on the pikeman to exult. The cry was echoed all across the Downs and found echo beyond. Others were closing in.

Escort-Captain followed their example. He shouldered past all obstacles to have at the beast, losing his hat but gaining admiration. Lunging in a scarlet streak underneath wild flailing claws, he buried his foil deep into the rampant crotch.

The thing's erection shrivelled. It spoke loud of its pain. Two hands extracted the sword, drawing it gingerly forth, and then put a right-angled kink in it. Two more limbs took Escort-Captain by his shoulders and massaged them to jelly. Even his disdain for show could not survive that and he threw back his wig and howled to the hills.

The sound touched Guy's heart – and bowels. He stood forward and gave a bullet to each cable-fingered hand. Their hide peeled back, reluctantly but obliged at such close range to admit the visitors. Escort-Captain was released.

There were still arms to spare. One came down to clip Guy's ear and darkness fell on him like a sack. His last recollection was that the blow smelt of previous dinners.

Then the world came again and he was pleased to be there – for a second – softly catered to by turf for his back and a woolpack somehow crammed into his head. All thought was crowded out, though distant thunder heralded the coming price of this holiday. Guy would have liked to remain thus, new-born, eyes not yet opened, but there was too much noise outside. He remembered his name – which was progress – and then his age: it transpired he was an adult and ought to face bad news.

Languid lids were raised and there it was, right before him: all the disgusting facts you could wish for. The temptation was to shut them out again and lie back, somehow hoping not to be noticed.

Bathie's yell brought him round immediately. Guy recalled that sound. He looked and remembered more. The girl wrestling with a demon was something to him. He couldn't

94

yet say what but it grew in importance by the second, as more and more faculties revived. It seemed important that he should arise and save her before she was past saving and whatever value she bore went beyond recall.

Some metal was heavy in his hand: a gun. Guy could remember what it did – and then what it had done. It was empty. He threw it at the horned head but might as well have blown a kiss. Surely, though, there *had* to be options. There was the strong sense he'd been the sort of person to have both belt and braces – and a bit of string in his pocket too. The last thought make him look. He detected weight around his waist: a scabbard. Long fingers flew to it and drew out an elegant stiletto. It would have to do.

Guy set to remastering his legs. One after the other: that was the way. The process, repeated, would bring him and the weapon closer to the fray. Once that was mastered he could look for a promising point of entry for the wicked needle.

Bathie saved him the trouble. Her peril disciplined the mob of her thoughts into an army, drumming out all doubters. However fleeting, she now owned a coherent, shiny, world-view – and informed the demon of it, via her tiny hands to his breast. The world saw it as a blue flash.

The thing said nothing, but slumped, half the fiend of a moment before. Eyes wide and wounded, it gently set her down and shuffled back a step. All serviceable arms were cradled over its chest, nursing a hurt no one else could see. Great tears fell to the grass.

Bathie took Guy by the – stiletto-grasping – hand and led him past. The huddled creature stood aside, reproachful as a kicked puppy, and let them go.

The field, so recently a concert of inhumanity, was hushed. Even those poised to strike or shoot held their hands. Sorcery was the one of the remaining great unknowns, its boundaries not even sighted. They had no idea what she could do.

In contrast, Bathie was all too clear about it. That overwhelming clarity was gone, its parts slithered back to their irrational homes, a jigsaw disassembled. She had no more left in her; not for the time being anyway. Her talent was periodic. All the more reason therefore to make good their escape by light of its afterglow.

She raised her hands against those enemy still showing above the Way. Scarlet sleeves fell back to reveal pearl-white arms and those they were aimed at did likewise. Everyone in their path shrank away.

'Now we run . . .' she told her husband. The rest of the party could follow if they liked but they weren't her concern.

Guy was not entirely Guy Ambassador yet but sufficient was in place and working for him to demur.

'Escort-Captain . . .' he told her.

The man was on his knees beside the monster but unaware of it. Both were lost in contemplation of crushing internal wounds.

Bathie pursed her lips.

'Must we?'

'Oh yes. D-d-definitely,' Guy assured her.

She told two soldiers to fetch their captain. Surprisingly, they went, even returning a touch nearer the demon to do so. Eyes carefully averted, they reared him up, the pain of it giving him merciful entry to oblivion. That was as well. A single scream, however justified by agony, might have broken the spell and ended the truce.

They all bypassed the thoughtful monster, avoiding eye-contact with his abashed allies and hurried on. Spirits rose with each bounding stride and they became once more a *purpose*, still prickly enough to inspire caution. Rifles were borne at the ready, pikes led the way. It looked as if they were clear and laughing.

Certainly somebody was. Now there was peace they could hear it.

Gentle amusement came down from on high. Guy, hyper-sensitive on the subject, was among the first to search aloft.

And there they were: two supercilious spectators suspended high above them in every sense, held up by effortless will, cruel children drawn to misfortune. They looked down as though upon the squabbles of ants.

Guy was even more awake now. Here was the one subject that could still his kindness and sponsor grinding of teeth. Yet he held on to the remaining strands of fluff and wool in his skull since they served to calm and slow his brain. He embraced the roaring ache that was coming to supplant them. His thoughts must be dulled, his emotions uninteresting. There must be no cause for an angel to rummage in his being and discover the new vein of gold within.

Seeing the game was over, the two flyers frowned. One drew a fiery sword from nowhere.

'Whose is this?'

It spoke in every ear, a personal question promiscuously asked. With it arrived an inner image of the constructed angel outside Lewes. An angel-donated picture proved more vivid than unassisted memory; almost over-coloured.

The silences, one set relieved, the other fearful, served just as well when answers weren't forthcoming.

'We will *not* be worshipped,' said both angels: a simple, uninvolved, statement of fact.

'But respect?'

The foe proved to have their own bold captain, a shepherd of the Way-wolves, so far unseen. He stepped into view atop the Way, revealing a dandy, glorious in green and gold. His atheist insignia was more prominent than those of the rest.

One angel conceded a smile.

'That,' he or she said, with a voice filling every head, 'we *insist* upon.'

'Go!' hissed Guy, going so far as to shove members of his stilled party forward. 'Run!'

They went reluctantly and slow at first but he was insistent. Guy had had more angelic dealing than most. What seemed like dangerous fidgeting or unsanctioned departure to the uninitiated, he knew the angels might not even notice. When he hunted he paid attention to the generality of birds, the consensus of the flock and thus the best target, not every peripheral set of wings. Even in the throne room of the Null-

King in Paris, it was sometimes possible to quietly slip away.

Every yard, any increment of distance between them and centre stage blossomed into increased speed and confidence. They were leaving the unfolding play behind them, even if its lines were still received loud and clear.

'And *why*,' came an extra-imperative query, 'are you so implacable?'

For a horrible moment Guy thought it was they who were addressed – but happily there was more. They pressed on.

'It is not *normal* to assault the Way . . .'

Guy happened to be looking back as he shepherded any stragglers on. The Christian captain had doffed his feathered cap to bow low. Despite the widening gap, they were made privy to his reply.

'Our general rule is to take eggs but not strangle the chicken; agreed. However, under *instruction* . . .'

Guy could not see, but as an Ambassador he knew when a voice issued from a sweating man. This conversation was thwarting a higher priority. Guy could guess that much, if not the motive for overweening urgency. All the more reason to scamper whilst they could. Their escape might well be observed by mortals who could be fascinated by such trifles, but for the moment there wasn't courage enough to mention it. Survival cupped strong hands around the enemy's balls and gained their undivided attention.

The angels lifted their serene heads and consulted, not with each other, but something beyond.

'Not our *instruction*,' came the definitive reply.

'Yes,' came direct contradiction. 'Really.'

More attuned – by training and experience – to human duplicity, Guy thought he heard a man on firm ground – but to contradict the master race was to invite the fiery blade. Therefore, what here was more important than life? It was a puzzle: though an eminently portable one. Guy panted on.

The skyborn two had conferred again.

'*No*. We expressed no such wish. Who did?'

Chief atheist indicated the stricken monster in the Way.

Feebly, almost pathos worthy, it tried to raise its head.

'Our prophet. He speaks with angels.'

This time they were emphatic.

'No. *We* are your fountain of revelation. You need *no* other.'

And the words had not ceased to resound in each ear before the creature was a red smear across the green. No part remained more substantial than liquid and rivulets ran back down the bank to puddle below.

It was a grave loss to the Way scavengers, no doubt of that, but Guy heard a buttoned lip in the ensuing exchange, a higher cause even than prophecy.

'One here carries blasphemy!' The enemy dared to protest. 'We were *told*. One here sows the seeds of a false god!'

That was enough to call down the feather touch of scrutiny on every fugitive. The angels need not be near to pry. Guy blessed and nurtured his remaining concussion. '*Please God*', he prayed, '*don't let them probe too deeply*' – and then tried desperately not to think even that. Either way, his plea was answered or else sank home when expressed. An invisible spider alighted, crawled briefly under his scalp, and then was gone.

'One is an Ambassador,' came the broadcast verdict. 'That is all. He has safe conduct – if we are watching. Do not kill him – unless by accident. Carry on.'

'No' said his/her partner. 'You forget the effigy. There must be *sorrow*.'

No one had ever observed lasting disagreement amongst them – alas. The breed had discovered the secret of harmonious life, albeit savagely restricted to themselves.

'That is right. And that was wrong. Half of you may continue. *That* half.'

An angelic arm indicated one side of the Way.

'But *you*,' it traversed right across, transfixing the unfortunate others, 'you must return and *repent*!'

The second angel descended there to wreak fiery vengeance.

The last Guy saw of those close companions of the last hour was as scattering figures across the sward, growing ever more scattered to their best of their ability. A white and gold figure in pursuit caught who she would and made them ash, letting the wind do the work of *scattering*.

After that he was fully occupied, face front. They had put a good distance between them during the angelic conversation but the remaining attackers, still numerous, were motivated enough to at least keep pace or even catch up, should any weaken. Guy took Bathie by the waist and conformed her to his jogtrot, joining his strength to her faltering reserves.

The pursuit turned day long. Occasionally, someone – self-sacrificing or tired of running or just plain tired of it all – would drop back and gain them seconds before being trampled. Most unlike him, but fuelled by exhaustion, Guy came to *hate* the enemy for their mindless persistence. If it had been much further to safety, or if Bathie weren't faltering, he would have been one of the volunteer stay-backs. He longed for the simple – and life-long in the circumstances – satisfaction of making his opinion *really clear* to them, with full force behind a stiletto. The gloating angel escort, drinking it all in, only strengthened that wish.

By the time they sighted New-Horsham, temptation had grown almost too strong to bear. The mildest of men can still weary of persecution, even if they have miles in their legs to spare. By then, his feelings had transferred from the pursuers to that which enjoyed all from above. Guy could no longer consider the future as anything likely. Before he left this life he wanted, just *once*, to speak his mind to the smirking new masters. At the end even Bathie was merely a weight on his arm, an anchor holding him back from that joy.

He could resist no longer, he released her and turned. Guy opened his mouth to speak the truth, to tell it like it was.

Three things alone saved him: dusk, guns and the vision.

He knew what he saw would come to be. Only that stilled his lips.

It was not a dream or delirium but a proper *vision*, taken between one step and the next. Guy was granted it like a heady draught. He drank deep, greedily, embracing that future. There were foul tastes, true, but compensatory intoxication. It went down handsomely. He swallowed – and his veins were afire.

The battle – another battle – was over and won. This was aftermath: pure pleasure time.

He had pistols in both hands and yet a bright sword also. Somehow that was possible because the arms that wielded them were multiple. They came kaleidoscoping in from different occasions, different times, all his own but combining to a blur. Every suppressed ambition arrived at once, all mental padlocks torn away. He was still *Guy Ambassador* and yet could not be – for he was also become *Guy Destroyer*, a myriad-limbed god, death-dealer without pity.

Briefly Guy wondered where his abundant mercy, the quality he'd always admired so much, had gone – but that cavil was drowned, held violently under the wild ocean of his joy, until it stopped moving. This vision was too wonderful, too real, not to leap into bed with wholeheartedly. This was no day for '*yes, but . . .*'

These were no guns like he'd ever seen or owned. They fired like cannon, issuing a great spout of yellow light which burned the angels. They tried to flee, to fly, but the weapons sought them out, plucking them from the sky, dragging them back to earth in a plumage of flames. Their burnt-feather smell was glorious perfume to him.

With an excess of zeal he tracked some all the way down, needlessly keeping the trigger depressed and the beam flaring, till what reached ground was barely cinders. Others he merely blackened so that they hit hard, twitching their final moments without dignity. Some glorious lips opened to scream but their words and throats were all burnt away.

There was an army with him – but they were smaller than he; mere spear-bearers. He did not even feel the need to look upon them: they babbled around his mighty feet. Alone of himself, *Guy Destroyer* sufficed. Careless, he walked on, huge strides straddling the North Downs in a single step.

Over the Hog's Back, by New-Ash and New-Wanborough, he found the angelic reserve regiments in serried ranks – and he *burnt* them. They danced a last jig in his rain of undying fire.

Then he was smaller, by his own wish. He could measure himself against individual enemies. A barely damaged angel had crashed athwart New-Wanborough's ancient tithe-barn. Its wings flapped and stirred, further scattering the sundered oak-beams.

Guy wished for his sword and it was there. He stood over the wounded cherubim, legs and groin and parts thrust forward, dishonouring it. There was still sense in those unbearably beautiful golden eyes. Then he belaboured it for a long while, with grunting, chopping, blows. The blade scorched, turning white flesh brown wherever it cut. Only when the creature was like autumn leaves would he desist.

Then Guy exulted, raising arms and swords and guns to the Downsland sky. His ululation blew away the clouds. It brought down fleeing angels. The pygmy army around his feet, humanity victorious, clapped hands to ears in awe-filled pain.

Guy grew wings, great white feathered augmentations in satire of his intended prey, and followed the surviving enemy. If need be, he would pursue them to Heaven and Hell and burn them out of there also.

The vision was more satisfying even than speaking his mind for one last moment, but it left him when fortress Horsham's guns spoke over their heads. They were enough to wake the dead.

None hit at that range but there were close calls and their time would surely come, given enough chances. And thought of *time* at last leeched the fire out of the enemy's inexplicable zeal. It dawned on them their prey had a bolt-hole but they were facing no warmer welcome than night in the *Wild*.

So they slowed and then stopped and watched their intended victims stagger on, pace by pace further under the protection of ambitious marksmen.

Whilst they hesitated one sniper got lucky – or fully exercised his gift. Horsham's great wall guns, three times the size and bore and charge of the largest musket, yet nimble when swivelled in the hands of their hereditary custodians, were up to piecing the weirdest of the Wild half a mile off. One demonstrated by exploding its target like an overripe puffball. What was left wasn't worth burial, even had his Wild friends gone in for such sentiment.

Only then, when they'd surveyed the remains or wiped them off, did the enemy slink away: a day wasted – prior to a night full of excitement. Yet even so, they marched slowly, with backward looks and longing. Guy could sense the antipathy on his shoulder blades all the way through Horsham's triple gates. The green and gold Dandy even felt it worth the risk to linger and shake his fist: an impotent judgement on the civilisation he'd forsaken.

Truly, Guy concluded, though still under the wonderment of his vision, there was no hatred like the hatred of atheists and Christians.

Grim and spiky Citadel-Horsham was the fortified gateway to New-Wessex, both martial mistress and chastity-belt of the *Way*. Beyond it and the earth-shaking *boom*, *boom*, *boom*, of its wall-guns, things grew markedly calmer. A day's stroll under heavy escort along the Imperial perimeter road took the party within sight of the promised land.

In thanks for that, they paused atop Blackdown, anomalous

sandstone high point of the North Downs, to survey the wonder of New-Wessex four hundred feet below. The contrast between forest behind and fertility before could not have been any plainer. They could turn their back on the *Wild-Weald* to face home and holy ground.

Song sprang naturally from their gratitude. It wasn't clear who raised voice first but they weren't lonely for long. There might have been more pause had they known the words were lifted from a hymnal of the hated Professor ('*may his name be blotted out*'), god-king Blades's blackest enemy, but that inconvenient memory was long lost. The sentiments had been just too appropriate to lose, regardless of parentage.

Guy's voice was delicate and reedy: Bathie's higher and more fragile still. They were rarely heard above the soldiers' bass roar.

> '*And did those feet in ancient time*
> *Walk upon Wessex mountains green?*
> *And was the holy Lamb of God*
> *On pleasant Wessex pastures seen?*
> *And did the countenance divine*
> *Shine forth upon our clouded hills?*
> *And was* Jerusalem *builded here*
> *Among those dark satanic mills?*'

His feet *had* walked there. They knew it for a fact – even if they were unclear what a 'satanic mill' might be. It was enough that those same feet would do so again – most clung to that promise. But only Guy Ambassador cherished hopes of it happening shortly, or even within their lifetime. Therefore his smile was the firmest fixed. He knew it might be a mere matter of days.

The survivors of the *Way*, limping, wounded and unwitting – bar one – bearers of good news, finished their song of praise and descended to New-Haslemere. They were glad to be home and willing to be gathered to the ample bosom of the Motherland.

'Step forward, Shepherd of scum . . .'

Shepherd of the Saved was his actual title but the Dandy answered anyway, entering the fetid hovel. The mother of his – former – finest ally was in mourning and he wanted to appear respectful; properly brimful of commiseration. That included not shielding his nose from the stench, – a major penance. It smelt like the squatters she'd captured her home from had never left. Presumably they were amongst the whitened bones everywhere underfoot.

She had even more arms than the fruit of her womb: that gross mould for making more currently exposed for their delectation. Beyond her present control, bunches of limbs twitched ceaselessly like scrawny snakes beside and around her, perhaps in grief; more likely lusting after employment.

Though the brick-red flesh was dulled with age, her hunger and malice were greater than her son's had been and the stylish *Shepherd* knew it. It was she that had sent her boy out to hunt with humans – as well as *for* them – inspired by the better rations that cooperation won. That was the beginning and the end of the two species' relationship, the alpha and omega. The Faithful received brute-force aid and prophecy and in return their Shepherd would stun his conscience enough to funnel fellow-men the monsters' way.

The pleasure in mere survival of the Way battle was now past. He looked dully upon the tasks of all the days to come.

'My baby. He is lost me. He is *lost* me!' Her lamentation was solely in the words and nowhere else. The tusked-sunburst face was unmoved, her tone mere unchanging hunger. She was bemoaning an empty larder, not a son. Shepherd disapproved, though he knew this was neither time or place to let ethics out to play.

'He was angel-taken,' he said, as sympathetically as a gagging man could sound. 'And wounded by wizardry before. A two-fold treachery!'

105

'Angels give, angels take away,' said the monster-mother, suddenly reconciled. The Shepherd-dandy just as swiftly discerned what she had in mind. Their breeding cycle was swift; she would have more – and in the meantime rely on him for sustenance. His good heart rebelled against the conscience-coma that would involve.

'An angel led him there,' he objected. 'Misled him, only to be betrayed by another. They contradict themselves. He was told: "a new religion is on the Way". He was *told*.'

The Mother found a bone to suck on, to assuage her longing and stem the dribbling.

'There are angels and angels. My lovely son eavesdropped on any he could. Sometimes one sort, sometimes the other. What of it? His words were true but their interpretation is yours alone. You have no grievance. What's another delusion more or less? You *meat* are fools. Why the longing to bow the head? Why fall to your knees except to *feed*?'

A good question from a bad source. As he daily drew further from his original ideals, becoming a mirror mercilessness of the Empire his ancestors had fled, Shepherd posed that one himself often during the sleepless early hours.

Fortunately, there was now an extra richness of distraction from such unanswerables. For instance, after the Way debacle and that diminishment in strength, he must worry about their ability to hold ruined Lewes. A fresh arrived colony of *Owlmen*, who hunted by night and wouldn't hear about conversion or alliance, were pressing them hard already. Sunset had brought a nightmare of ambush and talons even before. Now the perimeter would be tighter, less well defined; the sudden twilight onrush of feathers still more to be feared. So there it was: a reality as deplorable as the angel-spawn splayed in her filth before him. They needed this abomination and her brood. There was no way round the disgusting fact.

She rightly took his abashed silence for acquiescence and slavered all the more.

'*So*, scum-Shepherd, rib and trotter fetcher, sweet greaser of my chins; bring me the *wergild* for a lost child. Bring me deep

106

and bubbling joy . . .'

Betrayed on every side, by fate, by his faith and angels who spoke lies, the Shepherd of green and gold was well lubricated and ready for unconditional surrender. Though he'd deceived himself all the way there, he'd truly known right from that day's dawn what the accommodation would be. Outside, the tethered Assyrians and slaves and Imperials were ready marshalled. He whispered for forgiveness.

Then, over his shoulder, he beckoned for them to be brought in.

'*Omit verses twenty to forty-three,*' said the voice of God, percolating like distant thunder through the Castle walls.

That left only one remaining, which suited Guy well. In the presence of the Almighty's viceregent on Earth his stutter threatened to rise from the grave, despite all the stakes driven through it.

He lifted his face from the ground to sing with more vigour now that the end was in sight.

> '*The Ancient, the Witness,*
> *and Face of all Days*
> *the Abaser, the Guide,*
> *the Deserver of Praise.*
> *The Watchful, the Gatherer,*
> *the Subtle, oh, guide us to see*
> *through thy light, ineffable,*
> *which parts us from thee!*'

Having stated most of the 999 names of God, the prone congregation could scramble to their feet to greet him.

'*We declare,*' they roared in easy unison practised from childhood, '*that there is no God but God. And Blades is his shadow!*'

The great silence, a marvellous, pregnant *gap*, was confirmation enough. Their statement was allowed to ascend in echoes up to the far ceiling, uncontradicted.

Of course, in one sense the actual Blades was gone from them, risen back home, but his every successor bore the same name, so there was no violence done to the truth. Once a lone survivor emerged from the dreadful winnowing of the Imperial selection process, he or she took the name of Blades in addition to their own and stood in his divine shoes till he should come again. They weren't *quite* the real thing but the centuries had dulled perception of that. The second-best arrangement would do.

Then, by lone voice added to lone voice, from dark galleries high in the walls, there resumed the hymn of praise, building rapidly back up to tremulous concert. A school existed just to breed choristers to it, its tones and words and sentiments, as their life-long vocation. Relays of them praised God by day or by night without cease – save when, as now, God himself spoke. Those rare moments alone went unaccompanied. It would hardly do to interrupt an answer to your prayers . . .

The revived ubiquitous sound became almost unnoticeable; an eternal backdrop blending in to the sights and smells. Every sense was beguiled, whether by music or colour or incense, or even a certain tangible *tenseness* to the very air. The goggling visitors were left hanging a while to drink it all in. That was a mercy for few of them were likely to pass this way again.

Each had performed some signal service and had come for their reward in very much a *tell-your-grandchildren* sort of occasion. Divine kindness now allowed them to properly attend to the harvest of memories-for-later. Dull indeed must have been the soul that didn't gorge itself, for here was an embarrassment of opportunity. Every way you turned was a month's worth of diversion.

First off, Guy settled on straight ahead. He liked silk: on himself, on Bathie, or deliciously separating him and Bathie, but today he had to ponder it less lubriciously. A bow-shot before him, ninety-nine wide-spaced translucent screens of it interposed between the worshippers and the godhead. A dimly glimpsed throne shape was at the far end of the monstrous hall and, with the eye of faith, a figure might well be seated upon it, but there was no clarity, no particularity allowed. That was deliberate and thought out long ago. Imagination was to be allowed to play without parental restraint, thus maximising awe better than any jewels and pomp.

Despite earlier bidding, he didn't even need to withhold his eyes from one portion of the scene. The affront of an angel-shaped tunnel burnt through each successive screen was refused entry to the conscious mind: the lesson they'd thought to impress failing to register. Decades of domination had rendered many tokens of servitude invisible like that.

The Imperial staff hadn't dared to repair the pointed angelic point, but neither had they unduly worried. Day after day they saw its blasphemy slide off the armour of conviction. In a way faith grew only the stronger, a benefit lingering on long after the event's transient humiliation. The conquered, as in all times and places, were learning to cherish tiny victories.

Guy was exalted and free of such cares. He had only known the presence once before, when confirmed *Ambassador*, and on that day had been just one of a large throng, a collective of likewise nervous youth each in turn waiting to be dubbed *Gunner*, *Taxman*, *Pirate* or whatever. Today's gathering was thinner, older and more select. Yet the urge to remain knee-bound remained just as seductive: perhaps even stronger when not merged in the mob.

About them like a cloud of fireflies, there were chamberlains and acolytes and Imperial flunkies of indeterminate role, more numerous and gaudy than the gargoyles and tapestries which festooned everything. The place was *huge* and active, as busy in purpose and puzzling as a dream, but less escapable. A golden line delineated the box wherin the invitees might walk and prostrate themselves and being strictly raised in their religion they no more thought to stray from the path than spit on it.

An army of menials, rendered deaf and dumb in infancy but nevertheless silver-and-lace resplendent, trawled each surface without cease, seeking out impudent dust and uninvited life. Guy looked from them to the looming stone titans lining the walls and the *Golden Huscarls* standing sentinel in-between each, and he felt like an intruder in the most wondrous of anthills. There was no place where the eyes could rest and not be amazed. The far distant roof itself, all chandeliers and corbels and iron effigies, was like the vault of Heaven, dragged

110

down – but only a short distance – to be improved and fashioned into greater glory.

His gaze intercepted that of one of the Imperial soldiery and rapidly disengaged from the smoking, angry eyes looking out from the crab-like helm. They were said to be driven mad by their infinite devotion, taking even an innocent glance as an affront to the Divinity. Being delegated their Lord's power of life and death to correct any slight to him, people avoided them, seeking invisibility in their sight. The Golden Huscarls lived their lives channelled, fast-flowing, down a dead-straight track. They had no families.

At length, Guy found respite for his face in a truly monumental tapestry, a story written over dozens of paces, so huge and richly threaded and thick as to require support at myriad points by oaken beams. There he lost himself and his fear and awakening impediment in its story.

At the beginning a portal opened in dazzling white and yellow and orange and thread-of-gold, and Blades stepped out of it from his paradisaical home. He bore in his arms the *musket*, stylised but recognisable to any son-of-Wessex beyond first schooldays. A few yards on, he set his weapon of majesty aside to raise up *Lord Null-ear Firstmet* from his abasement in animal-skins and life in a burrow. Following on, he shot down a party of Null, a delightful little spout of red-thread emerging from each muscled, purple, chest as it admitted a bullet. Then there was the *Closing-of the-Burrows*, when Blades ordered the ancient entrances sealed, obliging Humanity to live upright and under the sun, as intended. Next he was mounting the Ladies Boudicca and Jezebel and creating the princes Sennacherib and Arthur and . . .

'*I summon Guy Ambassador!*'

Lost in reflection for so long, he'd almost forgotten they were in the presence. Called by name, Guy's thoughts and guts liquefied. The rich tones, so redolent of all-knowing and secrets perceived, came from everywhere and nowhere, as much from floor as roof or walls. It was in the air, *was* the air, like its creator.

Others about him, even high-generals and arch-mages of the Empire, looked on Guy in surprise, not knowing whether to envy and pity. It was, they didn't doubt, a beautiful thing to come under the audit of God – but at the same time an honour best avoided till death made it obligatory.

Guy avoided their eyes as he had the mad guards'. He was prepared, as best could be. In his heart he knew that this must happen, that there must be some exchange between the infinite and himself, but no amount of preparation could make the happening moment easier. The obedient limbs of the living God converged on him, a kaleidoscope of courtiers urgently penetrating the multitude to seek him out.

They bore before them slender wands of Sussex marble, polished and sanded till they shone white. These saved them from the contamination of human contact and served to separate Guy from the herd and then drive him on. They had no words for him, these pale-visaged exotic blooms: perhaps put beyond speech by mutilation like so many servers in the Castle-sanctum. Alternatively, it might have been piety that would not permit any mere human addition to the summons of God.

Guy was shepherded beyond the golden bounds, leaving the realm of ordinary mortals behind. Ringed by silent, sun-starved functionaries, he was marble-prodded along a long and ever darkening path. It took them beside the feet of the statuary which lined the audience chamber where, as the islands of candle-blaze thinned and the pools of shadow between them deepened, Null and human-hero alike took on a equally threatening obscurity. Ambassador or no, Guy felt dwarfed by cyclopean stone, its lumpen weight pressing down on him as much as his mission.

Then they were behind the titans, entirely divorced from the great playing field of the chamber and its comparative light and noise. A narrow, inky passage revealed itself running behind and alongside: a discreet means of communication for those in the know and sure of their footing, out of sight of the uninitiated. Though not numbered amongst the *illuminati*

112

Guy was strongly – silently – urged to walk that way.

Guy had already surrendered, unresisting, to the flow. The past few days had left little option. He'd soared from depths of danger on the *Way*, through the too-brief plateau of pleasure in homecoming, then up to the dizzy heights of a palace summoning and all the vertiginous thrills that went with it. There he'd found the confusion of mixed signals: the furious honour of selection contrasted with a close regime of fasting and purification before admittance to the presence. Even as they *milord*'ed him this and *master*'ed him that, the Imperial servitors hadn't spared the purgatives and pummelling with aromatic oils. He hadn't demurred and submitted to all with good – or lip-bitten – grace. Others, higher than he, set an example. Guy himself witnessed the *High Admiral of Mankind* acquiesce to a rose-water enema with barely a whimper. All around him, the very cream of New-Wessex had meekly subjected themselves to savage treatment to become fit company for the eyes and nostrils of their God. Who, therefore, was he to protest?

The fear of crashing face-first in the black corridor almost overcame that philosophy. They were pressing him on too fast, making him rely on nothing but good luck for his footing. To them, a broken nose or purpled face was an insignificant less-than-nothing compared to keeping the godhead waiting an unnecessary second. Intellectually, Guy might agree but the stubborn, impious flesh-he wanted the brakes on. Blades had given him but one beautiful straight nose and wouldn't bestow another.

In the end their fear was more than his and the whey-faced ones overcame their revulsion for contact and lifted Guy bodily up. He was skimmed, fast and helpless as a missile, onwards towards Divinity.

But, as ever, nothing was straightforward. Just as he was getting used to child-style portability again, they whisked him aside, seemingly towards collision and a squashed nozzle after all, right at an implacable wall. Guy promised himself a reward – a brace of whores and flagons of wine and a big horse flutter at least – for acting mute in the face of disaster.

113

His leading boots met stone – which melted painlessly before him. Whether that was magic or cunning pivots or both he never knew, but the solid-seeming barrier admitted him with less resistance than a petticoat. After that, no surprise would be sufficient and he allowed himself at last to relax. Here the rules of existence were abrogated and reason was as much use as a glass hammer – or even less, for even that could be used the *once*.

They were in another corridor, parallel to the last, but broader and better lit; a hive of activity. Guy saw alcoves packed with people: soldiers and flunkies, even oiled women, all of them waiting upon one will.

Individuals of less obvious purpose but clear, peacock, importance, lined the walls. Some even deigned to study him as he was hustled past but were plainly unimpressed. Proximity was their fountainhead of status whereas Guy, even a Guy *Ambassador*, was merely a tourist. He might come to bathe in the presence but it would only be a swift dip: these courtiers were become almost aquatic.

He was allowed his own feet now that the improved light let him step more sprightly. Yet still the wands goaded him on if he so much as hinted at pause or spectating. Therefore, wonders passed him by in a half-glimpsed flash; memories to be reconstructed later and treasured, however incomplete or enigmatic: the backdrop to many future dreams. What precisely those *wonders* were he would never know but he was sure they were wonderful.

Then suddenly he was awfully alone, carried on by impetus only. Guy sensed it in the absence of jabs, the lack of anxious bustle. The herder-courtiers had dropped like stones to prostrate themselves and he was solitary-erect. He turned for guidance and it came in abashed silence. Eyes averted in the dust, flapping white hands waved him on.

'On' was a monstrous door: monstrous in both size and decoration. From top left to distant bottom right, the 'Scourging of the Null' was shown in beaten copper. At the beginning the vermin were deep cut and many and top-dog.

By the floor they were shallow and few and only humans bearing Null-trophies stood proud. Guy chose to read it rather than act. He had not been summoned – not lately – and initiative was beyond him.

The courtiers' distress drove him to reconsider.

'He waits. He waits!' they keened in chorus.

Their sense of danger stiffened Ambassadorial sinews enough for him to walk. Guy approached the barrier looking for entry.

'No. *No!*' Their anxiety was amplified to hysteria. 'Not *Doom. Blessing!*'

And then he saw they were urging him to another way: a tiny door beside the other, rendered insignificant, almost invisible, by its brazen neighbour. It was more his size and plainly-handled. Guy took it.

The little opening opened into space and echoes and accumulated sanctity. Ant-like, he was back in the throne and audience chamber, but at its further and more austere end. His stomach dipped and rose of its own volition but the orders to his feet got through and were obeyed. Another Guy Ambassador entirely found the wherewithal to reach back and shut the door behind him.

With no obvious welcome awaiting, he gained valuable seconds in which to orientate himself. Even after the extended and headlong race he had still not come to the room's utmost extent. It carried on a way, ending, he suspected, in distant shadow. Nearer to, there were chambers within a chamber, rooms big as a Downs-Earl's *Great Hall* or cramped as his meanest kennel, presumably entered into from the passage he'd just left. The lustrous double doors of brass Guy had hesitated before and read, accessed one such – a hollow box as he now saw it, albeit glorious in white and blue tiles and stucco, but a box all the same. That was true of all the sub-chambers in that they led nowhere but to themselves: silent and mysterious and self-contained – whereas only his humble little door opened into echoing glory.

Guy had never felt more alone – and repented of the

sensation. He knew he *should* feel bathed in the aether of the Almighty but it would not come. He was a cockroach lost in a giant's kitchen, awaiting the shout of detection and the crushing heel to come. Shutting himself in was the limit of his courage. He could not force his body further on into the void.

'Hello.'

Guy's head span round faster than it was designed to do. He would pay for it in days to come, but right then ignored the rending of delicate fibres. A man had approached from the gloom beside the tiled container. His gown of gold was mere plain fare here: it signified nothing. Fussiness and a weak moustache countered it in any case.

When lost in uncertainty, Guy had always found repetition the best course.

'Hello.'

His study of the puzzling enclosed tiled space had been observed.

'You don't want to go in *there*,' said the stranger. 'A *bad* place.'

'Bad?'

'Yes, bad: that's what I said.'

Guy's echo-act occupied the passing moment but the man seemed to expect more. He raised an average eyebrow in an unexceptional face. Guy mirrored it – and then a thought occurred. He prayed as never before that it was not true.

'How are you?' said the man, clearly making a concession.

'Very well. And you?'

'My arse hurts, but otherwise so-so.'

'Oh . . . I'm sorry to hear that.'

The man pursed thin lips and a cloud shadowed his flat features. He seemed quick to feel impatience. Guy's horrible suspicions grew and grew like a disgusting cancer.

'I . . .'

'You?' countered the man, more amused than angry, though the proportion was swiftly inverting. Hands on hips he waited for more.

Guy was struggling. 'Are . . . ?

116

Colour flecked his vision. In that dreadful dawning, Guy quailed.

'Who else?' the man replied.

Guy Ambassador crashed to the floor and worshipped.

Twiddling his thumbs, the Almighty waited for it to end.

The throne was just as legend described it: huge and intricate and crystalline and, as the god-king Blades XXIII had hinted, probably very uncomfortable.

That spark of divinity was loathe to reascend it.

'An hour of receiving praise on that and it aches like *buggery*!' he told Guy – and kicked the hallowed thing with a silvered slipper.

Though they seemed alone in the stupendous stone cavern it plainly wasn't so. Somehow the monarch of humanity's lightest wishes were conveyed to those poised to fulfil them. From some unseen entrance – a trapdoor perhaps or obscure tunnel, a gaggle of lubricated beauty charged lithely on to the scene, all nodding head-dresses and eagerness to please.

'No, *no!*' said the Emperor of New-Wessex . 'I don't *want* it. I said I'm *pained* like it. Metaphor. And don't send doctors either. A period of solitude.'

The painted ladies skidded to repose and then reversed. Ordinarily, Guy would have enjoyed the show but it today it could not be. They were in a rush, their speed defrauding the voyeur eye, whilst he had – even – greater distractions. His god was talking to him. *And*, distracted, he hadn't heard!

How to apologise to a divinity? The truth or a bluff he could surely expose?

'Pardon, Lord?'

'Yes, if I *could* have your full attention, I'd be grateful. Don't worry; you can taste one of them later – though they'll have to be strangled after. I'm not allowed second-hand goods, you see. Did you know that? The doctrine of *Pristine Creation* – or something. Maybe *you* could explain it to me because I'm bugg . . .' He stopped himself and frowned and Guy saw that there might actually be drawbacks to wishes as commands. 'No, I mean I'm *damned* if *I* understand it.' He sighed heavily. 'Still, there you are . . .'

The Lord of that same *creation* paused in reflection. He was studying Guy but the compliment wasn't returned. Guy dared not look for fear of what he might learn. Already he was having to pretend he couldn't feel sickening shifts in the foundations of his certainties. Everything was exactly as before, he told himself – and did injury to the truth because it wasn't.

'. . . and now *here* you are,' Blades XXIII concluded. Another quizzical look and then he took the first few steps up to the quartz throne and signalled that Guy should follow. 'One is told that you had problems on the *Way*.'

'A mere fracas, Lord.'

The god-king's brow furrowed into an intimidating concertina.

'No, *truth*, not courtier-speak. It's relevant.'

So Guy drew breath and came at it again

'Terrible. They were at us like a dog with a bone and harried us all the way to Horsham. We left people and possessions like a trail of blood. A close-run thing, if you'll excuse the pun. I've never known anything so bad . . . Lord.'

Blades XXIII looked up in sympathy.

'No, nor I. It's puzzled my event-interpreters too. *Way-wolves* are not normally so ferret-like.'

'There was angelic salvation, I'm afraid.'

A sneering of Imperial lips to mirror Guy's own

'Yes . . . we heard that also. Fortune and misfortune mixed in the same pudding. Its sweetness is marred by an aftertaste. Why were both enemies so motivated, I wonder?'

'The bandits dared to dispute with our winged rescuer. They said they too were angelically motivated, their fervour the product of instruction . . .'

Blades's horror said one thing, the dismissive flap of his hand another. Guy didn't know which to believe: contradictory indications in a god-king were a torment and

118

trial to their believers. Could two opposites be sincerely accepted at the same time? Was it a test?

If so it was a swift one, with no marking of the paper. Blades had swept the issue aside, for the present exchange at least, though he seemed additionally burdened with things to think of later.

'Never mind. You survived, you are here intact. That will do. So, what do you *make* of it all?'

Guy pondered as ordered but found no useful words. He could raise his face no higher than to regard the ninety-nine veils. Muffled by their distorting discretion he heard the unceasing praise and supplications from the throne-room and beyond. Conveyed through miles of voice-pipes threading snake-style through the castle walls, tears and whispers and thanks percolated to him like voices in his head. He saw the smeared shapes of the throng he'd left, now the further side of the gauzy veils. He saw and heard and felt but he could not credit it was *really* he. The disassociation was frightening. From somewhere else, the real Guy Ambassador was looking down on a hollow shell and wondering when it would be safe to return home. And worse of all, his god was disappointed in him.

'Ah . . . it's . . . very nice, Lord . . .'

The god-king was indeed disappointed, though not bitterly so, for his hopes had not been high. Yet the latter-day Blades still deplored the added increment to his loneliness. Every day brought more proof he could never *descend*, not even for a much needed moment, not even to a mundane so singled out by history. He would ever be the prisoner of the role he doubted, a captive in the web of adulation and dependence. Blades XXIII, Divine Light and Upholder of New-Wessex, the Pontiff of Humanity, sighed again.

Melancholia was a mortal man's affliction. Surprised, Guy raised his face at the sound – and the god-king mistook it as a good omen. He re-opened his arms to hope.

'See that?' Blades XXIII pointed to a battered tome resting on one of the throne's myriad stone-storm of arms. 'That's *His*. Go look.'

Guy was up to simple discourse now: the jabbing nerve that had unmanned him was burnt into silence.

'*His?*'

'The very same. My predecessor. True god.'

To look, to see, most certainly to touch, Guy needs must ascend the throne. He told his legs to do it and, after one or two false starts, they did. From its prominence he looked back down, taking in the spectral host beyond the veils. The same as he, they would only behold a grey shape and thus be deceived. Their worship was being blasphemously misaddressed. The target god-king – down below and looking up at *him* – saw and understood.

'Don't worry,' he laughed. 'It's the thought that counts!'

Deliberately aborting *thought*, Guy grabbed the book and descended at speed. He almost missed his footing on the treacherous polished slickness.

It felt just an ordinary thing, though crumbling-ancient. It had binding and pages like any other set of fossilised notions. Guy tried to keep that anchoring realisation foremost in his mind. He looked for permission to the god-king and it was granted.

The split cover flaked as he turned it. There, set down in plain writing just like any old hoi-polloi hand, was its story, accommodating as a whore, on the title page.

The Journal of Emperor Blades I, Downs-Lord Paramount, Emperor of New-Wessex and its dependencies, Protector of Assyria-in-Sussex, Despot of New Godalming and the Holy of Holies, Sultan of the Marches, General of Hosts, Firer of cannon, Musket-Master, Keeper of the Citadel keys. Redemptor and Defender of the Faith. Bane of the Null.

Guy looked up, unable to riot-control his imagination any longer. The weight of the book was no longer an easy burden, the pages had become molten to his fingertips. He silently appealed.

The seventy-ninth and eightieth names of God were *the all*

merciful, the reviving. Guy had sung it not long before, in choral unison. Blades XXIII now lived up to his reputation by coming to the rescue. Gently he disengaged Guy's hands and took the tome to himself.

He, or someone else supremely favoured, had marked certain passages with strips of gilded Null hide. The book groaned as one was selected. This successor-Blades loved it but was not careful of it. Within was material for use, not gloating over or preservation.

Guy couldn't help but think otherwise. He wished the pages turned with tweezers, wielded by reverential hands. He felt the keenest stab of pain as one already wounded leaf gave up the ghost after four centuries and disengaged, lilting leisurely down to the floor. The god-king ignored it. He had what he wanted.

'Look,' he said, and so Guy did.

'The Null are a disgusting and oppressive race. I have decided to exterminate them all.'

Guy got ahold of his breathing, which threatened to stampede. He remembered *that* famous resolve from school lessons. The monsters had slaughtered a human convoy and some of the god-king's most beloved concubines amongst them. Blades had appeared – as the divine was more wont to do in those golden days – on his balcony and howled his decision at the populace. The youthful Guy's blood had been stirred and channelled in the right direction by tales of the consequent angry issuing of mankind-militant, streaming armed from every gate of Castle Blades, out to wound the Null. It had been the turning of the tide, their finest hour. Thought of it put fire in the veins of true Wessex men.

Guy was that or nothing. To see history encapsulated, on a page, in the very script of its begetter, shook him. He looked up.

The god-king was still beside him, though Guy could not have answered how many moments had passed whilst he was rapt.

'There's more, much more!' said the author's descendant, and grasped the volume violently to his heart, speeding its ruin. Dry shreds of paper and binding sprinkled down. Then, by contrast, he brandished it like a weapon. 'Here is validation. Here is hope!'

Guy's face withdrew from the fervour of it all. His Lord's eyes were hot and ringed. He had travelled down paths Guy had not and never wished to.

'I *doubted*, I admit it,' the Almighty went on, as much to himself as anyone, 'but ran the race to the end. I was rewarded and showered with comfort. There *was* wisdom within after all – to a god-king, that is; not to you..'

It was the first time he'd stood on ceremony or pulled rank. If he'd been consistent from the start then Guy could have taken it, being fertile ground for imposition. Now the plain statement felt like a rebuff. He had been gathered in and then thrust away. Resentment flared before being slapped down.

The god-king hadn't noticed: his eyes and thoughts were elsewhere: centuries as well as miles.

'So, you shall go and fetch him to me. He and I shall talk together. Then he can save us all. You understand?' It was more accusation than query. Guy flinched but indicated agreement.

From passion Blades XXIII subsided into weariness without warning. Amongst all the other lessons queuing for admission to his head, Guy learnt that even god-kings could have tethers to be at the end of.

Suddenly, without an intervening second for acclimatisation, the god-king was avuncular again.

'There's more here, never fear – even for you. Trust me, I've read it all. And you could too.' Then he had abrupt second thoughts and looked shifty, a secluded man ill-practised at deceit, used to the inscrutability provided by walls of stone or silk. Against Ambassadorial abilities he was as open as the book he held like a lover. His capping words were hasty. 'But that's not needful right now. You know it exists and that should suffice – for you.'

All these *you*'s – they were distancing. Blades swung from humour to humour like a barn-door in a storm, capricious and violent; and his actions matched each ever changing mood. Guy had to fight not to accord with them.

No longer the god-king's best and only friend, the book was flung to land in a flurry of fragments on the unwelcoming seat of the throne. The slave of his swings Blades XIII had forgotten its material existence in favour of the notion alone.

'Mind you,' he explained, perhaps noting Guy's wince of distress, admissions now pouring out, unthinking, in an unheralded flood, 'it's mostly battles and orgies. I'd almost repented of my trouble to get it. All those miners' lives, burrowing under the Castle: unstable strata; wicked traps – such a waste. I did wonder. But the ending though, *that* spoke to me. I was in despair till then. It was soon after . . .' With a nod, unwilling to speak of it, he indicated the angelically singed corridor through his veils. 'Oh, but there was humiliation then – and I was made to drink every drop, believe me, right to the dregs. It *insisted* – and others gathered to see. So I was low – until I read and *He* spoke to me – through that.'

Guy was glad to disengage glances to register the abandoned journal.

'*I* think,' said the god-king, in measured tones, wholly in soliloquy now but cunning still, 'that was a sign. I should have had more faith. I strayed and so he spoke to me – and now I wish to speak to him.'

Without warning, Guy was reincorporated into the conversation. Blades turned to him as if for the first time. 'He's back, you know. Back with us. Did you know that?'

Guy constructed a hybrid nod-cum-bow.

'I do, Lord. You told and summoned me.'

'I did? Oh yes, I did, didn't I. That's why you're here: *seeing* me. Not many do, you know. I want you to go and fetch him. You're my most intrepid man – *chosen*, too. And you're blood. You *are* blood, aren't you?'

'Direct line – by a second-circle wife. The descent is

authenticated by the College of Ancestry. I have the papers if . . .'

The god-king brushed that aside.

'Of course you're blood. I can see it. You bear the mark. This is work you're made for. I've thought of everything.'

In his flailing impressions, Guy foundered on an objection. The Divine couldn't help but think of everything. The fact needed no special statement. So why was he being told?

'*I* can't go,' Blades gabbled on, 'can I? *They* visit me – often. I have to take things to dull my thoughts so they can't read me. I'm sober now – for this, for you; but it mustn't last. Oh no. Wine and distillations – that's me this evening. Hours of swirling visions. Can't be helped.'

Guy rebelled against pity for a god but couldn't help his mutinous kindness. The sinful feeling was there, not willing to be denied.

'But *you* can go. Yes indeed. You're meant to wander. They won't think that strange. You have the excuse and spirit. Ideal. That's why you're here. Do you understand?'

By restricting himself purely to the practical aspects, Guy was truthfully able to say he did. The Imperial summons had left him in no doubt of the wonderful fact even if it gave no supporting detail.

'Good, because I can't spare you too much sobriety. I'm overdue a visit.'

They both knew what and whose visit he meant. The danger of being witness to a terrible disillusionment made Guy's wish to be gone all the stronger.

'Lord, tell me what I must do and then, if this flesh and blood is able, consider it done.'

The god-king breathed out through his nose. Here was a burden he was just longing to shift on to other shoulders.

Blades XXIII was again a tired little man, though more optimistic now. At long last he recalled his position and the need to intimidate. Lulled by the years and worship into laziness, he'd blithely assumed blind obedience.

'Good man. Your Lord is pleased with you. You shall not

124

falter, in this life or the next. I see myself beside the open gates of Paradise beckoning you when this poor shadow-dream is over. *"Come hither Guy,"* I shall say, *"thou good and faithful servant. Come into the gardens of your reward: rest your self on this divan of delight. Ten thousand ageless maidens are waiting to serve you in this eternal portion that is now yours of right."*

It was standard stuff, dictated by the ream to supplement the scriptures brought over by the first Blades. Those were all very well in their way, but a bit milk and water, especially in the later sections. All that *loving-kindness* business was less than helpful in welding or wielding a realm and so later god-kings had acted as conduits for some more practical revelations. Blades XXIII could quote or create it by the yard as required.

Chore done, he was back to normal: his usual solipsistic self.

'I knew I was right to chose an Ambassador,' he mused, just chatting to Guy, like he would a good gardener. 'Dependable sorts. Well done. Therefore, accompany me.'

The damage was already done: cracks appearing in the edifice. Guy was so far out of awe that he dared frame unsolicited questions.

'What for . . . Lord?'

Again, unwisely, the god-king compromised himself with explanation and reason. He pointed.

'To the window, Guy Ambassador. I'm going to show you the way to God.'

'Good shot.'

Guy disagreed but stayed silent, allowing the retort and powder smoke to be his counterfeit reply. It was no feat of marksmanship to hit a target so large and so close with a swivel-mounted musket. They were sitting ducks – or sitting Null: an amusement rather than challenge. If Blades had not commanded him he would not have played. He didn't regard his kill but looked to the green Downs beyond.

The tethered captives in the corral below, already de-fanged and clawed, didn't have that option. Their alternatives were either high walls or the open sky and so they raised dulled yellow eyes to the distant window that dealt death. A fallen comrade bled his remaining life away unregarded, a winner in their poor lottery of fates. Those not struck down by the *meat*'s god-king would only survive to suffer worse fates. The rite of Sacrifice in the Cathedral was slow and drawn out and calculatedly insulting. Those too old or imperfect for that would be processed, drained and diced, for winter cattle food. Therefore, of all the futures, a quick farewell to the light was best.

'More?' asked Blades XXIII, thinking he was offering a rare treat: merely a post-breakfast, post-passion diversion to him, true, but surely tales-for-grandchildren to a mortal man. 'These are loaded too.'

The golden muskets, all perfectly poised, all shined and carved and waiting, stretched away for some distance along the ledge. Guy tried to recall his earlier bedazzlement and recreate it. '*An honour too great*' was the facade he was aiming at: child's play for Ambassadorial skills. The sham construction duly came and apparently it worked, deceiving even the Almighty.

'Or the *parliaments*, then? More of a challenge, eh?'

The leathery, cawing, beasts never seemed to learn their lesson and leave the Castle alone. Perhaps the rewards were too great, the temptation overpowering: choice leftovers here, a careless nurse and juicy baby there. Whatever the impetus, heedless of the relentless toll, they continued to wheel round the turrets year after costly year, prime targets for a bored monarch. Their mounted heads, green and beaky, were endless around the chamber's walls.

'I fear to miss, Lord,' answered Guy, lowering both his gun and head, 'and thus gain an eternal embarrassment to recall in years to come.'

The god-king couldn't see that – surely all men fell short in comparison to him and shouldn't mourn it – but he'd already had enough of the solicitous-host charade and didn't pursue the flaw. Whilst Guy was occupied with Null-murder he had been perusing the *Ambassador* file: impeccably printed page upon page from the Imperial *eyes-and-ears*: agents-like-ivy, so close to everyone of significance that they couldn't assume their mildest burp went unheard.

No respecter of fine work, he mangled its thick, high-quality and Emperor-worthy, leaves. It was something to do whilst he kicked his intellect into sullen action. There were loose threads: strands within that caught attention and piqued his curiosity and he ought to have prized such finds in a life whose greatest threat was satiety. They should be probed, they really should, and yet his mind was sleepy. He did so wish answers would oblige and come to *him*.

'How is your wife?' he enquired at last.

Guy allowed the golden gun to return to upright and stepped away. The liquid voices of the Null, raised in unguessable lament or anger or despair, followed him, diminished by distance, into the room.

'Exceedingly well, Lord. Your choice was perfect.'

That got to the heart of the matter. The god-king recalled now. With nothing better to do one day, he'd drawn up a betrothal list whose lightest suggestion was law. Not only had it cut through the nobility's intricate tapestry of marriage plans, thus taking them down a salutary peg or two, but also introduced fresh breeding lines into an aristocracy gone stale. Blades XXIII had noted the frequency of idiots and high-strung heirs: the mad-girls and sad-boys, neatly rendered into numbers for him by his clever elite-stream bureaucrats. He'd reckoned a bit of new blood would do New-Wessex the world of good.

The measure's randomness was only qualified by a certain – understandable – indulgence. During a long afternoon, when even the thought of food or sex or executions appalled, it had amused him to construct some stunning mismatches as well as healthy bonds. Lusty wenches were spliced to timid men and vice versa; bookish types tied to roaring-youths and the devout to crypto-rationalists. Those who worshipped the female form were betrothed to brides of similar opinion and voluptuous venuses set to hopelessly compete with boys for their husband's affections. Even Lady Deb-deb, his favourite erotic dancer, was placed on the altar of fun and given to a man whose sense of adventure skidded to a halt at *two* glasses of wine. Despite the sacrifice that involved, *oh*, how the god-king had laughed!

It must have been the same spirit of mischief which made him marry an *Ambassador* to a *Fruntierfolke* – and in particular, archetypes of both – to see if one could tame or tilt the bland mask of the other. He'd selected someone said to be an especial handful (though not in the amorous sense) and another smooth and amiable as butter (when not stuttering): a devotee of horse rather than woman-flesh. Many were the sleepless nights when the god-king had the distracting thought of that particular – presumably well ruffled – marital bed. Now it rather spoilt things to learn he'd done right for the wrong reason. Guy's reply seemed to contradict and spoil all. Many a quiet chuckle was devalued in retrospect. A *perfect* choice? Surely not.

'*Was* it? Really? Is she your first wife?'

'And only, Lord.'

'Well, well, well. So she's a hit, is she?'

'The love of my life, sublimity. We can't thank you enough.'

Unaccustomed to any shrouding of reaction, the god-king's disappointment was as plain as a pike to the face.

'Oh. And to the exclusion of all others, you say?'

'Wives, yes. I have neither need nor desire, Lord.'

'Not even some subtle little Ambassador minx lined up for you, eh?' He winked conspiratorially, most un-godlike, watery eyes streaming to focus. 'Someone of the real true-blood to carry on the line properly?'

Guy straightened up from the window-ledge, suddenly recalling he was leaning in the presence of his creator.

'I am my father's to command, Greatness, and the

Ambassador elders likewise – but they know my wishes.' Guy never bristled, thought irritation beneath him and unnecessary, but the very suggestion of the ghost of the embryo of both floated upon his voice now. 'My *strong* wishes . . .'

The god-king read it correct and turned aside. That avenue had proved to be barren, swept clean of the slightest amusement.

'Good, *good*,' his voice was insincerity itself, even to the hard-of-reading. 'I'm gladdened to hear it. Well then, to business!'

He joined Guy at the window and directed his attention outwards to the Wessex heartlands spread like a carpet below their high eyrie. A thin arm draped round Guy's shoulder and overlooked the shrinking of flesh. The Ambassador controlled himself but felt another nail sink into a very important coffin.

With his other hand, Blades XXIII pointed far away into the haze.

'God is sixty miles off,' he said, 'in that direction, over there in the Wild wood. Go and bring him to me, please.'

The great brazen doors opened and blood came out.

A team of naked, perfect, women – such that would never have wielded mops in normal life – were toiling away to stem the flood. Guy had been shaken from deep sleep to be present, but was suddenly, fully, alert.

The god-king's voice interrupted the sterling work and put the seal on Guy's wakefulness.

'A *bad* place, as I told you,' he informed him, resuming seamless conversation as if they'd not been parted for a day. The Ambassador said nothing, merely grateful he'd initially encountered the Presence via the humbler door.

'Traitors, the misguided, angelic lickspittles . . .' Blades XXIII dismissed the piled corpses. 'Formerly trusted folk: hard to arrest at home amongst friends and fellow malcontents.

129

They are summoned and deceived. The glorious portal deludes them, they enter – and receive justice.'

Guy now noted Amazon-huscarls – the fabled night-shift of the Imperial Guard and sole remnant nowadays of Blades I's egalitarian reforms – straining at huge copper wheels to either side. As they prevailed against evidently strong forces, he saw the departing tokens of a phalanx of spikes recede into the floor.

'Spring loaded,' explained the god-king, obviously proud of his toy. 'The unfaithful see me and ooze in. The doors close and . . . they get my point. Do *you*?'

Guy observed with horror that he was standing over a cunningly obscured, finger-thin, inlet into the floor. They were everywhere at the front of the chamber, brilliantly blended in with the pattern and lay of the mosaic pavement. Each mythic eye, each excuse for a circle of black, concealed a launching tube. Guy's groin was poised over just such a threat, a slim orifice masquerading as the eye of a Null being brained by an earlier Blades. It took Ambassadorial strength of will to stand his ground. He must have *faith*. He must: and show it – to convince others as much as himself.

'I reveal this not for your education,' his Lord reassured him. 'Oh no, but because time is short. *You* do not belong in here, rest assured, but there is much to do. My cruel schedulers combine appointments. Take it as no comment on yourself but mere coincidence. You are my favoured servant in whom I am well pleased – or confidently expect to be. Come in without fear and meet another of your number. Mind you don't slip.'

And Guy found he did have residual faith and strode on, edging round industrious mop- and axe-wielding women. A few still-moving bodies were being finished off, and the mess they made likewise sent into history. Looking neither up or down or around, Guy crossed the room and remained unpenetrated.

Once safely past the stressful zone and atop more innocent mosaic themes, he was the master of his eyes again. He saw

130

that in addition to the customary cloud of heart-aching concubines and Golden-Huscarls, Blades XXIII had the company of an incongruous man: an obvious *out-Wessex* poured into civilised raiment. Guy spent his professional life tolerating foreigners and thus didn't thank them for intruding on any rare spare moments. He caught the man's gaze and mangled it and yet made no impression – which caused the ever-amiable Guy to warm to him.

'This is *Hunter*,' the god-king introduced him. 'An idealist and former Wild dweller: not orthodox – but monotheist. He believes in the first god-king, but not me, naughty man. *Blades-Bible Standard* or some such heresy. But he'll rejoin the fold, you'll see. We've been working on him.'

Someone obviously had. There were no marks visible but at the light lash of that remark 'Hunter' liquefied for a moment: a mere human who'd had too much asked of him. His recovery was swift: almost impressive – they bred them tough in the Wild; had to or else the line ended there – but Guy spotted it. He'd been broken and then repaired but the mends weren't quite set yet. Guy *Ambassador* saw that and marked the promising pressure points.

'Hunter, this is the Ambassador you've been told of.'

He didn't bow or even dip his head. Wild-manners or Leveller-taint, most probably. The purist sort of heretic tended to radicalist neuroses: they stripped away every construct till they stood naked before their God – only to be punished with reckoning themselves alone, standing talking to nobody. The abyss of despair was their lot and occupational hazard. Guy had little sympathy.

'The fellow has a story for you,' said Blades XXIII. 'Let us adjourn to more charming surrounds for you to hear it.'

They left the beautiful-but-false box of death by a door evident only to a god-king. Where only a second before was just wall, they walked through unhindered. Guy smelt crystallised sorcery.

In the great throne chamber beyond, they turned aside to an even smaller self-contained portion of seclusion. Until it too admitted them by mysterious means, they were assailed by the continuous hum of praise and prayer. Hunter had clearly not heard it before. He turned and swivelled, looking for its source and was abashed. Second time around, Guy was less vulnerable. He had not prayed since the first interview and refused to debate the matter with himself.

A fresh set of walls silenced it again. Inside there was renewed peace – and bubbling water and divans and layer upon layer of every kind of opulence. To step on to the floor coverings was to surrender to luxury and languid thoughts. Even the air within was heavy and incense-fat and drug replete, though strangely not a whiff had foretold its presence to the wider world.

'*Tell* him, misguided-man,' said the god-king, stepping familiarly to a nearby blowsy couch where courtesans awaited, splayed in welcome with shrieks and shrills. 'Tell him. I *shall* be listening, I assure you.'

He turned his back on them and unhurriedly mounted one of the far-from-loath women. Her nigh identical sisters, triplets or else painstakingly moulded look-alikes perhaps, gathered round and joined in as best they could. Each simulated noisy ecstasy, far too soon for it to be true. Blades XXIII didn't care: his face, when visible, was bland and elsewhere.

Hunter turned his back too – but on the unfolding, giggly, scene. Guy had heard that the self-exiles tended towards primness; the harsh life of the Wild prejudicing them against any surrender to pleasure. He also recalled that the first Blades had often fulminated against the *Puritans* found even in his Paradise-home – which was another good reason to despise the revivalists. Guy felt no such pressure to hamstring desire. He looked and merely wished he was there.

Hunter might have suffered much but his voice kept the authority born of Wild-survival.

'Ahem!'

Ambassador-polite, Guy smiled, bestowing at least half his attention.

'Yes, please, *do* go on.'

Hunter spoke: a surprisingly melodious whisper from so uncouth a face: all harsh winds and rains-looked-into, tanned by sunshine borne undeflected.

'I have seen him,' he said. Matter of fact, something definite: clearly recollected from recent experience. 'I can take you to him.'

Now Guy's full and undivided focus could be nowhere else, even had there been a dozen Bathies beneath Blades on the sofa.

'I have seen God,' repeated Hunter, hammering home the point, pinning Guy to the moment. 'I have beheld the Lord our God walking in the garden in the cool of the day . . .'

Time passed: a mixture of sacred and profane. On the one hand, the sweetness of scripture fulfilled and hope ascending like a fiery chariot, on the other, the time-killing pointlessness of a god-king rutting away on the sofas-of-Sodom. Guy embraced the first and blotted out the second.

So now he knew – and believed again, with all his heart. Promises were not in vain and prophecy false. He longed to go right *now*, even at the price of being in amongst the Wild wood, and draw close to salvation. Parched by the dryness of Castle Blades he would go to quench his thirst from the true fountain of wisdom. Each step on the way would take him further from this incremental disillusioning, the bleeding away of faith into the sand. Though not normally a man of strong emotions, he wanted that very badly. Here, now, enclosed and trapped, he felt his stutter beginning to waken. He knew it was only the vanguard and trumpet call of much worse things.

Feminine whimpers of feigned amazement and the slaves' fresh stoking up of the incense braziers dragged Guy back. The wafting scents, rich purple and ocean-floor-black, re-assailed his nostrils, making him recall the cloying moment. He was not approaching the throne of grace: he was still in the house of its Sussex-marble substitute, that which pained the 'arse' of its occupant. *That* pale, poor-man's god-king remained with

133

him, an oblivious and undeserving master. Guy forced himself to regard the bobbing backside without thought. He feared the conclusions lurking just across the border of remaining belief.

Finally, tired of portal probing but still unassuaged, Blades XXIII looked around for fresh diversion. Whilst cringing body-slaves cleaned him, his unhappy eyes swept the room and recalled Guy and Hunter. After a second's debate it seemed they would do and, with a train of still-dabbing menials, he returned to them. Guy realised that whilst he was diverted it was assumed that they had remained in stasis, only operational whilst bathed in divine proximity. That at least was impressive: a proper shouldering of the mantle of godhead.

Again, it was as if conversation had never even paused.

'It *had* to be you,' Blades stated – which both worried and pleased Guy, for that very question had been framed if not stated in his head. Perhaps this dismal, sallow, man did pull the puppet strings of divinity after all. Yet, if he *did* wander in the thoughts of his people, admiring blooms here, deploring misgrowth there, then surely he ought also to be aware of Guy's mutinous crop?

Apparently not – or, if so, he showed no sign, lingering neither to harvest or weed.

'*He* knows where.' Blades XXIII flicked a finger at Hunter, who flinched in instinctive reaction to an Imperial's – *the* Imperial's – attention. '*You* were chosen. So shall it be.'

That was a flashed furry-hoop just too tempting to pass. Guy leapt in.

'Chosen?'

Previously sure-footed, the god-king went wrong from there. He showed every sign of surprise at having his pronouncements questioned, and yet inbred careless confidence led him another step or two down from the mountaintop. The correct response was to have blasted Guy with simple commands. That would have been understood and respected, but obligingness simply didn't fit with pretensions to godhead.

'It was revealed to me in a dream,' he foolishly explained.

'How so . . . Lord?'

'By an angel – yes, *yes*, a dubious source, I agree – but no call to pull such a face. This one was of a different kind: doubtless a personification of my inner talents. I trusted it. It named you.'

Blades frowned, at last some trickles of misgiving finding their way through the dam of arrogance.

'I *can* trust you, can't I?' he asked, leaning very close.

Guy could answer truthfully. When not wielding Ambassador skills he was pre-eminently a man of honour.

'Entirely, Lord.'

Blades batted away the still ministering flunkies from his privates and reddened brow.

'Good. I don't want my dream proved wrong. I believe in them.'

It was evident that the shelves in his meagre store of industry were growing bare. Blades XXIII, God's vicegerent on earth and – in some subtle way as yet undefined – also his very essence there, wasn't used to long focus on individual pieces on the board. He thought he'd done well to devote himself this much. Guy saw doors swinging shut against him behind those wet eyes.

'Of course,' said the god-king, mustering up a final effort, 'you can't be an *Ambassador* any more. Oh no, that's out. No, I think you'd be better off as a . . . monk.'

Then, noting the slightest tinge of opposition, he sighed and signalled.

The world opened up under Guy's feet.

'Utterly, finally, and definitively, I renounce you, I renounce you, I *renounce* you.'

In stratified and stable New-Wessex, roles were rarely changed. It was a decision of such magnitude as to need ratifying before the High Altar.

With each renunciation, the priest's flail of holy water showered Guy, pattering his newly-shaved head, sealing his promise with a libation. Blades XXIII himself had drawn that draught from the river Wey, and blessed it. It was surpassingly potent: pure sanctity in droplet form.

'Ambassador no more,' intoned the Bladian priest. 'You are free.'

Guy didn't feel it. *Long-locked no more* was the only thought that surged into his brain. He felt no different, felt no wrenching movement of fate or being, but distantly recognised the severance of his name. The mark was gone. No prying angel would puzzle over an *Ambassador* in the Wild now. There was that comfort – but it didn't touch him or ease the pain.

Right from the moment Guy and Hunter had plummeted down the chute from the god-king's presence, dismissed by his boredom and trapdoor, he'd felt very little at all – not even when, his will and patience replenished, Blades XXIII came to them in their opulent cell to explain. It should have been a monstrous honour but Guy had looked up from his silken divan with Ambassadorially dead eyes and no confidence in his tongue. Fortunately, he was not called upon to speak and stutter.

'An Ambassador does not risk the Wild,' the god-king had decreed. 'Seeing the mark upon you an angel would *enquire*. You must be something else.'

Had he pondered on it for all of a second before deciding?

'A monk. As I mentioned before. A brother of Perpetual Search. *They* might well be Wild wandering.'

They might well. Equally to the point, they might well be castrated and fingerless besides. The idea was that the brethren set to search for the lost original Blades should be single-minded and beyond the temptations of the world. Suitably streamlined, deprived of hair and other extremities, they started their vocation in the actual palace maze of his disappearance and then roamed ever further afield, till success or death (invariably the latter, via grateful Null or Wild-life) overtook them. Such was the exciting career pattern thrust upon Guy. Newly nameless or no, it was only Ambassadorial skills that sedated his reaction.

That same mask was maintained even now, when he'd shed at least half that which was him and made unfelt promises to put on other clothes.

The proffered habit was of ill-combed wool and bristled from the very first touch. The *brothers* were not meant to be at ease, and discomfort served to add urgency to their search. Magnanimity enough had been shown in waiving the castration-shears and digit-snippers. In the quest for plausibility, there could be no further concessions.

Obedient still, he accepted the grey bag and covered his nakedness with its purgatory. The priest, likewise god-king commanded, then formalised the insincere conversion.

'On, *on*, dear brother,' he ordered Guy, in a now time-hallowed formula. 'Seek *Him* without fear or tiring or cease, till you find our Lord, in this world or the next.'

To be positive, of all the thousands ordained to the task, Guy was the first in four centuries to have a real prospect of success. Alas, that didn't console his spirits which limped, prematurely aged now, far behind his body. Without his true name he was naked still. The chill in the Cathedral bit as though he remained unclothed.

He looked the part, he had committed to memory the brotherhood's stock phrases and prayers and Blades XXIII was confident that would suffice. '*The mark's the thing,*' he'd said, in that lap-of-luxury holding suite where they'd plummeted down to a cushioned fall. 'They *see only superficialities. Unless they pin you to a board, they no more mark our differences than we do the different shades of beetle.*'

It was probably true, would probably work, but the wound left within Guy by the rough surgery refused to be healed.

'On, *on*, dear brother!' The priest's voice went right through Guy, recalling him to the blessing of dismissal. It was the last formula he'd rote-learnt and so was foremost in his mind. He heard and recognised it and turned on his way.

137

'On, *on*, go forth to find your God!'

Instead Guy went to find Bathie and weep dry tears in her lap. Then, when he had explained, her own bitter lamentations rained down in turn.

They slept apart, despite Bathie's wishes and hints, for fear – distracted by greater cares – of a tardy, *casual* coupling. It was an *inauspicious* occasion, both – eventually – agreed, and neither wished something so desired to be born from despair. They'd not yet lost hope and wanted a better morning-after to wake to. Consummation could wait a while until a more smiling moment came along.

So, after kisses and embraces hard to break – surface-smoothings threatening to breed into something else – they split their generated warmth and went separate ways. Bathie stayed in the palace room allocated them, doubtless spy-holed and mirror-revealed for spies and others, and put on a show for the presumed *voyeurs*: a slow peeling off of scarlet to reveal sights which were Guy's by right but beyond his strength to see. True, it only worsened her own below-waist pangs but some other frustrations were assuaged. There was an appeasement offering to Bathie's Fruntierfolke spirit in taunting spectators with what they might desire but never, ever, have.

A silken Ambassador still, to cursory glances, Guy's long prowl ended in a guardroom beside one of the lesser palace gates. He paused before it, the night air dancing on his naked head, before plunging in, confident of finding no-questions-asked refuge within. The huscarl-sentinels were even kind enough not to enquire about his savage scalp and strange distraction. It was yet another reward reaped for being an affable friend to soldiers and the lower echelons in general. Other noble-houses, the more haughty and stupid, were careless in speech both to and before their inferiors, opening up a seam of spilled gold for Guy to mine for information. In years past he'd both made and broken plots that way and no one ever suspected. Canny Guy Ambassador was accredited with supernatural antennae, whereas in plain fact he merely talked *to* people, not at them.

Accordingly, with memories of tips in both coin and horses, the huscarls there recalled and liked him. His needs, firstly a soldier's bunk and supper and then solitude, were cheerfully provided. The changing of shifts and challenging of strangers lulled him to sleep – but he was cold, despite the soup and brandy and fire, and also knew he would *dream*.

His dreams were cold too, and filled with shouting. The army blanket he'd drawn over his head became his enemy and suffered a dreadful mangling. The huscarls beyond the door exchanged glances but would not go into their dormitory to see. It was common knowledge and school-taught that the Ambassadors were god-touched, and this one was troubled, for all his easy laughs and talk of racing and women. Rather than interrupt his communing, they slept on the floor and prayed for him as best their poor education allowed.

It was a bad night, richer in memories than sound sleep. Nevertheless, Guy arose fresh and false and shiny, bowling out of the soldiers' dorm full of chat and compensation for monopolising their accommodation. His cover was intact, his explanations and words a smooth-flowing river, innocent of rocks or rapids. He was out into the town before they could even form a strong impression, taking his dream with him like a shameful thing; uninterpreted.

Bathie, a born huntress, missed her quarry by minutes. But for her reasonable assumption that – quite naturally – he'd spent the night with a maid or some of the 'pay-companions' who thronged the Palace, she'd have had him. As it was, she wasted time tongue-lashing lacy ladies and painted boys before picking up the true trail and arrived at the huscarls' post just too late.

As befitted his – now renounced – name, Guy Ambassador had taken steps to cover his tracks but Bathie's money was as good as his and her name that much nearer the military lineages. Like a buzzing hornet far below the hulking great huscarls, she got answers out of them.

139

With the informed eye of a wife, she also detected the disrupted cot, for all that Guy had straightened and tidied it. She sniffed out his night via the sweat-reek and read the ravished covers.

With all her heart, Bathie wished it had been made in joyful joint cause; in their own room and cot. She mourned the vain night and wasted wrecked bed. She wished it was their own, combined, perspiration and her maidenhead mark instead.

A night wrestling with some bought fun, that she wouldn't have minded – it was only to be expected from a worthwhile man – but agony: that was different and angering. Enemies ought to be faced *together*. Her black eyes grew blacker still: a frigid inter-stellar shade.

For a while she smoothed down the covers with her small hands, cleverly coaxing them back into a semblance of as-before. Then, in sudden change of plan, she furiously ripped the blankets free and bore them off like trophies, scattering pacifying coins behind her.

The huscarls said nothing and picked up the recompense. What were a few rough covers more or less? Also, Fruntierfolke were *meant* to be wild like the lands they precariously held. Likewise, it was all-too-plausible that Ambassadors wrestled with unknown forces by night. All was as it should be and these practical guardians of tradition approved.

Bathie laundered the abrasive squares in rose-water and then stored them in her private case, the one she'd cheerfully started after losing all in the *Way* chase. Packed with sweet herbs and aromatic oils crammed into tiny, baroque, bronze coils, they were *hers* now, to be brought out again on a happier occasion. True sprig off her tree, she didn't count this battle lost or the past unalterable. The struggle of the previous night would be re-run – and won – some other time.

'Fine leg, good striated fetlock muscle and hocks to die for. No outings yet but she's a goer!'

Guy concurred with the Stud-master's judgement.

'I'll take her. And her.'

Stud-master chuckled.

'I was referring to horse, not handler . . .'

Guy smiled.

'So was I – but then flung the sales pitch wider . . .'

The yearlings continued to circle their little tree-topped hillock, a gift pimple of perspective amongst flat green fields and gallops, each horse led by a stable hand; a prancing show purely for one man's delectation. Guy Ambassador's purchasing visits to New-Godalming's best racing stud were keenly anticipated, both for pleasure and profit. He was good company and a free spender. The Stud-master looked for nothing more in a man.

The chosen racer, all free-of-concern vitality rising like sap, reminded Guy of life as it ought to be, and its handler recalled Bathie – insofar as she possessed two legs and was feminine and desirable. The Stud-master knew both had been included in the appraisal and approved. It seemed . . . *in keeping*, despite the early hour, with the racing fraternity's rakish spirit. He also liked an educated eye once in a while, a certain collusion with shared knowledge, even if it minimised his mark-up. The lordling Guy knew his stuff and would ask the right questions if information wasn't freely offered first. Thus, deprived of his predator role, Stud-master could relax and go with the flow rather than steer it. He was confident a deal could be struck regarding both purchases.

'Mind you, she's free; you'll have to *ask*.'

Since it was of no import, Guy permitted his surprise to show. To escape the charge of automatism, Ambassadors were positively urged to show emotion in the little issues of life: the dropped pieces of toast and stubbed toes. It deceived and calmed the fears of the balance of humanity about their actual lofty perspective. Then Guy recalled he was no longer an Ambassador and had to suppress a give-away facial tic.

'Free stable hands?' he queried, covering confusion. 'That's new: an innovation, no less . . .'

'Not mine, Lord, but the times. Even artisan families feel the pinch now we're packed in and piled on top of each other. The frontier's set and opportunity's limited. I mean, *I* shouldn't complain: you get more work out of free than slave – you're not responsible for them, *they*'ve constantly got to impress. But still, you have to sympathise: it's a wrench for some. Amongst the lesser sort it's all hands to the pump, I tell you: girls and boys, young and old . . .'

'Slave and free, yes . . . well, well. Poor girl, I must talk to her.'

He set down his fortified wine on the elegant little table specially provided and made his way back to the stable. Studmaster, with shouts and signals, brought the show to a close and directed Guy's purchases after him.

In the straw- and dung-layered yard, he made closer inspection, prodding and prying; for form's sake really. He knew full well when the Almighty imbued speed and courage into a mould of flesh and here it was, hot under his hand. Barring disease or a fall or hungry Null, she would do him credit. Sometime in the future, God willing, this animal would strain for the winning post and bring him joy and coin for more joy. The buxom blonde girl looked mettlesome too.

Another punch to the stomach, painful to conceal. Old and easy certainties about the great author of this beast and decider of its racing fate were now lost, along with his own surname. Only his unassisted judgement on women remained dependable, answering the helm. He kept forgetting a new day, grey and unpromising, had dawned in his head – until it reminded him with internal rain.

Guy looked up suddenly, releasing a cupped hoof from scrutiny, feigning instead absorption in the mangy Null heads adorning every horse box in the square. It was odd: he'd never seized upon them before.

'Draw up the papers. I'll sign.' His tone was curt, lightly spread with gall.

Stud-master raised an eyebrow at such uncharacteristic brusqueness, and left swiftly, not wanting to hear more to subvert their proto-friendship. He puzzled that the Ambassador's humour should have departed along with his silky locks.

Back at the paddock, dark night of the soul or no, Guy was still Guy. The girl was detained and taken on the straw bales of the horse's home.

Likewise, she took him, both his kind words and best efforts, but not his coins. Those she rejected out of hand – or cleavage, which was where he'd slipped them. She was a free-born Wessex-girl and thus as much a thoroughbred as any of the racers she tended. She took her pleasure when it suited her – and it suited her to have a crack of dawn work-out, the same as Guy, the same as the spirited sprinters all around. Her jodhpurs and riding boots came racing off – with Guy's assistance but her connivance.

The people of New-Wessex were not modest in making new people, or pleasurable dry-runs at it. Blades, the first and founding god-king, had initially tolerated and then later commanded that leftover from burrow-life and Null-prey days, seeing wisdom in it. The rate that life and the Null used up his *People* left no room for primness or sloth in breeding reinforcements: to that extent the shedding of shame was mere common-sense. However, altruism supported the policy too. Blades was happy when his children were happy and so chose not to expound too much on the debatable; crutch-freezing, prohibitions of the Blades-Bible he'd brought with him from Paradise. His new creation remained free of the *Puritanism* which soured faces and lives in the old one. It was some small compensation for having the Null instead.

Blades had privately concluded you could never regain Eden: the Bible fables seemed correct on that much at least. It was always one damn thing or another. Of course, he never

143

voiced such views in so many words – save in his journal, and he'd planned that safe buried under the Castle, out of sight for ever . . .

The lanky man already breaking his new monkish vows, the pink wench under, on and around him, were innocent of such worries. They were stealing moments from mundanity; treasures not to be wrenched back, excused from life for a spell whilst potholing tunnels of delight.

Long equine faces looked curiously over at the strange beast-with-two-backs as Guy entered the final lengths and drove hard towards a neck and neck finish. Guy's handler's cries saluted that prospect of success as she locked strong legs around him to spur him on. Even the Stud-master smiled and paused outside when he came back with a vellum scroll – befitting the luxury buy – for signature. He was quite content to wait until the finishing post was whooped by. Delight alighted on every shoulder around the premises that morning.

Guy left with thanks and his normal facade restored and everyone was misled. Whilst the girl was distracted, packing herself back into tight white cloth, he did not neglect to hide some gold in her scarlet jacket. He might have lost much – like identity and belief and hair – but still owned his good heart. That constituted ground enough on which to make a last stand.

Leaving his acquisition and – did he but know it – fresh-forged son in good hands, Guy strode off, red-eyed, back towards the City and breakfast with Bathie.

They re-met in the vast Palace banquet hall where the rations and company got more refined and the tables cleaner and more colourful-carved, the nearer they drew to the Imperial presence. Down one end, amidst hubbub and simple energy intake, bacon and eggs were served like-it-or-lump-it. At the other extreme was cautious talk and calculation and whatever dainty you asked for, bought piping and swift: *silver-service*.

144

Gargoyles and banners and former god-kings in gilded wood or greening bronze loomed over all.

Annually, a forest was martyred to feed those deathless cooking fires; daily a holocaust of beasts – for the feeding-frenzy was unending, one meal blending seamlessly into another. Even the hours of darkness, when others and betters presumed to rest, were a busy time for cooks and scullions. Night was made precious by the Null sleeping in writhing heaps, making it safe – or safer – for far-ranging Castle labourers to issue abroad, after ample fuelling. Come dawn and breakfast-time they'd return demanding 'dinner', rendering the feast immortal, a serpent devouring its own tail, keeping the menials too busy to think.

Perhaps that was just as well. It wouldn't do for people to realise that Mankind was regressing, returning to shadow-skulking for fear of what prowled outside. Slowly but surely, they were slouching back down the centuries towards burrow days.

Arguably, the taskmasters erred on the side of caution. Here at the hub, things were better than at the fringes. You might go for months without mishap – but then, suddenly, shockingly, you'd find yourself a man – or many men – short. The Wild-stuff wasn't the problem here – the Fruntierfolke absorbed all that – but individual Null, driven to daring by insatiable urges. Despite the toll taken getting in, a residual purple drizzle survived to prey, neither savagery or skill serving to dissuade them from the sweet taste of domesticated *meat*. The great larder that was New-Godalming drew monsterdom like moths to flame and a consummation in either death or dinner.

So, it was just easier, on the nerves and everything, to develop night-vision rather than chance your arm – or neck. Through the best and most understandable of intentions, the retreat slipped another ratchet.

Still, for the moment, that process remained incremental: easy to ignore in such a vast achievement as the banqueting hall. There were soldiers of every rank and mages and chamberlains and it seemed inconceivable *they* would allow the rot to continue. Here, if you ignored the possibility of angelic gate-crashing, the illusion of competence was maintained.

The Fruntierfolke tables were almost empty as usual – they having pressing duties elsewhere – but still Guy paused, as tradition required of a mere outsider, for permission to be seated. Bathie, the sole occupant, graciously granted it.

He kissed her hand, she brushed his brow to straighten out the unsuspected frown in occupation. She scented straw and horse and woman whilst he detected on her fingers the blanket-aftermath of his night. They barely spoke, for there was no need for talk when perfume and looks had already revealed all. She was glad he had been cheered; he was cheered by her concern.

They shared a chicken who had clucked hello to the rising sun that very day, whilst Guy was in up to the hilt and Bathie laundered. It was delicious and, for play, they fed each other with sundered wing and breast, each proffered handful bearing an incense passenger-reminder of the past hours.

'Was she good?'

'Scrumptious.' It could have been answer or reaction to the tender portions supplied.

'Did you dream?'

'Vividly.'

'Violently?' Bathie added.

'That too.'

'Tell me later.'

Guy nodded, his pleasant digestion suddenly soured.

'As soon as I admit it to myself, you'll be next to know.'

Bathie found the wish-bone and shared the greasy thing with him. Try as he might he won the tussle and obediently closed his eyes, even though it only encouraged the siren call of sleep. When those weary lids lifted again it was to see that his wish had been granted. Bathie was still there.

After their joint and several ordeals, but before the inevitable explanations and tasks and the years to come, they agreed – by silent looks alone – to make a day of it in New-Godalming, the still throbbing blood-pump of humanity.

Bathie, with borrowed huscarls and a hired haggler, succumbed to the suck of the *souk*, that riotous and labyrinthine sunburst of free enterprise clinging to the city's edge. There she shopped for house pewter and silver hair-braids up to the task of taming her black thatch, as well as a fresh supply of scarlet gowns.

They parted at the souk's round and guarded orifice and Guy surrendered, with Bathie's blessing, to a parallel call. He went to answer the siren-song from atop the Frith Hill precipice, where joy-factories perched on high. There, on yielding divans, money and imagination mated to make hours as sweet as the viscous cups which fuelled them. There life was sweet – albeit suspended high over a fall just like the villas-on-stilts which housed it. All discomforting notions were refused entry.

Guy, however, was made *very* welcome. He was known there: the stage scenery already prepared. They knew what he liked and could – at a price – arrange everything. Nothing was too much trouble for one of their most valued customers.

For the mere bagatelle of a mortgaged Ambassadorial farm (around double the lifetime wages of a ploughmen in its fields) his favourite and most thrilling tableaux was procured. A naked houri of impeccable lineage extracted wild music, both sacred and profane, from a church-style organ. Guy lay back in the swirling sound's embrace and lost himself in it and, subsequently, her. He really couldn't ask for more of life – but still did.

Afterwards, Guy played backgammon for startling prizes and won whole moments of excitement and distraction. Just for the day, life was like a dream, enabling him to forget his actual dream. Even so, it was still there; the thing that occupied and tainted his mind, that beast of the previous night, prowling round his perimeter, peering in through the chinks in his feverish postponing. It asserted its reality and importance whenever Guy's concentration faltered. The Ambassadorial exterior was threatening to crack and he knew the circling, roaring notion would have to be faced some time, to be confronted, and then tamed or shot.

Memory of deicide was not something you could placate forever with organ-joy or won-duchesses.

'*Tear it all down. Tear it all down!*'

In retrospect – or maybe even during the delirious moment – Guy realised that this was more than mere dreaming or the boiling over of a troubled mind. It was perhaps less than prophecy but definitely a parasitic feeding from the future. Not even his wildest nightmare would have him entering the *Holy of Holies* – and pissing everywhere.

Right now, Guy had a miraculous sword that could sunder doors, even the thick-skinned and iron-studded doors of churches. His acolytes flooded in over the gash he had made. They were implausibly little, like imps or ants; teeming, tumbling through the breached hymen. They ravaged everything they touched like a plague of locusts.

Then he was beside the High Altar. First he heaved over it and then heaved it over. Beneath was bare earth, leached bone-pale over the course of its half-millennia white-marble night. *Guy the Destroyer* wanted light on it, the kiss of the sun after so long a famine. He thrust his hand – which could somehow reach – high up into the roof and tore down the timbers like twigs, punching his way into the cleansing air.

'*Burn it all down. Burn it all down!*'

His swarming assistants, all black as sin and swift as wrens, could produce sparks from their tiny fingertips. His own sword was now replaced by a blazing torch, dripping globules of molten heat. Swept round his titanic form it soon had all he required in flames. Even stone walls took light at his behest, old granite and bargate melting down like honeycomb to puddle on the ground.

Conveniently man-sized again, there was just time to defile the Holy of Holies – entered god-like but left besmirched, its angel-guardian sliced, its sacred glow snuffed out – before the whole edifice tumbled into ruin round his ears. The destruction was so complete it could surely never rise again.

Outside, in the smoke darkened day, the priests were being massacred, waiting patiently in lines for the executioner's garrotting wire. Racehorses galloped by on fire, unregarded, unmourned.

Guy belaboured some of the already fallen with his reappeared blade, carving great slices off the bulge-eyed dead and howling hatred at the sky.

All New-Wessex heard him, right from Thames to Wight, all the way to the beleaguered dependencies of Kernow and Guernsey. Even the red-throned Null-King in Paris turned his head at the sound, not understanding but recognising the cockcrow of a new dawn: a fresh day not necessarily to his advantage.

Then the scene shifted to a glade, though all else was the same: his burning rage and disappointment remaining pristine. Guy left a road through the forest in his wake, edged with blistered trees. Nor did his sword sleep in his hands. On the contrary, it fidgeted with plans of its own in his palm, wanting *more*, as a lone figure glided towards him. It was Blades-the-god – a perfect Blades – coming at him, serene and shiny as a statue, not even troubling the grass with his passing.

Suddenly, the dreaming Guy was no longer so wonderfully *sure*. His resolution and despair died on him just when he needed them.

He travelled towards Blades-the-first-god-king to meet him and ask some urgent questions, not knowing what else he would do. He was conscious of both his knees and sword, sensing the potential use of either.

149

Blades opened his mouth and said . . .

And Guy woke in a sweat-drenched Huscarl's cot; the one that Bathie would strip and save a few hours later, after she missed him and just missed him. The wasted hours of misplaced bed-wrestling. He screamed.

And then he woke *again*, this time in reality, and realised he's been reliving the night before. He was high on Frith Hill and opiates.

'Dear *boy* . . .' said the aristocrat kneeling before him. 'Do not rejoin the world reluctantly. Here, let me wake you so that you *smile* at the light . . .'

She took the lolling dice-cup from his limp grip, and the drained drug-cup too, before burying her bee-stung lips deep into his lap.

It was a far better surfacing into the days to come and whilst it lasted his nightmare fled before the flare of her lip-service. But she was good and he was weak and so the holiday was not long.

Overhead, a flock of *parliaments* cawed interest in the westward-wending convoy, diving to see if they had any babies or limping folk they could spare. A waved pistol from an Ambassadorial retainer was enough to see them off in search of more toothless prey.

Guy resumed.

'And how long have you been a hunter, Hunter?'

'Always.'

'Goodness, as long as that? It must be jolly interesting.'

'Not really.'

'No? Oh, well – rewarding, then.'

Hunter let the full light of his disapproval shine.

'Do *you* reckon deer and rabbits "*rewarding*"?'

'Delicious animals in their way . . .' said Guy, battling on.

'Liar. Lamb's better. I'd sooner have *lamb*.'

The fleshpots of New-Godalming boasted that treat-meat as

standard and Hunter had apparently dived in. The grease still visibly sparkled and stiffened his beard. True, it was less shaggy, more pointed and satanic, than when he'd arrived but it took longer than a few days of civilisation to drive out a life of Wild.

Guy treated him too – with good food and the revelation of fresh sheets: acts of disinterested kindness without thought of thanks – which was as well, for there were none. Lamb-chops aside, the little luxuries of life failed to seduce Hunter. Servants reported that he wore boots in bed and sold the soap. Guy tried the man drunk and tried him sober but found Hunter the same either way. His rough treatment in Imperial hands (and implements) seemed already transcended, or else buried so deep only he knew where the body lay, but ample obstacles remained to make him a rough road to travel. Guy finally concluded he was just a rocky route, a pitted path, and drive as you might, your wheels would jolt as you crossed him.

Metaphors aside, their present path was fairly smooth by modern standards. They were high above the *Weald*, privileged overseers of the toy landscape both sides of the chalk ridge, lone travellers on the ancient North Downs trackway. Men had walked – or dashed – here forever, wearing a path even in burrow-days, before the great *Standing Aloft*, before Blades and muskets and ceasing to be mere Null food. Then, in the ensuing glory years when day-business no longer had to be furtive, traffic had flowed like blood, spreading nutriment right from Canterbury to Winchester; sufficient to require a proper road and metalling. That was still around, only slowly degraded by the passage of time and frost, though without the patrons to do it justice. Nowadays, there wasn't the same impetus to travel or trade and self-sufficiency was the new ideal. Aside from the occasional military column or powder train, or noble wanderers with nothing better to do, the roadway was left to solitude and decay for days at a stretch.

That was so today and Guy's party had the strange feeling of being pioneers on a major thoroughfare. Some of the byways off were in a shocking state, probably only passable in high summer.

151

Guy refused to be shocked. He thought he should be used to bumpy rides: conversational or otherwise. Compared to Null negotiations everything after was a stroll in the park – or so he kept telling himself.

'Well, lamb is all very lovely, my man, but where we're going we shall have to acquire a taste for *your* cuisine, shan't we?'

'Or starve. Hope you like giblets . . .'

Guy grimaced – and to his credit, most of it was down to the awful itch. On quitting New-Godalming he'd been obliged to take on his new role in full, visible, form. A tailor in the capital had put a cleverly disguised soft lining into the monk's habit, but it still shrilled Guy's skin like the pox he'd caught long ago at Ambassador's College. Shift in the saddle as he may, it only moved the guerrilla war on to some other sensitive part. His whole body was war-weary and suing for either peace or retaliation – one or the other, *please*, it called, but no more mere endurance!

A rising wind lifted their hair or teased their headgear. Its bellow provided welcome excuse for Guy to abandon Hunter and adopt a silence befitting their lofty route. Less happily, it provided reminder of his lock-less state.

Finally, within sight of the Ash and Aldershot bastions, they took a road off the high spine of New-Wessex, down into more sheltered climes. A trackway of sorts wound on, scruffily kept now they were in the Ambassadorial fief (a consequence of preoccupied and often absent masters) but still clear enough between the fields of their tenants. Autumn rains would seek out old familiar ruts to make them pools again and transform the rest to mire, but today it was hard and solid and dusty, as good a travelling surface as Humandom provided in present decadent times.

From the crossroads where actual Ambassadorial land began and patient horsemen waited to escort them, Guy felt a growing sense of fitness and home. It grew by the hoof-step even though it was not now strictly his to own. He was no longer a precise fit, his grey gown a cause for discreet second looks – though, of course, not words – from their chaperones. These were generations-in Ambassadorial retainers, men bred to say '*oh really?*' if told giant golden caterpillars were coming to dinner. Therefore, their mere raised eyebrows betokened storms ahead, inverse harbingers of blood-family reaction.

The adverse review only made Guy cling all the firmer to his true, inner, identity. A test of it was to persevere with the poor conversational harvest.

'I suppose this must seem very tame to you, Hunter.'

An elegant wave of the arm, only partly negated by its dowdy covering, indicated the fruitfulness and order of the land they traversed. Square copses and straight hedgerows divided patchwork fields. Free and slave laboured away in them even at midday, ignoring or bowing to the passing troop respectively. Mankind had worked hard here for half a millennia and it could hardly get any better or more utilised.

For once Hunter agreed – but again threw his questioner.

'Gorgeous,' he said, nodding, an incongruous judgement to come from such an unsoft physiognomy: a talk-killing surprise. Even Guy lapsed into quiet.

Along their path were pollarded elms, planted by a very early Ambassador, marking a no-nonsense path to his door and providing beansticks for his peasantry at the same time. Lightning and greedy over-use had done for many over the centuries, but enough remained for Guy to feel that he was in a funnel feeding him back home. Aside from the spreading raw regions between him and his saddle, aside from the gaping crevice in his firmest beliefs and recollection of a dream and a vision too awful to contemplate, apart from a bowel-clenching mission ahead, he was as much at ease as circumstances permitted. It helped that Bathie was with him, allowed to ride just a modicum ahead so he could admire her split and offered haunches, tightly scarlet spread, atop bucking horse-flesh. Sight and reminder of his two favourite hobbies combined, lit by summer sunshine in his own homeland, could hardly fail to cheer. Guy's spirits got up off their knees and contemplated satin-thighs and twelve-to-one winners.

Home properly announced itself when the faded elegance began. For sure, the first Ambassadors must have had *some* refinement for them to gain their title and pass it on. Yet, in Guy's private opinion, from all he'd heard or read, they seemed to have been about as smooth as coal-bunkers: rough men with direct ways suited to their times. Only later, polished by the sanding effects of success and centuries, could he see himself in, and identify with, those who came after. Gradually, hard-learnt lesson by lesson, they learnt to sever the connections between face and events, finding a rock on which to stand above the torrent of sensation. Their lives and achievements came to reflect detachment from the pell-mell world: not any over-obvious, cold distancing, but a charitably ironic one: the sane reaction of a thoughtful man to an often insane universe.

That non-aggression treaty with life was reflected in their works. What they had built was restrained – neither utilitarian nor overblown. Their understanding with fate showed in their houses and estates, the very layout of their productive lands. Guy perceiving a calming, intelligent distancing from the ephemeral moment. Just rambling on horseback through an Ambassadorially-created landscape calmed the soul, or at least sedated it. At that stage in his blameless life, he stood in powerful need of at least a horse-dosage of that medicine.

Travelling past picturesquely built – and now just as picturesquely decayed – watch-tower minarets and the rose-clad homesteads of market-gardeners, Guy's death-grip on the reins loosened. He lost the iron bar across his shoulder blades when they sighted the famous elegantly arranged pyre of Null-skulls that heralded New-Farnham's domains. The ancient faith betokened by the crowned spire of Waverley Abbey gave all his burning questions quiescence. Everywhere he looked, he found reassurance. Friendly, familiar, childhood-hallowed sights. He was home.

The place itself lay not far from the chalk ridge, down a gravel turning off the road, through stylishly crumbling twin pillars. On each was the heraldic shield of the Ambassadors: two white hands poised, upon a field of black. As a boy Guy had wondered whether they were set to embrace or yield or strangle, and only later learnt it might be any of those, or all, as tyrant occasion demanded. The figures and colour were incidental, for it was the *ambiguity* that was the thing, the true core message. There was inner wisdom there, for those that could see. Guy could see.

The twin shields were peeling now, their hands skeletal, the background black a matter of faith, but through love and ten thousand beholdings Guy saw them as though on the day they were painted. They were long ago etched upon his heart, where wind and rain could not age or trouble.

The drive to *Ambassador Hall* dipped into a bluebell hollow and then rose from the delightful wood to emerge into the broad daylight of civilisation and sight of the house..

Matching the lines of bluebells there were crucifixions, but Guy refused to let them spoil things.

'AAAAAAAAAAAAAAAAAAAAAAAAAAAAAAAAA AAAAAA!'

There was a massive gong, employed since time immemorial to summon the Ambassador clan to dinner. Guy disarmed his father of the hammer used to strike it – or treacherous sons – and by the bending back of fingers in the same action, also killed his war cry.

'Yes, hello, father – and how are *you*?'

Purple and apoplectic and murderous was the answer: that much was obvious without speech. In other words: little change. One of the great luxuries of final retirement from active Ambassadorship was the untrammelled expression of emotion. It was recognised as a great gift for the sunset of days – and one turnable to family advantage if employed right. Aged Ambassadors became the bludgeon and battle-axe of the family battle plan, complementing the inscrutable

155

youngsters' shield and stiletto. It could be a formidable combination – except when turned in on itself in civil strife as now.

Tusker Ambassador knew *exactly* how he felt and said so, with word and deed. Whereas Guy, his son, a still-practising professional regardless of wrapper, had to corral his reaction, passive under fearful siege.

Papa had gone for the throat at first sight of the monk's gown. He'd sighted it from a broad upper window as they came up the gravel drive and the arrivals heard his reaction, bansheeing ever closer as he brought the nova down to show them. Intervening rooms, stairs and servants were cleared in short order, most un-old-man-like, whilst the rest of the family followed, duckling-style, in his wake.

Younger brother Nicolo sidled in, already smirking from one ringleted wig edge to the other; a private universe to himself. Step-mother number seven – whose name presently eluded Guy – arrived and made cooing placatory noises – that being, pre bed-time, her precarious role. In fact, the world swam in a warm alcohol-bath before Lady Ambassador's eyes and nothing seemed all that serious any more. The visitors wavered ghost-like before her, just as she did before them. Fortunately, there was no call for introductions: Bathie had met her in-laws before. She knew their names and they her's. A stable armed-truce existed.

Guy held on to his begetter until they were both worn out by struggle. Bathie, ever a calming influence on Tusker, stroked his brow meanwhile. Hunter looked on from on horseback, amazed by it all, as though nothing he'd seen in the Wild could cap *this*.

'That's right,' said Guy, when the writhing ceased, 'no longer an Ambassador. A *perpetual searcher* now. Sorry. Direct Imperial command, I'm afraid.'

Straightaway, all the Family-head's fury went somewhere else: presumably compacted to fit into the already crowded larder of disappointment in his brain. Periodically, that door-catch broke under the strain and boiling rations seeped out to scald those around – but at least it was now stored back in the proper place. The Ambassadors were Imperium loyalists or they were nothing. To be an effective mouthpiece and deceiver one first had to *believe*. Remembering that cradle lesson, Guy's stomach took a leap and came down only sullenly, under command.

'Right,' said Tusker – and that was it: no more to be said. He turned round, recalling he had two sons, only to turn back again, disillusioned. Nicolo was still grinning. '*Ambition revealed is ambition aborted*' ran the forty-fifth clan precept, taught, kicked, cuffed and persuaded into Nicolo no less than Guy. So how did it turn out that one son should be a sponge, the other a rock, under the water of instruction? That might well be a mystery of mysteries but not so the basic tenets of diplomacy. Here, on Tusker's very own threshold, were nursery lessons wantonly set aside. Displayed thoughts in an active-service Ambassador were all round embarrassing as split trousers at a funeral.

Tusker Ambassador growled again, but no one knew the cause. That opaqueness consoled him. Evidently he was still up to it, should the need arise. And with these two products of his privates, it looked as if it would.

'Oh well, then,' he said, 'least said soonest mended. Come and drink some wine and watch your mother slide under the sofa.'

There was no appealing novelty to that daily event, but the travellers were dry and croaked with road-dust. Guy signalled his people on. Tusker stood to watch, bemused, like a plough-boy before a menagerie.

'Never seen a monkey ride before,' he remarked, as Hunter dismounted. 'Years of training I expect. *Very* clever. Did you use whips or nuts?'

Guy turned.

'No. That is Hunter. He comes from the Wild – but is a man, nevertheless – and a monotheist. He is of our party.'

Again, part of Ambassadorial-ness was the bland acceptance of the fantastic. Tusker merely nodded and called his own retainers forward.

'Soak it in water; then scrub with vigour. When livestock-free, give it a bone and let it rest in the kennels.'

As a loyal son, Guy wouldn't argue with his father's under-his-own-roof arrangements. He allowed Hunter's protests to be forcibly silenced. The disruption dimmed as the Wild-man was borne away.

They swept in via the ancient steps up to the fortified door, filing betwixt two rapidly assembled lines of servants. The honey-coloured bargate stone of the house beckoned above and around to the limits of view: turrets, battlements and fields of fire, all framing one window for each day of the year: as welcoming as a fortress may be.

Then, as Guy paused to bestow a word on old, familiar faces, Bathie drew her father-in-law's attention to the first-sight less-than-open-arms welcome. Initially he didn't catch her drift but then light dawned and he looked back at the line of crosses down the drive. *Those* open arms were still and black, their occupants mostly gone on. Only a few sunburnt remnants showed twitchy signs of life. Plainly it was all shakily-recalled water under the bridge to Tusker now.

'Spring-cleaning.' he explained, and Guy heard.

'What?' he queried. 'The Estate-workers? *Again?*'

'S'right,' confirmed the old Ambassador, pulling a face, as age and retirement privileged him to. 'Christians. An absolute *infestation!*'

Down in the dog-house, Hunter reconciled himself to the accommodation. It was dry, there was meat and drink – if you fought well – and at least the company was dignified. Or rather it would have been but for their distressing manner of greeting each other.

There again, Hunter could transcend even that. Doubtless Guy's family did the same or worse in the privacy of their own home.

Secure against an evening shower, with a bone to gnaw and

warm fur to lean on, Hunter reckoned he had the choicer choice of companions. Given the option of either Ambassadors or hounds, luck had lodged him with the more humane company.

'Rhododendrons. From Lord Maxted's villa in New-Godalming. The 'Byron Conspiracy'. I took a clipping the night of his arrest.'

'I remember that. You threw a party. We were allowed to stay up.'

'Children? Parties? *Love* 'em. It's the adults I can't stand. Can say that now. Bastards. Mean-spirited, mostly. Self-seeking. Shame we have to grow up. Still, it's nearly over now. Be dead soon. Can rest then. So I'm easy. Reconciled even.'

You wouldn't think so to witness the passion with which Sir Tusker Ambassador directed the little world within his estate walls. The portion beyond them might no longer be his to sculpt but no one incarcerated within was left wondering. For instance, he abandoned books and bottles – and presumably the thoughts that went with them – where it suited him, left open for him to carry on with when – if – he passed again. And woe betide anyone, blood or servant, who tidied or closed or stoppered either, be they left in never so inconvenient a place. The previous night, Guy and Bathie nearly broke their necks over a flask of port and slim folio on the principal staircase leading to their divided beds.

The old man also had strong opinions about chatty intruders in his beloved '*Perfidious Garden*' – but kept those more muzzled. Guy got a conducted tour and the make-believe of innocent paternal conversation was played out a little more rope.

'Party? Celebrate? Did we? Hard to believe. Party every time we *had* someone? Ruinous. Too expensive. Your mother-of-the-moment would have had to go out to work. Earn money on her back. Cheaper to make a garden.'

159

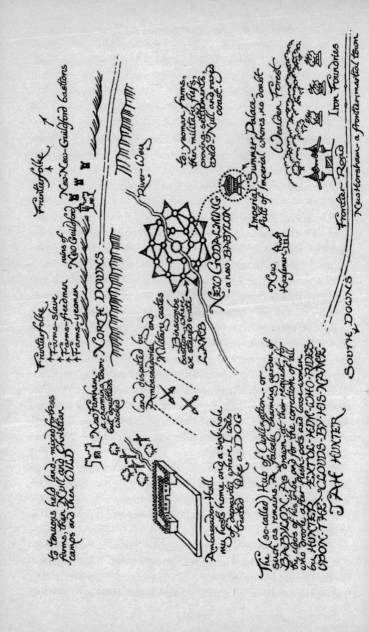

'Quite. And those?'

'Fuchsias. From the 'Glittering Star Recidivists'. More Imperialist than the Emperor (peace be upon him). Or so they said. We hugged 'em close, stoked 'em up – and then sent 'em against the French Null. Never saw *them* again. Angels didn't approve – or the Null. You can still see the skull stacks at Dunkirk, apparently. They had a prophetess called Fuschia. Strange skin: paper-white and cool and smooth as parchment. Yum. Also weird as a mad-rabbit. Bedded me and cursed me. Lovely woman. Always think of her when I scent them. Flowers, that is – not rabbits.'

He stooped – cautiously, taking account of all the ensuing years – and got one bloom nominally to his nostril.

'Mind you, she was sweeter.' Then he paused to reminisce, independent of his son's promptings. 'That was my very first sole charge. They were *my* heretics. The god-king himself supplied me the line to feed them. I stood on Beachy Head and watched her ship burn. And her – probably. Fire or water: one of the two.'

Suddenly he was back up the tunnel of years, remembering reality and back to strict staccato.

'Imagine that. Me only thirty. Conveying *divine* lies!'

Painfully, he struggled back to the vertical and pressed on, arm in arm with Guy, showing him the stolen plantings that celebrated each triumph. Here was his glorious career, summarised and expressed in the private language of flowerbed and petals. He walked it every day, perhaps exulting, perhaps communing with the back-stabbed and fallen. His feet had worn pale paths.

Guy knew it almost as well as Tusker, never tiring of its stories in colour. As a child he'd absorbed a lot from here, back when it had served as a roofless schoolroom for young Ambassadors. To him it was both library and monument, though sightly more than either. He'd vowed never to add to it – for all he was well qualified to – but leave it perfect, as a memorial to one of the great – and stylish – betrayers.

Tusker Ambassador stopped dead in his tracks, forgetting

that their disparate vigour would allow Guy to drag him on a pace or two. The effect was spoiled.

'Damn y'eyes. Stand still. You've nothing left to learn from here. This is all weeds and dead stuff. Your turn to teach. Where're you going?'

Guy lifted his head, wondering if was possible to lie in a temple of deceit, right in the face of its high-priest. He sampled the heady mixed scents: only slightly soured by the acrid-crucifix stench from across the way.

'To the Wild, father; as I said. At *his* command and direction.'

There was no – loyal – answer to that, they both knew, but Sir Tusker scrabbled round the bottom of the barrel looking for one anyway

'But why the woman too? Batheseba's no monk.'

Guy passed over that, considerate of his father's feelings. It had been a leaden, peasant, question; unwelcome reminder of a slowing intellect. Bathie and he were joined at the hip; a shock success from first glance. Everyone knew that.

The old man regrouped unworthily, unable to think of anything better.

'And why no belly-swelling yet, eh? Is it you? Then tie a stick to it, boy. Or dropped off, has it? Ploughing the wrong field, a? Thought one of the mothers had the *talk* with you . . .'

'Give it time, father. We're trying our best.'

In his distraction, Tusker Ambassador clipped the edge of a bed of thistles that commemorated his liquidation of an *Over-Thames* (or *Scot*, as the first Blades had termed them) slave rebellion. He yelped as they took their revenge on the margin between sandal and knee-britches.

'All right.' he grumped. 'But take *milady* with you too. That's all I ask. Oh – that and a bloom from out there.'

Guy understood and nodded. Since Nicolo insisted on a wig six inches longer than the norm (and was rumoured to be merciful) his father always described him in the feminine. Blooding him was Tusker's inconvenient price for loss of the family name and a god-king-ordered knife between his own ribs. Likewise, it was only fitting that the Perfidious Garden be concluded with something appropriate to mark the designer's own betrayal. It would serve as the artist's signature.

Guy could ride it, even as he ached to *tell*, even as he prided himself that his father, *his own father*, hadn't guessed. It was not the end of hope and final betrayal that Tusker thought. *He* saw his only two sons, a no-longer Ambassador and a not-up-to-scratch, unaccredited Ambassador, heading off to death, alongside his only chance of legitimate grand-spawn. In his weakened old age he was thinking that hope left with Guy – and was to be congratulated that his shoulders still bore that weight unbowed.

Out of love as much as duty, Guy would have given all his future winners to tell his father he went to *fetch* hope.

As their horses were brought round to the front, they took wine and traditional way-biscuits in a parlour with high roof-to-floor windows flung open to the garden. These were inserted by a long ago Ambassador before the angels came; in a hard-to-credit, lost golden age when defence was subordinate to comfort. Now they were a precarious innovation and thick panels were bolted in front when the sun fell. For the present, the incursion of flower-blessed air outweighed additional worry by night, but it might not always be so. Their continued life hung by the thread of Tusker's pig-headedness and ancestor worship, and he would not be around for ever. Nowadays, strange things slinked past the Fruntierfolke and stranger religions took hold in hovels. Older architectural priorities were coming back into focus.

Hunter was refreshed through those gracious portals, recently released from his tether and temporary home with the hounds, but not suffered to actually enter the house. Tusker was willing to be tolerant, so long as it cost nothing, but there were still residual standards to observe.

'He might be concealed Wild-life,' he'd told Guy when his

release was petitioned, 'poured into human-form.'

True, such things weren't unknown, but that particular type of new-breed was too ravenous to keep up the deception for more than minutes. Guy explained as much and so Sir Tusker simply drew back to a second line of defence.

'A Fungoid then: under all that hair who'd know? Or a Christian. No, let him linger with the woofs . . .'

And so he had, uncomplaining (not that anyone listened or cared) until brought forth into the light on the day of departure. Now Hunter peered into the parlour at the silkily confident gathering and concluded he'd never seen anything so beautiful and yet so cold; so bland and yet so . . . *fitting*. Here were people who were quite at home in the world. He didn't approve of that.

Ambassadorial good taste dwelt particularly on veneers. They were felt to be somehow appropriate to a calling that hid away true feelings under a glittering facade, and, over the centuries, the clan's patronage had nurtured a mere craft into fine art. Barely a surface in the parlour was not expertly overlaid and then baroquely enhanced – rather like the occupants, in fact.

Panelled, enamelled or 'japanned', the bright lightness of the furniture matched the overall scheme, and only an occasional wall portrait, some dead Ambassador or famous victory, blazed into colour amidst the prevailing pastels and gentle creams and blues. Ordinarily, conforming to the standards of princes and courts, the Ambassadors would have been contrasting peacocks too, all primary colour coats and rainbow wigs and buckles, but today was no ordinary day. Very shortly, some of them would venturing into the virgin Wild and so, instinctively chameleon, all now conformed to more mundane hues. Even Bathie's scarlet was dimmed to mere brick-red.

Hunter chuckled, knowing they were deceived, all-too-aware that the actual palette of the Deep-Wild was more startling than they conceived. In fact, the party could have gone as gaudy as they pleased and would still be put to shame

164

by some of the blowsy blossoms he was used to. Out *there*, the lush emerald of the Downs was replaced by shocks catering to angelic taste. Even so, he didn't disabuse them yet: it proved they were virgins in all this, which was useful to know. Also, in practice, one camouflage was as good as another in a kaleidoscope. For someone accustomed to the vision-tiring variety of the Wild, present sights were like a calming holiday for the eyes. Here was peace and proportion and rationality. He couldn't imagine passion erupting here in Ambassador Hall when faced by so many discouragements. And so he too was deceived in his turn.

Even the biscuits were veneered. When Hunter bit into his first a thin layer of icing made a doomed bid for freedom in the mouth. He had to mush it back into marriage with the whole before swallowing.

Guy had come to the window. It would be a sour man indeed who'd not soften at sight of his so solicitous features. The pungent kennel-nights and canine meal-melees were forgotten.

'We should be going soon,' he said, not venturing over the threshold, but coming closer than the minimum required all the same. It was a democratic gesture and appreciated. 'Are you quite sure of the way?'

Inside, all the Ambassadors were taking seats, the babble dying as refreshments were set aside and heads bowed in silence. It was immemorial tradition to briefly reflect before a journey or mission or new beginning.

Hunter's upbringing hadn't time for such indulgences: he didn't understand and feared the outbreak of *Imperial* prayers. Turning his back on them he looked towards home.

It took a minute but he found what he sought, above and beyond the scent of beech woods and bluebells, of washed humans and house-brick. There, riding the breeze, was just the slightest emissary of what he knew best. It was humid and cloying and neutral, even to him, and worst of all, it was incoming – slowly to be sure, but inch by inch and year by year, ever more pungent.

Hunter knew where the Wild was all right. If they but waited long enough it was coming to them, though these painted bigwigs might live out long lives and still not see it lapping their manicured lawns. Yet, come it surely would: he could *smell* it on its way.

'Oh certainly,' he told Guy. 'Quite sure. I've only got to follow my nose.'

'There. There'll do.'

Guy's lips said it but they lied. His mind was telling him it wouldn't *do* at all. He liked the Wild to begin imperceptibly, shielded from decent people's sight by a wide band of Fruntierfolke fief. When it struck like a knife the affront to every human pretension was explicit.

Here, where New-Liphook and New-Alton once were, only an angel-made moat divided them from nature-in-nightmare. Even from a distance, the water was visibly alive with flapping, snapping things. The perverted forest came right to the water's edge and the very sight appalled them. The Wayside Wild was one thing, but this was full-blown. To all save Hunter, it came as revelation

They were four: Guy, Bathie, Hunter and Nicolo; five if you counted the bearer-slave who had no name. The vista welcomed them without distinction, a low hum emanating from its depths: the ceaseless sign of lusty life unseen.

Each reacted according to their own lights: Bathie gaped without shame, the slave wept, whereas Guy stumbled only a second. They all knew this was taboo ground by Imperial edict; an order that normally required no enforcing. A leagues-long high stockade fenced off the offence from New-Wessex proper, until gradualism and Fruntierfolke land began again. Truly, they were strangers in a strange land. Even the little gate by which they'd entered through was rusted stiff with disuse. Hypnotised by the act of trespass, they paused when it would have been wiser to press on.

It was their own decision. There *could* have been a slower introduction to horror, and a retracing of Hunter's route in, via land held down by Bathie's people, but they hadn't the time to secure safe passage. Even in the zones directly gripped by her blood-kin, the welcome was uncertain. Fruntierfolke were inclined to assume the uninvited were pseudo-humans and fungoids – since mistakes could not be rectified. They fired first – and second and third and twelfth – and shrugged over unfortunate errors later, if at all. Just penetrating their tamer fringes to ask Earl Rage Fruntierfolke for his daughter's hand had proved an adventure in itself for Guy. He'd returned with all his limbs and pieces, admittedly; not to mention the perfect bride. Conversely, he'd had years and grey hairs put on him and seen sights he couldn't un-see, much as he might wish to.

So, a diversion and swift plunge in had seemed the wisest course. A wide circuit round the Wild-focus of fallen New-Reading and then a day's march north ought, all things being equal, to take them to the outskirts of Hunter's knowledge. Thereafter, he could guide them straight 'home'. Then, on the off-chance they were successful and spared, they could always take the shortest route back. The Fruntierfolke looked more carefully at, were more discriminating to, incoming objects, even if only for cataloguing purposes, than those who sneaked up from behind.

Viewed from on high and on a map it had seemed merely daunting. Now '*disgusting*' stepped up to join that description. The naked reality of it sneaked lead into their boots and sneered at all their clever plans. Even the fauna were part of the conspiracy. A flight of parliaments mocked them in their ease to skim the awful jungle – till something swift and red and tongue-like emerged from the sward and drew one in, protesting. The survivors wheeled off sharply.

They had discussed it along the way but no amount of preparation could prevent the collywobbles, or the wish for privacy and a bush. Every child of New-Wessex was raised on Wild tales and had its paths as their default bad-dream. Guy

167

felt the bowel-churning no less than any there but it was up to him to set both pace and tone. He'd often observed before that speed and recklessness were the way forward in such situations. You either prevailed or perished through carelessness: and either way *there* was an end to things.

There was also a means to their end. Beside the little and little-used gate through the stockade was a pontoon, left for the urgent or suicidal. Guy was going to offer a prayer of gratitude to the Emperor who thought of everything – but then thought better of it. It was . . . inappropriate. The ready-made transport was taken without thanks, hitched up and dragged along behind them.

At the hungry water's edge Guy shot a horse and the rest were set free. They bolted away, shocked by the sudden noise and murder. The creatures might survive a spell pinned behind the stockade, ready and waiting conveniently for their return. Alternatively, they might not, and end up as Wild dinner. Whatever transpired they'd be of service, as transport or hunger-assuagers. Their fate was the least of Guy's worries at the moment.

The latest addition to that list was how to shift a dead horse where you wanted. The victim plain refused to cooperate and Guy's own efforts proved about as useful – and dignified – as flogging it. Finally, one by one, the party's unified strength was deployed, purple-faced and rumps aloft, to heave the still bleeding beast in. Straightaway, the water began to boil in a feeding frenzy – that being merely the chance-passing minnows of the moat. Larger wakes arrowed towards the spot as unseen krakens scented a free lunch.

Guy had hoped to have the rest already on the pontoon and well launched by then, with him dashing back to leap aboard. As it was, given the recalcitrance of horse-flesh, they all had to sprint there and make frantic efforts to be away. Hunter and Guy's joint industry propelled them afloat and then Nicolo and Bathie punted from the edges. In the middle, the bearer-slave looked on, a dull-eyed and passive spectator, expecting absolutely nothing of life, and none-too fussed about its continuance.

The distraction served them awhile, even as the new motion and stabs of the poles betrayed their presence. Guy had chosen the meatiest steed to provide maximum diversion, but the short-order surfacing of whitened bones indicated it was not enough. Mere inches under their feet, held at bay by a flimsy barrier of lashed planks, there lurked voracious appetites, now beginning to consider them with cool marine thoughts. Some of the surface trails lazily turned their way. They were less than half across.

Hunter took the pole from Bathie – without asking. Eyes widened, she rebounded from the shove aside to poise ill-intentioned hands above the unsuspecting Wild-man's straining shoulders. Her fingertips fizzled brightly and there were sparks amidst her hair. Guy had to scream 'No! Please . . .' when he'd rather not have drawn attention.

Nicolo was too diverted to look but Hunter saw – and to his credit did nothing. They were now putting speedier distance between themselves and doom and there was his justification. Bravely relying on Guy's influence for deliverance, Hunter simply carried on and, after a tense second, Bathie withdrew the threat. Sullen but no longer murderous, she shared the middle of the pontoon with the slave, still-effervescent hands crossed out of harm's way into an armpit each. Guy breathed again and decided to overlook Hunter's insolence – should they survive the crossing – by way of thanks.

The water round their raft grew livelier than justified by their furious pole strokes. Half-seen mouths and glassy eyes appeared just below the surface to observe them and draw unguessable conclusions before submerging once more. There came ominous bumps and testing probes against the wood beneath their feet. Nicolo and Hunter drove on ever harder.

Guy hadn't wanted to trumpet their arrival in the new land, nor present his credentials as (ex) Ambassador. Apparently however, his wants and wishes didn't appear on destiny's menu today and he had to eat what was put before him.

Coincidentally, at that very moment in fact, he beheld something that wanted to eat him. It was sleek and greeny pink and all teeth, rising to the surface with urgency.

Guy drew out the ancestral shotgun from beneath the folds of his habit. As best anyone knew it had been Great-grandfather Chopback Ambassador's to begin with, as famously employed by him during the negotiations between New-Wessex and Camelot-Kent. The legend grew year by year but Ambassadors took it as an article of faith that Chopback and 'the impasse gun' had cleared Canterbury Cathedral of both life and sticking points, beheading the insurgent statelet. After the smoke cleared on that bloody day and the colonial war which followed, Kent was once again an honoured but subordinate slice of core Humandom, benignly guided from New-Godalming. Countless souls were saved thereby. Guy held the weapon as a hallowed object; a good and faithful servant of his family. He also peppered the water with it as though spreading bait.

The ascending thing took one discharge full in its spreading mouth – which dramatically spread it all the more. With rocketing momentum it still rose, red, from the water, until the pellets tore down its gullet and exited at the tail, wrenching all back in ruin.

The deceased's colleagues weren't much for wasting time. Without pause for mourning they were on the slivered remnants and tucking in. The water boiled with orgiastic pleasure and Guy's fortunate shot proved their salvation. The pontoon was buffeted but not mounted during the remainder of their journey. Things attempted seizure of the poles, teeth gripped them and tentacles curled, but sharp metal was equal to their dissuasion. Seconds passed like hours, even with all the entertainment, but they made progress.

Finally, upon hitting the far bank, the humans bounded ashore like youths on heat. Only Hunter was collected enough to linger and drag the vessel on to dry land but as a solo task it was beyond even his hawser arms – noted for the first time now by Guy when drawn out from the modesty of a leather coat. The Ambassador brothers returned, slightly shamefaced, to heave on the draw ropes as . . . things continued to snap at the pontoon's retreat right to the last watery moment, full of insatiable anger and greed.

The Wild jungle was orange, a vivid hue painful to the eyes, leaving an afterburn which coloured all else. Bathie shrinkingly parted its fronds so that the pontoon and poles could have a shade of concealment and the men then grunted them into place and out of sight. All in all, Guy thought they were doing well to employ foresight right then. The group were gasping and had only just begun to digest the experiences of the last moments. Except perhaps for the slave they were cursed with enough imagination to see alternative endings and themselves in a circle of spreading red; treading lively water. Their lurid landing-stage wasn't a place designed for comfort and relief about dangers past. Guy saw good cause to be kind to themselves.

By virtue of some angelic decree, as soon as the moat was crossed the air became humid to dripping point, and Guy shed his hairy monkish gown for a looser – and at the same time, more fitting – coat of many colours. That was his own little indulgent luxury, well worth Hunter's disapproval of the brief show of flesh. He felt safe in making the change as well as less sweltering afterwards, confident that, should they bump into an inquisitive angel, it would be the mental mark that was examined, not the outer human. Experience had taught him that the new masters declined to scrutinise the markings of each and every insect. So the habit was added to the slave's already heavy burden, to be brought out again when it was time to deceive more cunning, human, eyes.

'I think we should be away,' he then suggested. 'The gunshots, you know. *Such* a fuss – not very discreet.'

Hunter shook his beard.

'Don't you worry. Anything peckish would have arrived by now. Anyhow: bangs deter: it's smells that attract. Your nice clean bodies say you're here better than a proclamation.'

'I am *not*,' declared Nicolo, for the umpteenth time, to

everyone's weariment, 'going to cover myself in filth, not for any reason.'

'And I'm sure the Wild-life will thank you for it, as they enjoy their dainty dinner.' Hunter was already smearing himself with handfuls of his native soil, even diving it beneath his shirt. 'Go to Hell and digestion in your own way, then.'

It wasn't the united front Guy had hoped to present to the Wild. He too declined to degrade himself with mud, however safe-making, but there was no call to state opposition so bluntly. Nicolo's relentless *honesty* was a great disappointment to the Ambassador clan.

'To foot, gentlemen, if you please,' interrupted Guy, posing instruction as suggestion. 'And less bickering would be *so* appreciated.'

They went as bidden, and silently so, finding the orange excess surprisingly easy going. It was weak stuff, the angels' invention perhaps failing them at the borders of their control. The disgusting luxuriance gave up at the slightest footfall, tumbling in on itself like something of no conviction. In the shortest while they ceased to look for paths and forged their own.

Hunter led the way, seemingly at ease, with Guy close behind, impasse gun slung on a Bathie-embroidered sling from his shoulder. Nicolo, looking all about and pausing to make notes in a little silver-backed pad, brought up the more and more dawdling rear. A fascination for the natural world was another high-numbered feature in Sir Tusker's litany of his son's faults.

They hadn't marched for more than a quarter of an hour when Guy saw good grounds to let their spirits rise.

'Look,' he said, as general announcement, 'this isn't *so* wicked a place. We shan't want for drink!'

Hunter looked and was underwhelmed.

'Where?' he asked, though Guy's pointing glove was as unambiguous as a poke.

'There!' answered the ex-Ambassador, ever patient with other's games. 'The stream.'

Hunter looked again and then laughed.

'Oh aye, I see now. Well then, Wild-tracker, go and drink your fill!'

Just to prove a point Guy thought he would and drew closer.

The legs of the vast millipede did indeed flow like a river, a ceaseless blur of motion deceptive to the distant eye. Its armoured carapace was indeed a shiny, aquatic blue.

Hushed, the party came close and looked – and looked – but could see no head nor tail, nor beginning or end.

'Well?'

Hunter looked puzzled. 'Well what?' he asked Guy.

Their first camp was commencing awkwardly. Guy and his wife and brother stood before Hunter, blithely assuming he would know his duty. When he only looked blankly back, seemingly happy for the pause to live forever, Guy had the embarrassment of actually having to put wishes into words.

'Shelter . . . please,' he explained (this last a concession) and spread his hands to signify their nakedness before the Wild. 'Then warmth, then food.'

Hunter continued to feign incomprehension – or just possibly it was the real thing – before these suddenly helpless children. Then he chuckled.

'Aye. *We'll* plait a windbreak. *We'll* gather wood. Then *we'll* cook rations.'

And so they realised they were in his world now and the face-losing subject wasn't raised again. One of the more endearing Ambassadorial traits was an abhorrence of lost causes, a willingness to be reconciled to revolution. Their settling for the night became a cooperative, democratic affair.

Soon after though, Nicolo gave evidence of the depth of his shameful delicacy. Unguessed at, from the bowels of his slave-borne pack, he drew out a folding travelling stool and collapsible cup and matching tiny set of cutlery. He perched

173

on the first and employed the rest to pick at his supper. It was pronounced *'inedible and insufficient'* and the slave had grovelled to ask forgiveness. Then, despite all Guy and Bathie's entreaties, the sole true Ambassador there strayed with perspective glass and notepad, to play peeping-tom on the fauna. Even Guy blushed and Hunter raised both eyebrows.

Then, an owlman, plate-eyed and mindless, came to roost on a nearby tree and Nicolo rejoined them with a crashing of slain vegetation. Without a word, Hunter arose and shoo'ed the visitor away. It thought a while and then rose into the air with dignity, taking its dead dog to dine elsewhere.

New respecters of the Wild, their mood had changed. After conforming to the leviathan millipede's pleasure, put in their place by patiently awaiting opportunity to cross Guy's *stream*, they had a fresh sense of its potentialities. Aside from Hunter, who'd had never lost his awareness of them, only Bathie was more prepared than the rest. Her childhood home was no stranger to improbable things striding across the lawn, taking many muskets to fell; or scream-worthy many-legged life lurking in cupboards. It was just that the welcome respite years of education and 'wife-prep' in New-Godalming had dulled her recollection. No one would reproach her for that. It was only natural and human to cleave to a normality where life came out of broadly non-stomach-churning moulds.

Save, perhaps, for Hunter – and with him there was no telling the difference – they were hushed. That first Wild-night they sat round the disproportionate campfire he recommended, sleepless and in silence.

Later, whilst Guy and Bathie snuggled together close as symbionts, a 'flight' of flightless birds, huge as chariots, came to visit, circling tirelessly round them, pounding with their claws, desperately curious – or maybe carnivore – but not daring to come in. Night-long they were kept at a safe distance with blazing spars.

When dawn came and the stupid things were still in sight, Hunter had Guy shoot one. Its comrades looked and mourned in strangely human voices but did not retaliate. After five reloadings and ever closer tries, the chosen one finally lay still and the rest stampeded away.

Red-eyed and tired, Guy set aside his hot gun and lay a hand on the gleaming beak. The expected pleasure of revenge for lack of rest failed to show. Here, beneath his fingers there was warmth departing, even as the shotgun's was, away to add its infinitesimal contribution to the creative cauldron of the Wild. There, added to the whole, it might spark some new thing, a fresh birth, that very day. The relentless cycle would go on and nothing ever be wasted. Wild-undergrowth would grow stronger on this spot next year for the bird dying on it today.

Guy looked down on the rainbow feathers and limbs he'd stilled, the story he'd ended, and, for a moment, wished himself off the thoughtless treadmill of life. He envisaged the courage contained in squaring up to nature and saying '*I won't play* . . .'

Then Hunter joined him with a knife and set to work, aborting with a flow of avian innards, the very possibility of fine thoughts.

When they finally resumed their travels, the pack-slave was burdened by two drumsticks, massive as a giant's club. The ending of *their* walking days would fuel the party's feet into days to come.

'An army in the Wild is just a larger banquet: it lends no great advantage. If you've come to find and not conquer, then far better to pass small and unnoticed.'

Hunter was explaining the strategies of Wild survival to an enthralled Nicolo. Since its annexation was not even a distant ambition to the New-Wessex state, Guy barely cast an ear. His main attention was focused on exercising discriminating vigilance. Too free a trigger finger the last few days had left him low on shotgun cartridges. It was all very well for Hunter to preach '*shoot when I say: I'll tell y' what's hungry or not*', but the encounters weren't like that. Fur or flesh launched themselves at you just beyond reaction range if you were lucky, at reflex distance if not. There wasn't time to consult Hunter-the-walking-bestiary before deciding.

'*That's a shrill-bug – harmless . . .*' was of no use after the event, when every speck of Wild-life came from an evil child's nightmare and moved fast, powered by a wealth of limbs and wings. In the end, his nerves shredded into permanent tingling, tired of being told the shuddering horror by his feet was '*harmless*', Guy relinquished the role of vanguard and moved Nicolo forward. His revolver shells were no less precious than the impasse gun's cartridges, both equally expensive products of the overstretched Imperial armouries on the Downs, but Nicolo Ambassador was an incompetent shootist, slow on the draw and brimming with qualms. He spared things that proved harmless, if unsightly, thus husbanding their firepower. Guy didn't think he'd given in to frailty. '*Regard policy like water*', ran the twenty-first clan precept, '*sometimes hard as ice, sometimes flowing; sometimes invisible as vapour. Use it in the form that suits*'. He was both going with the flow and still steering: the highest manifestation of Ambassador behaviour, and Bathie showed that she *understood* in looks. Should his brother's judgement chance to turn septic, Guy was still standing by, not far behind and beside Bathie, ready to remedy things and extract revenge.

Orange and then purple and then vomit-coloured jungle had given way to a mad parody of Wessex countryside. Some parts suffered from uniform gigantism, others were stunted dwarf versions of familiar landscapes; still others looked normal but for the inhabitants that surged out from hedge or lane-ditch. There were even signs that madmen lived here and attempted to grow crops. Their fields, edged by monstrous, abandoned produce, clung to the remains of pre-Wild roads, but of the cultivators there was no sign. The things Guy and Nicolo, and occasionally even Hunter, shot didn't much look like agriculturalists.

Conversation, never strong, died on the second day, soon after novelty expired and the weirdness ceased to be comment-worthy. All Hunter's favourite chats were held inside his head and the slave's wit was bred out of him. Guy and Bathie had long since said all that was needful to each other and Nicolo knew he was disapproved of, however little he cared. Accordingly, for hours on end now, they moved through the pseudo-Wessex in trudging silence.

It was only when they stumbled on the remains of New-Reading that the hush became purposeful. The undergrowth died suddenly and was replaced by purplish tendrils that matted the ground like some corded carpet. When their eyes grew used to that – or as used to it as they'd ever be – and the dramatic extension of view, they realised they stood upon the works of man.

An open vista spread before them, in contrast to the few score yards perspective of the last days: a plain of low hills and enigmatic blocks, all tendril enveloped but recognisable as non-natural. Before the angels came and blessed new ways, man had built and lived here. Those regular lines had been houses, that pinnacle, though now purple-coated, was once a cathedral, beneath whose roof serious questions were pondered. Under tendrils-rivers slow seeping forward, searching for support to climb to the light, there the party presumed broad thoroughfares. In imagination a ghostly throng of citizen-humans arose to walk again, blithely confident in their trading and praying, Null-free, fear-free: little knowing the tricks time could play.

Their living, humbler, successors stood in proper, rather than wearied, silence before the view and took it in. The sun was declining behind the lost town, giving variety of shade to the uniform purple, and the little party drank it all in. There, neatly summarised by either cruel or benevolent fate, was everything they had lost and wanted. Better and more lasting than the drumsticks, it gave them sustenance for their journey.

Bathie stepped forward and raised her hands. Dull scarlet

cloth dropped back to show skinny arms. Her voice was awed and sincere.

"'*All that is, and therein, shall pass, shall perish*",' she recited from The Book of Blades, word-perfect, "'*And there remains only the Face of thy Lord . . .*'"

Guy was saved from having to look within and assent by the sudden dimming of the sun. The others' *amens* were also stillbirths, miscarried by the dying of the light.

They looked up and saw that a prodigious butterfly, acrewinged and beautiful, had shaded both them and a vast space into temporary dusk. It dwarfed them, their thoughts, dead Reading and everything.

When it had gone in stately motion – though lingering long in view, further, deeper into the Wild; a glorious kaleidoscope against the sunset – they remained mute.

It was an awful, undermining, even treacherously *subversive*, thing to learn that angels sometimes rendered fair exchange for all they had taken.

The pursuit introduced itself with human voices, far away and raucous. A mob was baying with hatred for something they could scent but not see. They wanted to see it very badly.

Hunter turned on his heels with more animation than they'd had out of him since Sir Tusker ordered his guest scrubbed. Wide-eyed, for once careless of expression, he communed with the sound. Even in those few seconds it seemed to have come noticeably closer.

'Tomfools!' he told the air and himself and, a chance byproduct, the others as well. His amplification of it was to take to his heels, regardless of whether he was followed or no. Naturally he was.

The pace was such that Guy needed his breath for keeping up and leaping what could not be trod. He drew abreast of Hunter and spared the minimum possible air for speech.

'What?'

The single-minded man didn't even turn his head.

'You'll see.'

At this rate, Bathie and the burdened slave, and even Nicolo with his less than practical boots, would soon be left far behind. Guy wasn't having that and drew his long *seax* blade. Held before Hunter like an unwelcoming winning-tape, it slowed him down to reasoning-speed.

'Forget *w-w-what?*' gasped Guy. 'Answer *why?*'

Hunter chested the levelled cutter, applying pressure but not yet defying its instruction. Behind them the hue and cry was worse and nearer.

'Maybe we can outrun,' he shot back. 'If we go *now!*'

'No.' Guy was assured. In his cool head he'd done the calculations, comparing their distance travelled as against the greater proximity of the hunt. Even at best speed the end was only minutes away. Twisted lips expressed a negative. 'Wouldn't work. You probably. Me perhaps. Not them.' He nodded back at the laggards. 'So, no.'

Guy respected their guide's sudden possession. If something impelled Hunter to rabbit-style flight, then it merited every respect. All the same, rationality had to be invited to even such a short-notice party.

Hunter looked and did the same sums, only more slowly. Realism and manhood returned.

'S'true,' he concluded. 'So: refuge or fight. Let's look.'

He led them on a more sustainable rate. They remained a party, strung out but still coherent, inspired by the howls at their heels.

A sublime woodland path, almost normal by Wild standards and sunken through long use long ago, led on. Sunlight filtered through the beech-leaf cover to variegate the shades of green, crowning all, even decay and fungi, with brief beauty. In usual circumstances, it would have been a clear and savoured route. Now it was a death trap, a funnel to the abattoir. They would be sighted long before they reached its further end.

Hunter huffed at its glorious show, unappreciative.

179

'Now, *there's* a stroke of luck . . .' he said, disgusted.

'Over the edge, I suggest,' said Nicolo, already attempting the high bank, digging his still vaguely polished heels into its soft earth and accumulated leaf mould.

'But what if they guess?' Hunter asked sarcastically, pointing at the child's-play trail he left behind.

The chase were taking on individual voices now. They didn't sound like pleasant people.

'Minutes from now is better than now,' Guy told him – and followed his brother, linking arms with Bathie. They didn't see Hunter's longing look down the lane or pondering of *individual* salvation. Between his solo speed and the signposts the rest had left, there was a chance *he* might still make it. He could be away whilst the hunt were dining on red meat. It was very tempting . . .

Then Hunter recalled the maxims of his faith, that thing which had led him from Wild to Wessex and now back again. There was the higher cause, the longer view and eternal life to consider. '*Greater love hath no man* . . .'

With a wry smile Hunter resigned himself to his *wyrd* and assisted the poor laden slave over the rise.

Straightaway he was rewarded with a sign from above of having done the right thing. It was rare that the Great Teacher's marking tick came so soon upon the event. Usually it was delayed by years, decades even, or – so he was assured – postponed until the school report of the life-to-come.

Need and danger had inspired Bathie, and her hair and fingertips were alight with cold sparks. She returned to the bank's edge and by the passing of hands raised a tempest amongst the leaves and soil-creep. When it had passed it was as though they never had. Hunter could not have done better, even with hours of application.

The extra-life then left her and Bathie fell back, diminished by and for a spell. Normally anarchic black locks lay disciplined and lank around a further-whitened face and the ground became a doubly necessary home. They all joined her and hid down below the bank, not daring to run further for

180

fear of each footfall betraying them – for the enemy were with them now, entering and surveying the lane as they had. Puzzlement and fury changed the octave of their clamour.

Guy pressed back into the never-disturbed mould, a comfortable bed in any other circumstances, and held his breath. The rest did likewise – bar one. Noting it when looking across to check on Bathie, Guy saw unfamiliar sentience in the slave's eyes. The man was calculating whether betrayal might be a good career move right now: that and the likelihood of finding freedom, or at least a better master, amongst the Wild-folk. One shout, one clearing of the throat, was all it would take to launch a new destiny down the slipway. Once over the bank, he might be free or he might be dinner, but it was probably worth a try. Given his present lot, Guy could hardly blame the chap for considering a fresh – if risky – roll of the dice.

Sympathy or no, he also couldn't permit it just then. The impasse gun was across Guy's chest, its line of fire fixated on the slave's – presently closed – mouth. Guy let it be seen; conveying a wealth of information with a knowing smile. It tipped the balance of decision the way the former Ambassador required. The target lips clenched closer.

Neither need have bothered. Treachery took another route.

Over their heads arrived an apparition. An angel. Past caring, Hunter let his groan be heard. It didn't matter: they were already given away.

'Here!' sang the angel to their unseen seekers – and even pointed from its sky vantage. 'They are here!'

And yet it was no plain song or easy telling, for she or he or it was grievously hurt – and burnt – and breathless. The gesture conveyed more sense than her gasping words.

Save in his dreams, Guy had never seen an angel distressed – nor had any human as best he knew. Some other time it would have been a wonderful sight. Scorched and blistered all down one side, this one was clinging on to grandeur by its fingertips. Even the great wings they liked to materialise to

181

impress lesser breeds were not with her today. She was at functional minimum; a basic, *urgent* angel. Blaming the party below, she looked down on them – and at the same time honoured them – with hatred.

'*Here!*' The screech filled the forest and the world and all their powers of hearing. 'They are h . . .'

A new arrival both occupied and negated her space, as swift and terrible as worlds colliding. They were a matching pair, equally wounded, and once one covered the other, both were gone in mutual annihilation. Even the resulting flames were consumed away, like water departing through a plughole, leaving only a great sadness.

Humans were up to transcending that particular tragedy and moving on unmoved. Survival also proved to have precedence over miracles. Guy's party fled into the forest without comment, as their pursuers, shocked into silence, followed on up the bank. Neither hung around to gawp, absolved by each other's sound effects from any need.

Naturally, he had one or two other things to think of at the time, but in the portion of his mind that could be spared, Guy tried to fix his most recent memories in amber. The sight had been fleeting, almost too swift to grasp, but he felt convinced – sure as any racing hunch – that the hurtling nemesis, their salvation, had *also* been angel-shaped. There was joy and puzzlement in that in equal measure: a heady brew to be sipped at later.

Unhelpful foliage and yielding earth prevented them from making much progress. Meanwhile, behind, some powerful urge was inspiring the foe to heroic feats. Guy heard the race result prophesied in their now audible breath and little sounds, like snapping twigs and branches brushed aside. Some, he thought, were silent and intent on their work, content with the prospects. Others amongst their persecutors were banshee-like with joy. The second variety sounded the closer, and gaining by the second.

They wouldn't make it. Bathie was waging a losing war with briars which reached to snag her billowing dress. Every bushy

182

assignation, though spurned, lost her a pace or two. Bathie's eyes were wide and wonderful – but reconciled to the likely end. It was said that Fruntierfolke feared barring from Heaven unless they brought a fresh-dead enemy with them as proof of identity. Guy took thought as to how he might provide that last service for her.

Then Nicolo had lost a heel and, even worse, paused to look for it – which was another burden for Guy. Not only was he about to lose a brother, but the full weight of the family's hopes would descend, like a rock-fall, upon *his* shoulders – for the few moments before those shoulders were stilled forever. An axe was coming to their branch of the ancient Ambassadorial tree, to cut it back to the stem. There might be new growth, but it would have to be a foreign grafting. An old story was about to end here in this falsely beautiful glade.

Hunter and the calculating slave were well away, respectively a practised woods-fleer and someone in search of a better life. They needn't be involved in the debacle unless they wanted to be.

Guy didn't have that luxury of choice. He turned on his heel, the impasse gun foremost and willing to serve, for first sight of the clinging enemy. It made such an impression that he almost forgot to fire.

When the angels arrived and the Wild descended on humanity like a guillotine, those slow to leave or insufficiently grateful – or just unlucky – had been deprived of their senses. Whilst the *new-life* burgeoned all around them, whole populations were left bereft of understanding, left to live – or die – like animals. When they wandered, starving and anguished, aware of some great loss but not what it was, they were turned back or, later, shot, by the horrified border guardians of Wessex.

In due course, the soldiers' consciences were salved by Imperial decree and the newly-dubbed *Tomfools* had their citizenship revoked. Thereafter, they were fair game for either mercy-killing or charity, the god-kings of remnant humanity expressing no preference. In those difficult times of adjustment, both geographic and spiritual, New-Wessex had too many people for too little land as it was, and in the first winters even aristocratic ribs could be counted. Thus there was scant compassion to spare for beasts, for all they might look like men and wear scraps of clothes.

Occasionally someone might recognise a friend or relative and take them in, but there was no helping them really, no way back to the intelligence expunged out by angelic decree. When they bred they passed on bestiality and the children – or whelps – were worse than their sires. On the whole, sentient man preferred them out of sight and thus out of mind. To see a brother brought low like that was only sour reminder of the whole species' humiliation.

In the Wild some survived, learning four-legged skills and shedding scruples over choice of menu. Noses acquired fresh sensitivity, sight became keener: they speeded up enough to bring down sprightly prey. There came to be packs of them, mutual assisting clans and tribes and dominant males. The Fruntierfolke got to hear confident howling close-by and by day.

As an angel once said to Guy in Paris, you had to hand it to humans; whichever way you threw them, they landed on their feet – even if it was sometimes all four feet.

And sometimes their new skills were recognised and they found patrons.

These were leashed and muzzled but the leashes were slipped and muzzles loosened as they raced towards the party like human-shaped lightning. Though a poor use of scarce ammunition, reflexes from the savannah and sabre-tooth-time made Guy turn his fire on the animal-enemy first. Blasts took two in the chest and somersaulted each back. Then Nicolo limped over and used his *pepperbox* pistol, twisting each barrel round in turn to fire.

Guy was rather impressed. His brother ignored the siren call of Tomfool targets, instead sweeping the bank's edge clear of atheists. Indeed, he even paused, pretending to fumble over his gun, in order to let just the right number of new targets

184

ascend into sight. Then, one, two, three and so on, he knocked the skittles back down, exactly as Guy had at the ambush in the *Way*. Clearly, they had more in common than Guy had thought – which was to say, anything at all.

Suddenly there was anger and pain aplenty, invisible, in the lane, but no present threat. The Tomfools, bewildered by their masters' loss and prevented from full use of their teeth, were struck still and comical. With his Ambassadorial stiletto, Guy made the nearest brace go away – forever.

'Actually,' commented Guy, once the powder smoke was slightly abated , 'I didn't think we'd survive that one, did you? Nicolo? *Nicolo!*'

'Sorry,' said his brother, looking up, a little way off. 'What did you say?'

'Would you just *forget* your lost heel? Please? Right *now?*'

'But I like these boots,' Nicolo pleaded. 'They have senti-mental value.'

Guy gathered him by the arm and forcibly aborted his search. A fresh wave of atheists were coming over the top, issuing instructions to their man-hounds. The chase was on again.

Their victorious skirmish had allowed Bathie and the rest to put some decent distance between themselves and the pursuit. Guy sped to catch up, as best a linkage with a limping brother allowed, and, with nothing more pressing to occupy his mind, ran through an inventory of resources. Nicolo might well have a few shells left but for the present his *pepperbox* was unloaded and there was a great deal of foreplay involved in getting that model raring to go. Patting his own Null-skin ammunition pouch he felt a bare two cartridges remaining inside. That pittance had to be spun out not only to preserve them from this threat, but get them where they were going and then safely back home again. It was a tall order: a silver sixpence to last you all your life.

Having despaired of them and then been surprised, Hunter turned again and came back to assist. His bow flung shafts past the brothers to produce satisfying cries. Then shots spat from the opposite direction, inspiring the sullen earth round Guy's pounding feet to dance. He hated it when things came down to just luck. When calculation and cunning had no role to play, an Ambassador felt unworthy even if he prevailed. Whilst recognising Lady Fortune, Guy would not bow down and worship her. Horse-racing had made an atheist of him in that one specific respect.

The Tomfools were getting awfully close again. Hunter's fire was being directed nearer and nearer to his friends. A near miss caressing his ear then made Hunter exclaim and duck. They couldn't go on like this.

Happily they didn't have to. The landscape abruptly changed, as the Wild so often did. Generally, Guy found that disconcerting but today he blessed its ever-changing moods. Woodland suddenly gave way to jungle: not even orange or pink jungle but blessedly normal coloured stuff that could swallow them up and enfold them in its blowsy bosom. Of course, given the nature of the flora, there was the possibility of being swallowed for real, and then digested – Hunter said there were flowers that ate horses – but the chance of that was better than the racing certainty of it not far behind. By gesture and exhortation, Guy urged everyone into the vegetation.

'On you g-g-go – and thanks be to Blades.'

They heard that back in the forest and cursed him and his God. Without turning Guy waved them a cheery goodbye. A bullet passed between two spread fingers.

There was the danger of losing each other in the richness of concealment and so they stayed in contact by linking hands, a ragged morris-troupe rioting through the riotous growth. Whoever was least impeded took the lead, pausing to regroup should a link be torn from the chain. Guy found himself hand-in-hand with the slave of questionable loyalty – and so kept an extra firm grip on him. He was still needed for his broad back and brawn and so the day of reckoning wasn't just yet. Guy caught the now dead-again eyes but was no longer deceived. Although bred to a blind spot concerning slaves, he now looked on this one in a fresh light and, as a man who

186

relished his own freedom, saw how even this jungle, with peril snapping at your heels, might seem preferable to endless servitude. Guy dug his fingers into the horny palm, passing the message on.

Bathie's alabaster hand, now limp and sparkless, was entrusted to – and enfolded in – Hunter's paw. He dragged her on, threatening to dislocate the limb, but she was too spent to protest. Guy tried to work his way up the formation to assume the role of guide but stubborn tendrils and uncooperative trunks thwarted each attempt. From behind, he heard evidence that the muzzles had been flung away. The howls were whole-hearted now and they could hear the champing of jaws. Hostile speculation and instructions from more rational mouths interjected into the few quieter moments.

Hunter, in the lead, expressed surprise, copied in turn by those who blundered after. The ground was turned plashy underfoot. It was bearable for the moment: more moisture than standing water to start with, and no more of a problem than squishy shoes could pose. Very shortly though, they were wading, fearful of their footing and wrinkling their noses at the unseen things they brushed through. Linked hands gripped all the tighter for comfort, leaving nail half-moon signatures. Each conscripting their one remaining free limb, Guy, Nicolo and Hunter held gun or bow aloft to save them from ruin.

'Press on or hide?' hissed Hunter back down the line at Guy, his target audience.

'Or stay and fight?' added Nicolo. He'd broken the line and, with an extra hand to spare, was worrying away at his *pepperbox* pistol, all fingers and thumbs. Presumably servants had loaded it for him last time. As many shells were going into the water as the weapon.

Guy paused and followed his example, albeit more economically, sliding the last two cartridges into the impasse gun. Meanwhile, he filled the respite brimful with thought. Looked at one way, swamps could be great mufflers of sound, making some eventual hidey-hole all the more discreet. Also

187

the pursuit would be slowed. On the other hand, so would they – with splashing sounds inevitably added to offer a dead give-away. Bathie was pretty winded in any case. Therefore, flight was probably just postponing the evil moment.

On another hand – a third, if such a thing was possible – here was a piss-poor place in which to make their stand. When it came to wrestling with the Tomfools, as it would when the bullets were all fired, then any wild-fighting would be aquatic rather than in the dust. The animalistic once-men would be at an added advantage. Likewise, the lack of visibility that was presently saving them would make musketry a matter of luck rather than a considered pleasure. A few seconds of mad frenzy and it would all be over. Guy foresaw bodies bobbing in the green water and Bathie's red dress ripped from her by Tomfool teeth – and then the atheists would approach and see her snow-white corpse and . . .

That still-living lady had been lost in strange admiration of a scatter of reeds, but at that moment she looked up and at her husband. The breather had worked wonders. From somewhere she'd obtained a fresh reserve of strength and confidence. It showed its face to the world in a smile.

Thus it didn't *have* to be here. It could be whole minutes or hours later and Guy wished to maximise their time together.

'On,' he told them and led the way.

There were slight rises which tempted them to divert and walk dryshod but each proved to be things of mud and floating earth, little false-islands of grass and trees designed to deceive by the spirit of the Wild. Each gave way under the exploratory foot and lost them irreplaceable seconds. Their allure rested upon the fact that the water was growing deeper, its scum now lapping at their midriffs, or higher still against Bathie's flat chest. Guy had to deny parentage of that defeatist, half-mournful, half-gloating, spirit which is born from a wrong decision. He ignored its cradle cries but soon expected to hear it grown to lusty adulthood, in possession of another's voice – Hunter's most probably; or else Nicolo's, speaking sorrow out loud – or soft in their present danger.

That it was absolutely right made the sound none the sweeter.

The *halloos* from behind were now close and clear. The chase was firing randomly through the jungle to display their bullet-wealth and hopeful of the blessing of a little luck.

Not before time, Guy took delivery of a small slice of that delicious substance himself. They came up against an island, blundering into the causeway which led to it. The thing held, rather than floating mockingly away. Its emerald covering stood firm against their impact. At the further end there was a roundel of solid ground covered with a hat of gorse and thorn in which giants might hide. It was a gift and Guy blew a kiss to Heaven

'No!' said Hunter, brusquely, ungratefully. 'Not safe. It's a *Slither-house*.'

There was the option of pursuing the clerk-ish approach, of saying '*why* . . .?' and '*what's a* . . .?' but here and now was the time, if ever there was one, for nimble dance-steps.

'That's as may be,' countered Guy, in the voice he reserved for broken-spirited enemies, 'but it's *our* house now.'

The tone carried Hunter with them when sweet reason might not have. Guy urged them up on to the causeway and then, to some silent surprise, back down the other side. Only the thought of presenting easy targets when aloft reconciled them to quitting the lovely firm ground. If anything, the water beyond was deeper still.

'Now on. Heads down,' Guy instructed. They splashed on beside the line of the causeway towards the islet. Hunter's shrinking reluctance grew.

Guy drew back to him and put his head close.

'Bad?' he asked. He'd intended to whisper but the noise of the pursuit demanded something sturdier.

'Very.' Hunter's eyes would not leave the crown of gorse.

'Would *they* know?' Guy nodded his head in the enemy direction.

'If they've lived this long – bound to.'

Things were coming together. The ingredients gathering in

189

Guy's mind fell into order and made a recipe.

'Follow me.'

To both his and their credit, they did. He led them almost to the island and then out a shade, till they stood shoulder-deep directly behind it. Judging by the libretto, their unshakeable friends had just discovered the causeway too.

Since Hunter was the only one who understood, Guy fixed him alone with the gaze his father taught him. It said '*trust me*' – an unreasonable thing for an Ambassador, of all people, to demand and thus only to be secured through domination. To date Hunter had seen just stutter and lace, horse and Bathie-worship, so Guy had to crack the door ajar and let the inner steel be seen. Pondering that shock held Hunter to his place for the required spell.

Guy then paddled forward and swallowing all anxieties and revulsion, he took the islet's gorse and thorn to hand and agitated it with all his strength. Nature's barbs bit back till blood ran down his arms, but still he continued. Motion travelled down the ancient interlock of vegetation until there was good semblance of activity within. He continued with it, putting the pain aside in some internal place else for later consideration, until he heard the sight acclaimed. He also caught the word '*slither*' buried amidst the barbarous Wild-dialect insults hurled at them. It was done.

He waded slowly back to the others, easing the water gently aside like a hymen, to minimise its protest.

To those who badly wanted to make their acquaintance, it had been a long and costly kiss-chase. Now they thought they *had* them. All their pent-up frustrations came pouring out in the form of lead.

The islet and its hair-do positively quivered with the weight of musketry rained down upon it. The tight-arcing cover snapped in places, giving the place a neurotic, dishevelled look. Sparks struck like brief-living fireflies or like Bathie's black hair when she was possessed, but they failed to catch. The island was grossly assaulted but would not die.

Whilst the concert lasted the party kept their heads low,

almost to revolting water level. They saw now what Guy had in mind. The atheists shared Hunter's misgivings about the little refuge and declined to enter in. However, they thought Guy and co. *had* and on that assumption were content to fling in death until their end could be reasonably assumed.

It lasted a long while but, midway, the New-Wessex contingent saw something to liven their wait. On their side of the islet, away from the shootists, the brush gave a convulsive heave and something huge and midnight-hued oozed from underneath – a viscous pancake sliding from the pan. It entered into the water and dived deep below the surface.

'A *slither*, perchance?' asked Guy – and gave thanks for his stutter's sleep.

Hunter gulped, nodded and, eyes closed, began to pray. Probably they all did; even the slave, if such could bring themselves to speak to a Deity who did them so few favours.

They waited; five curtailed statues, cut off at the chest, their submerged portions anticipating the first feather touch of something vile. When, by and by, it failed to arrive, their postponed breath was expelled like rifle-fire but, fortunately, the display of the real item continued across the way, removing any danger of being heard. The foe persisted a creditable – or maybe cowardly – time, persevering with a policy that bore no visible fruit. Gradually though, enthusiasm and perhaps ammunition diminishing, the whiplash sounds slowed and above them they heard the order to desist.

Almost scraping the waterline, to dampen the retort, Guy shot the slave. Then he hurriedly dressed him in his own coat, medals and all. When the gently bobbing corpse looked the required part, and his useful packs were recovered, Guy launched the good ship dead-slave in the atheists' direction.

Only Hunter was bumpkin enough to protest the action, and even he did so silently: a matter of gaping mouth and owl-eyes.

'He might have given us away,' Guy whispered and lied – and convinced.

The sacrifice rounded the islet and the enemy assumed he'd come from it. They whooped the sight. That 'mission-accomplished' disarmed Hunter's outrage.

'Right, all aboard!' commanded Guy, and, in what was becoming an ingrained habit, led by example. Hunter was now content to meekly follow. The tongue-tied addict of horse and woman-flesh had won his spurs.

The islet proved to be glassy smooth, laminated with layer after layer of some hardened gloss. Opaquely beneath could be seen the original tussocky surface, now bleached and flattened and quite dead. It was difficult to retain a purchase on its armoured successor and they made a meal of clambering on. Happily, there were slipways in the brush, low flat paths worn by the previous owner, that permitted access without causing the cover to dance. Eventually, and as discreetly as possible, they were gathered atop the central point, huddled together like Null in a sleep-pile to retain their footing.

There had been more glorious claimings of fresh provinces for New-Wessex, not to mention more glorious provinces. It didn't merit the raising of a Wessex *Long Man* flag, even if they had had one. All the same, at that moment, they *loved* their rock-of-refuge as they would the hub of Empire.

Their grips held, their luck and courage likewise: whereas that of their persecutors faltered. *They* weren't up to investigating the work of their hands and guns, and chose to *presume* victory. Guy had gambled on that, more confident of it than the result of many a steeplechase. With but one life to live and one only, cursed with no hope of futurity, the godless were reputed to be . . . cautious creatures.

So, in their own dry way, they'd done their calculations and failed to arrive at any outcome suggesting survivors. Between them, lead storm and original inhabitant ought to have handled everything. However, checking that might involve meeting a wounded – and presumably rather tetchy – slither. Therefore, the enemy decided to put faith in human reason. To himself, Guy chuckled and blessed their naivety.

Hunter heard and smiled at him: unreserved approval. Use

the pursuit to kill the slither; use the slither to kill the pursuit. Very clever. Very *Ambassador*.

'Your God is *no* God!' called the never-glimpsed leader. 'And Blades is *not* his prophet!' They could have recognised his voice but there were better things to think about.

His minions joined in with repetition or howls.

Maybe that was just their tedious expression of joy, or possibly a final testing of success. The forces of piety on the islet refused to be drawn – thus losing the chance for re-acquaintance with their dedicated follower, the Dandy from the Way.

Then, after savouring the ensuing silence, he and his besiegers withdrew, chatting happily. Angel advice had again led him far from home and habits – and once more failed him at the climax.

Guy saw them a good way off before he permitted speech – though Bathie waved a mocking cheerio with overconfident finality. No one was racing for the privilege of initial comment in any case, each too busy in their own way, reeling in the shock of continued existence, to put feelings into words just yet.

Thus, Guy Ambassador spoke first and for all. He lent back against a mutated gorse and yawned, earning infinite admiration.

'It's all *g-go*, innit?' he said, languidly.

Guy might have felt less flippant later. He also might have felt a hundred hungry mouths attached to his feet – had he not been so heavily sedated.

The slither returned by night, when it felt sad and homesick and unfairly evicted by the *two-legs* with *fire-sticks*. Some of their stinging shells had resisted expulsion and the creature moved less sinuously for their lingering. Enraged by pain, it had skimmed to a Christian fishing village and dealt quite roughly with two of their beached boats, by way of revenge. No fish for them tomorrow; but a hungry restoration day instead!

Then, limping back, it found home wonderfully stocked with food and repented of all the earlier fury. The pink two-legs weren't so malicious after all. Their thoughtful, pleasing, penance, saved further agonising travel to fetch supper!

One shuddering heave up on to that home sweet home was rewarded with a veritable feast. Flowing over the sleepers like nightmare, nimble lips covering the slither's belly nibbled away cloth and leather coverings and gently attached themselves to *feed*. Slither-spittle, a calming gift of kindly Mother Nature, was meanwhile released into each bloodstream to save the meal from waking and distress.

Everything flowed smoothly, providing payment in kind for the earlier unprovoked attack, and the slither felt justified in draining at least one husk down to empty: a giving in to gluttony rendered right by his injuries. Also, without such ample intake it couldn't hope to combat the poisoning of the metal left inside. The slither needed to rest replete for a while if it wanted to see still more centuries. It was all very *sad*, but life lived by absorbing life – and it wasn't he who had started hostilities. . . .

Bathie and Nicolo were already anaemic by the time Guy's feet were reached. The multiple mouths tasted – and then paused. Conveyed in some inexpressible way, it imbibed knowledge along with the blood, tasting a higher call than survival. The slither prayed apology and what it had already swallowed it gave back. Myriad teeth stitched shut the joins.

It was still hungry, was still gasping for more in the urge to cheat death, but stronger than that the slither knew right from wrong. Here was a two-legs with a mission, something that, albeit unknown, it could and should approve of.

Though a monster now, the former mayor of New-Reading till the angels came and changed him and many things – and a devout monotheist still – knew his duty.

Slipping off its supper, relinquishing food and home to

violent squatters, perhaps relinquishing life itself, the slither slid back to take its chances in the swamp.

When they woke, their clothes were stiff and shiny and crackled when they stirred. Overnight, most garments had become a crazy polka-dot of holes. Covered in love-bites, Bathie was more pale and interesting than ever. Nicolo and Hunter arose like wan ghosts.

They looked from one to another but said nothing on the matter, wordlessly deciding to never, *ever*, refer to it again.

'*Lord God, Creator of the Universe, thank you for keeping us alive, for preserving us, and bringing us to this moment.*'

The Prayer of the Passing Moment – the Dandy had never said it with more zest. It should properly stem from joy, not relief, but right now he clutched for it like a drowning man. It felt good to reconnect with the only fine thing amidst all this vileness. Dealing in Tomfools and Wild-life – and death – made it easy to lose sight.

Nevertheless, despite swamp and conscience, each step felt lighter now that the deed was done. Spirits rose and the water, though still deep, dragged less. It seemed that the more wrongdoing you had under your belt, the sooner memory of it faded.

One click. Unnoticed amidst the Wild-opera.

The Dandy took comfort in the knowledge that he only did ill to do good and had hope of forgiveness therefore. The angel – of the righteous party, not the other sort – had poured reassurances over him on that score. Its abrupt disappearance didn't negate those promises. They were curious creatures, answering a not-to-be-denied beck and call. If the *summons* came it wasn't reasonable to expect polite goodbyes.

In the merely material world, he had light enough to see.

Within the bounds of keeping his footing, the Dandy could look around at the Wild-swamp and behold all he wanted to and more. The greater reality, though: *that* remained shielded from his eyes. Dandy peered harder in hope of catching the sparkle of the God in which he had his being and moved, but, as ever, *He* stayed cloaked in the interstices of the mundane.

Two clicks – a sequence still not perceived.

Clearer to the Dandy's mind's eye were the ancestors: those who'd preferred life in the Wild-fringe to falsehood. Escaping in ones or twos from 'Babylon', they'd refined true religion from the crude ore of emperor worship and extracted the pearls of Christianity from the swine-feed of the *Blades-Bible*. Their heroic example was often his solace when up to his hocks in wrongness, as now, wading through this fetid broth boiled out of tortured ground. At that moment the Dandy felt their smile on the back of his neck.

Such is the sharpness that can be put on steel, he never felt the sword slice through the same place.

Three clicks – crystal-clear but far too late to care about. The last thing he heard.

The Dandy trod on, one, two three, steps more, head less attached than hitherto, thoughts dying without knowing, on into the trap and whatever lay beyond.

Beyond civilisation, it was a mutilation offence to converse other than in Fruntierfolke finger-click speech. Centuries of usage had accordingly developed a vocabulary amply rich enough for Wild use: mostly permutations on *kill* and *don't kill*.

The senior-youth in the 'spur-earner' party had indicated that Guy's party be allowed through. They'd been on the point of getting short-shrift – and spear and sword – till Bathie was spotted. Her gamy gait marked her out as Fruntierfolke and kin, as plain as if she carried a flag. Obviously, since her breed never gave or took quarter, she couldn't be a prisoner. Logically therefore, she must the soft-folks' leader.

The skinny soldiers were clicked back into cover, behind bushes and trees or underwater once more.

The first time, the Dandy's party received similar dispensation. The Fruntierfolke boys didn't wish to spoil whatever game their sister was playing. She'd seen the reed-stem air-pipes. She'd even smiled in greeting and yet still hadn't called for aid. Her family had been happy to play along.

Second time around though, during the return, propriety was restored. It was neither polite or kind to chase Fruntierfolke through manky water, no matter how degrading their company. The 'spur-earners' were out there to do just that and their leader addressed the meal set before them.

Three clicks made the water erupt and suddenly the world was full of Fruntierfolke.

Headless, down in the water the Dandy fell. One by one, his party joined him.

All passion fled with the dying of the light and each last-sight was a square of sky, framed by streaming youths. Their blank gaze escorted *Atheist* and Tomfool alike off to Paradise.

'It was sweetly done, Ambassador,' said Hunter, '*that* I'll grant you – but nothing else . . .'

Guy sighed and Bathie remained lost walking her inner landscape, very probably an even weirder vista than their present Wild-stop. Meanwhile, Nicolo leaned back and closed his long lashed eyes, the downpour waterfalling off the brim of his flat hat. So long as any deed, for good or ill, was done stylishly, then that sufficed for him. He couldn't or wouldn't assist with further analysis. It was another part of his embarrassing liberality that he could calmly sit and hear *hoi polloi* question the actions of their betters.

For three days after Guy and the slither saved them, it rained as if God was lamenting over Creation, and Hunter chose to take it for a sign. He would not let the useful murder of the slave lie, worrying away at it like a Null with a bone.

Once the subject of the angel erasing was worn threadbare by their pacing over the thin evidence, then they became sitting ducks to Hunter's monstrous integrity.

Of course, in response Guy was as polite and urbane as ever, but even he wearied with the repetition. In vain he pointed out some fortuitous examples of Wild-life: a slimy thing slow-devouring a screaming two-headed dog, vocal in protest from both muzzles, or a flock of mega-rooks persecuting one lone white mutant aberration amongst them. Guy's thesis was that it was impious to strive to be *more* just than God – who permitted such sights. Whereas Hunter insisted, with words plainly not his own, that man was *of* but not *in* nature, and should draw wonder but not example from it.

In the end, Guy had to fall back on his last ditch *try to think of me as a loveable rogue* defence but even this normal killer failed to do the trick, leaving him armed only with smiles and shrugs. His religion had warned him both about the endless cavils of the sophisticated and the beauty of simple faith, but nowhere did he recall guidance about implacable virtue in the lower orders. Clearly, strange things came into being when plain men pondered deeply away from good counsel.

The Wild's jungle, then forest, then grassland, then landscapes less definable altogether, was no shelter at all. Within moments of the cloudburst's birth they were drenched and then stayed that way. Having sacrificed his coat in a good cause, Guy suffered especially; a shirt, even one of peerless embroidered elegance, proving no protection against the deluge. Water bullets drummed on his hairless head, a constant reminder of his new, unwanted, status. He was almost – but not quite – minded to don monkish garb again, and its bulge in the pack that he now had to carry himself, after dispensing with the bearer's services, beckoned like an unlikely temptress. Fortunately, the sight of Bathie, soaked to the skin, dress clinging and black locks plastered down, was some – if not enough – compensation, strengthening his resolve.

They made slow progress, less than invigorated by their

blood-loss, the pallor in their cheeks remaining longer than it should. Then, to cap it all, at this midday stop a few inadequate bites served to finish the last of the food. A fire was out of the question, not that their meagre larder justified one. Rock-hard bread remnants were held up to the rain to soften them and then crumbled in the hand to eke out the feast. Even then, they could only stretch it out a moment or two. Stomachs queried as to when the rest was arriving and everyone licked their lips for the last taste of dried beef before the rain washed it away.

'Well, God alone knows the truth of it . . .' countered Guy to Hunter's perseverance, deploying one of his huge library of profound but non-committal conversational parries.

It failed to put a cork in the flow of cant. Hunter showed his lack of breeding by taking all speech at face value.

'He does!' he agreed. 'And one day shall judge you by all he sees. Depend upon it!'

'Then I am content,' lied Guy bravely – for he was very far from it. 'The Divine Emperor knows the rough gales of fortune that buffet us. Therefore he will excuse our sometimes in-elegant gait along the path of life. I am confident Slave and I shall meet at the gates of Paradise and he will shake me by the hand.'

'Or neck,' said Bathie, just when they'd discounted her from the exchange. It served to shut Hunter up when reason wouldn't.

'Sweetly done, I say,' he mumbled, '*but* . . .' and left it at that – for the moment.

'So now what?' asked Nicolo, waking once all the agonising was over. 'I mean, does our lack of ammunition condemn us to *grass* as dish-of-the-day – and tomorrow, and tomorrow? If perchance we encounter more big-birds should we ask nicely for one to commit suicide? Or maybe we could all link hands and try to strangle it . . .'

He still had his collapsible chair and spoke from its slight prominence. He'd even fastidiously brushed the seat with a sodden kerchief before alighting. Together with his cutlery it had been preserved through all their chases and troubles, to be brought out to grace even this graceless meal. Doubtless the heel-less boot was also still with him, tucked away somewhere. It was somehow a rebuke to the others that, wherever he might be, Nicolo effortlessly brought New-Wessex with him.

Although he looked airily into the middle distance – five or six feet in present conditions – there was no question who he was addressing. Guy might be their strategist and saviour but all still looked to Hunter for a dry bed and stuffing in their tummies. This was pre-eminently *his* nightmarish labyrinth

Pinned down to mundane matters Hunter remained dependable. He seemed fairly sanguine.

'We'll not *starve*,' he said to them all. 'The Wild provides a living to those who look in the right place – who ain't too squeamish.' Here he looked straight at Nicolo through the curtain rods of rain. 'It'll slow us down but we'll live. Hope you like insects . . .'

'Not *really* . . .' Nicolo's brow was troubled, his negative response apologetic in tone, as though the enquiry had been actual and solicitous.

'No? Oh well, master, let me see what else I can get you.'

Hunter rose and stood by the trunk of the tree that inadequately sheltered them. Till then it had been just another Wild-wonder and little regarded save for the cover provided. Guy now saw it was a particularly unpleasing sight, like a giant stem of coloured glass, heated and twisted and then adorned with leaves: an old-ladies' gaudy mantelpiece ornament with unwise life breathed into it and blown out of all proportion.

For a moment they thought Hunter felt the same way. His knife hacked at the brittle surface with venom, digging deep below. The contents proved to be pulpy and spattered the Wild-human with oyster coloured stuff, soon washed away. Then, up to his wrists below the glassy bark, he found justification for his violence to something that had done them no harm.

Distressingly organic wrenching protests accompanied the

drawing out of a long tuber from the body of the tree. It was purple and glossy and fat.

Hunter turned to show like a stage-magician. The expected applause failed to arrive.

'*That?*' exclaimed Nicolo. 'It looks like a Null's cock. My dear man, don't delude yourself I'm eating *that!*'

'Well, don't then,' replied Hunter, and took the obscene tuber to himself. Guy and Bathie watched, reluctantly fascinated, as it was held out to be washed by the rain and then slashed viciously along its whole length with the oversize *seax* knife. The already barely contained flesh leapt for freedom and a brief second in the sun before being gobbled up. Hunter then tilted the deflating thing to his face and squeezed the last of its goodness into the vicinity of his mouth.

'Delicious,' he told them when he was done, smearing most of the sticky pap from his beard. Enough remained to construct strange spikes and spires of hair. 'Eats a treat, I reckon . . .' His voice said one thing but his face another. The others knew which to believe.

'I had always hoped,' said Nicolo to Hunter, 'to get through life without seeing a Null fellated. Now you have dumped the image in my lap. Till I forget it I can never forgive you . . .'

The others weren't grateful for the picture either and drifted back to their own thoughts. Bathie blew a consoling kiss at Guy.

Hunter's vocabulary didn't stretch to refinements of love and so he was merely puzzled rather than offended. His audience lost, he also threw the drained and flaccid organ away.

'They're better when cooked,' he assured them through the pelting rain, seeking in his undesigning way to pierce their dejection. 'That's the way they're served by my people. So come on, you lot. Just think: two more days and then warm food and a warm welcome!'

Preferring motion to exhortation, especially from a yokel with guck on their face, Guy arose. Bathie naturally followed and even Nicolo moved to stow away his seat and redundant cutlery.

'*That's* the spirit, Ambassadors,' said the Wild-man, deluded his sermon was met with success.

'Ambassadors and *former* Ambassadors,' Nicolo corrected him.

The distinction didn't touch Hunter. 'Everyone,' he confirmed. 'All. On we go – with a spring in our steps. Hold it in mind – a warm welcome!'

Guy smiled and waved Hunter foremost – on the principle that he was less likely to preach with no one in view. It also allowed him to quietly jettison the last of the slave's now-empty packs – and thus all memory and memorial of him.

'*Warm*? Yes,' said Bathie, who had an intimidating memory for conversation. '*Welcome*? No.'

Hunter recalled and ate his words. It would make a change to their disgusting diet of late.

The crowds and their excitement probably added to the natural – if that term could be properly applied – armpit-ambience of the Wild. Cannon and musketry donated their own little portion to the oven-temperature too, but, those external factors aside, Guy found confirmation of his theory that the Wild climate conformed to those under its sway. For instance, when on their way to Hunter-town their spirits could not have been trodden any lower, the continuous rain suddenly stopped. Likewise, the present excitement and danger was reflected in feverish heat. There was some presiding – maybe just meteorological – deity. Now was neither time or place for superstition but Guy framed a silent prayer to sometime receive a balmy summer's day from it.

For the moment they were safe and mere spectators of the assault on Hunter's hillside home. Wave after wave of attackers threw themselves upon the stockade defences at sufficient distance to be entertaining. Hunter himself could not be so detached. You didn't need to be an Ambassador to read his almost overwhelming desire to rush in or at least snipe from behind. Guy kept within restraining distance to ensure he did neither.

It was all highly educational, as well as un-put-downable, innovative, stuff. Nowhere, not in history or legend or even winter-fireside yarn spinning, was there previous mention of joint human/Null operations. True, they were charging in as separate species but their project was a joint one. Marshalled by wizened Null elders and peacock atheists respectively, they were making a combined, no-nonsense, request for entry to the settlement. It was being declined just as forcefully, the message conveyed via shot and spear, but the gate-crashers would not take no for an answer. The bodies of those now past caring about admission were piling up and Guy spared a thought or twelve about the remainder's *powerful* motivation.

He needn't have bothered. The answer to every question appeared suspended above the melee – briefly, horribly, before its swift removal. The New-Wessex voyeurs instinctively ducked, as though mere trees and bushes could save them from angelic detection.

Their true salvation was the invader's brevity. The earlier miracle-in-the lane was confirmed and duplicated for their delectation. No sooner had the angel appeared, blackened, stricken as before, then a double arrived to blot it out. He/she/it had only seconds to scream orders and encouragement before the same scream registered the pain of negation. '*There. They. There!*' was the constant, constantly snuffed-out, always renewed, angelic refrain. They drew their conscripts' attention to the unseen beyond, over the walls. Then angels embraced, one eager, the other shrinking, and both were gone in fiery annulment.

That process was repeated again and again until, confidence growing, the party tentatively extended their heads from cover, like timid tortoises, to enjoy the show. Each fresh angelic touchdown had only a few seconds in which to assess and direct before cancellation. They pointed, they exhorted, but in the time left them there was little they could do. Frustration and haste were etched on their beautiful faces alongside the scorch marks. Guy, in particular, more angel-afflicted than most, fairly *lapped* it up. Mutual destruction. Two for the price of one. He could have watched the conveyor belt of sacrifice all day.

He also knew that pleasure had to be assessed even more vigilantly than pain, for one lulled whilst the other sharpened. Guy tore himself from the delectable play to attend to the wider world.

Atheist artillery. There was another first. Never encountered before, the fruit of theft or secret Wild-foundries? What other surprises and secrets did they have stockpiled, awaiting their day? The merely annoying horsefly had acquired poison and thus new status. With those brazen tubes they were more than Way-nuisances and brigands and cross-fodder; they were become City threateners, meriting extermination. New-Wessex could be wonderfully clear and single minded when some new fist was shaken at them. It was the over-compensation of once-rulers for their present impotence. Guy made mental note of the right generals to talk to if he ever returned home.

Likewise, the Null/human thing. Presumably it was only given life by angelic decree, a loose and sullen coalition, cobbled together for the urgent day. Guy noticed that a band of space was kept between the two contingents and that when *meat* intruded on it the Null scratched them. The angels disapproved of that and, if fleeting time permitted, burnt the offenders. Therefore, their analysis must be that an united front was essential to get their way. Guy pondered that conclusion in his heart and rejoiced over it at the same time. In what, for centuries now, passed for the normal run of things, angels came, saw and took, unaided. If they now required mortal hands and claws to achieve their aims, then that was a mighty diminishment. They were constrained – limited. They were *so* distracted they couldn't even detect prey beyond their immediate focus.

'Oh happy day!' he murmured.

Hunter – a less thoughtful man – couldn't see that. His people were under bombardment by an appalling alliance.

'Speak for yourself!' he hissed and tightened the grip on his bow to fingerprint proportions. 'It's all right for you: my wives are down there!'

Hunter badly wanted to be on those parapets, *higher mission* or no, far more than an unworthy, inner Hunter was glad to be safe way out here. He knew full well the despatch of good-news messengers to New-Wessex – and his solitary arrival of all of them – had reduced the ranks to famine thinness. Adolescents in arms, plying sling and javelin from the walls, were proof of that. Cannon and angels and atheists and Null were now pitted against a poor, depleted people who only asked to be left alone to love their Maker.

'I do beg your pardon,' said Guy, recognising his untimeliness, transcending the intriguing admission of polygamy. 'It's just that *we're* not in there.'

Hunter's frown deepened to storm-indicator level.

'By which I mean,' Guy expanded, hurriedly, 'that angels should *know* it. "*The world is theirs and the fullness thereof*" – normally. Today – *happy day* – they are blinkered – and dying!'

Scripture pacified Hunter where smooth words might not have. Also, both Bathie and Nicolo thought on and made *he's got a point there, you know* faces. Together, the two factors kept him in his place.

'Your people,' asked Guy, as the latest pink and purple wave hit the log walls and received rough treatment, 'can they hold, do you think?' It was no material concern of his but he'd rather have Hunter happy than not. There was also the question of whether they should press on direct or delay to see the ending. Conceivably, there'd be food and dry clothes amongst Hunter's folk, should they survive, whereas the Wild held only gorge-rising cuisine and samey apparel. Nicolo had been true to his word and refused all roots and tubers and was now visibly shaky on his feet.

Hunter looked on and appraised. 'You'd be surprised. We've had good practise. The fungoids attack most years when they're sporing and we've thrown *them* back. There's walls behind and traps and other surprises. I see hope. Worst come to worst, we've tunnels to retire to.'

Three sharp intakes of breath. That offended against one of the deepest New-Wessex taboos. Before Blades, in the *prey-days*, humanity had cowered away from life and the Null in burrows. Their first god-king had drawn them out of there, set them on their feet and bunged even the most time-hallowed warrens. Within a generation it was held the lowest of shames to take refuge under-earth. '*Better one day on the Downs*', went the saying , '*and death, than long life like a rabbit*'. In the early days, many – very many – lived out that precept literally and went down, musket in hand, rather than go under. To defy it was to deny every ancestral sacrifice, not to mention divine instruction. One – just one – of the charges against Christians was that they hacked out *catacombs*, to do whatever it was they did when people weren't watching.

Guy shot out his hand to curtail any comment. Part of Ambassadorial training was the bland acceptance of other cultures – however disgusting. It was formally tested early on, with displays of gluttony and incest and worse. His stomach acid rose just like the others, but he ordered it and them to be still.

'I see . . .' was all that emerged, all the world got to know of it, the very iceberg tip of the entirety.

Blithely unaware of his social suicide, Hunter's attention was elsewhere, looking for more signs of hope. They graciously arrived.

Part of the wooden wall gave way, splintering under the impact of shot and Null shoulders. Angelically urged on, they surged over, some coming to grief on the jagged remnant; human whoops and monster ululations making strange joint music. Joy then swiftly turned to dismay as they came up against fresh opposition. The way forward proved more than just literally uphill, leading only into a blind alley and further log walls on three sides. From atop them cauldrons poured sand heated red-hot down upon upturned faces. In the breach a tragi-comic Null and man folk-dance commenced.

A new angel, brown and flaking all down one side, showered cooling balm and eased their suffering at the expense of her own. Then, as she was cancelled in a puff of flame, the surviving besiegers turned their attention to the slightly thinner and thus more amenable inner stockade. Agile purple bodies began to ascend, claw grip by claw grip. More pedestrian *homo sapiens* brought up scratch-constructed scaling ladders of Wild-wood and tendrils.

Guy could hardly forbear to smile, nor Hunter, for all his anxieties, with him. They saw their game: the faith in sheer weight of numbers and commitment against a few fortress-huggers. Likewise, from the high vantage point they could also see over the walls and gain insight into the planned reception. Guy cautiously agreed: there *were* grounds for optimism. He witnessed the defenders stride confidently across them.

They'd done this before. They rushed about without instruction from one prepared position to another. For the attackers, every height climbed or corner turned was a shocking encounter with swift or sharp metal, either shot or prodded. When the required toll was taken, the garrison – male and female alike Guy noted – scampered back, only occasionally overtaken and slashed to quivering meat, off to occupy another killing opportunity zone.

Casting his eye promiscuously abroad, Guy saw yet more lines of defence, sparsely manned, true, but in great and morale-sapping depth. Then, at the very top, just before the dwellings and presumed children and oldsters, was a trench network, all zigzags and dead-ends, that would be the devil to take if stoutly contested. Beyond them must lie the tunnel refuges of nauseous mention. Hunter's people might be few but they'd made the most of not much. If the choreographed retreat went according to design, then all the victors would inherit was empty passageways carpeted with their own dead.

And, best of all, *they* would not be in there, even after all

207

that wasted effort. Triumph piled upon triumph.

One of the split-trunk partitions tumbled down under the weight of Null boarders. Waiting spears wedged upright in the ground broke their fall. Then the survivors stood and stared aghast at the last tiny serpent's tail of fuse leading to a powder barrel, *just* beyond reach of their intervention. Too late to quench, too late to flee, they could only await the cleansing blast.

It came and removed the front twenty paces of the attack. Protected from its caustic clasp by yet another line of deadtrees, the fur- and leather-clad defenders jogged back to prepare fresh horrors.

Guy felt like applauding, although, of course, he didn't. He could foresee the upshot, and even if it should be in *burrows* then it was still less than ignoble. The shaggy heretics were accumulating a great host to accompany them to judgement. He prayed to Blades that it would be a forgiving one. They might *believe* wrong, but in the end, they had *done* right. Justice – and what was the Divine if not justice? – demanded the latter outweigh the former.

Hunter must have read his thoughts.

'No,' he confided, whispering along the concealing line of earth. 'It doesn't finish here – else I'd be gone to share all with them. The fall-back is shapely: it coheres. They'll gain the tunnels and there are far exits from them. Most will live: I am content and will still walk with you. I shall leave here.'

And, since the show was far from over, that's what they all did – with rumbling bellies but cheered hearts, creeping on those same bellies away from tumult. Preoccupied, the enemy who strived and died solely to find them, did not see their passing.

It was still there. Although he had said nothing, Hunter's heart was in his mouth for the entire day before they at last arrived. His breath came in short, inadequate stabs at respiration and everything was coloured by his anxiety, all perspective banished. It was a poor frame of mind for an under-nourished leader of an expedition to be in. He made mistakes and took detours he hoped the others didn't notice. Guy had to use his very last shotgun cartridge on a outsize turtle-scorpion hybrid into whose pond-world Hunter led them blundering. The weight of history was bowing his shoulders and draping a sodden blanket over his mind. Only good fortune saved them on that last day because Hunter couldn't.

And yet it *was* still there. He need not have worried until his empty stomach upchucked the bile that was all it could offer. In the centre of a sudden clearing the portal remained: dependable, a rebuke to his *little* faith.

Strangely, upon that relief Hunter's sickness still refused to go. His body and mind had reached a feverish speed that wasn't to be slowed in a moment. He had no words but turned and gestured to the others.

They drew level with him. The portal was pretty and pink, beyond pretence it had no fleshy parallels. They came closer and poured on awe. It surely wasn't only wish fulfilment that made them think the orifice dilated just a little in pleasure.

There was no living god to go with it, but you couldn't have everything. The path *He* had taken was clear – they had Hunter's word on it and that was now proven true beyond doubting. *His* path was clear – and thus so was theirs.

Or rather Guy's was. He resumed his monkish gown and they exchanged equipment with him, as agreed, delving deep into packs for buried treasures. As the foretold one: someone, at the very least, Imperially-chosen, and the only one who had changed his name and being to stand here, the path ahead was his alone. That had always been the arrangement. Nicolo was wilting in any case, for lack of food and moral fibre. Hunter was too humble and in a state, to even conceive of penetration. Only Bathie might have stabbed her dread and come as well but she was ordered otherwise. Her affection for Guy was so unconditional that he was able to *command* her.

So, he now commanded her to come forward and the others to draw back. He ordered her to be with him for the final moments, and that far and no more she could be complicit. They wrapped arms and pressed faces as if they were trying to merge (which they were), seeking to vampire out essential essence, a scent to last in memory forever, for fear of the worst.

They knew there was no point in delay or even resting. What was beyond might be entirely different, not bound to mundanities like fatigue and longing. When each's imprint of the other was tolerably lasting they disengaged. Only their fingertips, extended, continued to brush, loathe to break contact.

In some ways, on rare occasions, she was the stronger – or coarser. She nodded past Guy to the salmon doorway.

'Go on,' she urged him. 'Hop in . . .' – and then the same idea was given to both simultaneously.

Hunter and Nicolo were invited to turn their backs. Scarlet gown and monk's habit were torn skyward and Guy bore Bathie up on ramrod arms. The pressures of the moment exorcised all history and worries. She wrapped her legs around him and, as though it was the easiest thing ever, not something that had eluded them in pain and shame since marriage, the key fitted the obliging lock. It turned with ease. The way was free, Guy entered in and Bathie was there to welcome him.

She gave the tiniest of cries and buried her head against his chest. His face was full of her hair and it crackled with light magic and they both knew there'd been no finer moment than that since Blades created the Universe.

All was sweet and brief and brutal, though it seemed to them they remained ages that way, draining each other and the experience dry. Such a time couldn't come again and they wished it exhausted before they were. The remaining divide between the two – invisible to all save themselves – was bridged as, like continental plates, they moved and then meshed, never to part again.

Wild-man and brother were still patiently and pretend-

210

incuriously turned away but plagued with cramp. Hunter radiated silent disapproval. Nicolo faked a cough.

There could be no good way to end it. So Guy simply withdrew and left his wife – insofar as he ever would now – to back away through the pink portal into a new world.

Which proved to look very much like the old one, as it happened. Akin to a fairly standard suburb of New-Godalming, only hotter and duller.

His parts were still exultant and moist and, once immediate safety was assured, stowing them out of sight was the first priority. Even with so much for him to see, he didn't want their waning enthusiasm to be the natives' first glimpse of *him*.

For there were natives: people much as he, not angels – which was a relief. Better still in his understandable nervousness, they took little notice of him or his emergence from a blank wall. Either they hadn't spotted that facet of his arrival or such occurrences were normal in Paradise.

Or wherever this was. Guy had half-expected Heaven and some immediate interrogation about what he was doing there prematurely. Or worse still, the murdered slave with some pretty probing questions. Yet straightaway he sensed his mistake. Here looked just too . . . *normal* for that: people were too preoccupied with their own business to enquire into his. There was the strong sunlight and friendly warmth he might associate with Heaven and eternal rewards, but little else. Did Heaven have need of houses and streets and a harbour?

When all was safely gathered in, he had his first proper opportunity to devour the scene. The portal was gone, its place taken by a high blank wall; apparently one side of a moderately grand dwelling. Guy stood two paces in front of it, the very same two stumbling steps, dress unadjusted, that had carried him from wife and Wild. There could be no mistake. He felt for the means of retreat but found only the blush of brick blessed by a sunny day. No way back.

The ensuing pang of alarm was ruthlessly dealt with, like an inopportune peasants' rebellion. He'd come to fetch God and with such a travelling companion transport home ought not to be a problem. In any case, problems were only *opportunities in disguise* – or so ran one of the less inspiring Ambassadorial precepts, the hundred and twelfth, down near the barrel-scraping tail-end of the litany of advice. Thus this was just another incentive to succeed and he stroked the warm wall in thanks. Its uncompromising hardness needn't unman him. He was a Wessex-stoic and proud of it. Guy turned to face the – new – world with shining face.

And so it was a shame that all that novelty spat back at him. The humans smiled at his greetings but it was only a sham. Their hatred for foreigners was such that his friendliest, most Ambassadorial, *what can I do for* you? bow was met only with obscene gestures. It was such a guts-punching disappointment to find no manners in God's own country. After the fifth or sixth affront Guy gave up.

He turned again to check the contents of his pack. There, amongst a brace of Hunter's tubers (or *Null cockers* as Nicolo dubbed them) and his proper clothes, was the appropriate response to such a graceless people. Guy's ancestral revolver had been in Bathie's keeping since its use in the Way battle, reserved for some honour-saving end of things. Before it was passed to Guy for his trip, she'd fastened a scarlet strip torn from her dress as a love-token around the trigger guard.

He didn't trouble to conceal his loading it with the five sole remaining cartridges, the last obtainable for that particular calibre gun. The firm that made both was fifty years gone under, long swallowed by the encroaching Wild. Null now wandered where once the safety of New-Wessex was manufactured. After those precious bits of metal were lodged in deserving homes then it was either unreliable, explode-in-your-face, hand-made shells for their spitter or else honourable retirement to a glass case hung in Ambassadors' Hall.

For the moment though, it still did the trick; when swung

casually in the hand the Paradise-dwellers were awfully impressed – and shocked – but not frightened, for they made the vile crossing gesture all the more.

Guy steeled himself to just go with it and not be offended, though they might cross themselves right in his face. He focused on the smiles instead and pretended they were genuine.

'Hello. Hello. Yes, you. Could you t-take me to God, please?'

She was a lovely girl, olive skin and white teeth, a black *mantilla* for decorum but cleavage for cheering show. Yet she, the picture of innocence, insulted him no less than the rest. Mockery was tipped on top of it with a curtsey.

'*Padre?*' she said to him when her fingers had left her breast, but those wide eyes were all on his gun.

Guy repeated his simple request.

'*Inglese?*' she ventured, aping a sincere desire to help. Then an apologetic shake of her black curls, like Bathie's but tamed. Fingers were raised to her face again but not to make the Christian sign. She mimicked a speaking mouth and deep regret. '*Soltanto Italiano. Scuzzi . . .*'

It might as well have been Null chimes to Guy and he indulged in a little retaliation for her insolence. A waved revolver sent missy on her way in short order.

The sun of this novel place was like the old one in that it beat down on unprotected heads. Guy drew up his cowl and from its shadows looked round for guidance.

He found it not in the passing crowd giving him a wide berth or any help of man, but in the lost path he had trod. A shadow, detached from visible facts, loomed huge against the house wall which somehow hosted the portal. It slowly traversed, pointing like a road sign, to show the way. And the shadow was angelic.

According to the Emperor, an angel had set Guy on this road and so it was fitting the breed should speed him along it. Once, Guy would have said that only poison water could come from *that* well, but in the Wild he'd witnessed angels

213

doing good – or at least killing each other, which served just as well. So, though far from joyful about his tour-guide, he took the path indicated and the shadow fled.

At the next parting of the way it came again, projected against a church steeple. Guy was given pause by that. What need was there for worship in Heaven? Why pray to what was beside you? Seeds of doubt were sown in his field of certainty. It was both good and bad news. If this *wasn't* Paradise then it was less likely Blades was here. On the other hand, he was glad Paradise wasn't so mundane.

For example, this little township was *woefully* under-gargoyled and austere as an accountant. A few baroque flourishes and finials to the roof edges, a hanging basket or two, and that was *it*. The rest was whitewash and thatch and daub. And as to the inhabitants: Guy had seen more gallant costumes pulling a plough. The New-Wessex peasantry prettied their plainness with ribbons and blooms. Even slaves and gleaners wore enhancements gotten free from Mother Nature. Here, a spot of lace was the height of their ambition.

Seen one way, his developing thoughts were actually welcome confirmation. Right from the start, Guy's heart could not accept that this place of dull dwellings and boorish people was Blade's throne and footstool. Perhaps it was some sort of *ante*-chamber to Paradise, a resting place for people of limited imagination. If so, the question was to find the main door and knock politely upon it. Accordingly, he scouted around in search, squinting against the sun.

Evidently, Heaven had few enemies. The marble blue waters of the harbour were innocent of anything more martial than a pleasure yacht or two. Fishermen tended their humbler craft alongside. Indeed, the entirety was rustic, from bland villas to crazy-paved roads. Guy had seen the like a thousand times in the dilute fringes of Humandom. Once absorbed and accepted he thought it kindest to just pass over the parallels without comment. Blades *knew* what he was doing – and naturally that wasn't always graspable to his creations, imprisoned in the flesh and limited by single life-time perspectives.

214

Guy accepted shadow shepherding in the same spirit, even if it were framed in a sinister shape. He presumed there was nothing here that was not of God, right down to the ill-mannered locals. After all, it was clearly written that Blades moved in mysterious ways his wonders to perform.

Guy emulated him in his own little fashion, allowing the sudden angel shape to be his guide. Flitting, unpredictable, from wall to wall it led him through the whitewash glare to one particular harbour-front home. Its valediction was a unequivocal finger, distorted to yard length by angle and sun, singling out the door. Then it was gone, leaving Guy alone again – save for the throng who stared and insulted but avoided him.

Their blessings removed any hesitation he might have had and, glad to be shot of them, he gained the cool of the sunken doorway and hammered upon it with the revolver.

In their own sweet time, after much exchange dimly heard within, someone consented to answer. The rustic plank construction gave way to reveal, appropriately enough, a rustic woman.

She saw fit to insult him too, fingers nimble to face and magnificent bust – till she saw the gun. Then her eyes widened like a gorilla was at her.

'*Padre!*'

Guy declined to upset even the gratuitously rude and so stowed the metal away behind his back – out of sight if not out of mind, still serving its motivating purpose. He smiled at her – another stick-jammed-across-the-mouth construct, but passable.

'Hello. Is Blades here, please?'

Her beaming was falser still, a yellow and black dental display. She expressed incomprehension as only stubborn peasantry can: an all-encompassing '*I ain't got no nuffing about nuffing for no one, never.*' You couldn't argue with an act practised and polished for centuries.

You could however raise your voice; the embarrassing last resort of the true Ambassador: a demeaning of their talents, but sole weapon against stupidity.

'You. Get. Blades. *Now*.'

It worked – or so he thought. She raised her hand – in pause, not insult, this time, and turned back into the house. More unseen debate followed and then at last she returned – and forced a few tiny coins into Guy's palm. He was so shocked he accepted them.

'*Soldi, padre*,' she said, the while flicking him away like a troublesome insect

If he hadn't been a life-long, *what's bred in the bone comes out in the meat*, Ambassador, Guy might have felt a tinge of anger then. In his current monkish persona he was quite at liberty to indulge in it, but the true he, regardless of grafted titles, won out.

He expended his frustration on the coins, staring at them as though they'd been impudent to his mother – whoever she was. Then he put them over his shoulder in a bronze shower, provoking an urchin and fisherman scramble in the street.

Peasants revere coinage: they deplore slights to it. A deep V appeared in her brow, as impressive as her cleavage.

Guy's frown was better and drove her back. One step, two steps, then an easier and rapid three and four. He was in the cool of the house now. His words were polite but could have been used to store ice in.

'Excuse me. I'm looking for my God. You may know him as Blades. *Emperor* Blades.'

'*Babble*.'

Again, the wench only had eyes for his revolver. Guy concluded they were disinvented or never known in this poor-man's Paradise and thus comprised a gross distraction. He again hid it away behind the folds of his monk's habit.

'Me.' His spare hand pointed chestwards to put it beyond doubt. 'Me *look*.' It was then held level across peering eyes. 'For God.' One arm waved to inadequately express omnipresence. 'Blades.'

'*Babble babble babble babble*.'

An Ambassador never wearied of discourse or cut short

dialogue. Talk was not war, or at least spun things out whilst those whose job it was prepared for war. Guy's sigh was a secret one.

'*Dear* lady,' he smiled – one of his very, heart-dissolving, best; one that had even stilled the Null-King's growl. 'Do you speak English?'

A light dawned in her perplexity.

'*Inglese?*' she said, relieved, in obvious *why-didn't-you-say-so-stupid?* tone. '*Aspetti, per favore, padre. Aspera aqui . . .?* – and turned and sped away.

The threshold was his to possess but he wisely withheld conquering feet. Lingering there he could see further within and was shocked to note a crucifix hanging upon a wall. It provoked a revelation of his own, awful as infidelity. The gross insults of the population were now cast in new light. Maybe this wasn't Heaven but some dull purgatory where Christians were sent once they'd sloughed off their timid and unwanted lives.

The man who appeared seemed far from timid. Guy knew an intrepid spirit when he saw one. There were people who filled a room regardless of how big God had made them.

'No, he's *not*,' the man told the peasant woman. 'You – you – *daft* Dolly-Daydream. He's a monk, for gawd's sake! Whoever heard of an English monk these last two centuries? And you got me off me mistress for this? Damn your eyes. Get rid of him.'

The woman didn't feel up to it. She mimicked possession of a gun.

The red faced and coated man laughed in *her* face – and then Guy's. He pushed back his tight-curled wig.

'Save us. Do I have to do *everything* me-bloody-self?' He came closer to Guy, average in everything but soul and thus still capable of intimidation.

'You – Ut!' he told him. 'Me C of E, *capisce?* Church of England – no bloody good. You Papist: worse still. Don't care if you're the Pope – the *Papa, capisce?* So you *ut!*' He held two surprisingly elegant fingers before Guy and made them do a rapid little trot. 'Cheerio, *padre.* Go with God – but for God's

217

sake just *go*!'

Guy understood most of it – and that was like rain on an enemy's funeral. He could even overlook the brusque dismissal.

'How do you do?' he replied, with a medium grade – status not yet established bow. 'My name is Guy . . . Ambassador.'

The man recovered his jaw from his chest and stepped back as if shoved. The flighty maid flicked his shoulder and grinned, as though to say 'told *you so* . . .'

'An English monk, by God. You were right, Stella: *good* girl. I shan't smack your bum for a whole month!'

He scanned Guy, still disbelieving but highly delighted. 'An *English* monk by Christ . . . Well, I'm a Dutchman . . .'

Then he remembered himself and bowed, even more fulsomely than Guy, in return.

'Theophilus Oglethorpe, junior; at your service, sir. By *God*, sir, I'm pleased to see you, even in . . . that garb. What part of England do you hail from?'

Guy was frowning, head cocked forward, in his effort to keep up.

'I am equally pleased, sir. But I wish to be candid with you from the genesis of our converse. I am not English – although that is the language I speak.'

Oglethorpe bluff visage fell, like a child's whose present had been whipped away. 'Oh . . . shame . . .'

'I regret I know of no such place.'

Guy regretted with cause for his host exploded. Brick-red features turned Null purple.

'*No such place*. No such *place* is it? Let me tell *you*, sir . . .' Guy fell a step backwards whilst Oglethorpe spluttered to a halt and then rallied to charge in from a different angle. 'Just because we're ravished and abused by Dutch and then Kraut kings, *don't* you tell me, sir, *father* and bloody foreigner, that there's no such . . .'

Guy feared for his safety and thus mission. He didn't understand the offence given by his ignorance and thus could rush to mend it with demeaning humility.

'I am a m-merely a man of Wessex. I do not travel much.'

Easter came a second time to the stranger. He wheezed, resting one hand on his knee.

'Don't do that to me, father. I'm getting too old for disappointments – had too many of 'em. Drop your Jesuitical specifics. What's Wessex if not England? The very heartland, God stripe me. So I'm *not* a Dutchman after all: you *are* English and bloody well bless you for it!'

Remembrance unfolded like a glorious water lily in Guy's mind. How could he have forgotten? Book six – or was it seven? – of the *Sayings of Blades*: the epiphanous *Monologue of Lulworth*. The first god-king had laid claim to Englishness, amongst his many other titles. So perhaps it wasn't only a language but also a state of being!

The log-jam now burst, his memory released yet more recollection-reinforcements. Hadn't the great theologian Brixi always chosen to locate mankind in the *spiritual* state of 'England', with Wessex as its mere province? Critics had cavilled at that but he'd been right rather than eccentric all along. Heaven clearly concurred. It all hung together.

'Then I am English,' Guy happily confessed to Oglethorpe. 'For if God is English and we are his children – then we are all English!'

Oglethorpe abandoned fleeting '*well, that's putting it a bit strong*' hesitation in favour of simple gladness. Closing the remaining distance between them he clasped Guy in a heart – and ribs – felt embrace that made bones creak. Guy sensed more than just brute strength there, for good or ill, and geared up his caution even higher – once breath could return.

Whilst he was still buried in red cloth scented by man and alcohol and some additional smoky smell, they were joined by a flurry of silken sounds and a second female voice. At first it was just more babble, if joyful babble, spoilt by a welded-on edge, but Oglethorpe soon interrupted.

'No, don't get excited. And don't gabble *Itie*. This is an Englishman. Try out yours on him.'

Released from fragrant masculine imprisonment, Guy was

219

freed to see a vision in turquoise silk. For a moment, the awesome liquefaction of movement and hinted-at limbs reconciled him to being far from home. Even omnipotent God, whose mere handicraft she was, was momentarily shunted into an obscure mental waiting-room and forgotten.

Her hair was black as her skin was white. She was as Bathie might have been had her Fruntierfolke ancestors spent less time squinting for enemies and up to their hocks in blood. Guy knew without having to think that she was one of nature's unspoilt, uninstructed, bed-wreckers. He envied Oglethorpe his evenings.

That gentleman looked round to see her. Familiarity had obviously inoculated him against the fever Guy was suffering.

'This is Joanna,' he said, breezily. 'Who lets me lie on top of her in return for board and lodging and damn expensive clothes. Bloody good, though. And sometimes we talk over dinner as well. Fierce as a vixen – but less charity. Do you want to meet her ? Bit of a vow-stretcher for you, I would have thought . . .'

Guy wasn't sure what that meant but it became clear when the woman draped herself all over him. Cloth rather than vows stretched when insatiable, treacherous portions beneath his habit arose, sore but willing to joust even so soon after quitting wifely company.

'You got through the door!' she told him, in tortured English, blowing inflammable kisses in acclamation. 'I hear it. Never before. You are the first one. Bless you, *padre*. So, speak to the infidel. Reason with him!'

He fully intended to, but the girl got there first. For that she readopted flash-flood babble. The soldierly Oglethorpe first tried to stand against it with attempted '*buts* . . .' and '*ums* . . .' but then gave up and sheltered silent under a frown, waiting for the affliction to pass.

All things come to an end, and when at last she had to pause for breath he found opportunity for a firm, plain-English '*No*'.

The tornado then turned on Guy who had to restrain an involuntary flinch.

'You speak, *padre*,' she commanded him. 'Convert your countryman and save his black soul.'

When Guy only blanked her he got to see to see the steel beneath the silk.

'What is the matter with you *Inglese*? Cold-fish. You breed only fierce men-boys. Duels and bottles and the animal-killing. Foxes. Can you eat them? No. This one – look at him: he kills men and foxes and only laughs – but then he blushes over a little bed-play. Go on. I have made a start on him for you. He now takes off his hat when he passes the wayside Virgin. Go. Go!' She actually tugged at Guy's sleeve. 'To work, *Inglese-padre*. Convert him.'

When he didn't move and allowed a portion of bewilderment to show, she parted two dark lips to spit at his feet. The peasant woman resignedly crossed the hall to fetch a twig brush.

'Ah!' Joanna dismissed him angrily. '*Castrati*!' and then plunged a tiny hand to contemptuously grip Guy's parts. Their unexpectedly robust welcome repelled and surprised her. With a sidelong glance she signalled he wasn't entirely written off in her sloe-eyes after all.

So it was Oglethorpe's turn to again face the onslaught but the tidal wave was suddenly become a merely choppy pond, promising sweet bathing later on, if only patience was deployed.

She lifted one shapely leg and hooked it over his hip. Her hand curved to ruffle his stubble.

'If you take the faith, I would give you *such* a night as never man exper . . .'

Guy hated to disrupt domestic scenes. Indeed, some precept about avoiding the zone between husbands and wives and dogs and trees was set down amongst second echelon books of Ambassadorial guidance. Today though, time pressed him to apply a boot to ancestral wisdom. There was no saying when his visa to this demi-heaven might be revoked. He did not wish to re-emerge into the Wild clearing bearing nothing firmer than an erection.

He coughed politely. 'Um, *actually*, the reason I called is fairly specific. I am come to fetch Blades.'

And then wonder of wonders, they knew what he meant. Grappling man and woman looked round at him.

'Him?' asked Oglethorpe. 'The beggar? What on earth for?'

Joanna wouldn't let go, not in any sense.

'You see,' she told her prisoner, tapping hard on his red chest. 'True religion cares even for scum. Your Church comes from the balls of a bad king: its priests they fox-hunt and drink port all day. Here is difference. A servant of the King of love goes about his master's business!'

Oglethorpe had obviously heard it all before and had other opinions. He continued to look over the lustrous lover.

'Seriously though,' he enquired, 'why?' .

For the first time in ages, Guy really did feel lost and alone, standing aid-less before the tribunal of a mocking universe. God-kings *begged* for nothing: they were the antithesis of mendicants. Rather, they *dispensed* . . . everything to everyone, with open hand and heart. This was blasphemy beyond understanding or offence. It was past absorption even for the most open mind.

He therefore opened his heart and spoke straight from it. That organ, unused to daylight and license, started off tongue-tied.

'He's our Lord and God. We n-need him!'

Oglethorpe was shocked silent for just a space, and then shook off his lovely hindrance to double up with laughter.

Guy knew he sounded like a little boy, vainly pleading not to visit a mad auntie, but couldn't help himself. He'd been raised up and flung down once too often of late, and no longer trusted the ground to be there to meet him. There were limits to even Ambassadorial spines. He lifted his hands in placatory fashion, forgetting one ended in a revolver.

'My oath!' exclaimed Oglethorpe, not in fear but appreciation, and never taking his eyes from it, thus proving Joanna's every accusation. 'What a *beauty*!'

222

And so saying, he definitively shook off the beauty created by God for that created by sinful man. Joanna was left unregarded behind as he approached and worshipped. Her aura of disgruntlement failed to reel him back

'Age of miracles!' he said, wide-eyed, to Guy. 'Did the Jesuits invent this?'

Guy allowed the gun to be prised from his fingers and fondled. He felt in no danger, merely a civilised man permitting a mistress to go to her beloved husband. At last, he felt he had a bargaining chip in this baffling place other than appealing to the inhabitants' charity.

'Possibly,' he bluffed. 'Do you like it? *Would* you like it?'

Oglethorpe looked up from his love-making, his hands still smoothing the shiny surface.

'It has six chambers,' he husked, 'spun upon a central spindle. I see its cunning, *padre*. Six mini-barrels. It can speak again and again. But where is the ramrod? Where the powder pan?'

Guy gently retrieved the thing from hands loathe to lose it, and broke it open. Oglethorpe gasped in horror but then saw the wound was soon remedied. Guy indicated the five shells sitting snug as wasp-larvae in their temporary homes.

'Breech-loading!' Oglethorpe turned to Joanna, weak at the knees, pointing feebly back at the pistol. '*Breech*-loading!'

The lady was unimpressed. 'What of it, Theo?' she countered, and flounced at her competitor. 'So am I sometimes.'

There was no contest. Oglethorpe turned again to the summit of his desires.

'I do want it,' he croaked. 'What do *you* want?'

'Make him convert!' screamed Joanna, suddenly engaged again. 'Save his immortal soul!'

'Whatever,' agreed the Englishman. 'What do I say? *There is no God but God and the Pope is his protege*. Will that do?'

It wouldn't. Guy hadn't the foggiest what they were squabbling about nor the inclination to enquire.

'What I *want*,' he said slowly, so that even the hard-of-understanding might grasp this matter of infinite import, 'is

Blades.'

And then, taller than the Paradise dweller, he pointedly held the lusted-after treasure out of reach.

'Do you know where he is? Will you take me to him? If you will, this toy is yours.'

Oglethorpe looked up like a dog at a bone.

'I do. I will. Yes, please.'

Bathie's ribbon was not part of the bargain and Guy retrieved that, but the rest was slowly, almost lasciviously, lowered and delivered into Oglethorpe's cupped hands.

'S'wonderful!' said Joanna, bitterly, and turning so swift as to flash some heel. 'Now you can fight six duels at a time. I wish you *joy*!'

He already had it – clasped to his heaving chest. She saw and left the field, sweeping Stella the brush-wielder along with her. In babble-tongue between them they denounced the iniquity of the male sex. Soldier or monk, they were all the same.

Guy flicked fingers in front of the preoccupied eyes.

'The bargain . . .' he reminded him. 'Where is he?'

Oglethorpe surfaced slowly up from wonderland. In his mind's eye he'd just been refighting the battle of the Boyne with a thousand such distance-killers. William of Orange's head had looked like a colander.

'Where he always is,' he said, still not really with Guy. 'In church.'

It seemed reasonable. The Deity would abide in his own abode. What could be more fitting than to find him there?'

Oglethorpe took him by the arm out of the house and into the searing street. Guy's unacclimatised vision blinked at the sudden glare and he had to surrender himself to the madman's guidance and faith. It proved not misplaced. Though truly having eyes only for his new gun, Oglethorpe was at pains to see the monk did not stumble. He pointed out particularly hazardous horse and dog piles.

There was not far to go. They stopped before a door. So, Guy had been close to the living God all the time but had not sensed it. Perhaps the Lord Blades was still wrathful with his creation and withheld his presence – or was punishing him for his slowness and child-weak faith. On the other hand, it was quite possible that Blades hid the greater portion of his powers for fear of blasting the people of this place. Very probably, normal life would otherwise have been unendurable so close to the effulgent light. That might be a sign of his continuing mercies. Guy's hopes rose along with his nerves.

Oglethorpe wrestled with the door. Eyes adjusted now, Guy took the chance to look about. It was a high building this; the wall ascending up to a tower and . . .

Atop the tower was a cross. Guy's last meal urgently begged to see the world again.

The entrance was opened now and he was drawn within into the cool and dark. Once again his vision was languid to adapt. Darker-still suspicions didn't exactly urge him to speed.

'There you are,' said Oglethorpe, doffing his wig to show respect since he'd left home hat-less. He was pointing to the lighted eastern end of this cavern-within-walls but Guy was frightened to follow the finger. 'That's him.'

A scraggy old man, a bundle of rags – just like a beggar – was prostrate face down before the candle-blaze of the altar. Central upon it and the object of his abject worship was a crucifix.

Oglethorpe wasn't having Guy's strange last minute reluctance. He wanted the bargain fulfilled and he wanted the gun. In point of fact he had it and the mad monk wasn't getting it back now – but he was first and foremost a man of honour. Honour had led him into exile and joy at every passing stray countryman. It was too late to change his ways now.

'See?' he persisted, and actually directed Guy's averted head so there could be no mistake. 'There. Him.'

Guy both shook his head free and shook his head.

'Oh yes, it is,' Oglethorpe contradicted him, his attention already drifting back to the revolver. 'That's Blades.'

When Guy's disbelief remained intractable, Oglethorpe

even took the begrudged time to step forward and gesture theatrically, dredging into his thin stock of scripture to add weight to his words.

'There!' he insisted, and Guy at last had to look and accept. '*Behold the man!*'

A Transcript of a Curious Confession
(though with all reference to the sinner's name and particulars rightly purged).

Archive of The Congregation of The Holy Office and Inquisition.
Supervised Collection. Wall 12.Shelf 2.Folio 436.
Aquis.and Cat.anno.MDCCXC
Attrib.posthumously seized papers of Father A.M.Curare (Excom.), late of Sant' Antonio da Padova, Anacapri, Diocese of Capri. Abducted by Corsairs anno.MDCCLXX

Acuis.Supervisor's notes:
This document should *not* be, but since it is . . .
. . . this scandalous priest then took to setting down the more piquant sins and tales confided to him, in careless breach of canon law and his priestly vows. The rest of this weariness of lovers' boasting and tangled paternity I have committed to the flames and the obscurity from which they never should have emerged. However, one solitary outpouring of a troubled soul – suitably shorn of every identifying particular – I deem it more honourable to retain, for the edification of seminary students, that they may be forewarned. Such are the bizarrities that you may hear. Such is the infinite invention of Satan when he invades the weak human frame. Such are the monsters that emerge from the murky labyrinth of man's mind when faith sleeps.

If you have tears left, then prepare to shed them. This lost sheep sought to mimic Almighty God and fashion a new Eden (inside his fevered brain, though real enough to him), but brought forth only Hell. The gentle Christian reader may indeed wonder what was the fate of this sad sinner who received neither absolution or exorcism (as he sore needed) from a false prophet lurking in the bosom of Mother Church?

Capri is a humid and luxuriant island, conducive to the incubation of the more languid sins. I opine that none should minister there upward of five years. Then translate them to the seething poverty of Naples across the Bay . . .

Sinner: So you do believe me? The new world, New-Wessex and Null and all?

Priest: I do. I believe in the Trinity. What are your tales compared to that sublime mystery?

S: Bless you, father. Thank God!

P: Indeed.

S: You must understand that for years I did only good.

P; The slaves? The killing?

S: All towards a greater cause, Father.

P: And what of your stewardship? You say you were a 'curate' – of this 'Church of England' that I have not heard of. Did you therefore evangelise? Or was the light of the Good News concealed under a bushel?

S: Well . . . In the early years, we were pressed too hard. The Null would only have bitten a turned cheek. And then we had to stay above ground. There were hard decisions. I did bring Bibles – only they had to be . . . interpreted. I thought that when times were more easy . . . My church does not approve of 'enthusiasm' . . .

P: And all these women, my son? Why did you not stay your hand there?

S: But the temptation of it, Father: all those curves: God's architecture. Too much for a man to bear.

P: First Corinthians, 10. 13. 'God is faithful, who will not suffer you to be tempted above that ye are able'.

S: Really? So you're telling me that if you were regarded with limitless gratitude by every woman in the world, if every gorgeous, pouting, soft palmed and full-bottomed wench was yours to . . . [incoherent, drooling] you'd say 'Oh no thank you, get away from me you brazen hussies.' Oh yes, I'm sure you would, you bloody papist . . . [incoherent] *castrati. It's all right for you if the Vatican's chopped your bits off but I'm . . . Oh, damn your eyes, I'm going!'*

'The poor mad sinner never approached me again but begs a living in Capri Town, the lower end of the Isle in every sense, down where the sluggish air is injurious to all moral principle. There he finds charity in the household of the heretic *Inglese* cavalier, Oggy-throp. I am told he haunts other Churches there, prostrating himself and seeking cheap forgiveness by day and by night.

His slur on my chastity I cannot forgive but maybe God is more merciful than me. And I say I *could* have withstood the siren call of the flesh, however many hundreds of thousands of sweet, peach-skinned, apple-arsed maidens repeated it. I'm sure I could have . . .'

Joanna had never seen anyone so sad: not even the mocked widow of the general whose last words were *'they'll never hit me at this dist . . .'* So, out of the kindness of her heart and parts, she offered to console Guy in the way she knew best, as soon as Oglethorpe's back was turned. And if it chanced to be his peculiar pleasure, as so often with the *Inglese*, then she'd turn *her* back too. There was a price: he would have to convert Oglethorpe, but it would take a surgeon to straighten out his ensuing smile, she absolutely promised him.

Ordinarily, Guy would have bitten her braids off in his eagerness to accept. Being asked so nicely, he might even have requested she play *an* organ and his organ simultaneously – for he'd noted one in the church-of-shocking-discovery. However, of late he'd suffered a surfeit of hammer blows that numbed communication with anything that might be played upon for pleasure, be they trouser, skirt or church confined. The *laissez passer* to Paradise was declined. Now threatened with serial theological bereavement, he sat inconsolable at Oglethorpe's table, head in hands, criminally missing out when he might have grasped Joanna instead.

It's hard to worship someone who refuses to be worshipped, who behaves worse than yourself and makes too much noise consuming dinner – as Blades did now, right in Guy's ear. He was gumming and coughing his way through bread and water – all he would accept from Oglethorpe's lavish larder – and scratching at livestock whose existence, though unseen, now seemed far more credible to Guy than the god-king they dined on.

'And . . . that's about the s-s-shape of it.' Guy's voice was dead, entirely unsuited to wondrous story weaving.

Nevertheless, Oglethorpe apparently liked the *shape* of it. Compared to sitting useless in a Capresi kitchen sipping wine he liked it a lot. *It*, i.e.New-Wessex, sounded like his kind of place. He said so.

'This *it*,' he enthused. 'Lead-me-*to*-it!'

Guy paused for breath. His was quite a tale, difficult to *precis* to patience length, spanning centuries and more marvels than you could shake a stick at. It *extended* him to be simultaneously concise *and* eloquent, when all he felt was put upon and ragged, and in other circumstances he would have feared for his hold over the audience. Joanna had yawned through a mere ten minutes of the other-worldly saga before sliding out to go shopping, whereas Oglethorpe's initial mighty frown had been gradually erased by the desire to believe – plus childish pride in being right about Guy's monkish credentials and his womenfolk wrong. Slow but sure, acceptance seeped in, to be sealed when the *beggar* saw Guy's distress and had charity enough to expand on all his previous terse *s'right*'s and *mebbe*'s . . .

'And *so*,' Blades roused his rags to sum up, 'after all these adventures we've heard ably recounted,' he gestured in appreciation at Guy, 'and in conclusion,' – this to the enraptured Oglethorpe – 'as I've told you myself ten thousand times, only you've never bothered to listen, I am the *first* of a long line of Kings!'

Guy spat in the eye of despair – though she retreated only a little and straightaway started to edge back. He pressed on with the litany. Perhaps this time it would have a happier ending.

'And you are Blades,' he said neatly, like slipping a knife in.

The beggar conceded that at least.

'Yes, the very same. Thomas Blades, First *Downs-Lord*.'

Guy could barely credit he was sitting in a kitchen before the face that commenced every Blades-Bible, begging a beggar to admit his true nature.

'And *Burrow-stopper*, *Wessex-builder*, *Bane of the Null*: all the stories I've just related.' Guy crept forward one step at a time after the first guts-rending denial. Anything good in this world, he'd concluded, had to be sneaked up on.

'Yes, I am all those things.'

Then the great leap forward, plus blind faith that the ground would hold.

'And god-king.'

It didn't. It crumbled like wet cake beneath his feet. The abyss yawned beneath.

'No. Not that. *Never* that, may God, the true god, forgive me. Better to say, "*so-called god-king*".'

Blades looked up and around and, in the midst of his greater uncertainty, saw the need for more dramatic renunciation.

'I call on you and all here, and God Almighty himself, to bear witness that there is no God but God – and I am *not* he. Though made in his image, I am nothing but his lowest, most sinful, servant. As are you. As are we all: poor, insignificant worms, fit only for eternal sealing in a pit of our own filth but saved by the blood of the Lamb . . .'

Minds thinking alike, Guy and Oglethorpe simultaneously barred the conversational way. For a start they were getting splattered with vehement fragments of soggy bread.

'"*Lambs*"? "*Worms*"?' asked Guy, about to plunge head into hands again, before realising it was becoming a habit – and one to break as early as possible. I don't quite . . .?'

Meanwhile, Oglethorpe was ponderously shifting himself from their shared table.

'Listen. Listen good. I left England to get *away* from this – that and the Hanoverians. All this prattling Protestant hair-splitting cant. I ask you, why can't supposed clever people just look out at the world and *worship*? All these bloody words and emotional incontinence. Ploughboys don't feel the need, you know. They see the sun rise!'

Up to that point he'd been reasonable but suddenly the notion of being evicted from his own kitchen reached home. He turned back and surprised them by having borrowed a devil's face.

'Sort yourself out!' he purred. 'I'm not *having* it . . .'

That rang the curfew on theological debate – which suited Guy's drooping spirits very well. It also forced the issue, rocketing him to an unpleasant destination he'd have come to eventually, but at his own speed, schoolboy-laggard and reluctant. *Why* – came the unstoppable, dangerous, thought – *does the Almighty, all-loving, ever merciful and so on, put his fragile creations to such strenuous tests?*

'Come back with me,' he said to Blades the beggar, who'd now returned to worrying his cottage loaf. 'Reign again.'

The whiskery mouth was full of mumbled bread when it gaped open. The offer obviously struck a spark.

'You have a way back? I thought the portal lost.'

'I do.' confirmed Guy, primly confident. 'It is returned – along with your image.'

Blades shook his head, puzzled.

'News to me. *I*'ve not been back: save in – shamed – memory. Are you sure?'

Guy spread pleading hands.

'How else could I be here? And why else?'

Plainly, the beggar hadn't thought of that, and was in two minds as to whether he should.

Guy reckoned the door ajar and pushed.

'Return fully, in body *and* spirit, Lord. I implore you!'

Blades was tempted, that much was clear, but clamped

231

down on it and the dough-display alike. A firm 'No' emerged from gritted gums.

Within his weary head Guy sounded the charge. Forcing emotions to engage and face to flare, he leaned forward.

'But your people have *n-need*. They labour under a heavy yoke. Things are afoot – these eyes have seen the signs – the burden shifts. Now we dare to hope and from under that same yoke the afflicted call out for you!'

'No. Get thee behind me, Satan!'

'Their prayers besiege Heaven.'

'Then tell 'em to readdress their prayers to a true God. Maybe he'll answer them. I cannot.'

'*Now* is the time!'

'Not for me, it ain't. I've praying of my own to do.'

Guy sat back and sighed. It was as his father Tusker said: his great summation submitted for incorporation in the Ambassadorial wisdom books – and embarrassingly rejected, alas. '*Reason is the weak argument of the weak*'. The Ambassadorial elders – many of them insulted or cuckolded by Tusker in his retirement freedom, might tilt their noses over the precept, but how *true*, how disappointingly, predictively-useful, *correct* it was – even if deemed unworthy of immortality because born from rabid lips.

'May I?' Guy now addressed Oglethorpe who'd remained poised in fury throughout, looming over them. Mad and alien though he undoubtedly was, in present storms his was the only harbour in sight. Out of courtesy and caution, Guy signalled his intentions. 'Only a loan, I assure you.'

Guy – eternal Ambassador whatever his temporary name – had carefully noted in which Oglethorpian pocket the revolver was stashed. Very slowly, to prevent alarm, he now reached for it. Oglethorpe was indulgent, if watchful, and soon the barrel was taking the weight off its feet against Blade's head. Of course, Guy knew no god-king could suffer death – but their temporary shell of flesh might take some unsightly damage. It was by far the bravest thing he'd ever done.

'My Lord,' he said, 'forgive me but I m-must *insist*.'

'You wouldn't!' Blades quavered, not even convincing himself, let alone Guy.

'He would, bless him!' laughed Oglethorpe, who considered himself a fair student of men and who'd been studying Guy's eyes – the windows of the soul, after all. They'd deceitfully shown a no-nonsense landscape.

'I won't go!' screamed the beggar. 'I'd sooner die!'

For inscrutable divine reasons of his own, Blades was currently feigning vulnerability. He pretended to fears in this world and the next. Guy just had to think himself into the part.

'Would you? When so unsure of Heaven? Are you quite ready to give account of yourself *this* very day?'

Obviously not.

'I'll come,' said the god-beggar.

Blades spared the balance of the loaf its life and arose, having concluded this effete-looking young man might not be so merciful. Contrary to expectation, their other dining companion mimicked his motion.

'You too?' Guy asked Oglethorpe, when he'd shifted more than merely making way dictated.

'If I'm invited.'

'Why?' Guy asked, the gun wavering. 'You've heard the stories. The Null are *this* high.' He tip-toed to demonstrate. 'Angels turn people inside out for amusement . . .'

The exile conceded the possibility with a shrug of scarlet and lace.

'Mebbe so. However, upstairs in m' bureau is a newsletter from England. Gut-churning stuff. The rising failed. James III's fled back to France. German George reigns supreme.'

'Gracious . . .' said Guy, understanding nothing and caring less about Jacobite fortunes, but sympathetic to a soul in pain.

Anxious to unburden stockpiled woes, Oglethorpe wilfully misheard even that lukewarm response as '*encore!*'

'Banging your head against a brick wall, that's what it is. The riots in Manchester came to naught, and Ormonde's sea-raid on Plymouth was a fiasco. Preston's gone down in a welter of hangings. We only snatched a draw at Sheriffmuir, even outnumbering 'em three to one. Still, what do you expect when you pitch that turncoat *Bobbing John* Mar against Argyll – '*Red John of the Battles*'? Eh? Both called John but the similarity ends there. I mean, it's not the men in the fight but the fight in the men. Don't you think? You just can't get the staff. Not in the right place at the right time anyway: not when God's turned his smile off . . .'

'Absolutely . . .' affirmed Guy, as he supervised Blades's continued progress.

'And they'll have stamped on the embers and mopped up long before I could ever return. So I never shall: not in victory anyway. All there's left for me is Joanna and her successors till the magic flute won't play no more. It's that or insulting m' Dad's memory and making peace. No *thanks*; no biting y'tongue to the usurper and then horse-doses of port to dull the pain for me. Tried that under fat old Queen Anne. I'm no good at it: can't help the way God made you, can you? No, your place sounds best. May I?'

'And *very* welcome, sir,' said Guy, bowing low to usher him on first.

Oglethorpe's packing and winding up of his old life redounded even more to his credit. A mere five minutes of poking about and he was ready, armed to the teeth but otherwise burdened only by a small valise. It was perhaps as well that Joanna wasn't around to be farewelled, but Oglethorpe left a note for her, a brief scrawl whose large and open hand it was hard not to descry. In a few terse sentences there was *thanks for all the broken beds* and good wishes and every confidence in her bright future, seeing as how she was *sitting on a fortune*.

Under the cyclops surveillance of the revolver, Blades was compliant, continuing the pose of the broken old man he appeared to be. Guy wondered exactly what theological point was being made. Blades had tested his people before, for instance during the legendary *Professorial* invasion. Then too, he'd feigned collapse before rising in glory to crush all enemies underfoot. Afterwards, he'd been famously, graciously, forgiving to his flock-of-little-faith and Wessex men learnt to reserve judgement up to and beyond the last moment in future.

Guy tried to recall such strictures now. He only hoped his hijacking of a god was part and parcel of the intended – foretold, foreseen – lesson, rather than the grossest blasphemy on his part. He dimly recalled the Blades-Bible mentioned a parallel case: some *Judas* person, pre-destined to go wrong. Guy ill-recalled the upshot (they weren't encouraged to dwell on the latter parts of the book) but felt sure a merciful Deity would ordain all for the best. Like Judas, his intentions were good and self-sacrificing – which surely counted for something?

Capri had already been introduced to the novelty of a gun-toting monk and word had gotten round. Therefore, his reappearance with an abductee they also took in their stride. There was such a thing as the *Church Militant* after all, a concept ninety-nine percent of the witnesses were baptised into. If it had come to rounding up the poor at gunpoint to *force* compassion on them, then they could go with the notion.

Happily for the departing party, the Caprisi were notoriously non-judgemental and adaptive. Jean-Jacques Bouchard, a French writer and antiquarian of a century before (and possibly Capri's first tourist since Emperor Tiberius) had referred to the beauty and obliging nature of Capresi girls and boys alike. That tradition continued in full vigour and Christ-like they withheld the first stone as the *padre* chose to frog-march a beggar through their streets.

That Oglethorpe was along for the ride reinforced their fuzzy tolerance. '*Inglese Italianato è un Diavolo incarnato*': as the time-hallowed Italian proverb said – '*an Italianised Englishman is a devil incarnate*'. It was wisdom forged from the days of the *Condottiere* mercenary lords and hooligan bands of English made redundant by lulls in the Hundred Years War. The great

235

John Hawkwood (or *Giovanni Acuto*, as best Italian tongues could render it) was the exemplar of the breed. An Essex plough-boy made good, he was now immortalised by Uccello's fresco in the Cathedral of Santa Maria del Fiore in Florence, the City he had both served and dominated so well. There he sat in all his equestrian glory, staring confidently into futurity: a lesson in painted plaster for those who would be wise.

Acuto's descendant in spirit, and a tinderbox of under-utilised Jacobite energies, Theophilus had already fought two duels in defence of Joanna's spectral 'honour' and was well-known to prefer a fracas to breakfast. Thus, there was both ancestral wisdom and contemporary common sense besides, in deferring to Oglethorpian opinion. If he, a heretic and 'Protestant' could wear the padre's eccentricity, then so could the spectators.

Blades's *Via Dolorosa* was short if not sweet. He protested at first. If he hadn't – correctly – discerned that it would lead to the loss of innocent blood, he might have appealed for help from the throng. As it was, they parted like the Red Sea for the mini-procession and then put it from their minds.

'I called myself a god!' he pleaded with Guy. 'Six month's repentance is not enough!'

The sores on his knees and elbows testified otherwise. Oglethorpe said his every free moment had been spent in grovelling lamentation.

'You *are* one,' countered the Ambassador, wondering if he'd really dare fire should his Maker chose to bolt for it. 'And it's been longer than that.'

There was another flicker of interest. The beggar-deity turned his head.

'How long?'

'I was born more than four centuries after you left us. The angels came in year A.B . . .'

'*Four* centuries?' Blades interrupted, accepting the use of his name as datum point with ease. Oglethorpe – who wasn't so bluff and stupid as he made out – perceived just the very slightest stiffening of spine. 'Well, well . . . A long time. Six months here but there . . . a long time. Lots of repentance, really. Maybe enough: who knows?'

'*You* do,' said Guy firmly. Perhaps it was at this part of the pantomime that Blades transmogrified, only requiring some final feed-line. Once again, Guy ransacked his Scripture-store, carelessly hurling items out of the box till he found something to fit.

Then, lying there waiting right at the bottom, he thought he'd found it. 'After all,' he declaimed, 'is it not said: "*Whatsoever sins thou shalt bind on earth shall be bound in heaven: and whatsoever thou shalt loose on earth shall be loosed in heaven.*"?'

Apparently not – or not just yet. Blades shook his head.

'Would it were so. *Would* it were so . . .'

'It is. Your kingdom is yours to enter. It has burning need of you.'

That appeal to duty fared better than before. Blades chewed on the notion rather than directly spitting it out.

'I couldn't have gone *before*,' he explained and justified, hooked now and failing to watch where he was going. 'The portal shifted me too many miles and marooned me overseas. I found myself a stranger in a strange land – and time had passed. I don't know if my family live or not. Silas might still be around, I suppose. Yeoman stock, you see – takes a lot of killing . . .'

'But your *greater* family awaits, Lord.' It was a lot easier to accord respect and title to a being becoming more vertebrate by the moment. 'I might also add that I have the honour of your precious blood running in my veins . . .'

Blades's raised hands, a sign of surrender, were slowly lowered. Guy did not demur.

'*Do* you now? I suppose one – I mean I – did fling the seed far and wide. How goes my line?'

'Oppressed, Lord.'

'Is it now? Dear me . . .' He was so lost in thought that he overlooked a stumble and just carried blithely on.

'Call me prosaic, if y' like,' said Oglethorpe, just when Guy would have preferred no interruptions, 'but *where* are we going? Or can you walk on water? As it happens I *have* got a little boat in the harbour but surely we can't sail to where . . .'

'Here,' said Guy, with all the confidence of returning faith.

They were at the wall which concealed his entrance to this world. At the moment of their arrival it was still merely a high house, but then faith was rewarded in the way it so often isn't. A shadow nothing to do with the terrestrial day rose from the ground, taking angel-shape against the bricks.

Blades shied a little but Oglethorpe stood firm.

'Well, blow me!' said their host, primarily to himself. 'So it *is* true. A second chance. And I feared myself out for a pointless walk . . .' He blew a kiss at the sky.

Even Blades now looked at the shape with growing interest.

'Six months – or four centuries – of prayer,' he said, 'I mean, it *is* a lot. An awful lot, really. Maybe it's enough . . .'

'*Entirely* adequate,' said Guy, because it was required of him.

Blades looked back, beholding Capresi church spires and chapels and wayside Marian shrines with a mixture of longing and distaste. 'Of course, so long as I *couldn't* find the way . . .'

'In such a case,' said Guy, 'then your delay and . . .'

'Penance,' prompted Blades, to fill the polite gap.

'Then these things were only proper. Whereas now . . .'

He gestured towards the only way forward. The alternatives were harbour water or backtracking and defeat. Blades's eyes took the suggested route, but not the rest of him, not for the moment. He was wavering.

'And it was *me*, you say? My image that was seen?'

'One or the other, Lord: repeatedly ascending the portal to here.'

'That cannot be – I was constantly in church, save when this kind man fed me.'

'He was my countryman,' said Oglethorpe, seeking to excuse his kindness, 'and starving. Prayer doesn't pay all that well . . .'

'And was this a *youthful* me or as I am?'

A perceptive point, and one that hadn't occurred to Guy.

Hunter had failed to specify. Yet, thinking on, it *must* have been a sight approximating to the image fronting every Blades-Bible. The present beggar-Blades might have excited pity but not recognition.

All the same, such razor-sharp enquiries revealed he now had the *real* Blades, whatever his present outward shell. This mind had forged an Empire out of nothing, and in the face of satanic opposition besides. Signs of that spirit were beginning to show, despite all the dissembling.

'In your *full* glory, Lord,' Guy confirmed.

Play-acting objections remained. 'But my portal was in the New-Godalming maze . . .'

'Doubtless it moves where it wists, sire . . .'

'Doubtless . . .' The dry tone and cool scrutiny of the shadow could almost have been imperial: Blades *Null-Bane* cutting his way out of the 'Great Defeat', Blades of the second Runnymede Treaty hurling the Null out of Wessex, Blades of the Thousand Mountings – any one of the scenes from tapestries which had illustrated Guy's youth.

It had arrived for their convenience but Guy didn't wish to presume on its patience. The angelic portal awaited. He gestured again but still Blades did not move.

He was still looking back, re-calculating in the light of new developments, shaping passable continuity between old – sincerely held in their way – opinions and shiny new fresh-forged ones.

'It *has* been rather boring here . . .' he mused.

Guy sensed he was waiting for a shove from fate, some omen absolving himself of responsibility. And so, since fate is subtle and cannot be relied upon, Guy stepped in to deputise.

Guns can do more than merely kill. They also have the power to concentrate thought. Guy injected a dose of that serum via an imperative barrel jabbed into Blades's spine. Straightaway there was benefit: the fever of cowardice cooled.

'Let's go home,' said god-king Blades – and then led the way.

Straight into the arms of an angel. They were caustic and made Blades shriek. For the length of a smile she held him but then had pity and released the old man, his rags smoking.

The portal, the glade, were all as before, save that Bathie and Nicolo and Hunter were missing and an angel added.

Guy was straight there, in body if not in spirit. He made obeisance.

'Thank you, thank you, s-sweet one. For your indulgence, thank you!'

And all the time he was trying to still-birth his hate and not mourn the ending of everything at its very beginning.

The golden eyes looked down and he felt appraisal swarm over him like warm fingers.

'And what and what and what and what is an *Ambassad* – oh, you're not. My mistake. But these are *outlanders*!' She reared to her full height to regard Blades and Oglethorpe. The first was bewailing his lost skin, the second too ignorant to kneel and at least feign fear. 'Would you like me to remove them – amusingly?' This last was added solicitously, as kindly reassurance.

Guy pretended to consider.

'Might the pleasure be left to me?' he wheedled.

Guy had never seen a smile so wide and perfect and vacuum-empty of friendship.

'I don't see why n-' The smile was snuffed like a candle, not even fading face lines remaining. The breed were always perfect and wholehearted in whatever they expressed. 'Him.' She poised a translucent hand over the cowering Blades. 'This. If his years are peeled away then he becomes familiar to me.' The shining head swivelled like a slicing knife at Guy. 'Explain.'

'I. . . . ' He couldn't. An Ambassador who is lost for words is no Ambassador, is a castrated deflowerer, a handless juggler. Guy really did look for the right words, in the right order and at the right time, but – for the very first time – they were not even in sight.

The look flicked back to Blades and was awful. She loomed above him.

Her type's occupancy of the passing moment proved to be a thing apart, not something shared with their toys and prey. Her twin-sister's arrival could be observed in exquisite slow-motion, even though the humans hadn't the speed to react. The mirror image visited the scene and wrapped languorous arms around their persecutor. Two sets of lips met, one shrinkingly reluctant but compelled, the other ardent. Love in the eyes of one was reflected by rank fear in the other's, but both expired in lazy flames, coiling down into each other and nothingness like shed snakeskin.

Guy had the advantage of being on home ground and familiarity with miracles – if not understanding of them. He was first to move and gathered Blades up, rolling him in the grass to extinguish the remaining sparks. Oglethorpe observed, his glance moving from smouldering angels to burning beggar, not exactly floored by either, but all motors stalled for the moment.

Then Bathie and Nicolo and Hunter emerged from the concealment which had obscured them from angels and passing Wild-life alike during Guy's long absence. Therefore, introductions had to be made and Oglethorpe's too ready sword persuaded away, in tandem with recovery from horrible shock and singeing. Yet all of that proved child's play compared to overcoming scepticism about the mission's success.

'Yes, he *is*,' Guy insisted to the stay-behind contingent and Oglethorpe alike. 'I know how it looks – but he *is*.'

And they had to accept that because it came from Guy and he'd bought receipts in the form of obvious aliens – not to mention a miracle. Primarily though, everyone's jaw – metaphoric or otherwise – was on their shirtfronts because of the angel immolation. They'd seen it before but that made it no less wondrous. Compared to that, the arrival of a scraggy beggar, however exotic, was small-fry.

Moreover, they'd been expecting a Blades-in-glory to worship and, immediately after, all their troubles instantly rectified. This thing of burnt rags and whimpers didn't fit the bill and the best he got was hesitant genuflection. Nicolo, in particular, was underwhelmed and merely tipped his hat.

Fortunately, chewing on the feast of thinking set before them (and some bread from Oglethorpe's pocket to keep Nicolo going) saved them from too-soon conclusions. Something major was afoot – the signs screamed in your face and defied you not to notice – but it required pondering in the privacy of the heart rather than words out loud.

That suited Guy well, for he'd intended to dictate discretion about all they'd seen. Now awe silently did the job for him.

The march home commenced with Guy close by Blades's side, whispering necessary words of comfort and encouragement, but fate conspired against even that not-much-to-ask-for. No sooner had they started, trundling down another green tunnel of a lane, when a Wild-tree, hungrier than its brethren, leant over and tried to strangle them.

The first enquiring taps on the shoulder they assumed to be wife or brother or acquaintance requesting attention – but not so. When day was extinguished by a deluge of foliage they re-learnt that the Wild was empty of innocent greetings. Spindly branches sought out exposed flesh and attached bud-like mouths to draw forth man-sap.

The Wessex-folk were experienced enough, and Oglethorpe adequately, genetically, up-for-it, for them to snap the impudent probes and repel them, their only losses being hats and wigs and dignity and tiny circlets of skin. It had happened a dozen times before, supplying a life-long inoculation against wistful sylvan fantasies. Guy even remained sufficiently composed to collect a flowery cutting, as promised to his father.

Blades, though, succumbed to horror, allowing the green twigs to twist around his neck and bulge his eyes, whilst the tree struggled to lift the bag of bones and winch him home. His feet danced a jig, tippy-toed on the grass, barely adequate counterweight to the evil-oak's ambitions.

In the end, Hunter had to take a knife to the woody garrotte – but Blades was not to know the Wild-man was approaching, armed, with only his best interests at heart. He kicked and struggled and generally left all poise behind. Already freed, the others – Guy excepted – stood back and looked on with pity.

It was over in minutes, the merest occupational hazard of Wild-travel, and yet caused their visitor to revise all decisions anew. It was made very clear he no longer wanted to linger. Guy saw that a lifetime of knee-bashing before the altars of Capri had regained its allure.

Blades traversed the scene with fear-widened eyes, from enveloping Wild-jungle to the clear blue above – and failed to like it. His voice was throttled-husky, a temporary octave lowered but still well able to wail.

'What kind of world have you *brought* me to?' he asked.

Guy's reply was firm but intended to be heartening. His arm swept wide to indicate the green and blue entirety of it all.

'Yours,' he told the beggar.

'*He's* no god-king!'

A set of New-Godalming's finest false-teeth had improved Blades's diction no end. So long as you didn't actually move on to study the source of the sound . . .

Guy nodded agreement. Day by day, Blade's opinions were becoming more dependable. For whole hours at a time, you could truly believe in him. His successor, Emperor Blades XXIII, that pale shadow of the real-thing, had evidently been weighed in the balance and found wanting.

A delivery of sea-spray delayed but failed to deter the tirade.

'He asked me for *advice*!' scoffed the former beggar. 'His life

clean gun ✓
sharpen sword ✓
sharpen bat seax-knife ✓
wine ✓
cider ✓
mead wia ✓
poison ✓
say prayers ✓
More cider ✓✓

Not a
Word

Ye Realm of England
or a second New England,
'New-Wessex', so-called by its
aborigines.

As related to but
imperfectly understood by

THEOPHILUS
OGLETHORPE

(junior) Gent, of
Westbrook,
Godalming, Surrey
by divers natives of this
transmogrified and enfaeried
lande,
— in particular, MR GUY
AMBASSADOR, to
whom, for his sweet
patience and invitation
due gratitude, is
here expressed.

Antlered
Monsters
apparently

Killer-Trees, man-eating
fungi, titanic bugs and
general abominations.

My
amusingly
shaped
entrance
in

A barrier of SAVAGES
(from whom Mos Ambassador
hails) withholding purple
monsters and wild
excesses of nature

Scattered Humans,
it allegedly

no LONDON, or
only sad ruins, tis
said.

Ye little town of GODALMING
miraculously excellent to a mighty citizen
and home to a despot with
delusions of divinity

Casting dogs and
po-faced LEVELLERS
and other sundry
CROWBAIT

Cornshur
a few framets
ellegedly

Wight - the mons Venus
of England in shape,
bushiness and temperateness
- or so it has always seemed
to me, a sinner. Now a
fastness of wizards, hostile to
mundane mankind.

A chalk hill
titan and
symbol
of this
lande

To France and other
mainstays of Christendom
- all evidently
ceded to
MONSTERS

is *empty*, he says. Poor diddums. I mean, does a divine being *need* guidance? I ask you!'

Actually, Blades was doing no such thing. His questions were increasingly rhetorical and answered from within. A moment's thought revealed that such should be the nature of divinity-on-earth, transforming a tedious habit into yet another encouraging sign. Adding it to the still thin muster, Guy held his peace and looked down at the sea, whose instability matched his own ever changing mood. There he noted Hunter's head poking from a porthole, still being sick, hoarsely honking for two friends called *Ruth* and *Ralph*. Considerately – fastidiously – the once-again Ambassador turned his attention to higher things.

They weren't hard to find. A long looked-for god-king was to one side, his beloved wife of every-night-without-fail before him. Outlined by a glorious dawn, Bathie was at the prow of the ship as they neared Null-France, scarlet against aquamarine and gold. She was slow dancing the traditional steps with which Fruntierfolke greeted a possible final day. Her white arms kept time with the delicate placing of feet upon the deck, her flowing hair always a second or so behind, mimicking each motion but always in accord. The blow kept it free from her head in which music played for her alone. From rigging and half-attention to duty sailors looked on rapt or aghast. Even Nicolo's cool couldn't fully conceal his interest.

Guy had seen it performed by a parade-ground full, the delicate slow-steps looking strangely feline or feminine when performed by Fruntierfolke-men with mud-stiffened locks and two-handed swords. He'd been appalled then and was no less so today, although for different reasons. There'd been remote sympathy for warriors going against a Null incursion, but no real engagement of feeling. Now he averted his eyes from the alien beauty unfolding.

His concern was misplaced. Contrary to all outward signs, Bathesheba Fruntierfolke was thoroughly enjoying herself, relishing a rare holiday of seeing the world like everyone else did. High drama seemed a sovereign remedy for melancholia, keeping colour in her world for weeks on end. The cure was drastic, true: a bitter distillation of magic and death – but it did the trick. It was a price worth paying given the prize. Freed from the yoke, she danced on.

Guy turned back to Blades, looking for clues. Of what passed between the two god-kings in their interview after safe return from the Wild, little had leaked out. He only knew it had not been a success. Blades emerged full of contempt from the Palace at New-Godalming and Guy pushed at an open door when he sought Imperial permission to take the 'old man' away.

That old man's appetite for life was growing and returning, getting more lusty by the day. In the Wild, even cosseted by Guy and Hunter, he'd sought to blinker out every experience. Their blessedly uneventful progress he mistook for a nightmare, and even the safely distant sight of ravenous blooms or fungoids dining quite unmanned him. By contrast, after a few initial whey-faces, Oglethorpe had soon gotten into the spirit of things. Slipping from their Imperial escort at New-Horsham, he'd gone out alone to 'bag' his first Null and its ears were now pinned either side of his hat. He was having the time of his life, which – considering his previous history – was to make a bold statement.

Even with four ears at his disposal though, he declined to listen in now. Simple faith, imbibed in childhood and lasting for life, was good enough for him. He strode – or weaved, given the degree of swell – off to explore *The Lady Bridget*'s intriguing nether regions. Below decks, as befitted a veteran of the Sicily gunpowder-run, she was buxom with baroque-fashioned cannon, presently sleeping behind dragon-mouth gun-ports. There he would feel amongst friends.

'And pray tell, why are we so *alone*?'

Blades's curiosity was also risen from the dead. Queries kept on coming in waves, like Null against a nunnery. First, he'd wanted to know why shipping gave the Isle of Wight a wide berth. Why had the sea-Null the Solent all to themselves?

Towards a choreograph of Lady Bathsheba Ambassador-Fruiterfolk's "Death-Day-Dance" – observed and transcribed by her husband, aboard the Lady Bridget, en-route from Freeport Hastings to New-Dieppe and Null-France

Why were New-Portsmouth and New-Southampton just distant memories and offensively silent ruins on the horizon?

Guy dutifully explained about the wild wizardry which ruled Wight, and its violent distaste for *mundane* company. Blades then recollected he'd planted it there and reminisced about the academy founded at New-Yarmouth and the bizarre, deeply gratifying methods its graduates used to cleanse the Island of Null. Then, tracking along the chain of puzzlement, the divine intellect enquired about the paucity of merchant marine and Guy had to enlarge upon humanity's long retreat. There were still the ships, he said, there were still the sailors, but aside from Sicily and the gunpowder-run there were simply fewer places for them to meaningfully go. Dieppe and Sark only required so much supplying and the lighthouses were dark and unmanned now. New-Ireland lay empty, as best they knew, and New-Caledonia was even more of a mystery. Stray humans might survive here and there but re-establishing sea-supremacy would be way down their list of priorities. Guy himself had seen Freeport Pevensey chock-full of warships rotting away for lack of use. He'd shed no tears over that last particular detail but the overall picture irked. At the same time, he was conscientious and spared himself nothing: painting the portrait *warts and all*, as Blades demanded. Present decadence was fully confessed and it became an education for them both, in the exchange between query and response. Things he'd not cared to think about for years were admitted, whilst Blades received updates on his pretend-obsolete world-view. Guy's template of knowledge meanwhile got coloured in. Some of the shades were more vivid than he'd expected.

Then, when he'd had a dinner's worth of detail that required digestion, Blades communed with the scene and Guy kept silent. Nor was that just Ambassador-civility on his part. With each bout of information-intercourse the Bladian summations were increasingly worth waiting for.

'This world,' came the eventual verdict, 'has become a very *loosely* governed place.'

Blades's eyes might be resting on the Channel or Bathie but the Ambassador remained vigilant for any opening. Here was another.

'In the absence of the presiding deity,' Guy said to his deck companion, 'how can it be otherwise? You came, you created, you raised us up. Then, for a while, you dimmed your light and we have stumbled. Lord, I say to you again, let fall the disguise. Govern. Take up the slack reins and ride. You know that this is all yours to command . . .'

And once more he saw the flicker of interest in Blades's eyes. It had been sweet to rule here, Guy could tell. The flavour of it danced on the taste buds again.

Then, perversely, it was spat out, in favour of dry-as-dust rations.

'No, that's *nonsense*,' he told Guy, above the cry of wind and gulls and the snapping of the sails. The music of this world was still agonisingly short of beguiling him.

Blades straightened at the *Bridget*'s carved and polished rail, digging his hands in. His voice attempted strength but was cracked by conflict.

'No, Guy. No. Let me instead enlighten *you* with the precious truth.' He plunged, eyes closed, within, in order to recite. 'There is but one God, unknowable, intangible . . .' here he plucked and pinched at his own flesh to illustrate the point, 'omnipresent and Lord of all. And, that being *so*, we owe him gratitude for the mere fact of being and should seek to know his will for us. *And*, since he is good and the definition of good, he will show us his will via revelation. *And* that being so . . .'

Guy knew this was just more testing of him: wild heresies being spouted so that he should have opportunity to prove his true faith. He piously tuned out the false catechism.

The coast of Pevensey-Assyria was equally a matter of faith now, the shores of beyond-Humandom a fast approaching fact. They had come far: right from the portal and across the Wild, back through Fruntierfolke land where only Bathie and a wedding band saved their scalps a dozen times over. At the true border they'd felt like falling to their knees and kissing the ground. *That* turf wouldn't writhe beneath the heel or lasciviously return affection. It just lay there, like the lovely plain and simple stuff it was. They blessed the gorgeous grass and every ordinary, un-mutated sight.

It was the same with the works of man. For a while, every word said to them in civilisation sounded like 'welcome', every structure seemed a loving home. Even Ambassador Hall wore a smile; fragrant crucifixes and all.

There, back in almost-safety, his mood sweetened by Nicolo's vindication (as it was told), and presented with Guy's Wild-cutting, Sir Tusker relented about boarding Hunter with the hounds again. Then, back to normal, he frowned and ranted when the expected gush of gratitude failed to show. The Wild-man bore both inscrutably. His mind was settled, even as his presently sea-borne guts were not. Their route back to Wessex had included hellos and resupply at his battered but still living village. All wives and offspring proved present and correct, albeit some a trifle Null amended. Guy granted time for Hunter to dry their tears and garland his cabin door with new Null trophies. Meanwhile, the pious inhabitants left off burying their dead and sang psalms of joy when presented with Blades to worship; all wounds and troubles forgotten.

In dealing with more sophisticated folk, Guy decided against sudden disclosure regarding his wonderful find. For the moment, they could entertain their Lord unawares, reaping reward or punishment according to their lights. At Ambassador Hall Blades was introduced as a 'philosopher' who chose the Wild and, insofar as it was believed, mere survival out there bestowed some kind of kudos, just saving him from canine company.

In contrast, Tusker and Oglethorpe got on famously right from the start. The two men spent the short visit inseparably, uproariously together, shooting things.

All the time, Guy reckoned that arrival at New-Godalming would see some apotheosis and Humandom-wide revelation.

In that, though, he was gravely disappointed. After a day's private closeting with the Emperor, Blades was sent back to them; unrequired, unsatisfactory goods. Blades XXIII became as unavailable to Guy as he should have been from the start if he wished to maintain his mystique. What to do with the Lord of Creation was, by implication, left to him. A curt note from some under-under-Chamberlain merely ordered that he keep the Imperium 'apprised'.

Guy's foundations had shifted so far that he felt no obligation to inform the Palace of all he'd seen and the great good news of civil war in Heaven. Angel would continue to extirpate angel regardless of whether hapless Blades XXIII knew of it. All those that should know *knew*.

Thrown back on his own devices, Guy succumbed to selfishness for the first time since . . . he couldn't remember when. He wanted his name back, he wished for a warmer head than mere stubble allowed. So, Bladian permission was sought and casually granted and Guy surrendered his unwanted role before the same altar where it was draped upon him. The priests obliged, blissfully ignorant, for now, that they were losing both the worst and most wildly successful *Brother of Perpetual Seeking* there had ever been.

After that, an Ambassador again, it was no decision to hurry away. The god-in-waiting disclaimed any affection for the city he'd created, and Oglethorpe, though informed, failed to recognise his transmogrified place of birth. The others' hearts lay elsewhere and proved Guy's to command. Moreover, Blades developed a distressing desire to frequent churches and then bewail the Emperor (or self) worship he found within. In New-Godalming's Cathedral his bean-stick arms wrestled to fell a bronze figure of 'Blades-in-Glory' usurping the place – he scandalously alleged – where once a Christian altar had stood. Only Guy's strong arms – flesh and *firearms* – had got him out alive.

So, it was Null-France and Ambassadorship for Guy again: and where and what he should be. Moreover, he no longer stumbled amidst darkness: Guy Ambassador had the seed of a

251

plan. Their destination was the ideal obscure place in which to plant and nurture it. For a while they would hide away – and then emerge to overthrow the world.

Bathie – naturally – ever brushing and bumping intimately against him, came too, and Hunter and Nicolo also. One would not leave the Lord he had recovered and the other was now accredited Ambassador himself, by Tusker's decree. As Man's mouthpiece to the risen-Null, Guy was entitled to an entourage of friends – or '*flock-meat*' as his hosts charmingly termed them – even if he'd previously preferred to keep his friends and suffer alone. More relevantly, his father informed him that it was his dearest wish, albeit unexpressed till then, that he take his brother with him.

Oglethorpe was along for the ride, playing his own game in parallel with them for the moment. Guy felt sure he'd come in useful sooner or later. In any case, he'd warmed to this murderer of Null and bottles.

'. . . *And* the Church, through its apostolic succession, is the guardian and interpreter of that will. Do you see that now, Ambassador?'

'Absolutely, Lord.'

What he really saw were the towers of Dieppe, man's sole tolerated toe-hold on the continent. From yellowing maps and journals in Ambassador Hall's muniment room, Guy knew his ancestors had graced embassies in *New-Rome* and *New-Berlin*, before the angels had swept them out like an infestation. It was fitting that the means of regaining those glory days be brought to see the extent of their loss.

Null eyes were keener than human's. They'd espied the red sails and buxom green-and-gold flanks of the *Bridget*, long before its passengers saw their coast. Accordingly, they had time to prepare a lovely welcome. Tame humans were brought to cliffs and foreshores and lashed to prominently erected rough crosses. The sight and sound of humanity, slow-devoured, was the ship's musical greeting for league after league.

Bathie noted it but continued her death-dance to its

natural conclusion, an unbowed surrender to the inevitable. Nicolo looked but could not, of course, as a new-born Ambassador, react in any way. The others were luckier. Oglethorpe was blissfully ignorant down-below, caressing cannon flanks, and Hunter too busy adding his portion to the depths to worry.

But Guy saw; as he'd seen it all before – and was glad. He saw and heard and also *saw*, like revelation, that his feet were guided. His plan must have been divinely *inspired*: secretly so by the being beside him.

Where better than to strip away all games and pretences than here, where the meek were eaten to make points and the lion *laughed* at lying down with the lamb – other than to chew on its carcass? Here was his aim, before him his unwitting tools. When Blades saw what the Null made of the world he'd made, his true nature would surely leap, enraged, from the shell of ageing flesh.

Guy smiled and waved to the distant Null and dying men and looked forward to it.

'Oh *dear* . . .'

It wasn't the starburst reaction Guy had hoped for. Diverting here had cost more than a detour. He'd had to bribe the Null escort with a plump slave from Sir Samuel Musket's Dieppe establishment, topped with the spice of his begging them on hands and knees to devour the poor wretch out of sight.

He'd also arranged for Bathie to divert Blades with an indiscreet change of gown whilst the degrading bargain was struck, and that at least had worked like an answered prayer. There was nothing dozy about Blade's desire, for all that the bulk of his godhead remained comatose. Whilst his eyes were feasted on a festival of pink the deal was done.

Even at the feet of a towering Null captain, Guy had to work at control of his own gaze, fighting against the inexorable gravitational pull of Bathie's show. After liberation from its cage of failure by the wondrous deliverance at the pink portal, her sensuality had risen like yeast – and his parts met and matched it – so that their nights and idle afternoons were riven by cries. Neither cared the slightest who knew and shared their joy. Hunter might furrow his brow and feign deafness but few others were so incurious. Even Null heads were observed to turn and puzzle over the music – and then add a growling serenade to the love-play when understanding dawned. Human happiness was as unprecedented to them as it was unwelcome.

Guy looked upon the *Field of Bones* in much the same light. He'd thought himself prepared, since Sir Samuel had once glimpsed it, distantly from a daring ship, and forewarned him with a verbal sketch. Nevertheless, it was a shock to behold skeletons as far as the eye could see, laid out in the ranks in which they'd fallen. Here lay the last army of unbowed Man, the grand muster of those who'd demurred when the angels arrived. Some diehard general had painstakingly gleaned men from every land, thinking to debate the issue. The angelic host had sensed that unfurled impudence and came to see – and then waved fire over them. The charred poles which had borne their banners still remained: now mere naked spikes pointing pointlessly at the sky.

After that there was no more contesting the incontestable. The enemy had spared one man in every hundred, horribly puckered-red and burnt but still just about functioning, to go home and spread the *word*.

Albeit centuries late, transmitted through his mother's milk (whichever transient Mrs Tusker she'd been), Guy got to hear it too, as the story trickled down from age to age. He'd hoped it exaggerated in the telling, but now he saw – and saw that wasn't so. Right to the horizon or as far as they could bear to look, the land was black and calcium covered.

Perhaps some poison within the *balefire* which had showered down on those long-ago heads deterred scavengers from spoiling the neat patterns, or maybe the angels simply decreed it so. Whatever the reason, all was still as it had looked that day when the last flesh-fire fizzled out. Rifles of advanced design lay beside their former owners, an armament out of present New-Wessex's sweetest dreams but beyond modern daring to harvest. There was surely good reason for that, other than mere avoidance of painful recollection; enough to blunt a charge of cowardice. Even the Null hadn't wandered in to suck the marrow from thoughtfully pre-cooked long-bones. It didn't require a mage's sensitivities to detect an interdict lying over the scene.

'*This*,' said Guy to all, 'is where we were broken.'

Hunter and Nicolo turned aside and away. Bathie thought her own thoughts and soon wandered off at their prompting. Meanwhile, the Null, who seemed to have a poor grasp of death and none at all of an afterlife, showed no interest. Only Guy and Blades and Oglethorpe remained and pondered.

It was Blades who broke the silence once more, for which Guy was glad, since he had no adequate words himself.

'"*By the rivers of Babylon*",' the old man half said, half sang, '"*there we sat down,*

*yea, we **wept**, when we remembered Zion.*

We hanged our harps upon the willows in the midst thereof.

For there they that carried us away captive required of us a song:

and they that wasted us required of us mirth, saying,

'Sing us one of the songs of Zion'.

But how shall we sing the Lord's song in a strange land?"'

That was more *like* it. It pleased more than it puzzled. True, there was no river, no harps and willows; they were none of them sitting and the Null were unlikely requesters of song. *Babylon* and *Zion* were terms Guy vaguely knew but could not place to save his life. In short, there was much within that was inexplicable – which was just as it should be. It would do.

God-kings were wont to recite scripture by the ream, for such was their nature. Their truth and profundity would only shine forth to the enlightened – and that light had been dimmed for centuries and was only just beginning to flare

255

again. Left bereft, mankind's eyes were unaccustomed to the light of divinity, but the facility would return in good time. The lantern was relit. They need stumble in the dark no more.

Guy's chance inspiration had done the trick. Something had stiffened in Blades – and not just thanks to the flash of Bathie. He stood firmer upon the ground; his liver-spotted fists clenched and unclenched by his sides.

'Never again!' he said to Guy, or maybe himself. '*Never* again!'

And so it *was* worth the detour and all the horror and the drooping of spirits and the truncation of another poor slave's unpromising life. Here were the words and promise Guy had longed to hear.

Blades, a tiny, penitent old man, turned and *looked* at the nearest Null – and the monster took a step back.

'Here is our womb!' said the interpreter-slave, in tones of awed respect, expecting them to share his pleasure. 'Here is our fecund joy, our ever-renewing bliss!'

For all the old wounds on him and the jagged remnant of one snacked-off ear, the Null slave had so far absorbed his masters' outlook that he regarded the scene with almost erotic ecstasy. He, or his father or grandfather before him, had abandoned human identity in favour of being reprieved *meat*. He must surely know – and daily see – that when too old to serve he *would* be eaten or used-up as a practise-kill for Null cubs. The same fate awaited his children – *if* he got explicit permission to breed and wasn't castrated before. Even then, his infants might be wrenched from him as meat if he spawned too fast or well – but all that appeared forgotten or of no moment. The scarred man stood high over the Null *Hall of Mothers* and worshipped. It was sickening: even more than *all* of it was sickening.

As a signal honour and torment and to mark their return, the Ambassadorial party had been taken to view the very throbbing heart of Paris, acknowledged capital of the risen Null. As best Guy knew, no free-human – or *rebel-meat* – had been so honoured before. He wasn't all that thankful for it.

The rare-occurring female of the Null species were ten-times and upward the standard size, too bulky and perpetually-pregnant to be mobile on only normal-proportioned limbs. So, they lay subsided in their own blubber like huge, sweat-shiny, beetles, and bred and fed ceaselessly.

The creatures were two or three deep in some places, accumulating up the wall even as privileged Null warriors entered in to enter them. The mountings went on as constantly as the feeding and laying and since the Mothers' orifices were myriad, some were even unaware of being taken.

They had sentience, though. Many bulbous eyes were in the right direction to behold *meat* on the *Balcony of Viewing*. A chittering of ravenous welcome arose.

Null-mothers had grown too grand to feed themselves. Some, the older and more bloated specimens, couldn't even stretch claws to mouth and required their rations pre-jointed and then hand-fed. Other times, dainty treats were prepared and diced up on the viewing platforms, to rain down like manna from Heaven on the lazy ladies. The human visitors up on those narrow walkways trod in a slick of blood and residue from previous dinners.

Oglethorpe looked fit to puke and liquid-laugh over the revered ones below – and since that would have been a diplomatic incident to test even him, Guy gently ushered the man back from the brink. Hunter was sturdier, perhaps through familiarity with the breed or having already given all to Neptune on the trip over. His face, though, told a short but eloquent story. Doubtless, Bathie and Nicolo had composed similar tales but, as befitted their nobler descent, neither were made available for publication.

The Null tour-guide forgot them for a moment and leaned recklessly far over the abyss, spreading his hawser-like arms wide in an exuberance of affection. All Null *loved* their mothers, their devotion none the fiercer for uncertainty as to which one they'd slid out of. During the seasonal breeding frenzy that love grew positively rampant and careless, adding incest to the classical grounds for their extermination by Man.

Blades had drawn up these very precepts four centuries before. He'd heard them read to armies about to march on campaign. He even believed some of them. Now he felt the onrush of returning conviction as present sights and sounds unfolded. The Null mothers turned and rolled against each other, like some fleshy soup or slugs in a pit, not minding if fresh-born Null were crushed before attendants could rescue them. The penitent god-king's acid loathing dissolved every particle of Christian charity in him. His lip curled.

'They will sacrifice all for these,' he said, lowering his voice in deference to the traitor human present. 'I extracted the Treaty of Runnymede out of the vermin, through snatching a few such as this . . .'

Guy nodded. Ambassadors kept a beacon of history ever ready to illuminate or warn the present. *Runnymede* was a comfort word to him, just as the place remained a focus for pilgrimage even in present decadent days. When human fortunes were at a low ebb, the great Blades had raided the Null fastnesses, hitherto unknown to all save his own divine informedness, and put their mothers in cages of iron. Paraded along the Thames and pike-incited to sing, the sight and sounds of the matriarchs soon prised concessions from their children. A Null-free zone had been agreed and New-Wessex formally liberated. For Guy and Nicolo and Bathie, it had all been prime bedtime story material throughout their infancies. They held their breath (a blessing in the present clove and gore reek) to hear the tale retold by its only begetter.

'Take the bitches and shove something sharp where they're used to a prick – then you'll have the menfolk cowering like a Dutchman.' Blades voice was as bitter as the surrounds. 'Oh, aye . . . I *remember* now. Their general got down on his knees to me. We were face to face . . .' He exhaled forcefully and the interpreter-slave smiled, mistaking it for a sharing in his own pleasure. 'Ah me . . . happy days!'

258

The guide-Null might not understand *meat* bleating but he was sensitive to untoward noise. The *meat* were not sounding properly abashed. He turned and loomed.

Please, oh Blades, Guy prayed, *may Oglethorpe not reach for his sword . . .*

And Blades – or someone – heard him, for the out-worlder's right hand only twitched: insufficient even for Null to notice.

What he lacked in awareness, the Null made up for in excitement – in speech and parts. His member rose right at them and Guy, inopportunely, recalled that a feature of the enhanced-Null was their all-year-round lust, in contrast to their natural brethren. The party averted their eyes, on grounds other than good taste. There'd been a tragic fashion once: of dissolute New-Wessex types experimenting with taken Null cocks – stuffed and stiffened and lacquered – for their own perverted pleasures. It lasted till they found that weakling human flesh deferred to the more ardent Null version. Repeated brushes with Null-meat abraded man-membranes, leading to haemorrhage and some spectacular cancers. Of course, many non-indulgers took the long view, that the Null did unwitting service to humanity in purging the herd of its more degraded stock. All the same, remembrance of the infamous *Lords and Ladies' Pox* was uncomfortable, even to those whose family never succumbed or suffered. Guy and Nicolo and Bathie had each lost friends to it and so had valid reason for turning a blind eye. With Blades and Hunter and Oglethorpe it was more a matter of jealousy.

The chiming voice ascended higher than his prick. Though they kept no other of the ten commandments, the Null focused all the more heatedly on the fifth. They *honoured* their mothers. And if they, the master race, felt that way, then things further down the food-chain were doubly obliged.

Guy shuffled an unthreatening 'granny's footsteps' pace forward. He simulated speechless wonder and bowed thanks.

The guide-Null considered – and then was appeased. He merely reached out to release the tail-end of anger by gouging a fair canyon down Interpreter's bare chest. The human swallowed the majority of his scream, barely disturbing the sanctity of the Chamber at all. With commendable aplomb he crossed his arms over the flowing wound and radiated back injured love.

The Null had forgotten him already. He turned again to the view and shook the slivers of meat and blood held under his claw down into a waiting pink and purple mouth below. The other hand insultingly shoo'ed the visitors away.

Instantly, the suffering slave urged them out, even daring to lay hands on them. Oglethorpe, his nausea apparently overcome, was loathe to go, lingering to imprint the scene on his memory. The slave grew frantic and ever more pressing, and again Guy was on tenterhooks, fearing Oglethorpian retaliation.

Blades forestalled it. He observed the *meat* gobbets arcing down and then spoke.

'Time for a *new* Runnymede, I think,' he said, in a dried-out voice, inappropriate to a beggar. 'And a less forgiving one this time round . . .'

Guy's smile became entirely genuine.

The corridors were akin to the jagged twists and turns of a Null hunt, the sudden mad changes of direction matching the desperate attempts of prey to escape the inevitable. That similarity probably wasn't accidental, the Null architect, conscious or no, inspired by the roots of his being. Thus, just like a Null buck running down a fleet human, all the Ambassadorial party's weaving about was only postponing arrival at a fore-doomed destination.

The Null-King was waiting, the passageways held nothing to encourage lingering, but all the same their feet still felt leaden. If it wasn't for the lolling hordes along the way, salivating at them and play-clipping at their heels, their progress would have been slower still. As it was, they were hustled along, like veal calves to the crate or plate, down the narrow gullet of Null-Paris, straight towards its heart.

For some reason, all entrances to the City were high in the air; perhaps to simulate the first-unravelling, topmost portions, of an old style Null sleeping-pile. Down below, Paris presented only an austere blank face: a honeycomb of angular surfaces of wood and anything, glued together by obscene bulges of secretion. The only way in was up narrow and rail-less ways glued to the outer edge, leading to where circular orifices opened in the craziness.

Passing Null, an endless ant-teeming of them going in and out, barged past the *meat*, almost, but never quite, threatening to heave them out into the void and a short route to the ground. Also, there was the saliva and scratching problem and the insults to ignore, whilst pretending not to seek fingerholds in the wall. So, for a fleeting moment only, it felt good to leave the dizzy heights and enter into the great wasps' nest of the enemy. Then the gateway and guards were passed and the confinement began, the lack of anything but khaki translucent light filtering through the roof panels. Human eyes took time to adjust to the gloom and crush and clove-atmosphere, not to mention ill-intentioned bodies coming unexpectedly upon you.

The party, comprehensively put in their place, dribbled on and intimidated and disorientated, were led and driven to their gracious host. After what went before, his comparatively spacious throne-room, though bone-lined and perfumed, seemed to them like a breath of fresh air. That sad illusion soon passed. The floor was dark red and scrunched underfoot, releasing a sultry perfume with every step. Guy entertained – but didn't enjoy the company of – the notion of dried and powdered blood.

In impressive synchronisation, the humans bowed to the throne, causing Guy's coming-along-nicely hair to occlude his eyes. He swept it back to order and then they waited. Only Theophilus was out of step. He'd joined in honouring the Null-King but thereafter pointedly ignored him, concentrating instead on wringing out his wig. Oglethorpe thus discovered that Null spittle was mildly abrasive and clumps of hair deserted the cause into his hand.

Fortunately his manners and then chagrin went unnoticed. Presently, the King had – widened – almond eyes only for his friend, a young Null sitting in his lap. Guy paid no special heed, since the breed could be wildly affectionate for short periods, before hunger or mood swings changed all to snarls and competition. But then, when the two failed to converse and their subtle rhythm asserted a pattern, realisation dawned it was the youth's rather than the king's lap that was more imposed upon.

Unsure where to put their faces, the humans looked around or coughed politely, wishing the ordeal over. The few slaves of their own species present looked back at them, even more goggle-eyed than their supreme master, unable to quite credit humans who preferred selfish loneliness and rebellion to loving service. The very *clothes* they wore were taken only as signs of the shame they surely felt; mere fig-leaves to lessen the pain of swimming against the tide.

Blades discovered the slaves could not hold his stare, which momentarily pleased him, as it had been half a year – or maybe four hundred of them – since that was true of anyone. He partook of the flattering novelty, whilst Nicolo concentrated in enfolding as much of his thin face into a scented handkerchief as nature would allow. Only Bathie looked on, newly liberated and intrigued, interested in tips regarding the refinements of love.

A sigh proclaimed satisfaction, and then a growl its opposite. Perhaps the king truly hadn't noticed their arrival. Humans came – and, in lesser numbers, went – in and out of his presence all the time. He took no more particular note of them than he did the swarms of Parisian flies living like insect-royalty on what the Null left over.

The youth was pushed off, and stroked and cuffed, and finally limped away. The King then lowered his huge head down to his chest and drew in great gulps of breath. He might be committing things to memory or purging them away: there was no telling, and Guy, though he smiled like a suitor, didn't care. The old Ambassadorial adage of visualising opponents in their underwear didn't work with the ever-naked Null. Guy's personal variant was to imagine them with a slightly darker purple rosette adorning every breast, the sweet entrance place of a piece of lead burrowing down to their black hearts. That usually did the trick.

Unaware that Guy was killing him, but assuming it all the same, the King of the risen Null beckoned him forward. Guy shot to it, as keen as a ten-generations-in Null slave. He aimed for a mixture of meekness and dog-like stupid devotion. Its success made Bathie want to smile.

The sound of chimes and crystal clear water, babbling at the start of a promising spring day – and all from savage lips and flesh-speckled fangs. A slave interpreted.

'His Gorgeousness recognises you. Are you a serial visitor?'

Guy's bow almost butted the blood-red floor in gratitude for even demi-recognition. He presented his credentials, a vellum scroll enlivened with the coloured *initials* and baroque, flowing, script that New-Wessex calligraphy deployed at the slightest excuse. The Null would not sully his claws, naturally, but a collaborator was sent forward to accept and render it into pseudo-Null.

A response came back along the same route.

'You were here before. I recall your breeding-mate.'

Bathie curtsied and made Guy proud.

It made no impression on the Null. The intercourse remained unadorned.

'This time she may wander freely – and the other flock-*meat* too. The sight of you helps our cubs to hate.'

Guy kowtowed once more, as though accepting the most wondrous of gifts.

The King was not minded to note it and pressed on in distaste.

'What do you want?'

They'd been through this before too. Guy's answer was just

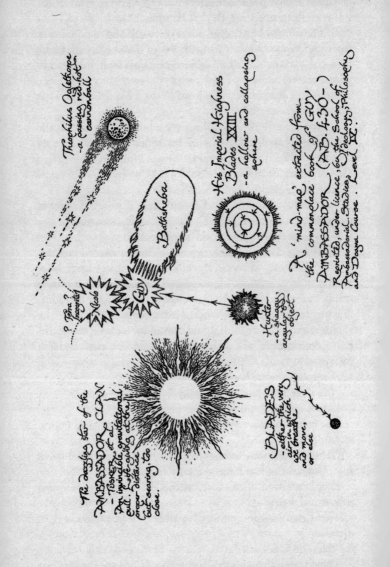

Theophilus Oglethorpe
– a passing red-hot cannonball

His Imperial Highness
Blades XXIII
– a hollow and collapsing sphere

? Terra Incognita ?
Pete

GUY

Batsheba

Hunter
– a shaggy, angular object

A 'mind-map' extracted from
the commonplace book of GUY
AMBASSADOR (A.D. 430–)
Reprinted, under licence, by the School of
Ambassadorial Studies, Theology, Philosophy
and Dogma Course. Level IX.

The dazzling star of the
AMBASSADOR CLAN
– Tooketh et al.
An invincible gravitational
pull. Safe giving at the
proper distance
but searing too
close.

BLADES
– either the very
air in which
we breathe
and move,
or else.

as polished and false as last time.

'Amity, majesty. Concord between our races.'

The Null never laughed – to Guy's mind the one defining difference between the two species. They might gloat or rejoice over horrible things, but honest merriment was forever off the menu.

What he'd never had the King didn't miss. The hilarious insincerity was passed over in silence.

'*I want . . .*' He ordered the open-ended demand conveyed.

Guy spread his hands and signalled he was the Null's to command.

'Anything, majesty. I'm all yours.'

'I want to *know.*'

Guy waited, wobbling on the precipice of still-born conversation. In the end he had to give in and prompt.

'And to *know* what, sublime devourer?'

The King looked around, as though he wished, for the first and last time, to speak direct to this cloth-draped ape, this larder-escapee, and not through a cowed and de-manned specimen.

'I want to know where the angels are gone.'

Guy's friction-free exterior retained not one droplet of the wave of interest which washed against him. Even Nicolo felt privileged to be in his presence and, better still, related.

The Ambassador looked about, mock bereft. Those who didn't know him or his trade might have thought him actually distressed.

'"*Gone*", Sublimity? Gone? Are you – we – deprived of their light?'

They played games – everyone knew. The angels listened in and eavesdropped and played childish games. Guy and the better informed humans half expected a presence to arrive and say all was well; they were back, and a little humble pie wouldn't go amiss, if it was *quite* all right with them . . .

But no one came. Their name was said and echoed against the cell-like walls and died without them answering the call. It was wonderful.

On the other hand, all this *Ambassador* business was angel sanctioned. Without them the Null had no need or wish for Guy's presence other than as another ribcage hung on a hook. Paradoxically, here and right now, Guy couldn't wish the new masters totally gone. At the very least they must linger like a bloodstain on the ceiling: a sign of something awful unseen in the room above.

'I cannot illuminate you, puissant lord. I do not know – but I weep with you . . .'

Oglethorpe snorted, even amidst his wig-wringing. He'd never beheld such a set of dry eyes. The hypocrisy was breathtaking: magnificent. Fortunately, he was ignored and failed to break Guy's stride.

'. . . and our distress at the loss is something we have in common . . .'

The Null looked at the human and the human at the Null.

'And the only thing,' came the eventual reply.

Guy Ambassador bowed glad agreement.

'No, I am *not*!' said Blades. 'How many more times? No!'

This was becoming the pattern of their Parisian days: a dialogue of the deaf or drunk. Guy allowed himself to be drawn from the former to the latter.

'So, I told him. I told King Billy *just* what I thought,' slurred Oglethorpe to Bathie, from their own table a little way across the room. 'And then I went low-profile, obviously!'

She was comprehending precious little of it but admiring all, agog for the next instalment.

'Really?'

'My oath, yes. Sold all me luxuries: well, all bar a few score muskets, and whizzed home to Godalming and me house at Westbrook to fortify the estate. Nothing special you understand, just a couple of little bastions, sweet for a seven-pounder each: just enough to command the Wey Valley and the London to Portsmouth road. But here's the cack on the bedsheet. How was I to know His Majesty was all the while preparing in St.Germain? Turns out they were still sending all the ciphers to me care-of Babylon – that's London to you. Not heard of it? Doesn't matter. Point is, I never got 'em. Wasn't told!'

He pushed aside another dead-man to join the bottle body-pile.

'So, there I was awaiting the call and not hearing a dickeybird. Naturally, the natives wouldn't breathe a word to me, not even if King James came down the High Street. Nice enough folk in their way, of course, but more than their fair share of po-faced Quakers. Not a Jacobite or Papist amongst 'em. "*Godalming: godly men but wicked women*" is the local saying, though I can't say I've particularly noticed the wom . . .' He suddenly looked into the nozzle of the current claret and found unaccountable mystery within. Solemn seconds passed.

'Where was I?' he slurred, when the vision was over.

'Godalming,' prompted Bathie – which was the capital of Humandom and Empire to her, but apparently something altogether different to this exciting blow-in.

'Oh yes. Well, anyway. A decent lot but a bit . . . you know, *hymn*-ridden. So I armed my tenants and cultivated my vines. Long south-facing walls at Westbrook: best in England. Dad planted 'em. Then I took a holiday from plotting and sampled the wine.' He frowned. '*Monstrous* imbibing, if I'm to be honest with you: several barrels a week, far as I recall – though it's all a bit of a blur. Oh yes, and I recollect a duel or two. And some pretty mounds to snuffle at, if you'll excuse me. But listen,' he levelled an unsteady finger, imprecise of aim, possibly at Bathie or, missing her, at Guy in hot debate at a nearby table, 'the *point* of the story is, that all the bloody time, unbeknownst to I, King James was equipping an expedition. I could have helped had I known. I would have gone. I could have argued. We certainly wouldn't have started things in bloody *Scotland* if I'd been on the Council, I can tell you. Skinny-ribbed men in skirts? Religion with a heart of flint? No *thank* you. Rise in England, that's what my dear Dad always

267

said, may he rest in peace.' – and here Oglethorpe brushed away a sudden tear. 'That's what he maintained. "*Rise in England or not at all*"'

Bathie nodded sagely, cheerfully ignorant of what she was agreeing to, enjoying the music rather than the words.

'And then,' Oglethorpe mourned, 'that's how it stayed, till I fell out with the next cuckoo-in-the-nest monarch and went on m'travels. What *happened*, y'see, was after thirty years of . . . lip-service, Queen Anne threw over her lady-lover: that Whig-witch, Sarah Churchill. Her Majesty had taken a fancy to Abigail Masham: suitable name when you consider. Anyhow: tremendous to-do, as you can imagine. Her husband, Churchill that is, the Duke of Marlborough – who's only commander-in-chief of the armed forces, that's all – was steaming fit to burst. All his decades of pandering to the Queen were gone to waste. There was the chance he'd deliver the army over to us. *So*, to pour oil on the flames, I got up in Parliament and proposed a grateful nation should present *la* Masham with a golden dildo; for services above and beyond . . .'

Guy had to tear himself away from eavesdropping on the alternative conversation. It was more entertaining than his own, for sure, but the task before him was of infinitely greater import. All the same, he couldn't entirely escape the sense of regret. Twice-bereaved of faith now, there was the impulse to cling to any promising bit of wreckage. Over *there*, so long as you didn't look at the florid man surrounded by bottles, over*heard*, was the voice of a true god-king. That sinful notion kept on occurring. If only Oglethorpe had been the one. Guy could have whole-heartedly invited *that* boisterous spirit back. He would have bowed the knee and said '*return with me, Lord*' and that would have been it. The angels and Null and infidels and Levellers would never have known what hit them.

And yet falsehood put on disguise. Oglethorpe was *not* the one: he mimicked it, in all innocence no doubt, perhaps through proximity to Blades, but he was not He. Guy repented of attributing improper respect. Like a boy to schoolwork, he

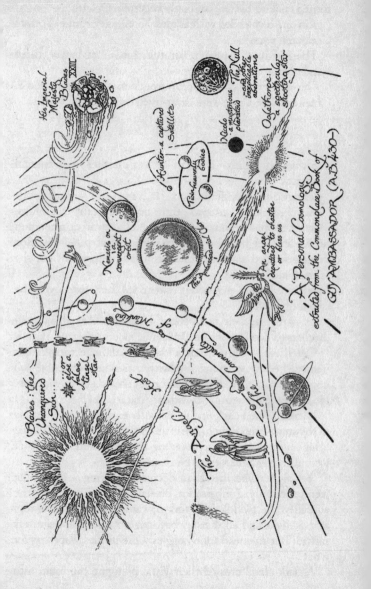

His Imperial Majesty Blades XXIII

The Null and other inexplicable aberrations

Hunter, a captured satellite

Twin-heavenly bodies

Nicda, a mysterious planetoid

Oolathorpe: a spectacular shooting star

Nemesis on a convergent orbit

The Ambassador's Sun

An angel deputized to chastise or bless us

A Personal Cosmology extracted from the Commonplace Book of GUY AMBASSADOR (A.D. 430–)

The Constellation

Blades: the Chaonquera Sun...

...or else a false tinsel star

of Madras

Fleet

The Fleet

turned back to his true and only begetter.

'Go on,' he pleaded with Blades. 'Confess it. Please. You *are* God, aren't you?'

The old man denied it for the third – or maybe three hundredth – time.

Guy cast a ear for a cockcrow from outside, but none came. Chickens, like hope, were short-lived things in Null-Paris.

Another pointless Parisian day, another continental breakfast.

'Disgusting. Wonderful!'

Guy couldn't follow the polar-different opinions. Oglethorpe had been warned about Null stew in no uncertain terms, and yet here he was consuming it at pace. The first verdict seemed appropriate to his meaty dinner, but not the second and opposite.

Nicolo leaned across and wrinkled his nose over the steaming bowl.

'Any recognisable body parts?' he asked. 'Are all Heaven dwellers so careless of cannibalism?'

Oglethorpe brushed that aside as he did the vapour. 'It's *mutton*,' he said, speaking from within a vacuum of doubt. 'You don't grow up in Godalming and not know sheep in your gob. No, I meant the set-up. Its rotten. And it's ripe!'

Nicolo leaned back and fastidiously exhaled every particle of the stew steam from his nostrils. His personal pearl-handled knife and fork were redeployed on the bread and cheese that were the only Null rations he trusted.

'Yes and maybe,' he at last decreed, speaking as though he were the only Ambassador present. 'The surrounds, the actuality,' he twiddled his fork upwards to indicate the roof and skylight and all that lay beyond, 'oh yes, most definitely rancid. But ripeness? One boggles. One puzzles. Ripeness for what?'

A dark cloud crossed their vista, plunging the room into

fuller gloom. As an especial mark of honour, shared with few other apartments in Null Paris save the Hall of Mothers and Throne-room, the *meat*-guest holding rooms were penetrated in places by glass. It was myriad types and shapes and even colour, doubtless looted from the works of man, but did at least allow a little light into their darkness. The cloud got black looks as much for diminishing that as being a poor omen.

Oglethorpe upturned a hand, grasping an imaginary voluptuous, perhaps even squishy, fruit.

'For change!' he exulted. 'For rebellion. Now I see why I'm here. I might not be able to unseat the king or put things right in England, but hereabouts is *begging* for it!'

They marvelled at his confidence: mere weeks in and already an expert on their world. That was what Bladian company could do for you.

Guy knew the man better than most there. He accorded him the respect of a hearing.

'What do you propose, Theophilus? I confess I did see your eyes light up in the Hall of Mothers . . .'

'Along with my guts heaving, maybe. Yes, I saw all right. I saw what a couple of cannon shoved up close could do. Give 'em a strip-down wash in jagged shot, I say. Ram 'em up close. See what's left of 'em when the powder smoke clears. You can't beat a good old frank exchange of views using artillery; that's what Dr.Oglethorpe prescribes. I remember this time in Canton and there were thousands of these fanatical Chinese. "*Kill the round-eyes!*" they were saying, "*Kill all the round-eyes!*" So I had a hole bored through this huge Buddha idol and put a *cannon-royal* right behind it. Then we let 'em in the temple and . . . Well, never mind all that now, but what I'm saying *is* it's the *shock* that does it as much as anything. Those you don't dismantle are left there like statues, black as a Moor and trying to remember what their name is. Aye, that's the stuff to give 'em. No problem!'

It was a glorious vista whilst it lasted and Oglethorpe's hands still waved over a sea of corpses, but his audience did not engage. New-Wessex culturally frowned on fairy tales of late; their predicament being too dire to give in to lovely imaginings.

Hunter had initially resisted the beggar = Blades identification but, pondering the matter in the quiet garden of his pious heart, had finally surrendered. Day by day his attitude to their elderly companion grew more reverential. It now pained him that others should weigh in when *He* hadn't yet spoken.

'And the total absence of cannon?' Hunter asked, speaking for his betters since they seemed beguiled. 'And getting Null permission to "*ram 'em up close*"? What do you propose about that?'

'Details,' Oglethorpe dismissed the objection. 'Mere details. Your armouries back home can supply those once the revolt starts.'

'What revolt?' Hunter was interrogating him. The disrespectful drop-in was usurping the Divine planning role.

'The slave revolt, dear rustic,' came the blithe answer. 'What else?'

Hunter had no need to reply. He could even show mercy and abstain from the communal laughter.

From outside came the liquid torrent that was Null anger. Their guards – essential to save them from passing appetites – might not speak *meat* but they sincerely hated human merriment.

Guy rather liked Oglethorpe and felt kindness towards him, for all he now doubted his true Heavenly citizenship. All things being equal he would rather not see his spirit abashed. He stilled his own spontaneous smile.

'Theophilus,' he said, above the slackening amusement, 'there are few certainties in this life: a little perception, some disillusionment, anything from a snack to a banquet of joy depending on divine favour,' – here he nodded towards Blades, who waved the respect away – 'and then it is done and we move on. However, one rock we may depend on is that there will *not* be a Null-slave revolt.'

'You've *seen* them,' said Bathie, shocking Oglethorpe, for

she'd never directly entered a debate before. He'd got accustomed to her as an enigmatic part of the scenery – which now spoke straight at him. 'They're broken reeds. The pre-emptive cringe was in their father's sperm and mother's milk. Bide here long enough and you'll see one eaten without complaining.'

Nicolo added his penneth. It was quite a day of novelties. No one had suspected him of strong feelings before.

'Yesterday,' he recounted, 'I observed an infant taken from its mother and consumed – no, worse – *half*-consumed by the Null. And yet she only watched and wept. Trust me, red-face-and-coat man, you'll no more see your cannon-day with those poor creatures than breed a family with a limp thing.'

Oglethorpe shrugged. 'You may be right . . .' he said, meaning *though I don't bloody think so*. 'But . . .'

'No *buts*,' interrupted Guy, anxious, through kindness, that their visitor shouldn't labour under any illusion. 'The slaves will not – *cannot* – rise. Their marrow has been sucked forth even before they grew bones. I know. My initial brief here was to seek their company and sow discontent, though the Null knew it and thwarted every chance and occasion. I did not worry, nor protest. I had already seen all that was needful. Be you the most convincing Leveller since Lilburne himself, you sow seed upon stone there. No crop will ever come; you will grow only tears.'

Looking within his stone bowl and meal, Oglethorpe detected some fragment that did indeed inspire disquiet. He pushed it and the notion away and fixed Guy with a *sit-still-and-listen* stare

'This is your world, ' he stated, 'that I'll concede. Yet you'll grant me that man is man wherever the Almighty plants him in his infinite garden. We all of us have a nose and arse and soul and they tend to much of a muchness. It's *my* experience that man is so ungrateful for merely *living* that you could raise rebellion in Paradise itself. Doesn't scripture confirm that?'

Guy didn't need to wonder when he had its author beside him. He turned and queried it with an eyebrow.

273

Blades abandoned the onion he was murdering and by myriad little signs conveyed that the man might have a point . . .

'I mean,' Oglethorpe then ploughed on, 'wasn't Old Nick himself snugly ensconced in the place we all hope to end in? And yet didn't he tire of bathing in the glow? There, sir: that's straightaway a dry patch in your wet blanket. No; I maintain that, given the right urging to discontent, even a Quaker will put his boot in your teeth. The *knack* is in stirring the bowl till it boils . . .'

Even as he said it, he wished for another metaphor, mindful of what he might have inadvertently tucked into. His discarded meal was still sitting there accusing him.

Guy thought on, and Bathie too. Their minds were the only open ones present – till they reached a conclusion and closed theirs too.

'*No*,' decreed Guy – and Bathie concurred.

Within New-Wessex, the definitive word of the Blades-touched was not contested. Even Hunter, a fundamentalist and heretic, baulked at that. But Oglethorpe was un-indoctrinated, as well as sprung from a stroppy strain. He persisted and raised gasps.

'No.' He mirrored their verdict with his own. 'I reckon you're *wrong* – or leastways history-bound. "*You never know till you've tried*", that's what my dear Father used to say. At Keynsham he charged three hundred cavalry into a rebel army of eight thousand, you know.'

'Really?' replied Guy, whose desert-dry tone should have formed a warning.

'And lived!' added Oglethorpe, as though that were a bonus.

'Gracious . . .'

'Anyway,' smiled the outsider-soldier, speaking like his argument was now warmly accepted, 'why are we on this earth if not to make mischief and put things right? You can't bounce on Joannas all your days, can you? No – there's debts to repay. I mean, what else are we here for?'

Guy had the answer to that – or at least the source of the answer, right to hand. He turned to Blades for it to be spoken, full of excitement. This might actually be *it*: the climatic moment of transfiguration, when Divinity-amongst-them split its chrysalis and blinded them all.

Blades would not speak or change. He shook his head and crossed himself but had nothing else to say.

Guy was crushed again, though no one saw.

'There will be no rebellion,' he asserted once more, his voice quite dead.

Oglethorpe winked back, the very epitome of irrepressible, fools-rush-in, cheeky-chappy-ness.

'Well,' he said, smiling as he spoke, 'we shall just have to see, shan't we . . .'

'Why-you-no-*listen*?' said Oglethorpe to their backs. If he had a pound for every time he'd said that of late, he'd be a wealthy man, able to *bribe* King George off the British throne, and still have enough for a life-time of Joannas and dancing bears left over.

The porter slaves carried on hurtling away, weeping in distress. An immature Null appeared and aided their progress with a taloned kick. Then he sauntered on as though nothing had happened. Passing by Oglethorpe he spat at his feet.

One of the pre-requisites of revolution was getting someone to hear you propose it. If all your potential Spartacuses covered their ears (when they had them – for the capillary-rich lobes were a favourite Null nibble) and scurried away at the sound of you, then you'd never burst out of the gladiator school at Capua, let alone take on the might of Rome.

Oglethorpe felt sure they could *understand* him – or at least some of them. The Null permitted a stripped-down form of speech to their skivvies, evolving upwards in complexity according to the tasks demanded of them. Whilst hereditary larder-stock might have less vocabulary than a parrot, the interpreter caste clearly spoke English as well as he – though less forcefully. With the former even Oglethorpe realised he was wasting his time, but the rest had potential – or would have if they didn't scatter before him like nuns menaced by a drunk.

The other difficulty was just finding a time and space to talk. The Null were everywhere, more prevalent than bugs in a slattern's kitchen. Even when you thought you'd found a corridor free or cosy corner in which to chat, then, lo and behold, one of the purple-vermin would unfold from some nook and slide over to see if he was eatable. He wasn't, of course – on balance and officially – though it set your teeth on edge to have it continually put to the test. Happily, the King's protection was upon him but that didn't prevent them salivating or drawing playful claws through his clothes. After only a few days of wandering Theophilus's coat streamed behind him in a gossamer of ribbons, like some rustic morris dancer on St.George's Day.

Oglethorpe wandered ceaselessly, whereas his companions more often lingered in their rooms, trying to speed the day when Blades would admit his true identity. The Englishman, however, reckoned *that* fact already well established beyond debate and so took his mission abroad, soon coming to know Null-Paris almost as well as Guy did.

The wasps' nest analogy proved sound and useful to bear in mind. Oglethorpe glimpsed hatchery-nurseries and food stores and honeycombs of resting chambers, all circling like fortress walls round the regal quarters and Hall of Mothers. The walkways and corridors might appear to dip and dive crazily but close inspection allowed Theophilus to perceive a greater pattern. Here was a design for life, self-replicating and boundlessly confident, coiled round a central core of preciousness. Cub-Null emerged from that, sliding slick and sticky from a careless womb-shute, to be gathered up and nurtured ever further from the epicentre as they grew, pending a first exit from the twilight city and presentation with a wider world. Some then left, seemingly forever, to spread the word, whilst others – Oglethorpe suspected the biggest and best – remained as permanent citizens.

The first and only heartening thing he learnt was that human slaves outnumbered all. The Null ate well and were lazy. They rarely built or made: they filled empty days with mock fights and sodomy. Increasingly, their food was brought *to* them, in dripping wicker hampers. Oglethorpe saw some go out to hunt, but by no means all. Their intake of wild flesh was a diminishing dietary feature – and perhaps likewise the spirit imbibed with it.

He'd read their history. Bathie gave him a *Blades-Bible*, which prefaced Scripture (not all of it rendered as Oglethorpe recalled from home) with a long discourse on the deeds of the first god-king. It was candid regarding early reverses and the ravening ferocity of the Null. The untold centuries of burrow-life under their heel were eloquently described and even Oglethorpe, who was only distant family after all, felt a surge of species-anger. Yet, most unlike him, he took a step back and so saw clearer. The Null may well have gained in being 'raised' – they no longer got wet in the rain, they lived longer – but they had also lost much in the bargain. Having witnessed in youth the court of William and Mary, Oglethorpe could scent decadence when it disported in front of him.

So, initially, he was heartened in his quest to raise rebellion. He noted the major slave stockades and committed to heart the pattern of their days. Surely, he thought, with one of the luscious and wholly wonderful *revolvers* plus a fiery brand in each of all those willing hands, he could have this place down to the ground in no time.

That the guns weren't there and raring to go was a mere matter of detail. Doubtless, the armouries of New-Wessex would churn them out, working overtime in sheer gratitude, and rush them over the sea for their date with destiny. If not, he'd go home and get some muskets himself – he'd read that Blades had done exactly the same, starting in a very modest fashion. That in itself should present no real difficulty.

Oglethorpe had more Jacobite contacts than teeth; frustrated men who'd gladly lend him weapons stockpiled for the glorious day of Stuart restoration. Since '*James III & VIII*' was proving a bit slow in obliging with that, the tools of the trade might as well be put to good use in the interim.

Meanwhile, he already had the initial wherewithal to hand. When the Null escort weren't looking, and to his companions' pursed-lipped distress, he'd gathered a posy of weapons to be going on with at the Field of Bones. 'Look. Good as new!' he'd said as he gathered guns like flowers – and because he was an ignorant foreigner and no one wanted the Null alerted, the others had passed over the desecration in silence and with averted eyes.

Preserved by angelic curse, the weapons looked fit to earn their keep, albeit a few centuries later than intended. In type they were still a mystery to him but their clips were full and a trigger was a trigger at whatever stage of technical evolution.

When his arms could hold no more and calls for aid got no takers, Oglethorpe had stowed the precious armful in their carriage, wrapped and concealed in a blanket, and again no one dared argue with him. The escort growled at the extra load but that worried Theophilus not at all, no more than their earlier disapproval of the dried Null ears stitched to his hat. It pleased him – and was a sure sign of right action – that what he did and was displeased monsters.

The poison posy was still with him, ready and waiting, stacked in the corner of what now passed for 'home'; but with the best will in the world he couldn't fire them *all* himself. Even the most ardent of spirits sometimes requires helpers: added voices to make life – which is deaf – hear clearly.

However, despite fervent efforts, he remained a choir of one. Just the *chance* of an audience became cause for celebration, and hope drew in its horns. Early promiscuous performances were replaced by more select auditions. In the beginning he cornered mere load-bearing slaves but they either ran, or when that wasn't possible, just screamed and pissed themselves with fear – once or twice even sending a golden arc on to Theophilus's feet. After that he no longer persevered with *them*.

Reason then suggested that the artisan-slaves: those taught a useful skill and a little speech to go with it, might be stauncher, and not spray him or emulate rabbits. So today he rejoiced to find a gaggle of the type and buttonholed them. They stood their ground – which was a start – but soon revealed it was solely for the purpose of gawping and then covering their faces. And then Oglethorpe realised, with a chill, that they acted not through fear, but *shame* at beholding one of their own so depraved, so *wicked*, as to stand in open rebellion.

Well, *everyone's entitled to their opinion*, he concluded – and gave them his with a V sign right under their noses. It was lost on the cowering half-men of course, but proved unfailing comfort to Oglethorpe, just as it had faithfully served his ancestors. In English longbow-man guise and of Crecy and Agincourt vintage, they'd employed it to show the enemy they retained their bowstring-loosing fingers – the Scots and French being wont to deprive prisoners of them when caught red-handed with the longbow terror-weapon. In all fairness though, those nations had good reason to act out of character. The innocent looking six-foot yew staves were a lash under which they'd suffered much.

Theophilus didn't know all that, not in his conscious forebrain, but deep down in his bones it was written right through, like as-yet uninvented seaside rock: wisdom from Oglethorpes long gone on ahead. It produced a warm glow, confirming to him on the instinctive level – which Theophilus ever took as his highest guide – that he'd done the right thing.

He moved on, following his nose until that prominent body part told him – not unequivocal good news in Null-Paris – that he was approaching a cooking area. Aromas barged past, the already fetid temperature rose and, closer to, tides lazily descended down the walls. There was every incentive not to investigate until an idea ascended the steep incline of his attention and put a flag on its narrow peak.

It was like this. All his other would-be insurgents surged off elsewhere when he mooted the idea, or even scooted at the mere offensive sight of him. Here, though, would be slaves rooted to the spot by the task entrusted to them. They couldn't move their work to a less subversive spot, nor hoist their cauldrons on their backs and find a quieter corner to lick spittle in. *Also*, food-preparers might be allowed a higher level of culture than most: given that they needed to converse on recipes and cooking times and myriad other things. Very likely, there'd be a hierarchy of sorts here: some grasp of sophisticated notions; perhaps even refined tastes. Oglethorpe's spirits rose for the first time in days. His feet had been guided. A kitchen was be ideal.

The mood changed directly he passed the – mismatched – double doors. The place was like the aftermath of a olden-days battle, when axe and edge were the sole ways to make people stay down. It was full of pink and red carcasses, many of which didn't bear examination.

Some of the teeming workers paused to notice him, but not much and not for long. They obviously had tasks to perform and only half the time needed to perform them. Most were naked, although that was probably not Null but heat-dictated. Mere seconds in and Oglethorpe was already flooding his boots. The place was like a sauna. He divested himself of hat and patchy wig.

Over one side were the butchery boards and cleavers to suit every arm and job. Oglethorpe mentally enlisted *those* for the day of the revolution. Running alongside and ultimately out into the abyss to splatter the side of the City, was a trough to carry those bits even Null and slaves couldn't face. Mercifully nearer to him, were kinder preparation tables, for daintier dishes or even greens. In-between were the stone-bottomed hearths, sinking into the weak floors under their own weight, with a cauldron above each and a scampering team to tend them. Into those went everything as it arrived, without thought, without measurement.

So much for high cuisine, thought Oglethorpe – and

indeed, so *much* . . . He witnessed what was basically a whole ox, roughly gutted and hoofs and horns knocked off, go into the largest example. There was no room for anything else and so there was the recipe for *that* broth. Maybe the Null-King would dine on such richness . . .

'Ahem. Gentlemen . . .?' he addressed them, loud and clear, in his best '*now, look here, chappies, this is for your own good*' voice. 'A moment of your time, if you please . . .'

They didn't. They carried on dismembering and broiling and all the rest, though some honoured him with the scrag-end of a gaze.

Not far away, a fat slave was straining over the lip of a cauldron to stir its obviously stodgy contents. Oglethorpe employed his more-beloved-than-a-spouse revolver (using, did he but know it, one-fifth of the world's remaining shells) to put the man all the way in, totally committing him to his work. Added to the existing cacophony, he felt fairly confident the splash would cover the noisy discharge.

Oglethorpe theatrically blew the powder smoke away into the coiling air. He had their undivided attention now.

'Now, *once* upon a time,' he told them, trying to remember how his father sounded when dispensing implausible but sound advice, 'there was this man called *Spartacus* . . .'

' . . . and after defeating . . . no, *destroying*, mangling, completely bloody pulverising, the Romans in five battles, Spartacus . . . um . . . Spartacus went on to capture Rome and released all the slaves in the world and, er, lived to an old age – happily ever after, of course – and then ascended to Heaven. Any questions?'

There weren't. He still had them fascinated – or rather his revolver did – but the glorious saga just recounted had failed to spark their souls – assuming the Null hadn't taken those along with their courage. Oglethorpe bridled at such a carnival of bookkeepers' spirit. The gun got waved like a baton, urging them to make some, any, music.

'Haven't you been *listening*?' he asked, a permutation on his constant refrain of late. 'Don't you *get* it? Spartacus, right? Slaves, down-trodden, right? They rise – like bread in the oven – do you follow? They kill their wicked masters and then can do what they like – which is called *freedom*: which is the birthright of every Engl . . . I mean human. Right? God *save* us, you bloody sheep, what could be simpler than that?'

For one exciting moment he thought he did have them. Their tolerance of him mutated into something better, their collective gaze become more focused.

Unfortunately, he realised it was focused beyond him, on a point behind his back. He turned to find himself in the shadow of a Null.

It smiled, as near as they ever did, a slow striptease of the lips to reveal row upon row of needle teeth, here and there overlorded by great rending fangs. The display was brought down close to Oglethorpe's face, bathing him in clove scent and body heat. When it had stooped very low they became eye to eye, two pupil-less almond slits seeking to dominate his plainer orbs.

Oglethorpe stood up to it. He was, after all, a man who'd given William of Orange a straight answer, (red) face to (corpse) face, when asked his opinion of the Dutch king's reign. Honesty had cost him house and home and fortune, whereas all he stood to lose here were his remaining years. Theophilus looked into the yellow depths and awaited a bite or kiss with equal indifference. He had his gun to hand; he might get in a shot before the jaws met and severed. If not, then he recalled that life had just been one damn disillusioning thing after another. He wouldn't be *that* heartbroken to leave it. There was hope of flying to a better place.

The Null wanted to indulge itself: it wanted to very badly, you could see and smell that. Most probably the kitchen had awoken his appetites: an imperious master even in the risen-Null. It sniffed Oglethorpe all over, inspecting his forks and canyons like a prospective purchaser in a market or whorehouse, taking its own sweet time. What seemed like an age passed before wisdom finally prevailed over ambition. Theophilus's red-coat, even in present tatterdemalion state, proclaimed him a protected pet, and fear of the Null-king's wrath – just – outweighed the temptation of the flesh. The Null arose and looked beyond him.

When it had silently entered the kitchen the slaves had been statues before Oglethorpe's oratory. That slacking was surely an offence of some sort, compounded by the wickedness they'd listened to. Now they sought to make amends by tearing at their tasks as if the past moments had never been. Oglethorpe saw and despaired. Here was their *true* heart, their only real reply to life's challenges. They were on their knees even when they appeared to run.

That wasn't enough to save them. If the Null couldn't strip the clothed human from his bones then it felt free to reinforce all sorts of lessons on mere sentient tools.

It brushed past Oglethorpe and savoured its position, high above the scamperers, judging them like a merciless god. All the while they pretended that nothing was amiss, but they were . . . smaller, each shrinking into their skin, trying to occupy less visible space.

The Null decided and reached once, twice, hauling two scullions in. Then it brought their heads together with a hollow stone-like sound – and then again, and again, till they were limp in its claws. The dreadful clock rhythm continued until the sound changed, becoming softer, almost pulpy. By then the examples were stilled for ever and their brains truly upon their work.

The Null released them to the floor and obsequious menials rushed to heave them away to the preparing tables. A horribly inappropriate memory flashed into Oglethorpe's mind: of his elegant Irish-harpy mother shoving an unfinished plate back at him. '*Waste not, want not*' she'd say – and then ensure what didn't go down at dinner, rose again from the grave, coffin-cold, to become supper. He took it askance that such a saintly woman be associated with these scrapings-of-humanity, scooping their comrades' brains off the floor and putting them

283

in the soup. It was another grave charge against them.

And still the show wasn't over. The Null beckoned two more slaves to him, specimens slightly more blessed with flesh than the norm. Obedient to the call, they came, though stumbling in fear and tears and dread, but the hand laid upon them proved to be a guide, not a blow. True, blood was drawn to trickle down quaking shoulders, but, by Null standards, it was a loving father's embrace. The monster drew them past Oglethorpe and chimed a signal that he should follow.

Theophilus followed on – post just a little point-making loiter. He knew his business here was done – or never begun. This kitchen, this life, and all the people within it: they deserved each other.

There was the fig-leaf of being *led* rather than driven, to cover his indignity, and Oglethorpe clung to that, no less than the Null clung to its prizes. Likewise, he travelled in hope of enlightenment, born of lack of anything better to do. Normal Null hospitality was just drool and abuse, but a tour was a *novelty* and thus well worth his time.

All the while, the two captives shot back pleading glances at Oglethorpe but he had severed all connection with them. His eyes held no mercy, his verdict was firm. If people made themselves sheep, they shouldn't then bleat when wolves came around.

Together the little group threaded their way broadly downward through the city-cum-heap. At times there was no choice but to climb, as the corridors or walkways obeyed some logic of their own, but the general tendency was towards descent and the outer air. Oglethorpe could applaud that and the prospect of it mitigated the ordeal of a Parisian promenade. Younger Null, lolling in groups, playfully tried to trip him up, whilst older, better disciplined, specimens settled for musical curses. Several times the guiding Null had to pause and rebuke his brethren. It clearly pleased him no more than they that a human should have a protector, but there was a story to be told and he was the teller.

Oglethorpe was willing to listen. This was a part of Paris

he'd not seen yet. It seemed thicker with Null: a concentrate form of whatever the City represented to the breed. Humans were thinner on the ground and, if such a thing were possible, even more cowed.

At last there was the open air and something sweet to combat cloves and sweat and blood. Oglethorpe drank it in like a condemned man at a tankard. They were still perched high above the ground but within plain sight of it. A precipitous walkway fell steeply down.

Theophilus could now glimpse the object of their stroll: something he'd previously overlooked, tucked behind one of the city's polyhedral sides. In its crazily irregular shadow was a corral of humanity: quite small and select and unaccountably parasoled against rain or shine. Oglethorpe had never observed such consideration over human slaves anywhere else in Null-Paris. Usually, so long as they survived their quarters still fit enough to serve, then that sufficed. These were pampered pets indeed.

His human walking companions seemed to know the place and feigned pleasure at the mere sight. Yet Oglethorpe could see neither heart nor soul were in it. Their poignant glances back increased in frequency, only to be rebuffed as before. His own view was that everyone – except maybe courtiers and, perhaps, Ambassadors – should say *precisely* what they mean, and then the world would be a simpler place. If these two skivvies wanted to pretend they were dying to arrive, then they should get on with it and pucker up.

'Hypocrites!' Oglethorpe accused them – but it was lost on prisoner and captor alike.

At length they reached firm ground. There was green grass to rejoice in, if one ignored the unpalatable gristle and body waste the Null decorated it with. Treading carefully, Theophilus alighted on Mother Earth and was duly grateful.

Not so his new friends – and now he saw closer and better he relented and didn't blame them. Here was a fattening pen for choice stock. It sat quiet under the weight of its destiny and the food forced upon it.

In his early days of exile, Theophilus Oglethorpe had passed through what he persisted in thinking of as the *real* France, before restlessness and politics and his temper urged him on ever eastwards. There, in some Gascon village, where a pair of shapely legs had beguiled him a while, he'd once seen geese force-fed. In the later stages they were even clamped under-arm to have rations rammed down them with a plunger, till the poor beasts lay stunned and the coveted liver, engorged to gross proportions, was already halfway up their throat.

Oglethorpe – a kindly man, at least as far as animals and children were concerned – was only strengthened in his opinion of the people he sought refuge among, resolving there and then to press on – after just a *few* more mattress-battles. Meanwhile, he abstained from *foie gras*, on that day and ever after, preferring rations killed with a swift knife to dinners bought with torment.

He was reminded of that long ago rustic French idyll now – and, curiously, of the long limbs that held him there. Perhaps it was all the naked flesh on display that prompted recollection – and so *much* of it and so shameless – but the Gallic girl's memory had no place here; nor that of any body shared through good honest lust.

Here was flesh too fat to stand – and too dispirited to care. It was feeding time for the sad elite gathering when Oglethorpe and the rest arrived – though that proved not happenstance but a constant state of affairs. Skinnier slaves, looking like another species, dived their hands into churns, moulding balls of butter to be passed through the fence. Null stood by to see every scrap was consumed with zest. If it was not, or if nausea intervened, then they intervened to make sure all was safely gathered – or regathered – in.

Oglethorpe both saw and had seen enough. He bowed his head and felt sick: a recurring theme in this visit to another world, he noted – which ought to serve as a warning. Now he saw the reason for the long trek. Here was a lesson against speaking to slaves and their listening to him. '*Here is where it all ends*', went the moral of the tale, for him, for the two

286

examples, for the kitchen slaves left behind and all they spoke to ever after. *'Here are the wages of dissent!'* Even the mere audience of subversion would reap only one thing from their attendance — that they would in turn be reaped and confronted with their true place in the food chain.

Even Oglethorpe, who was often hard of understanding, got the point — and it pierced his heart. He wished for temporary blindness and then blankets over his head in the fetid little room allotted him. *He* had brought these two wretches to this, and for nothing. That troubled the sleepy beast called conscience.

Wails brought him back, despite every wish, to see some more. His guardian Null had hefted two human burdens over the corral fence. They landed roughly and straightaway had to rise and fight for air. Writhing and elbow-work bought a bare sufficiency of space, allowing them to squat down, thigh to thigh; a bulky pair transformed into twig-men or famine victims compared to the company. Perhaps they vainly sought concealment amongst the meat mountains but placatory rictus-style smiles occupying pale faces only distinguished them further. Beyond those flimsy planks the rest of the herd was bereft and resigned, stunned by fate. Marked out in every way, Null and human waiters bore down on them, bearing butter and other good things, to start remedying their deficiencies.

Again, Oglethorpe switched off his gaze as the first grease grenades were piled down prised-apart gullets. There were incoherent sounds amidst the gagging and heaving. They were trying to express thanks even as they were fed.

'Behold the blessed,' said a smooth interpreter appearing, silent and the same colour as a ghost, by Oglethorpe's side, probably in answer to some earlier Null summons he'd failed to hear. 'When they are perfect their day will come. They shall bring the mothers joy!'

So that was it. Here was the mother monsters' private larder, a luxury supply of fatstock to keep them replete, the reward of love and for being . . . what they were. When spherical these once-humans would be building blocks for future nightmares: the essential spark in new little Null.

Thinking on at unprecedented rate, Oglethorpe still could not conceive of a more insulting fate. For a second, he wished his own Georgian kings in there too, but then repented of such cruelty. Even they, usurpers and misusers of his nation, did not deserve that, for all they'd already stuffed themselves conveniently Null-worthy.

Oglethorpe beamed at the new arrival, showing teeth which would have been an awful warning to anyone properly schooled in human nuances.

'Really? How marvellous!'

'Truly,' said the slave, looking as though he almost envied them their fate and rations. 'They shall be the fuel for wonderful breedings. The honour is theirs!'

'It *certainly* is . . .' said Oglethorpe, who had become a marble falsifying machine, just as good as an Ambassador. 'I mean, you just have to see. They're gagging for it . . .'

Then he had an idea – and his grin threatened to part skull from jaw as though unhinged.

'And so,' glorified the speaker-slave, obviously something of a poesyfier, called for that purpose to gild the lesson, 'they will live on in love and service, privileged, promoted, components of a superior race. In better form they will rise again!'

'Oh, *yes*, dear boy' agreed Oglethorpe, who now know what he must do and risk. 'They most certainly *will* . . .'

'There will be no rebellion. You were right and I was . . .'

'Wrong?' Guy assisted Oglethorpe.

'Yes. That word.'

'How very gracious of you, my dear man.' Guy bowed from a sitting position. 'Welcome to c-c-cold wisdom. Stare straight in the face of this world that the angels have made.'

Alarmingly literalist, Oglethorpe obeyed. He surveyed the

riverside and the sluggish, Null dotted, waters, and, sure enough, found little to please in his present mood.

He'd discovered Guy and Bathie beside the Seine, taking some much needed air and each other. A line of Null, tired of fish-dabbling and one another and every normal Null diversion, had gathered along the bank to watch. They could loosely appreciate the point of this human transaction, but not its length or the care for mutual pleasure. Null took their fun fast and where they found it and then moved on. Making new life was another matter altogether, approached as both duty and honour – or compulsion when the old spring-months madness came upon them. Making *meat* – and making a meal of it – seemed an unadventurous use of a summer's afternoon, and thus typically human.

These Null had vaguely heard of *meat* in rebellion – two samples of the breed lay before them – and the elders' tales implied defeat at their hands in the dim past – though that seemed hard to credit. Some of them had also glimpsed *meat* ships, distant upon the ocean, in arrogant defiance of their proper status. So, here then was a great puzzle. On the one hand, observed close to hand, these animals plainly had the spirit of wool-*meat* and were weak and considerate; whereas on the other, they demanded parity with the master race. It was unreasonable, on even the most basic of levels. The very impudent notion provoked Null irritation. Many a slave had a bite taken out of them soon after Null beheld a man in clothes. It really was *too* much . . .

As was the sex. It lasted too *long* and was uneventful. There was no pain – though some cries – and no blood. One by one the Null turned away or back to their catamites.

Those signs enabled Oglethorpe to find them. Nicolo had said they were '*out*', which was some – if not much – help. Hunter was giving his all to bow maintenance and thus even less forthcoming. Obliged to wake up Reason, the Englishman then retraced his steps at its sleepy bidding, heading back out of the City and wondering where *he* might choose to take a beloved wife on a sunny day. Since Paris-proper was short on places where a couple might frolic, far, *far*, away came the answer – with the cooler riverside as a second best. A line of Null watching but not attacking supplied a further clue. Expressions of delight once in audible range clinched the matter.

He coughed loudly as he breasted the rise – the same moment they did, judging by the sound of it. Then there were Null legs left insolently sprawled to climb over, and claws to avoid, which delayed him. By the time he hoved into sight, the couple were thankfully all packed away.

Oglethorpe scrambled down the sand and tussocks and said his piece. The closest he ever came to apology was graciously accepted – though Guy's magnanimity received little heed. Oglethorpe didn't care to be reminded, and was too busy noting how much better Bathie looked for a starburst of colour upon her cheeks.

'Why do you keep on at it, though?' Theophilus just *had* to ask; the question had been growing and growing in his mind for some while now. His brow was furrowed, sign of a rare spark of non-practical curiosity unconfined. 'I mean, the same person, the same thing. Don't you get tired? I got tired. Even my wife . . . whose name at the moment escapes me, got tired – I think. She left me in Paris – or was it Chepstow . . .?'

Guy clapped his shoulder and wilfully misunderstood.

'I shall never tire of *your* company, Theophilus. You may depend on it, even if I have other, pressing, things to do . . .'

Oglethorpe couldn't see past a compliment. The swerve was accepted at face value. His spirit of enquiry, ever a feeble being, sank back on to its sick bed.

'Hmm, well, thank you.' Oglethorpe tried to recall his purpose, looking from Null to Seine to City to jog it out of him. Laggardly, it finally came. 'Ah, yes. I wanted to ask you a question.'

Guy opened his hands and face. 'Anything, Theophilus. Fire away.' The last was inspired by sight of the remaining Null. A couple were mocking them, pumping away in imitation of him and Bathie a few moments ago.

290

Oglethorpe looked around – as though the Null would give ear to, let alone understand, the chatter of hairless monkeys.

'*This*,' he said opaquely, raising his arms to encompass something or nothing, 'it is *necessary*? Does it *have* to be? Would it matter if it *went*?'

Guy's understanding to date was that Oglethorpe left the room when matters turned theological. All their consciousness-raising sessions with Blades had only sent him out on long walks round Null-Paris to be dribbled on. Now he'd trekked a fair way just to put big questions imprecisely. It was most odd.

Still, Guy wanted to do his best. He considered.

'Well, first of all, I'd preface my reply by saying you'd be better off addressing someone from the Philosopher or Priestly clans with these questions, rather than an Ambassador. However, if compelled, I should reply that . . .'

One of Oglethorpe's hands rose and fell with a chop to stop all that.

'No. I meant the concord with the Null. *This* place . . .' He signalled back without looking to indicate the hive-city. 'I mean would you have great objections if it all went up in flames? The peace, the City, everything . . .'

No Ambassador ever expressed an opinion lightly when there was a fair chance of it impinging upon the material world. Guy sensed that with Oglethorpe the gap between *think* and *do* was as short as a king's gratitude. He had to tread carefully.

'Well . . .' he said, 'the present state of affairs,' a cupped hand was unfurled to signify it, 'is *externally* decreed . . .'

As with opinions, no Ambassador, or indeed any thinking person, would employ the angelic name recklessly. They listened and sometimes answered the flimsiest of 'calls'. Such was their whimsicality – and perhaps boredom.

'I know that,' Oglethorpe broke in curtly, causing Guy to wince. 'It isn't what I asked. I'm *saying*, does it upset the apple cart if matters change dramatically – and soon?'

The *apple cart* metaphor was not one that had made its way

from the old Earth with Blades and so didn't feature in New-Wessex English. It must have filled a need though, for the new world had forged its equivalent and so Guy could easily interpret.

'The strawberries would indeed go flying,' he agreed, pleased to see that cause a translation-frown on Oglethorpe's face – and serve him right for his obscurities. 'Such is the nature of radical change. However, in this instance, and to maintain the analogy, that bowl of fruit was not to our taste in any case. Nor did we order it. Much within the bowl sickens our stomachs. A significant many of the berries are rancid. A man may live on such rations but he will never prosper.'

Oglethorpe reeled in the metaphors one by one, his lips moving in repetition, and clubbed them till they divulged their meaning.

'So,' he said finally and slowly, 'what if a waiter came and cleared it away – and gave you a new menu?'

Guy sat down beside the already dozing Bathie and gently alighted his hand upon her mound. Oglethorpe snaked down too, and shuffled up close. The few remaining Null paid fresh attention, mistakenly thinking some refinement of *meat*-sex was imminent.

'Well, then,' mused the Ambassador, 'in such a case, we ought – by rights – to be delighted when the noisome meal is gone. And yet it is all we have. The proprietor, albeit a wrongful, trespassing one, true, but presently in firm occupation, dictates that we dine and smile. The kitchen seems silent; no rattle and bustle of alternative courses being prepared emerges from within. And we must live. *So*, perhaps, however unwilling, there is the chance of a restraining hand on that waiter, be he never so well intentioned. "*Leave this disgusting meal in place!*" we might find ourselves obliged to say. What if, the hungry customer must also enquire, the new menu proves blank or false? We do not wish to be ejected from the restaurant. That would be . . . embarrassing.'

'Quite.' Oglethorpe fully agreed. He painfully recalled being carried out, dazed and bruised, wig gone and breeches ripped arse to ankle, from Lloyds coffee-house – and all over an argument about the order of precedence between a *carbine* and a *musketoon*. He'd hadn't really known himself but it had seemed all important at the time.

'And thus,' Guy pressed on, 'on balance, and all other things being equal – which I agree before you say so, they never are – there remains a powerful case for gripping that well-meaning waiter's arm. And dissuading him. Using whatever means seem necessary.'

'I see . . .' said Oglethorpe – and he did. Warnings from the patient and urbane were always to be heeded.

Guy never liked to see a man left with nothing – just as soon as he'd got the point, whether it be conversational or stiletto. There were many, many, people who deserved better than subjugation.

'And yet,' he mentioned, in afterthought tone, 'if one *were* to see a fresh, delicious dish emerging through the kitchen doors; if its appetising aroma preceded it, and the server's feet trod inexorably to our table, then, *then* I say, yes perhaps we might call "*waiter, take this filth away. Bring us instead some of* that *delight!*"'

Oglethorpe thought on and arrived only a little delayed. 'Got you,' he confirmed. 'So you'd need to see the alternative dinner first?'

'Absolutely.'

'Only I don't want to leave you in the lurch, like . . .'

'How thoughtful. One senses your powerful urge for amendment; one is grateful . . .'

'Don't mention. "*One*" tries to pl . . .'

'And *one* urges restraint.' Guy let the steel sound in the third panel of his triptych. 'I see no such waiter. My nose, though it ever quests for it, detects no mouth-watering premonitions. It is for the god-king to summon the manager. He declines to do so yet.'

'Hmmmm.' Oglethorpe had seen Blades refused service in half a dozen Caprisi restaurants till he'd intervened and made them relent. *And* he'd picked up the bill, even if it were only for bread and water. He had no faith any waiter, however unlike-his-breed obliging, would take the slightest bit of notice of that particular carnival of rags. Blades would click his fingers and clear his throat in vain.

'But what if a nice platter does hove into sight?' he persevered. 'What then, Ambassador?'

'Why then,' said Guy, drumming his fingers on the gates of joy, 'I should be the first to take up my knife – and fork, naturally – to greet it. I should dine – being famished – with the very *greatest* of relish. On that happy day, Mr Oglethorpe, you would find me the most convivial of lunch companions!'

Oglethorpe struggled to his feet, patchy wig askew, disappointing the *Peeping-Tom* Null.

'Dear boy,' he purred. 'I look forward to it.'

'I too,' said Guy hurriedly, 'but cannot yet name a day . . .'

'Build up an appetite!' urged Oglethorpe, as he turned away.

Guy watched the retreating back stomping through the Null, and regarded it with something near to affection. Then he frowned, deploring the twists of fate. *What* a shame it was on a sunny day and after love, to have to plot the death of a friend.

'What-you-*want*?'

For this unprecedented interview the Null had obviously drafted in their top interpreter, a woman able to render questions precisely as they were spat from the regal fangs.

At that point Guy would probably have bowed but Nicolo was not his brother. He had identified an untried approach, a gap in the market, and wouldn't deviate from it, for all it might seem the door was closing. He'd grovelled the once on entering the charnel-house cum throne-room and that would do.

'No, what do *you* want?' he shot back. 'An Ambassadorial answer or the honest one?'

Top Null and temporarily exalted human consulted. Interpreter had absorbed the Null way, in both posture and vehemence. Nicolo admiringly recognised that imitation really couldn't go much further whilst she remained in a bag of pink skin. Even her answers successfully transferred the predatory tones of Null-speak into English. Nicolo might well have been interested in the female had someone not scarred her face and bitten her breasts off.

'Both,' she snapped. '*Ambassador* first.'

'I desire concord,' trilled Nicolo. 'I seek peace and harmony between our two great species. I hunger and thirst for the approval of our joint masters.'

'Now *truth*.'

'Well . . . the usual: power; position; women – oh, and *drama*, of course.'

The interpreter explained the concepts. The King continued to look straight at him.

'Stress *drama*,' Nicolo advised. 'I shouldn't have put that last.'

She also stared at him and, comparing the two, Nicolo couldn't see the slightest deviation in purpose. Here was symbiosis between meat-eater and meal. He tried hard to think of a comparable servility elsewhere in nature and couldn't. It was fascinating.

The response interrupted his wandering thoughts. He rushed back from the green woods of home to this tan and red place.

'We have *never* known counter-offer before. There has only ever been *one* Ambassador word. Should we be happy to hear two?'

'No – try *ecstatic*.'

'Why?'

'Competition. Negotiation. Advantage. The chance of a better deal. Take your time,' he advised the interpreter, friendly as you like. 'Expound those new concepts fully.'

She returned the offered aid with a dressing of hatred. Nicolo deferred. He knew, be she never so clever and loyal,

295

she'd end up as dinner one fine day. He could afford to be forgiving.

All the same, when her exposition went on too long, and the Null-King showed signs of resistance to its charm, the novice-Ambassador butted in.

'I *said* stress the *drama*. Therein is the very kernel of my policy. Elseways you are remiss: failing in duty. I will assist. Illustrate it thus: you attack, we respond: neither of us goes running to the angels. You land in Kent, we root you out – if we can – but none of us starts whingeing. Maybe you take Dieppe and eat it, perhaps we expand it. Who can say? But enough of *peace* and *stasis*. I see the consequences all too clearly. We grow stale, you – forgive me – grow lazy. None of it is good for us. Therefore, what do you say?'

The King said nothing, even after the full wonder of it was explained to him. He sat and looked at Nicolo still more, whether mentally tasting him or admiring a new future it was impossible to tell. Reply, when it came, was unusually subdued.

'I think,' repeated the interpreter, daring to occupy the throne of first person singular, even if only in translation. 'I ponder. So I ask again. What do *you* want?'

Nicolo sensed the pen hovering above the contract. He chose his words with uncharacteristic care.

'Your recommendation and support – and a free hand. Thereafter you shall see me but rarely, though you shall perceive my conducting hand. I shall make *such* sweet music, believe me. There will be grand opera – and *dramatic* drama. Depend upon it – and depend on me!'

Not one word of it had touched his own cool nature but Interpreter was convinced. In trying to be so clever they'd actually done themselves a disservice in deploying her. Even if she ever had understood human motivation, the very concept was long disowned. She was a pink-Null and thus readily deceived. 'A too *sharp knife can cut its owner*' ran one of the interminable Ambassadorial precepts, and Nicolo recalled it now. Sir Tusker would have been proud of his son – up to a point.

The real *point* was that Guy had both his job *and* Bathie, casting a long, cold, shadow in which to stand all these years; whereas faithful Nicolo, his brother, had neither – which wasn't *fair*, whatever way you surveyed it. He was not a greedy man, he'd settle for having either and wasn't *that* fussed which. Nicolo fancied each with equal detachment. However, since the Lady Bathesheba looked tightly clung-on-to (though doubtless have-able, given the right words, in the right order, said at the right time), then the least Guy could do was climb off one of the two desirable peaks he occupied. Nicolo didn't think that *much* to ask. He really shouldn't *have* to ask. So he wouldn't.

Also, Nicolo was acting in the true family spirit; was taking risks in the cause of equity – and drama – which was the *right* thing to do. One day, Guy would see that, if he lived and was reasonable.

The Null-King thought it reasonable. He extended an almost paternal claw and beckoned the human forward. Nicolo obeyed, clambering over Null youths and bits of ex-human.

'Close enough. His Wonderfulness says do *you* know where the angels are?'

'I do not,' beamed Nicolo. 'And that is how I am able to promise drama!'

Null sliver-lips split and a tongue darted out at a suddenly more *tasty* world. Talons urged Nicolo closer still. He was *there*.

He'd never been '*there*' before, just as he'd never been toyed with by a Null before, let alone a royal one. If you closed your eyes and bit your lip, the clawed fondling was almost erotic. That wise policy also edited out sight of the interpreter's green-eyed jealousy.

It could not, however, bar the sound of dripping hatred in her voice.

'The Master of Appetites *greets* you,' she said, and whatever her feelings, Nicolo knew he could rely on her loyalty for a true rendering. 'He greets you all afresh, risen-*meat*; and says

"*Welcome . . . Ambassador . . .*'"

Nicolo Ambassador opened his eyes and discovered that even a Null could look beautiful. He bowed a second time and surrendered to the embrace.

'*Dear* Brother. You are *welcome* . . .'

Guy even set his backgammon game aside, which should have proved it.

'Am I?' asked Nicolo. He might be questioning one or both of Guy's assertions. Guilty conscience squeaked ventriloquist-style from sea-bed depths, kidnapping his voice and making him speak when he'd prefer not to. Nicolo resolved to send an expedition down there, to root the last, unsuspected, remnants out.

'Oh, assuredly, b-b-blood-of-my-blood-most-probably. When I have a difficult request to make, your face appears like food after famine.'

Nicolo sat down in the little off-alcove within their quarters that Guy had commandeered for his base of operations. There was a crazy-legged and unlevel desk, the probably mocking Null answer to repeated requests, and excruciating chairs to match. The dark suspicion that the seat covers were human skin meant a sitter could never rest easy, even had the balance been comfort itself.

From somewhere, Guy – or Hunter, his volunteer man-servant – had wrenched a panel and wedged it into the alcove entrance, simulating a degree of privacy. Therefore, to enter the cramped court of Humanity's Ambassador, it was polite to knock and necessary to heave the blockage free. Nicolo had dispensed with the first but the second even he couldn't shimmy round. The effort produced grunts and loss of dignity – exactly as Guy had devised.

Seated – however angularly – and brushed down and composed, Nicolo could resume his normal face. It was bland and obliging.

'We are *Ambassadors*,' he replied. 'Between *us* to ask is to have. What do you require?'

For form's sake, though hardly needed betwixt two of their line, Guy's assumed a look of infinite regret.

'I may have erred,' he confessed, 'in bringing the Heaven-dweller Oglethorpe here to the real world. His conformity to plain facts is imperfect. Used to the greater liberality of Paradise he is too . . . exuberant.'

'*Far* too exuberant,' agreed Nicolo, honouring the custom of their family. As a counsel of perfection, the Ambassadors were exhorted to preserve – superficial – unity in all things. In the war of all against all that was the cold basis of their creed it was held vital that the outside should never 'know'. True, today there was no outsider there to see; Nicolo need not have bothered, but he reckoned it . . . nice to uphold the old ways when you could. Deep within him lurked a true belief in the Ambassadorial faith, imbibed along with the body fluids of his begetters. He even had the piety to feel a teeny bit hypocritical at that moment.

Guy was pleased. When two minds met, reinforced by ties of blood and faith, there could be a wondrous elegance in their exchanges.

'I fear,' he continued, 'that impelled by his – doubtless laudable in the Heavenly context – dangerous energies he may provoke some . . . inconvenience with the Null.'

'He *is* the type,' Nicolo agreed. 'I like him for it.'

'As do I. Alas, we cannot be free in our affections. Circumstance cracks the whip over us. Great things are afoot – perhaps. The angels are . . . mislaid and Blades is returned, albeit still shrouded. We must delicately *probe* at events: not give them a damn good seeing-to. Oglethorpe is the antithesis of prudence. Whilst we tread a delicate path, he threatens to cavort along it in metal-shod cavalry boots. So I'd like you to kill him.'

'Naturally. Just say the word.'

Guy smiled – and Nicolo too; though his wolfish amusement, impossible to swallow, sprang from a different and tainted well. He'd had a sudden vision, of a word here, a hint there, and then his brother and the out-worlder, breathing their last in each other's faces, impaled on one another's swords. It was a lovely, heart and face-warming, sight, and the road beyond the scene stretched gorgeously wide and clear.

'B-b-bless you, brother,' said Guy, and leaned forward to peck him on the brow. 'But do await that *word*. The time is close but not yet. Who knows, if Blades awakes, we may not even need to sip that chalice. Given the choice, and speaking for myself, I'd prefer not to . . .'

Nicolo tapped his sharp nose, signifying he understood both the timing and regret.

'Say no more,' he told Guy – and so Guy didn't.

As Nicolo left, the door took some shoving aside and revealed Hunter waiting beyond. Nicolo turned to query that with his brother and received reassurance via a shrug. If he *had* heard anything it signified nothing. The Wild-dweller was theirs. He would understand 'harsh necessity' just as well as, if not better than, a true New-Wessex man. Nicolo accepted that and left.

'The woman told me to come,' said Hunter, entering without being asked. Guy sighed but overlooked the irreverence. He recalled their location in the impermissibly frayed carpet-edge of the world. If proper titles like 'Lord' or 'Lady' were too much to ask for, then a bare minimum of obedience would have to do. Push come to shove, Hunter bowed the knee to the Bladian spark within a lineage. That must suffice.

'She did – and do, please, sit dow . . .'

He already had. His great plates of feet, swollen monstrous by wrap-around Wild-moccasins, were stretched out to the alcove's extremities.

'And?' Hunter queried, no sooner settled than wanting to be elsewhere. The Wild folk were like that: fast on the move, instinctive tricky targets, unlikely to make old age and thus careless of burn-out.

Guy checked on their solitude, searching out his brother's fading footsteps on hard Null flooring. He then pulled a face.

'Nicolo – alas and all that . . . He may have to go.'

Hunter looked after the departed Ambassador, as though his gaze could track round the dozens of twists and turns already between them.

'He already has.'

'I mean never to return. To a better place. Where no more tears will fall. To his reward – though not, I hope, his deserved one. Not yet, though. When I say. Will you do it?'

Guy was glad to conclude the short, barking, and profoundly un-Ambassadorial mode imposed on him by his audience. He quite saw the requirement for sentences like sword-jabs to the unsubtle or slow of uptake, but it still went against the grain: a disproportionate strain upon the trained throat. Happily, other considerations now dictated a pause – like consideration, for instance. Amongst family and plain-and-simple servants, one could cut straight to the bone and the when and where. With idealists and those beyond the punishment-and-reward nexus, a further one question diversion had to be tolerated. Guy didn't mind at all, glad of the rest. Also, he rather admired tender consciences.

'Why?' asked Hunter, sooner than expected. Guy shook himself from reverie.

'Oh . . . well, it's just that my beloved b-brother has been visiting the Null. It would appear that he has the – pointed – ear of the throne. He frequents its blood-carpeted floor. Nothing wholesome or to our benefit is cooked in that particular kitchen. One rather fears our Embassy is presently speaking with more than one tongue. Therefore we may require you to return us to a solo performance. What do you s-say?'

There turned out to be twice the expected queries – which was stretching indulgence a bit. However, Hunter had partaken in the pink portal moment – and thus was gilded by its memory. He was played out just a fraction more rope.

'How d'you know this?'

Inside, Guy was wearing the smug smile of those who know what they shouldn't and more than they let on. Outwardly, not a peep of it penetrated his profound regret.

'From my nightly inspection of his oh-so elegant and supple, needle-toed, shoes. I regret to inform you, my d-d-dear Hunter, that of late their soles are as red-coated as his deeds.'

Hunter considered – and then folded his arms

'Fair enough,' he said, 'if it be Blades's will. You only had to ask.'

Despite himself, Guy was touched to learn that the age of faith was not yet passed.

'Hello again. Only me!'

Theophilus hardly expected the red carpet for his second visit to the kitchen. There again, he also hardly knew what to expect. Given the disastrous consequences of last time, they might either fall or fawn on him. He intended to treat both extremes with equal contempt. He had his sword and a cheek full of spittle ready.

In the event, he needed neither and put both back. Perhaps it was a different work detail slaving away or maybe they were more supine than a cuckolded Quaker. It mattered not to him. A light sprinkle of black looks and muttered curses were easily lived with. Oglethorpe looked round for what he wanted.

It took some searching, a pacing round the labyrinth of walkways between tables and cauldrons. He even leaped the reeking channel that took away the off-cuts, idly wondering what on earth to do with himself if he fell within. Exile? A pumice rub-down till raspberry-red? How long would it be before he was fit for human company again? Those thoughts inspired him across with ease, making themselves redundant.

On the far side were men – 'so-called' in Oglethorpe's ethics – with cleavers and other sharp devices to part flesh from flesh. There were ample opportunities for any or all to practise their skills on the visitor and add him to the menu.

None did. Theophilus turned his back with impunity, he investigated without a care. If anyone got in his way he shouldered them aside like nothing – which was also their response. *His* glancing blows didn't terminate in raking claws. Compared to what they were used to, Oglethorpian rebuffs were like an old couple's embraces.

He ought to have foreseen, he should have foretold, had he not long ago divorced calculation for instinct, that his prize wouldn't lie amongst the quivering-carcass section of the kitchen. What he needed belonged more to its daintier portions – such as they were. He looked around, usurping master of all he surveyed, and saw some likely lads to chat to.

This time he crossed the blood and gristle canal on one of the bridges provided. Having conquered the further side there was no longer the need to display derring-do. He pretended to be unhurried, as though the intrusion of a Null were the furthest thing from his mind. In practice his steps were inches longer than normal. He feared the sight of a purple head intruding through the doors. For then he would have to come here again, and he didn't wish that. The whole grisly experience – human degradation seen in concentrate form – offended both nostrils and honour.

Oglethorpe arrived at those places where patches of green and yellow alleviated the general colour scheme. Vegetables for the bulking out of meals and for human-fodder were piled higgledy-piggledy, alongside herbs and spices to enliven Null-broths. The last were a recent development, arising from the monsters' enlightenment. Before the angels waved a wand over them, their height of gourmet pleasure was a still moving and fear-filled feast. Now, the foremost amongst them craved culinary fireworks in their mouths as well, the stronger the better. Guy had heard rumours that they actually sent trusted humans far afield, even over the sea, in search of new and piquant tastes. He likewise reported the Null-King eating garlic by the pail-full, and a red rain of chillies showered down upon the mothers as a treat.

Well, Oglethorpe wished them 'bon appetit' indeed. It

made him chortle – or would have if his face weren't on fire from the heat and his nose in revolt – that their dinners should be the instrument of their downfall. They should have stuck to plain honest rations like he did – and his father before him. Bread and cheese and the occasional pheasant had been good enough for Sir Theophilus, senior, even in his glory days of knighthoods and command of the entire English infantry. And if it was good enough for *him*, it was good enough for them – and anyone. Who did these monsters think they were? Bloody snobs!

Oglethorpe then paused, puzzled, to wonder how it should be his dear, fierce, departed father came to be telling the Null off when he'd never so much as sighted them. But then he gave up the paradox as too much trouble and promissory of a headache. It was just another item on the Null charge sheet, needing no justification from feeble 'Reason', thank you very much.

He saw what he wanted, shimmering like the Grail through oily air. A slave was pounding away at it, reducing what looked like mint to a paste. Oglethorpe shook him off it and the mint out. The pestle was taken too, snatched from shocked hands.

He studied his trophy. It would do, at a pinch, even if not perfect. This one was a shade too lady-like for what he had in mind.

'Bigger!' he told the ex-user. 'I want a bigger one, if you don't mind.'

He did. He wanted his mortar and pestle back and to get on. He tried to take it. Oglethorpe knocked him down into the pool of mint puree.

The one thing Oglethorpe wasn't expecting was tears. They touched his heart where no other response, be it pleas or resistance, would. He reached down to restore his victim to his feet.

'There, there,' he said. 'I'm sorry. I should have taken my ring off first. Don't worry: it'll heal . . .'

Amidst all the contrition he almost forgot his mission.

When he recalled it and looked up from comforting and applying a cold compress of lettuce to the wound, the nearby menials flinched back.

'Look,' he told them, 'I'm not a *bad* man. I just want a bigger mortar. Get it and I'll be gorn . . .'

He mimicked *bigger* – everything from expanding parts to windmills of the arms. The audience took it all in, focusing on groin or air as directed, but could make nothing of it. They just stood there catching flies – of which there were no shortage. In the end – which should have been the sensible beginning – he had to set down the no-good mortar and pestle and signify their enlargement with both hands.

They got it but he didn't. A spokesman slave – and thus the long sought for but now too late promising material for his Spartacist project – stepped forward. He said '*No*', as clear as one could wish.

Perhaps Theophilus should have been pleased. A bit of *spirit* was what he'd been looking for – but this was the wrong time and the wrong place. Oglethorpe purpled to almost Null proportions.

'Are you *bandying* words with me? Y*ou* . . . you licker of monster's arses, you carnivore of your own kind. I'll teach you to . . .'

But the instruction was coming all the other way. The slave, a big lad, stepped forward.

At long last some backbone – but only a sickening mirror version of it. Here was a hog saying '*three cheers for the slaughterman!*' An African chasing along the beach after the slavers' ship, crying '*don't leave me!*'

It served to anger Oglethorpe still more. If something didn't love itself, a nation no less than a man, it had no business *being* and should quit the stage.

'Oh, so '*No*', is it?' he roared, careless of fetching Null attention. 'A bloody '*No*', eh?'

'Yes. And yes,' confirmed the slave. 'It is for the beautiful ones, and their joy. You must not lessen our love.' Then, employing the element of surprise, he successfully snatched the mortar back.

Oglethorpe gasped – and then was on him, like a Dutchman on a boy. They rolled around in the gritty grease, a blur of red and pink. The rest spectated, too broken to even assist, blank faced at the all the *grrrs* and curses.

It was Theophilus who emerged first, minus wig and two teeth. The slave stayed down, enjoying a well-earned rest.

'God save me, but I *like* him!' a grinning victor told the crowd, just a touch ironically, even as he booted the fallen – just to make sure. 'Now, about that other mortar . . .'

It was brought to him, out from some obscure storage, bucket-sized and a behemoth of the breed: just the job. Theophilus took it with thanks.

Their faces crumpled as they handed it over, because a means of service was being perverted from its true vocation. They mourned it like a lost chance.

Again, weak-willed Oglethorpe sympathised, despite himself. He'd far rather put a sword in someone – for then there was an end of things – than hurt their feelings. He was subtle enough to know that invisible wounds can be by far the worst.

He also hated guilt. It was one of his major grievances against religion as he'd encountered it. '*In the beginning was the Word*', they'd always told him – and the boy Theophilus discovered that for the most part that word was '*no!*'. Fortunately, he'd had the strength to shrug off the killing tendrils of the C of E and came to know a more convivial God. Whenever they set to, Joanna always turned the picture of the Madonna to the wall – and he thought that showed respect enough. The Deity saw us naked and on the toilet and was surely past all shocking. In Oglethorpe's theology guilt belonged exclusively to the crueller sins.

So now he rejected it. He hadn't ordered it: the inner flunkey should take it away.

'You've only got yourself to blame,' he told the long-faced mourners as he left, letting them in on his earlier thoughts. 'If you turn yourself into sheep, you should expect wolves to call by!'

Then, adding insult to injury, he even took their few, tiny windows with him, prising them from the wall with a seax knife, enabling a cleansing air to waft into the kitchen from the world outside. It didn't take him long, for he getting practised by now. The lights were going out all over Null-Paris.

Bathie caught Oglethorpe red-handed – and then red-faced – in stealing their skylight. His sawing and grunting, perched atop a makeshift stepladder, could be heard half the corridor away.

By contrast, she could enter a room silently when she wanted, the upshot of a Fruntierfolke upbringing. On feast and birthdays their elders would await the children's arrival, faces to the wall. If their entrance was detected then they were sent away hungry and without. She'd soon learned. Once, she'd gotten right to the heart – via three incisions into sentries – of a Christian camp, before anyone so much as raised a peep. To her had been given the honour of felling the crucifix at its centre.

The first Oglethorpe knew of it was her cough and her eyes looking right up (and getting right up) his nose.

'What are you doing?'

That much was obvious. He'd hacked the secreted fixate from three edges of the pane and was murdering the fourth. What she really meant was '*Why?*'

Oglethorpe carried on sawing, puffed by having to extend his arms, robbed of dignity by being on unsteady tip-toes.

'Actually,' he said, in-between breaths, 'that's a bit of a long story . . .'

Bathie looked alarmed. 'Is it? Oh, well, forget it then.'

That wasn't the expected response. He looked down at her, at the risk of all stability. Only the bite of the knife into Null spit was maintaining him.

There was no outward sign to signify it but the Lady Bathie

had long dispensed with *long stories*. The one defining decision of her life was made, leaving no need for any others. The brick-faced man was a friend of Guy's. Until that changed she had no need to know more. Whether Oglethorpe lusted after windows or married a Null, she was free to ignore it if she chose. She chose.

Such glorious freedom left her at liberty to grapple with inner demons, confident the outer perimeter was well defended, even better than when she was a child of the Fruntierfolke. With it came marvellous dividends in terms of peace of mind. Her headaches and day-mares, symptoms of the moody magic within, were almost gone away. Every day, in her heart, she thanked Blades – and Guy – for it.

Oglethorpe should have thanked them too, had he but known. Bathie's forbearance spared him from explanations he wasn't ready to give. He just wished all women were so understanding. If only they – and everyone, come to that – would accept that life *forced* you into eccentricities sometimes, then the world would be a happier place. Having to explain them made things twice as bad . . .

'Er, right,' he said, as the pane came free and he lowered it down into captivity. 'So just . . . trust me.'

She looked up at him again. Two points of black loomed out of a pale island set in a stormy sea of frizz.

'I do,' she confirmed, simply.

Oglethorpe was taken aback again.

'*Do* you?'

'I do.'

'Why?'

'No reason.'

There was a lot else to think of, like getting down man and glass intact, but Theophilus's inner concern still outweighed all.

'Well, *don't*,' he begged her.

'Why not?'

For the second time in two days, the Oglethorpian conscience had gotten out of its cage without permission. He liked Guy – but he also dangerously liked the woman beneath him – and rather fancied having her that way on a regular basis. True, the individual components were unpromising: those almost mannish eyebrows, the sheet-white skin, the drip-pan of her lips, the minimal chin, all lacked appeal. But oh, the overall effect: an unquestionable trouser-tightener. Though it had been ages since he'd danced the mattress-pavane, though he would dearly love for her to study his bedroom ceiling, he knew he should resist. But there again, there were so many things he *should* do . . .

'Just don't!' And then in desperation. 'Look, I say it as a *friend* . . .'

Bathie wasn't worried.

'All right. But that means I'll have to ask why you've stolen our glass. I liked it there. At night you could sit and watch the stars. They reminded me that not all the world's like here.'

This last was soaked in distaste. She meant the Null and all their works.

'I'll put a tarpaulin up,' he said plaintively. 'you won't get rained on . . .' In fact, Oglethorpe was between a rock and a hard place, caught betwixt mission and the call of the loins. 'I *can* explain . . .'

'Go on then . . .'

He was down now, in more ways than one. She'd won, right had won, his cock had lost, though it still stood in the field. Oglethorpe didn't approve.

'All right, all *right*, damn you,' he said, stomping off glass in hand. 'Bloody well trust me then!'

She always had. Within minutes Bathie forgot anything had ever happened. With Oglethorpe though, it would take a great deal longer, and much energetic grinding in the privacy of his room.

'You can run,' she scolded, 'but you cannot . . .'

'Hide,' said the resigned old man, quite deliberately,

spitefully, spoiling the angel's valediction. So she scorched him.

Sir Tusker Ambassador took a last swift tour of his beloved *Perfidious Garden*, dressed in a new scarlet coat of flames. His arms flapped to beat out the fire but only served to fan it. Plants (including the hideous tub-thriving shrub Guy had presented, unexplained, as a *god-strangler*) ignited as he passed. It was *most* amusing.

Or rather it would have been, until the recent end to epochs of smiles and whimsy. Now days arrived lead-booted with the disgusting need for *care* and *concentration* – and insects that answered back. The word *caution* had entered the angelic vocabulary. It was all completely sick-making.

Further off, some of the household had been taken hostage. Clumps of singed people were gathered for discourse. They seemed little honoured by the fact, which quite killed all sympathy for their plight. Those still in possession of tongues or minds were told to employ them, for the sakes of their children.

'Why? Who? What do we want?' their guardian angels asked – and receiving no good answer cursed them. They were felled in neat swathes beside the charcoal-covered flowerbeds.

Then the presiding angel, whose game and quest this was, flew a circuit of burning Ambassador Hall and thought ruin upon those who sought refuge in the maze. The hedgerows grew razor-edged and closed in. She scented the ensuing juice.

There *was* something.

Next, the Hall at last surrendered, its roof timbers collapsing into the burning midst. Nearby stables took fire too, propelling sleek horses out, ablaze, on their last and best race. New aromas to add to the melange. She sampled it once more.

Again, the merest hint of . . . whatever it was they wanted.

'Ulalalalalalalalalalalalalalalalalalalalalalalalalal . . .' The unending wry-cry of martial angels. Her sisters rallied to her in the sky like white crows.

'There is. There *is*!' she exulted. 'I scent it.'

It was actually the mere ghost of something familiar and

disturbing: the whiff of alarm at the very edge of comprehension – though that was far indeed in angel terms

They weren't sure *what* they hunted; only that they *would* know when they saw it. Any life-form which has beheld the divine is instantly aware if threatened, even if it cannot tell how. No matter what the later life-path, one solitary searing glance of the effulgent light illuminates for ever. She was sure. The *disobedience* had passed this way. They were on its trail.

But there was paradox – and limitation. Golden bile rose in her slim throat at the very thought. They could draw close but not too close. To be overly successful was to invite extinction. Dull dogs from the other party, emanations of that *other* persuasion, mirrored and . . . dogged their search.

Each time the crown of success was raised aloft, then negation arrived: a willing exchange of atom for atom till both were gone in pain and regret. It was a moot point whether an angel could truly die, but of the lost ones there remained not a trace, not in any of the perceivable realms. If that wasn't the end then it was as good as. No more laughter and caprice for *them*. The angels quivered in thinking of that and held back.

Therefore they merely scouted now, their ambition just to sight the regrettable thing from afar. That alone should suffice. They were confident the merest *look* at it on that happy day would do the trick. Boundless anxiety had brewed hatred enough to fry defiance at any distance.

However, the spoor was ambivalent, gossamer-fragile – though followable with care. *Care*. Again that word: that *concern*. She loathed it – and looked nervously about.

Soon enough they would fly on, but first the angel had seen survivors amongst the greenhouses: sweet opportunity to break ancient vows.

Angels did not kill Ambassadors, not *ever*, as per the promises of old. Except today. Today was a special, *excusing*, day; absolutely gasping out for consolatory pleasures.

Molten glass fell as rain. The greenhouses' final crop was screams.

The sun smiled on Guy's mission in the same way as it did the City. Broiling weather made life in Null-Paris like residing within a well-matured corpse. The Free-human variety of maggot writhing inside longed for a breath of fresh air.

In such circumstances even the withdrawn Blades could be tempted out of its muggy, soup-like, atmosphere of part Null, part sweat and part fear. When perspiration coiled over the brow even at break of day, then it was a golden opportunity to drag the passive god-king off his knees and abroad. Guy looked for every chance to speed the moment of *admission*. He hoped a wider horizon might prompt confession of the truth.

When work on the City began, soon after the angels had shone light into previously sleeping parts of the Null brain, monsterdom had no experience of construction. Till then, right from when the world was hatched from the mythical Null mother that was the night sky, the intimacy of the sleeping pile was the limit of their skill. Now they aspired to reach that sky and kiss it. Tottering structures testified to that ambition – and also to its virginal inexperience. The remains of early experiments which had succumbed to gravity and poor workmanship were strewn around the older parts of Paris. Elegant long bones, once the scaffolding for bulbous Null muscle, protruded from many a ruin, a joyful sight for humans to behold. Here then, as much as anywhere in Hell, was a pleasant place to stroll.

That age of innocence had also been unaware that rivers had moods. The first risen-Null-King set his hive beside the Seine, blithely confident it would stay put, precisely as he'd first glimpsed it. Then floods had come, and natural shifts in the river's route. What was the *Ile de la Cîté* in Blades's world, a spit of tempting dry land athwart the water, turned out to wax and wane with the river's munificence. It had amused Guy from the very beginning to see Null structures soggy about the base and ripe to fall. It reminded him, though presently trapped in Null arrogance and power, that the monsters were fallible. In New-Godalming, Wey-side structures sank deep piles and built up revetments, intending to see out the long run, whereas the Null vainly reinforced failure, adding good material to bad, just enough to last the passing day or current inundation. He and all humans who beheld it took comfort in the true order of nature winning out. Only remove the angels' restraining hand, or put a rifle in mankind's hand, and you could soon have these shaky structures down. One decent *boot* should do. Down here amongst the sodden ruins that glorious day seemed more than just a dream. It floated like a mirage on the edge of vision.

It was also cooler beside the water; which was another reason for coming. The Null did not care for it greatly. Possibly the sights and gnats disagreed with them – for it was long observed that, paradoxically enough, monster skin was thinner and more sensitive than the human variety. In New-Wessex and Bladian heydays, human torturers had used that fact to great effect.

So, they directed their feet to beside the still waters, to where offshoot pools gathered round the remains they had undermined. Toppled towers split the waters like islands, creating rapids in one place and tranquillity in another. As they drew nearer, even the grass seemed cooler underfoot, the air less molten. The Null thinned out almost to absence. Here was as good as it got. And that was all the inspiration Guy needed to try once more.

He'd rehearsed his argument in the long hours of the night, when even he and Bathie had had enough of each other but sleep would not come, and the air in their room just *sat* there, slothful, as screams and weeping seeped in from outside. For the most part, even risen-Null still slept the night away, but some more advanced types would go padding past the humans' quarters at all hours, or else chime songs of praise to the sky. Afterwards, the beasts were usually moved to hunger – or maybe that was part of the worship – and then the soundtrack of their hunt and consummation was hardly a lullaby either.

313

Thus, if preparation meant anything, and Guy's mind was likened to a sword, then it had been applied to the grindstone till a feather falling thereon would divide in two. He was so sharp he hardly dared think, for fear of cutting himself.

They were seated on a sagging ruin jutting out into a little tributary. Their legs projected out over the void and Bathie hoisted up her dress to make full use of the air and freedom. Blades averted his eyes, with periodic success. Hunter and Nicolo and Oglethorpe were elsewhere, orbiting around each other, prisoners of mutual gravity and secret missions, did they but know it.

'So,' concluded Guy, 'you concede the Almighty graciously sent us a representative of his essence, in order that we might have a perfect picture of what was previously only hinted at, viz: his definitive will for us.'

Blades was all caution. He wasn't going to lightly risk everything gained in long days of bashing hard Caprisi church floors.

'Yes . . . that is the orthodox position – and the meaning of the Nicene Creed. "*God from God, Light from Light, true God from true God . . .*"'

'Which,' Guy dared to butt in, since he'd had enough of the dim labyrinth of this *Nicene* business before, 'could as well refer to a king as to this *Christ* person of the Christians, could it not?'

'It could,' Blades conceded, or so Guy thought, in a flare of hope. 'Insofar as Christ was a king. King of the *Jews*, I'll grant you . . .'

It was the barest toe-hold but the Ambassador put his boot in.

'*And* other nations,' he agreed. 'Like New-Wessex . . .'

'No,' snapped the shrouded god-king. 'Or yes. He is king of there too – only you don't know him. Or only some of you do.'

'Slaves,' said Bathie, dismissively. 'Wild dwellers. Atheists!'

The Fruntierfolke, in general, had a down on the Christian heretics. Abject captives of infuriatingly contradictory commandments, the wretches fought like mad things when

314

molested in the Wild but went all limp-wristed and peaceable in captivity. Fungoids feared Christians but no one else needed to. Broadly speaking, martyrdom was the kindest all-round option for them.

For herself, Bathie could hardly bear their current testing or to hear Blades spout slave philosophy, and Guy was required to secure and buy her silence with pep-talks and bed-fun. Bathie's faith was simple and unreflective, a slender tower of some beauty but untried foundations. At the moment Blades was having a go at them with a pickaxe. So, for the present, she preferred her own thoughts whilst in his company, and distraction in fantasy. However, his last statement had barged its way into her head and demanded instant denial.

'"*Atheists*"?' Blades denied in turn. 'How can they – we – be "*atheists*" when we bow to the living God and . . .'

'No. *Balls*!' she said, thigh to thigh with the god-king, turning to face him and forgetting herself. He, however, continued eyes front. 'I mean, how can people worship a God that won't show himself? And all those nudges and winks via a big book you can justify anything from? No!' She slapped the part stone, part panel, structure they sat upon. 'That lot don't believe in anything: it's just a smoke screen for *mildness*!'

Blades almost stood corrected – and Guy aborted his own rebuke. Maybe shock treatment was the answer; not that he would have dared, but Bathie was a holy rule to herself.

Less happily, Blades almost stood *up*. He had no good answer but he could always just *go*.

She hung on to his sleeve; unyielding enough to tear its wretched material. In that awkward, half-raised, half crouched position, he could see right down her cleavage, which was the situation's only attraction, though a considerable one. She was as flat chested as a boy and yet. . . . Blades was beguiled. He kept calm, though assuming a look of grievance. He even consented to slowly descend.

Guy exhaled. A reprimand could not be avoided but the debate was still alive. He would continue with its kiss of life once the storm clouds passed.

Blades tugged free his sundered sleeve. A relic was left in Bathie's hand.

'You *are* a forward *madame*, ain't you?' he told her, and, taking marital-telepathic cue from Guy, she wilted demurely under the lash. 'If you *truly* regarded me as a god-king, you wouldn't maul and abuse me. And if I *was* one – which I ain't – or your husband for that matter – then I'd up and give you a bloody good . . .'

The notions were blossoming too abundantly for him to give safe voice to. He wanted to take them away to pour over in privacy. Nor was it the only thing he wanted to *take*, god-king style. He could no longer trust his tongue – or at least not in the vocal sense . . .

'Just *don't* do it again!' he said, and Bathie cringed and coquetted perfectly. Doubtless there'd be a price for Guy to pay, but right now she'd handed him the right ammunition. The god-king-in-disguise proved to have retained god-kingly urges.

'And *so*,' Guy persevered, as though summarising a proven case – always a sound move against wavering foes, 'God sends representations of himself to Earth . . .'

'He does,' Blades echoed.

'And you are he.'

'I am not.'

'Or one such.'

'There is none such. Christ is our saviour. We need no other.'

They were surprised by a fish breaking the waterline below them. Even less anticipated, a Null head appeared in pursuit, rocketing from submersion to take the doomed creature. The master-race were sometimes known to toy with lesser meat, just to keep their hunting skills in. It joyfully crumbled the fish between rolling jaws, spraying blood and water up as far as the spectators. They involuntarily drew back their legs – and Guy saw Blades's eye track the motion of one particular pair.

Presumably, all they had said and done could have been observed and overheard: for the Null liked to prove the

316

strength of their will and lungs by lingering long under water. Yet, though there was disquiet in that, Guy's concern was only momentary; like the monster's presence itself. It directly swam away with bold strokes, parting the water Moses-style, chiming amusement at their fear. Cooling reason returned in its wake. Even had that particular Null been one of the few that understood *meat*-speak, it was barely conceivable that theological agonising would be reported back. *Meat* sentience was only grudgingly accepted by Null thinkers at all. Therefore, a lower animal's philosophical perspectives would hardly command rapt attention.

'See?' gestured Guy at the retreating purple back – which was redundant for he could tell Blades had. '*There* is your remit and justification here. *That* is why the Almighty breathed into you and brought you here as His vicegerent. You lifted us out from under them once and now the opportunity comes again.'

Blades only shook his snowy head.

'And from worse oppressors still.' Guy didn't name the angels, not wishing to try his luck and their lovely absence, but the god-king must know – as he secretly knew everything. He could not deny it: he had seen them in action.

Desperation now entered Guy's voice; a shocking indecency in an Ambassador, excused by his sense of urgency. 'Look, I beg you: I've pondered the matter long and hard. Consider the angels. It's been proved. They cannot harm you or those who seek you in faith. There are *signs* for those who would see. You are our weapon, the sword of God!'

'No,' the reply was firm. 'There is no God but God and Christ is his son.'

'But . . .'

The old man – or divine spark – chopped down with one arm. 'No!' He reached across with the other to pinch his ageing flesh. 'No. Look: this is just a bag of bones, a bladder of blood. The only breath of God in me is the same as you have. Worship some emperor if you must, but don't mistake him for me. I've had enough of nonsense, boy. I crave for *sense*. And

317

I've found it. Leave me be to be with it.'

Guy raised a finger to raise a point – but Blades wouldn't have it. He seized the digit in one claw, muzzling with sympathetic magic the doubtless silky words to come.

'No, Guy. You won't tempt me; you won't. "*Get thee behind me, Satan*". Which gives me an idea. I mean, how else can I put it plain enough to you when you won't listen to me? Lord save us, man, must I draw you *pictures*? *I-am-no-god*. What words will get through to you? Well listen to this, Guy Ambassador: I'm just plain old Thomas Blades, wicked curate of the "Church of England by law established": less than you, in fact. So, I tell you most solemnly and *beg* you to take heed: my arse is *just* as pink as yours!'

Bathie had only heard Guy sigh once before: on their wedding night when all went wrong and nothing wonderful would work. Now she heard the awful sound again and saw her husband, her proper-now and only-ever husband, perched high and dry in Null-land, looking diminished.

So that made her mind up.

'And, in the fifth chamber, it is customary to rend at least one garment, for here, encased in a filigree web of gold and jet, lies that portion of His (He needs not our blessing) sleeve detached at the *Moment of Transmogrification*, our second *Great Time of Testing*.

'For, in symbolically tearing our apparel, we piously hope for some tiny and retrospective participation in that holy moment; that crossroads of Revelation History, when humanity (or one humble female delegate thereof, who dared for us all) seized a prize which is beyond compare – namely, to know that the mind of the universe is breathing the same air as ourselves.

'Let the unbelievers, the Christians and other degraded, broken reeds, decry the fires that followed. The truly devout declare they only forged us the stronger. The smith may strike

hard and the sparks may fly but out of that suffering comes
steel!

'As to the ensuing massacres . . .'

*A Pilgrim's Compendium of Wisdom for those who would Glorify
their Earthly Life with the Jewels of Piety and the Silken Raiment
of Prayer*

Thane Brixi of New-Compton in the Province of Wessex,
United England. In the Year of Our Deliverance 457 A.B.

Bathie sat before the jagged shard of mirror that the Null had
provided in mocking consideration, fighting the tangle of her
hair. She took out the pain of all her contradictions on its
knots and the brush's insufficiency. A track of recent tears
further whitened her pale face.

She was a loyal wife – none more so – above and beyond the
strictures of the Fruntierfolke who fostered such virtues ('*A
house divided against itself cannot stand – and the fungoids will get
in*'), but there were even higher commandments for her to
obey.

To have so recently gained him, in joint entirety, only to
risk losing him so soon, tore her inside, worse than a Null's
ravishment. Yet time and again, for all she fled her
conclusions, Bathie was drawn back again, like a dog on a
leash, to the correct course.

Guy – who typified humanity and certainly all that was best
in it – lacked something that would make him and them all
they might be. Therefore, her greatest gift to her husband
would be to give him it: better even than giving herself. That
much she already did but the gale of events was blowing away
their too short, too sweet, interlude. It had become her
inescapable duty to risk all to gain all.

Over the scritch-scratching of the war against her crowning
glory, she heard a disturbance from the adjoining chamber:

Oglethorpe's designated space. It was surely a sign, and she thanked Blades for it (the same cruel bastard of a deity that forced her to this), for making things so clear.

The mirror was easily dislodged from its slave-botched setting. That sad breed had no experience or need for them and so had fixed it awkwardly, at an uncomfortable angle to use. Its loss would be the least of her sacrifices.

Oglethorpe was on the floor, winded by his tumble from the ceiling where he had been murdering another window. Still dazed, he was shocked by her presence when she leant over to present him with a second pane to match the one he held. It was accepted before he properly registered who was giving.

When he did, he sprang up, ever the gentleman, to make a bow. The razor-edged glass tucked under one arm hindered his fluidity, but the thought was there.

'Madame Bathesheba,' he boomed. 'And what can I do for *you*?'

'What you were thinking of doing,' she said, simply and decisively, every inch a savage mud-haired nobleman's daughter.

Disloyal ambitions reared up momentarily in the Oglethorpian breast. True, he'd been without so much as a hint of a Joanna for too long, but Guy was his friend and the wench was married. He slapped the ignoble impulse down.

'Refresh me memory . . .' he said, uncertainly.

Bathie wouldn't be drawn – for the simple reason she wasn't sure. It was something to do with glass and wicked grins, that much seemed clear. The balance didn't matter. She had complete confidence it would be good and exactly what she had in mind.

'No, not *that*!' Bathie could read straightforward men like posters. The image of delving hands and descending dresses had lightning-flashed across his eyes. 'I meant your *deep* desires. Do what you're planning,' she told him. 'Do it. All of it.'

Oglethorpe recoiled. How could she know? It was witchcraft. His parts withered even as a wilder hope soared.

320

'May I?'

It was better than that.

'You must!' she ordered.

Oglethorpe was brought up – strictly – to oblige ladies. He took her request as a pillow placed on the face of all his lingering doubts.

'As you command, madame,' he replied, and bowed again, extra low to conceal a wolfish smile.

In the war of feathers, Nicolo's hand but not heart was in it. As befitted an Ambassador, no one, least of all the Null or their human lackeys, would have been able to perceive a reduction in zeal, but *he* could feel it. The sight on the way in, of the Null-King's personal veal crates, crammed with immobile children, had quite robbed him of delight.

So, as his arm and quill tussled with that of the slave-interpreter's, contesting the precise line of surrendered Kent upon the map, only brute strength was his to call on. Cunning sat in its tent and sulked like Achilles. If it had been out there in the field with his other forces he might have saved New-Canterbury from occupation. As it was, aptly purple ink incorporated it in the freshly ceded overseas province of Null-France.

Nicolo briefly saw monsters defiling the high altar of the Imperial Cathedral there; that same violet-stained stone, dyed and hallowed by centuries of Null sacrifice, he'd worshipped before as a boy. Now, in a turning of tables and his mind's eye, he beheld those humans not across the Medway sharp enough, led to it to be made a holocaust and feast of. The claw would be on the other foot and all *his* own doing – which proved ample consolation.

However, although there was pleasure in treachery and the same thrill in naked ambition as with other moments of nudity, it was still a relief to focus again on the lesser purgatory before him. Even the red-floored throne room, the Null in

321

splendour and his retinue of over-sized braves and pathics in all their revolting reality, were an improvement on the horrors a decent imagination could construct.

Nicolo stepped – almost staggered – back from the map table. The Null-slave looked for instruction, as it did for almost everything bar breathing, and got permission to withdraw as well. The map, flayed and dried skin from a predictable source, was at peace as they had left it, a pierced and blotted and drawn-on-to-death representation of a changed world.

Nicolo Ambassador bowed to signify agreement, for the shaking of hands was not recognised by the *meat*-eaters. A dismissive wave was all he received in return – in addition to a free hand, some power and much *drama*. Especially the drama. He could almost taste that, a lovely antidote to present bitterness. Now he would live in *interesting* times and be at their forefront, at the sunny point of maximum intensity where he always wanted to be, and not in the shadow of an overly charming brother.

All the same, he wished the furtive side-door exit didn't take him past the cages of penned infants. Their eyes, all un-knowingly, accused him.

Of what? he asked them in fantasy. *Is it a crime to apply spurs to the horse of history?* Of course not. Silly boys and girls, what did they know? Very little, was the truthful answer, given they'd spent their post-weaning years penned like cattle.

Yet something unaccountable led him to shun their gaze as he left, crab-style backwards like a good courtier. Instead, Nicolo departed by the main door and thus met Bathie.

Shame is one of the hardest encumbrances to shed, even for an Ambassador. It lubricates every action and expression, making them overly facile. Nicolo's sliding from the Throne-room, his 'pleasure' in encountering his sister-in-law, even his sly smile; they were all overdone.

Bathie *knew* at that moment. The remedy was at hand. Her garter held up a stiletto blade as well as her white stocking. There could have been an end of it there. If she'd prevailed,

322

using surprise and what her family taught her, that was one way. If, perchance, dear Nicolo won the day, then Guy would soon eclipse it. She couldn't lose.

Something advised her otherwise. Reason had little scarred her life so far and continued to bless Bathie with absence. Therefore, her hand reached not underskirt but outward. All she planted on Nicolo's thin chest was five restraining fingers.

Nicolo looked down at them and then up. His own hands was still upon the double doors. Null were waiting to come in. They snorted like the steam trains of lost memory at being delayed by humans.

'He is a *good* man' she told him, not unfriendly, more like a sister than enemy. 'He doesn't deserve this.'

Nicolo had never contested Guy's sweet nature, merely his position. He opened his mouth. Bathie hushed her brother-in-law, a small spread hand still pinning him inconveniently.

'Think about it,' she said. 'That's all I ask. Just *think* about it . . .'

The leading Null would wait no more and leaned in to brush them both aside, guest-*meat* or no. They were hammered against the far wall but neither so much as noticed or took offence. Bathie's eyes still had Nicolo's.

'All I ask . . .' she repeated.

Nicolo bowed for a second time, but more meaningfully.

'And you shall have it,' he confirmed.

Blades slept on, oblivious to his visitor. Nicolo composed himself and then knelt and prayed.

'My *point* is,' he informed the Deity – who surely already knew – and thus largely for his own benefit, '*that beyond the great truth; namely that there's an universal sentience and order which we inadequately perceive as "God", there are lesser truths – which being true, by definition emanate from God. I mean, if you're not truth, what's the use of you? Nothing: you might as well worship the Null, mightn't you? Anyway, I accordingly take the lesser truths as additional commandments. It follows, doesn't it? I reckon I'm on sound ground there. We're talking about the observed truths of life: things you pick up and then can't really deny – not if you're honest. Like that we only have one word in this life and when we break it it's gone forever. Even if no one else knows and continues to trust us, we're aware of it and know every vow and show of integrity is hollow. Also, one day we'll be called on to give account of ourselves before a just judge. Ah – but is he also a merciful judge? Surely you're more merciful than me – and I can forgive all sorts of terrible things. I know the pressure people are under. But if you're less merciful than me, it's a mockery, because I can't be better than God, can I? That's nonsense and blasphemous. So, there's where it all falls down for me. Otherwise I'd stay on the straight and narrow and never stray and be happy with boring virtue and just a few wives and honouring promises. There'd be cause then, Lord. I must have cause, as you well know, since you oversee me . . .'*

He paused as the 'Lord' snored and turned over, restless in some dream.

'. . . even presently, in your current uninspiring shape. You put us to the test, I understand that, even though we're not allowed to return the compliment. You make the rules: I'm not arguing. True, I'd prefer a golden messiah: a fuller effusion of your essence than a cantankerous old scarecrow – but maybe that will be so when you split the shell – if you ever do. We must be patient and trusting, I know, but honestly . . .'

Nicolo recalled himself, not wishing to use up his portion of exclusive divine attention in repeating trifles. God knew all this and must hear it all the time. The 'Summa Nicolo' was more important.

'What worries me, as you're doubtless aware, is that along with one word, it seems to me a man only has one chance – one paramount chance – per life. I put those two things in the balance and they weigh exactly the same. Chance versus word: who's to choose? Where's the guidance? I mean, with me it's excitement and stirring things up and having people respect me, but everyone's different. Maybe for some it's a crack at some life-long object of

324

lust. Your life forks like her legs – you can go up one way or the other. Do you stick by your vow or stick it where you fancy, five times a night and all three ways and never forget it? Which is better – a lifetime of regret over missed opportunities but a reward after – or gilded recollection till you die, but then a reckoning to come – for coming, ho ho? I mean, it's a quandary, innit?'

There came no reply. Blades the curate and alleged god-king pummelled his pillow without knowing, a nocturnal Zeus hurling thunderbolts down from zzzz-Olympus.

Nicolo saw no other option than to press on. Sometimes the Gates of Heaven required storming with prayer.

'Fortunately, it's not women with me. Like Bathesheba for instance; she looks a lively piece; I dare say she'd be fun, but Guy does so dote on her. What's the point of causing all that pain for at most an hour or two of passion? Would it be kind? Would it be pretty? No. And she's right: he is a good man – if a bloody nuisance from my perspective. No. I have the harem and the mother-of-my-children back home and that's sufficient . . .'

Not any more it wasn't. They were black husks adorning the gardens of Ambassador Hall after the angels flew away, but the Almighty withheld that distracting news from him for the time being.

'I'll admit to you, since you know full well, that my failing is fun. If you'll excuse me saying, I don't think you've put enough of it in the world. The way I see it is that my valid role is to insert some more. Move things along, so to speak. Drama's the word I use but that's not precise. Do you get what I mean?'

Surely the silence did: no need to labour the point..

*'So what's the answer? **Now** versus postponed pleasure. Opportunity versus restraint. Is there a one-fits-all answer? What do you say?'*

Nothing. Not a peep or sign.

'A vigil, is that it? I remember a priest once told me that big issues are settled by vigils. Is that your requirement? If I pray long enough will you insert an answer along the disused tunnels of my mind?'

There came no guarantee, but since Nicolo never considered 'vigils' from one year's end to the next, he felt confident the thought must have been planted from outside.

'*Very well; thy will be done.*'

And it was. Nicolo remained on his knees throughout a long night, in growing pain and discomfort, and as dawn withdrew the mercy of night from the fullness of Null-Paris, he received his answer, through subtle channels. The ache of knees and toes and shins fled away, forgotten.

He applied fingertips to lips and blew a kiss of thanks to the ceiling – for to direct it at the curate in his wrecked bed was stretching faith too far. The scarecrow was only a conduit for God after all. His proximity had served its purpose.

Nicolo arose – creaking. Now he *knew* and could be glad again.

And soon after – directly following the next shoe inspection – Guy knew too, for he nightly dusted the god-king's threshold with chalk.

The last shards were turned to powder and Theophilus had started to cough blood. Obviously, the kerchief corners stuffed up each nostril during the work had been inadequate protection. To borrow the immortal words of the London goldsmith who'd underwritten his debts (until they threatened to ruin them both): *Enough already*!

Oglethorpe paused and puzzled. He ought to be thoroughly pleased. And yet . . . He gingerly looked within. No, he wasn't even halfway up the tankard with pleasure. Now why should that be? After only momentary hesitation, he leaned further over the internal parapet to find out.

All was ready and it would work – and, no, it was not *enough*. Oglethorpe sat down through sheer weariness, as though suddenly aged.

He was also bemused. This day was good, or it soon would

be. In fact it might never be bettered – and that thought only put Theophilus's head deeper into his hands.

He fought a desperate rearguard action – his very favourite type – against it but the revelation was too strong to refuse delivery. Its frigid message crawled all over him like some giant parasitic centipede. When positioned, it paused – and then pounced, and sank beneath the skin and *became* him. There could be no argument with unalloyed truth. Theophilus Oglethorpe understood now, beyond contradiction. The message was like an American visitor: too large and loud to ignore. It howled at him that all the years beyond, assuming he was spared, would only be repetition at best.

Why hadn't he realised it earlier? Why all the storm and stress and *put-a-brave-face-on-it* of previous years? Was it something in the air of this other world that invigorated the brain and made things suddenly clarified and crystal clear?

Oglethorpe scented it to test. He detected just his own unbathed body, plus Null-clove, plus *essence d'overcrowding*. So, no, probably not.

Whatever the reason, he was now as convinced as a dervish. The road ahead couldn't be any plainer. It stretched beyond his powers of sight.

Instantly he was scared. Oglethorpe feared neither sword or bullet, for they were only an end to all concerns. Torture perturbed him a bit more, mainly on grounds of dignity, but even that had a finite conclusion. Despair though, that ate men away, worse than cancer. He'd seen it: a ravening beast that never killed but kept on consuming.

An unchangeable son of the North, Theophilus couldn't just shrug his shoulders over the great life cycle and move on, just . . . . accepting. He'd absorbed the wine and lush morals of the warmer south but not its wider assumptions. There had to be a point or – or else there was no point.

Oglethorpe looked out of the – ransacked – window towards the oncoming dawn and pondered the origin of this sudden and awful wisdom. He'd have been quite happy carrying on for decades, ignoring that which he'd always half known, drifting from lost cause to lost cause and risk to risk, without undue reflection. Yet now, even in the Null-generated fug of the City, he was chilled. Someone had draped an icy wet blanket over his shoulders from a great height.

Look on the bright side, Theo, he told himself, taking another hardly-helpful swig of heady New-Wessex wine, *at least you now know what you really want. There's that much to be said for it. To thine own self be true and so on . . .*

He looked up, hollow-eyed, and shook a fist at the donor, whoever they might be, in ironic thanks.

There was nothing else for it. At last he was sure. He had to set down on paper the letter he'd been drafting all his life with his life.

Oglethorpe reached for quill and ink. He barely had time to scrawl '*To whom it may concern*' before there was a rasp (Null internal panelling not being up to hard knocks) on his door. He was heartily glad of the interruption – and doubly so when it proved to be helping hands.

Nicolo sidled in – he never entered a room straight-forwardly; there was always some angle to it – and spread those same hands.

'"*The Null are a disgusting and oppressive race*",' he intoned: one of the first god-king's most famous pronouncements and, ever after, a Bladian profession of faith, '"*I have decided to exterminate them all*."'

Oglethorpe didn't know that but he could hail the sentiments.

'Amen,' he agreed.

'I don't know what you're up to,' Nicolo continued, with a great big *hello-new-friend-well-met* smile, 'but I'd like to assist . . .'

Hunter, listening unsuspected outside, then sheathed his seax knife and went away to tell Guy.

Bathie tried to recall Guy's litany before she commenced. The heat wave encouraged every prevarication to any action, mental or otherwise. She couldn't help but slip-slide down every by-way offered.

Glow – that was it. Ladies *glowed*, men *perspired*, but *sweat* was the preserve of the Null. It glistened on them like a coating, and they loved to lick it off each other as a prelude to buggery.

Well, truth be told, she was emulating them now – speaking purely of the first part, that is. Along with the rest of the humans on the riverbank she was *glowing* like a Null on heat. Even the most languid motions resulted in waves of . . . glow from the hairline down. It was so tempting just to lie beside the cool waters and bask, forgetting there had ever been anything before or that something must follow the moment. Bathie liked oblivion, especially when it fell deep enough to soothe the pressure behind her brow. Then, when even her name was a matter of no concern, unknowingness was oh *so* sweet. During the best visitations, she wished it was forever – so long as there could be one man's company besides, a sort of known-of and nearby entity, a cloud adjacent to her own she could call on when she needed him – which would be often, even in Paradise.

Bathie peeled up the sticky front of her dress, desirous of a little circulating air, and registered the flicker of another sort of desire beside her. The god-king craved a better view yet felt obliged to pretend otherwise. Bathie retained a degree of insecure uncertainty even then, not wishing to be arrogant, but a bold wiggling of her brown toes confirmed the thing beyond doubt.

She felt honoured to be bathed in Bladian attention: especially considering her deviance from classical Wessex ideals of beauty. By those standards she was too pale and staring to merit a top notch match, too tainted by Wild-upbringing for any first rank alliance. Yet destiny – and the Emperor's whim, which amounted to the same thing – had decreed otherwise and she was duly grateful. That *He* should display even a spark of interest too was proof her *wyrd* was woven that way. There was no unpicking it or demanding another style or size, even had she wanted to. Two suns shone upon her that day, one as diffident as the other was scorching, but brothers in power all the same. It was just as she'd thought before: all that was left for her to do was *bask* in their light.

It also so happened that this gift brought all her other passing notions to a workable point. Nicolo, Oglethorpe, even her husband, revolved around the sun-that-was-Blades and a shift in him must be reflected in all their orbits. She might only be the fly-by shooting-star that aroused his blaze anew; she might well be consumed by it and never see the nova produced, but neither could she be absolved from her trajectory. It was destiny: her wyrd, and as meaningless to fight against as the pull of gravity. Blades had explained that particular notion during his previous stay – under his aspect-name of *Newton*, and then left them it in print for all to read and learn. His children had been made well acquainted with the laws he imposed on his Universe, arming them, even down to poor random-educated Bathie, with a richness of analogies to apply to their own little lives. They might have be left in servitude but not in ignorance and the path was clear to those who'd look. Bathie looked and saw. It led clear over the horizon.

So she forced herself and lifted her head. Sweat – *glow* – streaked hair sought to bind her to the ground till she heaved it free. Below, at the muddy river bank, there were Null disporting, splashing water and wrestling in the sheer joy of their strength. She pursed her lips at them. *They* did not know. If they thought of it all, they probably deemed the world a flat disc, an endless playground and hunting preserve, bounded only by water and Humandom. The purple killing-things lived unaware of what bound them to the earth or who set it and them in motion. Monstrous in deed as in thought, knowing neither mother or father, truly they were ignorant bastards . . .

It was a hot day, oblivion continued to wink seductively and there was always tomorrow, but *now* was her time. The moment had arrived, vouched for by instinct, refusing to take no for an answer. And rightly so, for impulse denied entry takes offence and calls less and less often. Some homes: accountant's neat dwellings or the rich mansions of the overburdened, never saw him at all and Fruntierfolke accounted such accursed, preferring even Null and fungoids for neighbours than them.

So, she'd only planned things in broad terms – otherwise Guy would not have been so close by, and Oglethorpe too, to see it: men likely to spoil everything with bravery. Also, if only her too-knowing husband was busy elsewhere, she could have stepped the death-dance and gone to the future with an easier mind. Still, it didn't matter: perfection belonged to God alone. Bathie turned to talk to him.

'I want to show you something.' She'd raised herself on one elbow, leaning close to Blades so that no one else would hear, but looking straight ahead so that her flattened black frizz almost brushed his cheek.

Already, he was alarmed as a rabbit, with just an overlay of arousal.

'What?'

Guy heard that and looked over. The dog-eared cards ceased to be shuffled. His interest seemed casual, but she knew that meant nothing. His scrutiny of the demon on the Way had been casual.

'You'll recognise it when you see it,' she whispered. 'And it's well worth the viewing.'

The god-king shifted a portion so that he could turn and see without touching her.

'Tell me what,' he repeated, but softer than before.

'Come with me and I'll *show* you.'

He exhaled hot air through his nose: old-lady-cautious.

'Will I have seen it before?'

When she wanted to Bathie knew the up-from-under-the-eyebrows look that could raise parts. They were part of the Fruntierfolke pre-nuptial course, given by smiling old wise-women.

'The type, yes, many, many times. But not this one.'

Most unlike him, he caught and held her eye, not happy about it, but hooked on an implacable line.

'This is all a bit sudden.' He was far from refusing delectable gifts, fearful that they might be snatched back, but at the same time . . . 'I mean, I thought you were a faithful . . .' To say the next word would be to queer the pitch. 'Just a bit *sudden*, that's all I'm saying,' he trailed off, weakly.

Bathie gave him another grade one *look*.

'Nothing less than a god-king deserves,' she husked.

For once Blades didn't demur. The stolen cap could fit for a moment or two . . .

'Where?'

She pointed, not looking, eyes only for him.

'There's Null . . .' he protested, his first proper show of doubt.

'They won't harm us; they daren't. They won't even look after the novelty wears off.'

Blades studied the proposal; he studied it like a diligent student.

'There *are* dunes down there . . .' he both observed and suggested.

Bathie rolled on her front and, looking back, slightly raised her hips.

'Smooth, rolling dunes,' she agreed, 'and private little valleys . . .'

Blades's voice was an octave above normal till he whipped it back under control and started again.

'Why . . . ahem . . . er, yes, why don't you show me?'

She nodded. 'I'll lead the way – to start with . . .'

Blades whipped a sideways look at Guy, busy wrangling in theological debate with Hunter. Oglethorpe was with them, contemplating the pair as he would lepers. No one knew – or much cared about – Nicolo's location. They were all absorbed, or pretending to be. There was a fair chance of sidling away, even by the god-king's safe-side calculations.

The two arose, side by side, and descended to the Seine. Bathie's agreed 'trust me' finger signal was received and returned by Guy without another soul knowing.

By the river there were Null, true, but also the promised sand dunes and cosy corners out of sight of anyone bar monsters. Both Bathie and Blades looked around and were glad, though otherwise their purposes diverged. She now desired the first and he the other. Bathie courted company, whilst Blades sought seclusion. A brief conjunction over, two planets went their separate ways.

'Where are you *go-*' he hissed – but it was too late. Bathie strode to the nearest Null who, shocked, stood unprepared to receive her. Water still streamed down purple, akimbo, legs, fresh from lusty swimming.

It realised this was protected *meat*, but such proximity was an insult. Grievance and fury rendered into chimes rained down on her along with a spray of Seine. From the river itself, other Null looked on and were amused.

Blades felt far from joining them and wished himself further still. He stood rooted to the ground, hoping along illogical primeval lines that inertia might be his salvation.

Under the shadow of the Null, claws looming three feet above her, Bathie turned and spoke. 'For you – and us all,' she told Blades – who with tiny, discreet, shakes of the head declined receipt.

As usual, the Null prick was urgent and straight at her. Bathie reached for it and applied all her hopes and hatred.

There were blue sparks and a smell of burning. The Null tore free and retreated with pulsing steps backward, his crotch a black mess. The Seine's waters, toppled into, came as a relief to him before he died.

She'd no assurance the magic would come. It had failed often before, even at times of direst need. Right now, it didn't greatly matter: the slightest affront would have done instead.

Either a girlish glancing blow or killing sorcery served equally to arouse the Null's rage.

In what was the greatest test so far, Bathie stood head bowed and hands clasped before her to meekly await developments. She heard the Null's reviews of her deed and the sound of splashing coming ever closer, but she would not deal with them. That was someone else's job.

'Run!' said Blades – which proved his entire, disappointing, contribution. Indeed, he'd already set an example by going a few paces himself. 'Run, woman!'

But she wouldn't. There'd been too much running by humans this last half millennia and she refused to add to that mountain. The man – or more – to do something about it; he who could cap that peak once and for all, was present. She'd arranged it so and slung awful reality right in his face. More than that she would not do.

And in any case, where would she *run*, even if she could sprint faster than the Null could pursue? Through France to the coast, and then over the Channel? Through the Wild and right to New-Godalming to ask if anyone one there would shelter her? No. Here was as good a place as any to wait and see.

'Help!'

She hadn't wanted that though. Blades might abandon her – for God moved in mysterious ways – but it seemed pointless to summon ineffectual aid. Bathie hushed him, backed up by a shaming look. Behind her, the scent of wet cloves was breathtakingly close.

Blades looked to the hills for his salvation – but there was none, nor any more martial types than he rushing in to sort things out. Aside from angry monsters they were alone. It had all gone wrong. He despaired and shed a tear.

Fortunately, Bathie never knew. In her piety and innocence, she believed he had singled her out as exemplar of his universal love, and an object for demonstrating it. High atop the pinnacle of preference he'd shown for her, she had faith Blades could intervene with full powers to be her salvation. If not, then he was impotent and untrue and the darkness would descend on Bathesheba Fruntierfolke as mercy.

The unadorned *truth* was that Blades accepted the old adage about gift horses and mouths – or any other orifices, come to that. Although no picture, Bathie was all that was on offer; and there was a decent chance of getting away with it after. So he'd gone along for the ride – and he hadn't got one. Now, instead of easing the long-blockaded tunnel of love, he was back to the bowel-churning menu detailing death and horror. His most cogent thought, insofar as he had any, was that it wasn't fair: it *really* wasn't.

So, it was all the more tribute to his Christian upbringing, that he found himself under the claw destined for Bathie. It must have been his elbow that knocked her aside, his the feeble body that interposed. Things infused in infancy must have taken him there all unknowing. Certainly, he had no recollection of the trip – which was just as well or he'd have retraced it.

There was the added credit of a knife as well. Whatever power drove him on was up to a martial show too. He waved it in the face of the Null like a pennant – inspiring about as much fear as an actual little flag would.

You could never really say the Null smiled. They just stretched their lips and showed some teeth, like lawyers amongst humans or dogs trying their best. Yet, as well they could, these Null smiled at his efforts. A little humour and a lot of terror added savour to a meal. They thanked the surprise *meat* for it. There was no one here to see and, between them, their appetite and the Seine would leave no betraying scraps. Guest-*meat* or no, it was they who'd set the tone – and now they could grace the table.

And doubtless that would have been the outcome, but for the angel's fiery sword. Though thundering down the slope at the risk of neck and ankle, Guy would have arrived far too late. The more ponderous and less inspired Oglethorpe and Hunter could only hope to attend the obsequies – and perhaps

335

form dessert.

That fiery sword lopped off the Null arm descending on Blades. It likewise severed the shocked monster's reserve limb, and then its head, just to put the god-king beyond immediate harm. She pursued the deceased's associates and boiled the water in disposing of them, till the Seine was angry red and bobbing with bits.

Guy's charge met with cursed luck and the solitary surviving Null around. Although robbed of enthusiasm for meddling with *meat*, the thing felt almost honour-bound with one fallen into its arms. It swelled, it growled – it fell apart.

The angel had returned, without deigning to occupy or visibly pass through the intervening yards, to save Guy. The Null was sliced, with blows that should have anatomised Guy too, but failed to loosen so much as a stitch or part his hair.

When every limb refused to answer the helm, the Null was forced to accept close of play and Guy was freed amidst much liquidation. He stood alone and aghast – in a cool Ambassadorial way – and covered in gore. Blades was beside him. They looked at one another.

There was joy and honour therein, certainly: the joy of vindication as much as survival on Guy's part, if not the god-king's. Significantly though, when continued life was finally accepted by Blades, a morsel of jealousy made a one way trip along the line of sight as well.

For whilst Guy's look was one of thanks to Blades for his deliverance, the recipient knew it was none of his doing and that therefore the Ambassador must be under the same protection as he. He recognised the reaction as mean-spirited, but it still rankled with him.

For the time being though, here was a *god-king* again. In the eyes of the witnesses – and minute by minute in Blades's view as well – here was a *Lord* indeed. Angels sped to do his bidding. They departed once he was served.

Guy tracked round to make sure of that. There were no angels, just as there were no Null; merely a ring of humans making obeisance before their saviour. Even the formerly sceptical Oglethorpe had doffed his hat to reveal a wounded wig.

Blades savoured it all, not least the demi-homage of his former Capresi host. He'd supped too much of abasement and forgotten how seductive justified (well, more or less . . .) praise could be. His chest and ambitions expanded.

From within, thankfully inaudible to any bar him, came a bat-squeak of reservation. Blades held its head under the oceanic notion of *the greater good* till the bubbles ceased and it was heard no more.

Annoyingly, a ghost remained, its spectral strands anchoring him to littleness.

'You must understand,' he told his once and future servants, 'I can't wave a magic wand and just . . . restore the past. No, er . . . that is not my way – human free will and all that. No, I tell you most solemnly, the Null and angels must be bent to *our* will!'

They were up to the task – under his inspiration. Guy's unbounded delight very nearly shone through to his face. He arose from one knee.

'And they shall be,' he assured his Lord. 'Never doubt it – just as we never doubted you.'

That was stretching things a bit. *Doubt* had flourished like fungi on the dampness and rot of Blades at his most abject. But that was a test, as Guy had always suspected, just as they'd been tested before in ancestral times.

He crossed to Bathie and took her small hand and kissed it – or would have had it not reeked of burnt Null privates. He cancelled that gesture in favour of brushing her white cheek. She returned the compliment.

'Wife.'

'Husband.'

'*Ahhhh* . . .' smiled Oglethorpe, sarcastic but approving.

Guy turned to him – swiftly.

'No offence,' Theophilus placated.

'None taken,' Guy confirmed. 'And now you may as well do it.'

Oglethorpe mocked a shifting back of shoulders, topped by a well-practised since youth *Who? Me?* expression.

'Do what?'

Guy was not deceived.

'What you've been planning.'

There was no point, and less dignity, in deceit before such an all-seeing eye. Oglethorpe gave a sunny smile.

'Fair enough. Right now?'

Guy spread his hands expansively.

'Why not? If not now, when?'

Bathie was beside him and unexpectedly well read.

'The Psalms of Blades, number 23,' she said to them all, '"*The Lord is my light and my salvation; whom shall I fear?*"'

Who indeed? It was an open question but none answered save its supposed author.

Blades mustered his own smile and said '*Hmmmm . . .*' – which the faithful chose to take as affirmation.

Together, they headed back up the dunes into the glorious future.

'Yes, it does bring a tear to your eye, don't it?' said Oglethorpe, examining the ruin Nicolo had made of his left ear in the radically diminished remnant of Bathie's mirror. The junior Ambassador had really gone to town with his knife in childish revenge after making a fuss about the comparatively minor notches Theophilus had made in him.

Nicolo looked but could see no signs of waterworks on the red face – which was another charge against the insouciant incomer.

'Does it? I can't say I noticed.'

But he had. As Oglethorpe had set about making him look authentically slave-like there'd been a spell when he could notice little else. The wounds had to be properly jagged, like a Null had carelessly dined there, since few indeed of the Null-bred humans were free of these marks of servitude and tastiness. The duo drew the line at whole body parts or wounds like canyons but, in those things open to influence during this one great throw, they wanted to leave the bare minimum to flighty Lady Luck.

Speaking of bare, Oglethorpe hurried to dress again, after dabbing off the worst of the sprays of blood. Nicolo had observed that before. The Heaven dwellers were more bashful than native New-Wessex folk and less inclined to be happy when just sky-clad.

Nicolo covered himself more leisurely. His body and the soul within was the greatest gift he'd been given. He would never disparage it, whatever the years might wreak.

'Now show,' ordered Oglethorpe, who'd usurped the role of officer throughout. This day was his creation, true, but Nicolo increasingly had to bite his lip as the social niceties were turned topsy-turvy.

'I beg your pardon?'

'Show me. Walk like a Null-slave.'

Nicolo obliged with a cringing shamble. Oglethorpe winced.

'No, no, *no*. Too proud. Too "*where's my dinner?*" Haven't you watched 'em? You've got to walk like someone's just kneed your balls. Here, I'll show you.'

Nicolo thought he meant to demonstrate, and so was unprepared when the kneecap was put into his parts. A new sun was born there. He doubled up and paid homage to it.

'*That's* better. Now walk a few steps.'

Nicolo was so astonished that he obliged.

'*Much* better. Keep it in mind.'

Nicolo would, for some time to come.

'No, no, don't thank me,' Oglethorpe waved non-existent sentiments away. 'Even if it will save your life.'

'And may I similarly serve you?' asked Nicolo, in a girly voice he hadn't been aware of owning. He drew closer. 'Just so that you may also be protected?'

All the affability fled like Scots before Cromwell. 'I wouldn't recommend it . . .' Oglethorpe could graft an unspoken snarl on to the most innocent of phrases. Nicolo retreated before it – and instantly the storm lifted.

'Thank you anyway,' said Oglethorpe, 'but the slave scamper is already installed in my dance repertoire.'

Nicolo left it at that, for there was little more that was safe to say. They'd done their best. The two men were mutilated, drenched in an infusion of herbs to look sun-browned and clad in ribbon-rags. Kindly nature had already provided them with an authentic coating of sweat. Once they adopted the '*ever so humble and so were my fore-fathers*' deportment of the Null-subdued, their ingenuity was exhausted on a way to improve the imposture. Both had made proper sacrifice – and of more than the virgin loveliness of their lobes. Oglethorpe was travelling without weaponry; something he'd not done since a boy. With an equally juddering wrench, Nicolo was leaving his dignity behind. Thus both of them felt more indecent than any mere nakedness could inspire. There was no reason to delay and every incentive to get it over with.

The candles were extinguished and then they were reliant on the full moon and what light translucent panels and random gaps let in. At first their steps were hesitant and slow, but gradually eyes adapted. A world of grey and darker grey materialised to greet them.

Oglethorpe took up his yoke and Nicolo cracked the door. Beyond, the night was as peaceful as ever hive-Paris would be. The out-worlder then took over to creak it open and Nicolo assumed his own burden. They moved out.

From the adjacent rooms came the sounds of their companions: Hunter mumbling prayers in a night vigil, Blades's whistling snores and Bathie's distinctive heavy breathing. The two men simultaneously wanted to be past and beyond them but also felt reluctance to leave the last friendly sounds they would hear for some while – or perhaps for ever.

Surprisingly, it was Nicolo who first snapped the strings and led the way. Oglethorpe cursed himself for at-the-brink weakness, even as he relinquished pole position. *To the strong the prizes*, he thought to himself – and then: *Let the boy earn his spurs* – as minor compensation.

The ways of Paris were a nightmare to them at any time, but when disguised as less-than-nothing and bearing cumbersome loads, the tight corners and womb-like narrowings were an especial trial.

Genuine slaves did what they could of their specific duties, and then sank to sleep when the sun fell. Come the dawn they would arise and carry on until old age and uselessness or Null hunger prevented them. Yet, whilst life remained, they also sank like the sun, slumping in spent one's or two's against the crazy walls, obliging Nicolo and Oglethorpe to step over them, balanced burdens swinging around their necks. The clanks and bumps of buckets and chains sounded like cannon fire to the two men, but the very nature of willing slavery came to their aid. The living-dead only stirred in their exhausted sleep and never heeded the pair's passing. After the strenuous story of their day, it would take a sound shaking (or the merest hint of Null speak) to rouse them.

The two pressed on, into less familiar portions and ever downwards, until, after a while, a degree of normal insolence returned. When one of the pails cannoned against a wall, they paid less and less heed, no longer starting like rabbits. It was not that care was abandoned but the growing realisation that their guise bestowed inconsequence. They had assumed the fate of the invisible. So long as it was only a flying visit, they found comfort in that.

There wasn't the slightest shred of comfort in the Null blocking their way. It stood at the head of an indispensable rampway and was wide awake. It saw them and contempt was no bar to full heeding. The humans hoped their instinctive hesitation would not spark a blaze of interest.

The Null uncoiled from a squatting position and rolled languidly in their direction.

Maybe it had been at its devotions or merely sought sleepiness on this most humid of nights. Perhaps it sought diversion and they were just the first candidates along. The two said their own fervent prayers in hope of that.

At the same time, each man was reciting to himself the same agreed litany to create the right frame of mind: *'I am less than least, I do not even deserve to be when every day I behold perfection. Yet I may serve perfection and spend myself in its service. I am less than least . . .'*

The Null loomed and scented. Nicolo's abject cringe could not have been bettered by a centuries-in slave – for it came from the very heart.

The purple beast emerged from the lesser moonlight into full illumination, and was rendered silver by it. Only the lemon-yellow eyes offered any contrast and those sloe-shapes regarded the two with unguessable emotions.

The Null continually licked their lips: it needn't necessarily mean hunger. Oglethorpe reminded himself of that again and again – and so stood his ground. He tried to empathise with the blighted life of the mouse-hearted and then mimic their crucifixion with heart and soul – even as he feared contamination and possibly lasting taint. Theophilus reached for the role with straining inner fingertips and averted face – rather like retrieving an item of value from a latrine. All things considered, the resultant act was fairly good.

Withering under the gaze, it would have taken more than Null imagination to see insubordination in two worms-for-a-night. After a few minimal sniffs and licks, the tormentor's attention moved to their loads.

It went to reach within and taste – and then hesitated. Nicolo aided deliberation with a quite wonderful display of fear. He even trembled on a hot and sultry night.

The Null withheld its questing claw, thinking better of it. If a cringe may express gratitude, Oglethorpe ventured the job. A hiss of hostility was all the thanks he got.

They dared to move one foot forward now, and then one more, and then several in sequence. There came no recall and soon the motion could be constant, putting lovely, lovely space between themselves and the Null who remained motionless, staring after them. They knew better than to rush,

342

although that was the summit of their desire. Eventually, normal speed took them on to the walkway and further and further from the time of trial.

After that it was never so bad. They met other stray Null but the first time was the most wearing. In a way, it was even better being a slave than guest-*meat*: you got mauled and dribbled-on far less as the prize for your mundanity. So, the two bypassed the honeycombed floors and water-holes that the Null favoured for their sleeping piles. They scurried by gathered middens of monsters without more molestation than the occasional sleepy look. Only a few restless slaves cast extra stares at them, detecting anomalies in their pose, but these were long bred to keeping opinions to themselves and would sooner go to eternal sleep than disturb the temporary one of their masters.

At last, Nicolo and Oglethorpe entered into the open air: high above the ground, true, but a commendable, significant part-way. All the entrance portals were guarded, whatever the hour, and so here was the point where breath in short stabs returned. Oglethorpe, especially, saw the sentinels in the way and wished to give them a different kind of *short stab*, but then realised that was out of part and might show in the eyes. He let go the gorgeous thought and embraced servility again. They plodded on.

Fortunately – essentially – Theophilus had made study of the ways of the feeders, of how they walked by day and night and of *how* they walked. It was their ceaselessness and sense of mission that had given him the idea. Thereafter, he'd always paid those particular slaves closer heed than a rip in a skirt.

Unlike most of his investments, it paid handsome dividends. The Null guards – indolent, arrogant custodians, up to nothing in the long empty hours but each other – snorted and stared but failed to pry. They allowed themselves to be persuaded that a great task should not be hindered by their over-vigilance. They lazily let doom down out of the City into the night air.

Nicolo freed and clenched a fist in celebration – causing

one side of his yoke to dip violently over the abyss, threatening to liberate its load. With that loss all would have been lost; for not even the negligent guardians could have ignored such carelessness.

Under his breath – recently returned to normal stately pace – Oglethorpe swore at him, employing words Nicolo did not know but could understand. Had he any shame he would have blushed, but the Throne-room encounter with Bathie had quite cleared him out for the moment. It was as well. Some things said were nigh unforgivable.

'Sorry!' he whispered, once control was regained, but Oglethorpe didn't want to hear. A sharp toe jabbed at a stretched ankle tendon supplied his opinion and urged Nicolo on.

The solid ground and grass felt better than a long-lost mother, and just as unconditional in its welcome. The temptation was to sink down and rest and luxuriate in something the Null had not created. They might besmirch it with their leavings and droppings, but one day they would be gone and earth would still abide. To tread it was to somehow link with that happy day.

This time it was Nicolo who set the pace. With a prod of the yoke, swung quarterstaff style, he dislodged Oglethorpe from his indulgence and air drinking. Nicolo only knew the way by repute but he was along it in advance of the true guide. Theophilus had to hurry to resume his proper position.

Under an overhang of the City, exactly as before, were the special feeding pens and the human-cattle destined for equally special maws. The doomed within clutched at the rough wooden bars or sprawled as they may, looking out at a future free of promise.

To his credit – or perhaps precisely the opposite – Nicolo took the horror in his stride. It never faltered but took him right to where the action was. Paradoxically, Oglethorpe, though he'd seen all before and supped his full, hung back at this, the very precipice.

Despite himself, he'd allowed his tunnel vision to slip and

broaden. He looked again and could not deny himself the story's sermon. There was, he saw clearly now, a hierarchy even within the rearing pens. Those larger than the norm or with residual spirit, those not stuffed to ball-proportions or dazed by forced-feeding, *they* cleared space to rest in relative ease. The others, the weak and feeble and dinner-ready, were bullied and squeezed into what was left. The wood-and-rope bars of their prison cut cruelly into them as they twisted and writhed for just a little comfort before the end: their final ambition a last luxurious stretching of limbs destined for gross conclusions.

For just a second, Oglethorpe paused and *doubted* what he was doing, and whether humanity in the round and general was worth risk and saving. There were *dozens* here, fairly flimsily held, tended only by a few of their own traitorous kind, plus the occasional supervisory Null. Why did it require an outsider to challenge things? Why did they make it worse for themselves? Even the Null weren't like that to each other. They might brawl and rape but their spirit was martial to the last sword-cut and drop of blood. You could sort of admire them even as you wished them scoured off the face of the earth. But *this* crew . . . they sat and waited and just *took* it – and meanwhile oppressed their even weaker brethren.

He didn't dare to meet the caged ones' eyes for fear of communicating too much and learning lessons he'd rather not. By force of will he swallowed his bile and pretended none of it was happening. Oglethorpe marched – or scurried – on.

Nicolo was already at the great butter barrels, emptying the twin churns he had borne into the greasy mass. At the cost of cut hands and much effort, the ground glass was already well mixed within before they even left their quarters, in what now seemed like days ago. He remembered not to meld it in too far to the general supply but mark its position for the harvest.

By the time Oglethorpe got to the vats Nicolo had armed himself with a pail and shovel and was scooping out the chosen portion. Then, bold as brass, he took it to the feeders and they began to dispense. He was cunning, picking his time so that the choicest, most Null-Mother-ready, specimens got what he had to give.

At the start, Oglethorpe entertained misgivings. They'd overindulged with the glittering venom on this first load, such that, seen in some lights, their butter glistened like the milky way with a million sparkling stars. He reproached himself for that impatience. The mixture would have to be moderated for further trips. Fortunately, it went down just the same. The condemned had long ago given up tasting or chewing.

There were no Null around just then. In that limbo time of night only the slaves who must be fed or those that must feed them were about, and both groups were dozy. They did not mark the newcomers or their little imperfections. It was dark and late and the work absorbing. Slaves came and went all the time and slaves knew it was folly to make friends or note faces. The duo's deadly dinner slid down alongside the rest, hidden within mouth-sized butter-balls.

Oglethorpe and Nicolo watched in hidden awe and rejoiced, for soon they could hurry away, with empty pails and lighter yokes and hearts. Also, they were hungry for open celebration and then sleep. Especially sleep.

Tomorrow night they would lose the night hours to come again – and again – for as long as it took for Oglethorpe to fulfil his vow. He, for one, had no choice. The slaves *would* rise: he had promised them and God and himself it.

'*You* will *rise again*,' he whispered to them, even though they mustn't hear or understand.

Accordingly, Theophilus drew a feeder-scoop and began to deal out death.

Red-eyed and careless, or maybe just light-headed through fatigue, Oglethorpe could not resist the temptation. When even sleep in a Null cot seemed like the choicest of delicacies, he postponed it to make oblivion a more considered pleasure. He asked, as a special favour, to see the Hall of Mothers again.

Single-mindedness can simulate innocence. Certainly, at that moment, he had no room in his head for more than one notion at a time. When he asked to see, he really *did* just wish to see. Insufficient faculties were up and operating to manufacture guile.

A senior interpreter looked him over and conferred with a taller, slimmer, Null than the norm, who granted the request. It even escorted him, as though showing off the glory of his race – which perhaps it was.

The mothers still swam in the sunken hall, like shiny maggots swimming in a pit: a harmless, ceaseless, war of all against all. Their chittering chorus assailed his ears even before he entered. Within, chance saw fit to make it feeding time when Oglethorpe stepped on to the balcony to waver unsteadily against the rail. A few more degrees forward and he'd have gone somersaulting down to join the quartered people, and yet that would hardly matter now, not even to him. He surveyed and smiled. For the bargain price of a sleepless week, the deed was done.

In the event, it proved not to be his time. The flimsy guardrail held and saved him. As did the sight. His handiwork ensconced within, red rations were raining down. He blessed every portion.

Was it just imagination or wishful thinking, he wondered hazily, or was that mother having trouble with her feed? She hawked it up but then returned greedily to her vomit, getting it down for good second time around.

Sluggish thoughts wandered round the notion, unresolved. Oglethorpe screwed up his eyes to refresh them for a final charge and then looked again.

There *was*. Amidst all the writhing there *was* a reddish froth to her upchuck. He was powerfully reminded of a certain Colonel Griff of his acquaintance – three bottles and two chicken dinners into an evening-out. But these vermin had less excuse, nor were they witty before or after. Oglethorpe had no sympathy.

What he did have was compassion. He commended the

regurgitation and the person it had been. He urged them – and all the untold martyrs – on in posthumous revenge.

'Rise again!' he commanded aloud, shocking the company.

'Rise again!' Oglethorpe commanded, rocking the company's beds.

Hunter could leap from sleep as though he'd never been there, but that was a product of his rough upbringing. Gentler folk like Guy and Bathie and Nicolo required a margin between sleep and wake before they could shine.

'What? Why?' asked his current victim, if only to make him stop shaking the universe. Guy had left a lovely dream and embrace behind and wasn't yet reconciled to harsh reality. His lashes were still gluey and limbs stiff.

'It's begun,' said Oglethorpe, succinctly. 'We should go.'

He'd thought of everything: had packed and ordered a carriage for a dawn ride. Refreshed after sleeping the clock round, he could afford to stand there, supercilious and formal in red coat and wig, his valise and guns beside him, whilst the rest stumbled about in nightgowns and fright-hair.

'You should have *warned*,' Bathie reproached. 'I could have packed.'

She threw two dresses and a hairbrush into a case, and that was that done. The one remaining scarlet topping went over her head and now she was Oglethorpe's equal.

'I apologise,' he answered, actually rather enjoying the chaos. He knew it matched, in its early stages, an anarchy that was hatching elsewhere in the City. That gave him a warm glow, better than the porridge he'd already eaten, better than this last dawn that he'd sat and watched. 'However, dear lady, you must understand the thing we've ventured is not an exact science. A tide of glass has ways all its own. I have merely observed the earliest intimations. We may have a while before the flood, it might be at our heels as we speak. Who can say?'

'I can,' said Guy. 'We go. No: not too much or they will

348

guess.' This last was to Nicolo, in the act of hauling out a huge casket capable of holding all his wardrobe and toiletries. 'Choose the choicest. We travel light.'

Nicolo looked aghast and then flicked a farewell to all, preferring to abandon every treasure rather than insult some with favouritism.

One thing they couldn't leave without was Blades. Post apotheosis, he'd acquired a suite of rooms all to himself, the others willingly cramming into the remaining space. His reward was privacy and dignity whilst the rest had the compensation of interesting sights. It also meant he got a lie-in as they prepared this moonlight-flit.

Guy knew he could leave his essential packing in Bathie's safe hands: his Blades-Bible, an all-weather cloak, a stiletto or two; that was all he cared to bring out of Null-Paris. The one really essential possession required more respectful fetching.

He knocked, waited, heard nothing, knocked again, and then on this rather unusual new day, dared to enter unbidden.

'Lord, you should rise.'

Repetition three times got some response. The shape beneath the sheets stirred and made a noise.

Guy pretended it was comprehensible. He'd often found that fabricating an false conversation could draw a reluctant party in.

'*Precisely*, Lord. So we really must rush.'

'Do what?' A creased face and halo of white hair edged from the sheets.

'The Null, majesty.' The Ambassador cleverly knew one phrase would tell all. 'The Null!'

Guy could turn his back on the lightning display of limbs that produced. The leader of humanity would be ready before they were.

The others were still milling under Oglethorpe's amused red-eye. Guy crossed to confer with him..

'Won't they think it suspicious, us all going together?'

'Yes.'

'And?'

349

Oglethorpe patted the bulge on his breast which showed his beloved revolver was at home. A stack of guns, bushelled together like harvest corn, stood beside him.

'Also, we are in the happy position of no longer caring *what* they think. The full menu of persuasion is now ours to dip into.'

Guy concurred. To grasp the advantages of freedom the very second they become available, is to have life itself blowing into your sails, leaving less wide-wake opposition far behind. Guy *liked* freedom, it being all he had ever worked for, for himself and for his people and species. He embraced the darling notion.

Therefore, Guy shot the very first Null they met beyond their rooms. The thing died as much of surprise as lead poisoning, retiring to a private corner to contemplate the shocking turn of events.

Some slaves watched, cavern-mouthed and horrified. They wept, as though by instinct, even as Oglethorpe offered them rifles. When they would not take, he left them by their feet, like some kindly uncle seeing beyond a passing tantrum.

Nor was it only 'Field of Bones' guns that he'd stockpiled for today. In various places they passed nooks where Oglethorpe had piled wood shavings and other inflammable materials. The Null were far from house-proud and had left them, whilst the slaves, lacking instruction, hadn't dared to meddle. They were mostly still in place for him to ask Bathie to ignite as they progressed. Theophilus's arms were heavily laden with armaments but sparks from her trembling hands did the trick worth a dozen tinder-boxes. The little bonfires sprang into life, garnished with unnatural kindling and burning all the fiercer for them. There were strange shapes in the flames which grew and a perdition-perfume to the smoke and fumes. Those tokens of magic dissuaded objectors from vital early extinguishing opportunities.

Oglethorpe, despite his planning, was proving to be the least successful of all. Guy and Hunter and Nicolo marched along, as happy as could be reasonably expected in the circumstances. The source of much of their joy was safely between them, matching their long strides and averting his divine eyes. Meanwhile, Bathie had her own tasks and addressed any place that she thought would *take*. They often did; the sorcery doing her bidding for once and producing a show even when it faltered or failed. She lagged behind the main party, walking the corridors in a coat of flames. No one followed them and smoke soon hid the growing audience from view.

By contrast, Oglethorpe was getting an embarrassing take-up to his great firearm give-away. He could hand the things out, show broadly how they worked (*'thin end, point, pull, BANG!'*), but the sales-pitch wasn't getting any customers. As soon as he ceased to cajole, the product was set down again, or worse still dropped like a stone. One such went off by accident and exploded another slave's ankle.

In fact, the whole show was going down badly, the audience wearing faces like grim graven idols. It called to mind a French opera Oglethorpe had once – briefly – seen, put on free and gratis for the costermongers of London by a philanthropist. Fortunately, this set of slaves' response was more passive – so far.

Yet they were roused sufficient to protest at Bathie's fire-raising. Ineffectual hands were waved over it till Hunter chopped one off and calmed things down a bit – other than for the donor. All the same, Guy knew it wouldn't be long before a bored Null heard the cacophony or smelt smoke or magic or both. It was as well they'd forearmed themselves weeks before with the directest route out.

Through the cloud of obscurity that now marked their trail, came a shot. A fluke success, it took off Nicolo's little finger.

It was not so much the pain he bewailed as the spoiling of his perfection. When the flow was staunched with a bandage from Bathie's gown (he declined to tear *his* fine apparel), the junior Ambassador's dearest wish was to relieve Oglethorpe of a rifle and pour out his opinion in the direction of the sniper.

Oglethorpe dissuaded him, refusing to issue the

351

wherewithal even as he deplored the incident.

'Bastards!' Oglethorpe called back at the – wrongly – risen slaves. 'Ungrateful bastards. Is this the thanks we get?'

Apparently so. On the edge of the advancing cloud, at the further end of the current long corridor, were glimpsed actively unhappy faces. Looking on the bright side, none were purple, though their looks were dark enough.

'M-move on.' The disadvantage of an urbane tone was that people were slow to pick up on urgency. Guy had to reinforce his point with some windmilling of arms.

Another agreed tactic prior to departure was a 'zone of discretion'. As they neared the chosen exit, all untowardness and arms were stowed away. Smiles hid the one and clothes the other. To the gate guards they became just guest-*meat* to be growled over, rather than the vanguard of a growing disaster. They were even provided with an escort, which doubly aided their cause. Not only would some monster guardians clear their way through the waking Null swarms, but each one subtracted from the imminent response. Though their pace had been quickened the smoke and slaves could not be far behind.

Full dawn was now breaking over the Seine, heralding the start, did most but know it, of a very special day, gilding the water and slowly unfurling sleep piles. From the precipitous rampway there was a glorious panorama to be seen, if spoilt in some respects by the figures in the landscape. Painfully aware it might be his last chance to appreciate God's daily miracle, Guy drank it in, editing out the less fortunate features whilst strictly moderating his pace.

Their carriage and horses and riders and escort were waiting at the base, as requested. It was not unknown for the *meat* to make little jaunts at odd moments, for it was also known – and amusing – that they found the sublime City too much to take. That they should all emerge together caused only a raised eye-ridge. Their cases were obligingly stowed away, excused in unsolicited explanation as hampers of milk-and-water human-food.

Guy handed Bathie in, as he would any other day. A pained Nicolo joined her, then Hunter and Blades and Oglethorpe and finally mankind's first – and last – Ambassador to the Null. They seated themselves in a protective huddle round the god-king, fidgeting about in search of comfort, as though this really was just a picnic and short respite from horror.

The slave driver looked back. He awaited their word.

Oglethorpe leaned over to Guy.

'Tell me,' he said calmly. 'You know this sort of stuff. Can a carriage horse out-distance a Null?'

Equine science was one thing Guy did have at his fingertips, though generally he focused on sleeker examples than those currently in front.

'Yes, I should think so; in the long run; if pushed. Why?'

The visitor to this world raised his head.

'Well, it's just that I suggest we find out.' He indicated aloft.

At the distant top of the rampway, men and Null and smoke broiled intermixed. Each seemed agitated.

Whilst Guy studied and pondered and concurred, Oglethorpe was acting. He swept the driver from the carriage and took his place. A hideous smile likewise persuaded the man's colleague to step down. Then, fully in the driving-seat, Theophilus used up a precious revolver bullet to kill the Null currently holding the reins and frightening the horses.

'All aboard the Skylark!' he called, and drove off like a lunatic.

One thing the Null could not be faulted on was the lubrication on their reactions. One look in either happening direction was all it took. Some went off to aid their City-in-distress, the rest sprinted after their errant charges.

The carriage had to perform its fair share of charges too. Its wheels, not designed for such ill-treatment, bounced high over a path that was purely intended for pedestrians. Oglethorpe lashed the horses like mutineers and, as a stop-gap policy, achieved some success. A little space was put between them and purple pursuers. Droplet-sprays of horse-flank blood flew back in their faces as appetiser.

In-between trying to stay aboard, Hunter and Nicolo broke out Oglethorpe's other contribution to the feast and speed-familiarised themselves with the ancient-but-modern guns.

'Don't make love to 'em!' their harvester called back. 'Use 'em!'

So they did and managed to strip away some of the worse offenders, once they got the hang of things. Still more were joining in though, issuing from unsuspected orifices in the base of the City or ill-met sleeping piles they passed.

'I've never tried this before,' said Bathie, her voice modulating strangely according to the bump and jolt of the vehicle. If she meant the general experience, then neither had any of them, but they listened to all her pronouncements nowadays, opaque or no. The wisdom of that policy was even now proven by sight of the blaze, whose Genesis she was, achieving adulthood and freedom, leaping over the top of one section of Paris.

'*Dear* lady,' said Nicolo, who was being excessively fastidious in his efforts to both shoot and spare his injured paw, 'don't let that stop you. We are all of us in new terrain now!'

'Well, actually . . .'

Hunter was going to dispute that because, strictly speaking, this was the route they'd taken to arrive here, but a Null streaking in, stage left, put pay to his pedantry. It laid claws upon the carriage and raked a horse flank far worse than Oglethorpe had done. The whole conveyance bucked and swung but then regained the ground after a sickening pause. The Null was still with them, clinging on, but so was Hunter and his gun, fortuitously deposited by the down-swing at just the right angle. He seized the moment and blew the pest away. As testimony to conviction and a desperate grip, it left behind one embedded talon as a reminder.

By then Bathie was leaning over the rear of the carriage, above the compartment where luggage and footmen were normally stowed. Not far behind and gaining, the Null were strung out in a line, unhurried and patient, confident of the ultimate end. They felt sure their hunger and hatred was stronger than the wind of the *four-legs*, even if they were whipped to the bone. They'd achieved a sustainable pace and it would do – and postponed vengeance would only be all the sweeter. It was worth the occasional brave who was knocked away. Null knew that fire-sticks couldn't speak forever. The *meat* grew tired or ashamed of employing their cowardly distance-killing and in due course would set them aside. That was the happy ending of all the old-time sagas.

Bathie's hair streamed back from her face as she looked at them and they looked at her. The pounding of the purple feet upon the green was as loud in her ears as the thumping of her heart. The only distraction was Blades's hand, nominally there to steady her in her seat, but creeping unnecessarily high, over *her* seat. Oddly enough, she found the furtive groping furthered her cause. Only a god-king could think of such things at such moments. Clearly, she laboured for the correct cause.

Bathie visualised, and purged all lack of faith. She *imagined* the razor-thin wire between her hands, as vividly as only a mage can – and then drew it out, flinging arms wide. She magnified it and let go, leaving it behind. Then she looked again into the visible world and, joy of joys, the wire was still taut and wide and *there*, if only to her eyes. The Null could not see and ran into it full pelt.

Some got away with just appalling wounds but others decapitated themselves, running on a comical pace or two, before the message got through that they need strive no more. They sank to their knees in the sward and fountained freely of that which had lately propelled them.

Those who'd stopped in time, looked and howled. For them the loss of purpose was as bad as losing your head. Either way you could no longer do that which you were born for. They stood, great arms handing limply down and useless, and they cried to the sky.

Oglethorpe, burdened with distractions, missed the full story but he heard the acclamation, human and otherwise, and slackened off on the poor horses. The distance between them and nemesis just grew and grew and he let the carriage have its way, no longer forcing it to the shortest path.

Emboldened by success, even Blades took up a rifle and, taking Nicolo's place, proved quite a dark horse and a far better substitute. He knocked off a brace of purple mourners before they got beyond long-shot.

'*That*,' he said, sliding down again, gladder than they ever recalled him, 'reminds me of the time I introduced guns here. Back then you could stand off and mow them down, one by one, and they still didn't understand what was happening. Oh yes. *That* taught them to not to eat my new friends. Ah, *happy* days!'

'And they shall come again, Lord,' said Nicolo.

Blades sucked his wooden teeth and considered and then a smile gradually lit up his face. All his wrinkles and imperfections were minimised.

'Do you know,' he answered to them all, 'I do believe they might . . .'

It was only then they noticed that Bathie had rejoined them in merely the technical sense. She must have turned her back on victory and resumed her seat by reflex action. Now she sprawled across the upholstery bereft of sense.

Guy was across like a rocket, indifferent to all other causes until he had established her condition. A Null mother could have joined them in the carriage and said '*how d' do?*' but he would have persisted with his wife. One ear cocked to her parted mouth, fingers probing up a red sleeve for her pulse, he left the world and other such minor matters behind for the rest to deal with.

Guy's breath was paused for as long as he thought hers might be. Then he felt the feather-fall of air on his face, an unequivocal rhythm talked to his fingertips and the wider universe could return and rejoice. She slept or else rested at low ebb: high magic was collecting its due.

He settled her more comfortably, tucked into one corner, arranging her limbs out of harm and the way. Only then could he look around in search of an update.

They were almost free of the City, trundling down the Null-worn track to . . . elsewhere. Nicolo had taken Bathie's place at the back, resting delicately on one hand, the other held clear for the passing air's cooling attentions.

'We're clear,' he confirmed as they bounced along, 'They're lamenting and retrieving heads.' He looked at his brother and smiled at both him and the day. 'And, do you know, by and large, I find myself rather *cheerful*. The sun shines – or will; the family is here together. There is *drama*, the Null whimper. I'm forced to enquire: what more could one ask?'

The enquiry proved to be actual, with response required. Accordingly, Guy wondered. All the minor improvements he could think of were mere ungrateful cavils, unworthy of mention. He was driven to agree with his brother.

'Very little, Nicolo.'

Nicolo Ambassador nodded and beamed again.

'You're right. You're in the way as usual, slowing me down, but you're right. On balance, I'm almost glad you're here . . .'

They came under fire and the top of Nicolo's head flew off. His final friendly face was frozen that way forever. He sat down with equal permanence, showering Blades with yuck.

Out of windows conveniently emptied by Oglethorpe, or perched on narrow ledges, slave snipers were giving their own verdict on the venture. The relicts of the Field of Bones were being belatedly used: inventions venomously turned upon their begetters.

Oglethorpe had to concentrate on driving, his attention more than occupied with reins and brake and whip. All the same he could see, in stolen glances, that his well-intentioned plans were being perverted. Also, Nicolo had moistened the back of his coat most uncomfortably.

'Well, damn your bloody eyes then!' he cursed the graceless recipients of bounty, the rejecters of liberation. 'I hope your balls retract and Null dig 'em out again. I hope your . . .'

'Enough.' Guy's command was quiet but sufficient. Oglethorpe glanced back and then roared no more.

Guy had his silenced wife to one side and an eternally

357

pacified brother, all passion spent, cradled in his lap. He held hands with both and looked into a private middle distance.

Theophilus and Blades and Hunter commiserated; each in their own way. They all had brothers themselves. The god-king had no idea how sullen Silas-Blades-of-so-much-good-advice fared, for establishing an empire in another world had rather preoccupied him and led to a drifting apart. All the same, he understood a certain sadness was now appropriate. Oglethorpe, likewise, had brothers galore, forever getting themselves killed in Marlborough's campaigns or imprisoned for Jacobitism. Yet, amidst a busy life of his own, it was hard to keep a close track of all their just as colourful comings and goings. Even Hunter recalled family, regularly culled by the Wild and just as regularly augmented by polygamy. Thus they could all sympathise to a degree but faltered over an excess of grief.

In one way – each thought it simultaneously but would never know – if there *had* to be death, Guy ought to consider himself fortunate. A horse was a bigger and better target than a slim Ambassador, but if one of *those* were to go, the rest of the party would follow in short order. They'd crash in ruin and the survivors would have to await the Null's pleasure. Thus, seen from one perspective, just losing a brother was a real result. As a racing man, Guy ought to appreciate that.

Oglethorpe squinted up at the rising sun and looked on the bright side.

Tumult rose like steam in the Hall of Mothers – a miasma of distress rising up to meet and meld with the concern showering down from above.

The elder males, those whose hearts had not already broken, remained and wept bitterly over the churning sea, wringing their claws or lacerating themselves: an outward sign of inner pain.

Slaughter above also matched that below. A constant

stream of humanity was fed into the hall and then dispatched on the brink to pitch bleeding into the void. Yet, for the most part, right up to the end, the slaves' distress was no less than the masters – though it did not save them. When they beheld the condition of the ever-recreating fountainhead, they wept too and added their various moistures to the flood.

The policy was as much impotent vengeance as wise precaution. After so grievous a blow the Null could not abide any reminder of those who had struck home. Be they clothed and treacherous *meat* or *meat* lurking behind servility, the Null would make no more distinction. All over Paris a cull was in progress, giving birth to mighty lamentation and even resistance at the very end, till all the great City was one song of misery and despair.

One wizened Null-elder had heard enough and stepped to the balcony's very edge. He would not look, he could not bear to, but his hands tore at his breast as if to extract the heart within. Purple slivers flew and went down to the inconsolable disaster before the rest of him did. He toppled over, distended face still averted, down to join that which he could not save.

There was hope, during the early stages, of diluting whatever poison was at play. A change of provisions to flesh supplied by self-sacrificing Null sought to oust the bad with good, pure food. Yet the Mothers continued to scream and haemorrhage and nothing would do. They could not understand or be coaxed and tore at those who approached. Even the gentlest comforting brought forth only worse agony until all that could be done was to leave alone and mourn. Mere fires could be quenched or sat out, but the wound to the soul of the City was beyond their skill at repair. Little was left to them but rage.

And so they resolved to spend that one remaining treasure which the *meat* thieves had left to them. They issued from the City of sorrow in a mighty purple flow, drenching the land.

Behind those issuing armies, the agony lapping the walls of the Hall of Mothers grew more peaceable and quiet and red. A hush settled, unprecedented since the angels' blessing. The black heart of Null-Paris slowly ceased to beat.

Disquiet rose with the noon of that same day and an unnatural
tinge to the horizon. Bathie, now awakened but still weak, was
the first to see. A purple crescent followed in their wake, its
extremities enclosing an ever-widening front.

'They come!' she told the rest of the carriage and then
subsided into delicious wooziness again. She'd raised the
concern and passed it on and now could leave well alone.
That was surely enough and quite creditable in the circumstances.

Hunter, taking his turn at driving, spoke for all in his usual
shorthand.

'Can we?'

Oglethorpe understood the question. He'd got the hang of
the vehicle by now and knew its ways and thus their chances.
He waggled a flattened hand.

'Touch and go. Not with him aboard.'

They'd retained Nicolo's body, despite the inconvenience
and mess, for lack of any strong reason not to. Warm day and
flies notwithstanding, no one had objected so far in deference
to Guy's feelings. Now though the time was come. They
looked to him.

Guy in turn studied the danger and calculated and, at
length, had to agree. He nodded.

'He might even help – you know, *delay* them,' said Hunter,
with all the hob-nailed boot insensitivity of the other-
worldly. 'If they pause to feed . . .'

Guy could only affirm to that, for it was the unvarnished
truth – though, significantly, he didn't dare risk verbal reply.
He was aware of being soft. Doubtless Nicolo would just have
ventured a wry smile over his final utility. Still, there it was.
In some ways Guy had always been the lesser brother.

Blades mistook his decent pause for hesitation. It rattled
the poker in his reawakened fear.

He reached over to brush the dead head.

'Go to God, son of man,' a reassuring farewell he'd heard good priests use. Previously, it had worked just as well on the relatives as the outgoing.

'Has he not already?' asked the languid Bathie, a genuine enquiry rather than probe. 'Can't you tell?'

The god-king's second apostasy was still fresh and sore. For the moment it was beyond him to pretend to consult the upper air and confirm '*oh yes, so he has . . .*' Instead, he settled for an opaque 'He's safe, never fear' – which only slightly pained the twitchy conscience and yet still did the job.

'Oh good.' Bathie fingered a kiss on to the ruined body and then recalled her brother-in-law no more. Guy marked the occasion with a single tear, discreetly swept away.

Oglethorpe assisted with the heaving over and the carriage did seem to leap forward more sprightly for the loss.

'Could you oblige?' Guy asked him, and Theophilus wondered what he meant for a moment, before the penny dropped. The Ambassador would prefer to respect his brother's memory and not see him graceless in the dust – but at the same time a fresh assessment was required.

'Of course, of course. You keep eyes-front and I'*ll* look. Take a moment to compose yourself, dear boy.' – and all in all he thought that very caring and Christian of him.

By then their pace had become Sunday afternoon-ish and mindful of taking the long run into account. They'd amply rested and watered the horses in the hours without evident threat, seeing no sense in flogging the beasts' guts out only to be left stranded when one or more upped and died. Now, Oglethorpe – who was more used to pursuing than the converse – had to reverse his calculations to judge the end of things. He pondered the purple harbinger for long enough to match its oncoming against that of Dieppe's walls. He assessed the potential for additional speed courtesy of dispensable freight. Everything pointed to the same conclusion although he refused to let it inform his face. Oglethorpe calmly resumed his seat.

'Home, James,' he instructed – and puzzled – Hunter, 'and don't spare the horses!' – which was all the answer Guy required.

The minarets of Dieppe were only slightly less detailed than the Null and yet, at the same time, as unobtainable as the gates of Heaven. The monsters' vigour and persistence were nibbling away at hopes of safety, till the very notion threatened to fall. Dieppe and its people and guns and teeth-thwarting stones were fast becoming a chimera; as fast as the leading Null's pounding, ceaseless feet.

The carriage was down to donkey speed now, the horses more than spent. Everything that could be jettisoned was gone – even Oglethorpe's beloved rifles, just as soon as they were emptied of venom in the direction of the foe. Even Guy's inseparable-companion playing-cards went overboard to puzzle the pursuit. Each sizeable loss permitted a little spurt forward, but with steeply diminishing returns. Like men of whom too much is asked for too long, the mounts had given all and had no more to give. From time to time one of them would look accusingly back, wide-eyed and froth-faced. It was mere cruelty to whip them now and Hunter threw the thing away. If the oncoming clove scent and easily audible chiming didn't spur the beasts on, then nothing would.

Oglethorpe, however, wore an incongruous smile. They were being driven to a dead-end which would remove all the tiresome business of options and decisions. At last, at the end of a long-enough life of worrying, relax.

He leant over and dug Blades in the ribs.

'Oi. God-king. Aren't you going to throw some thunderbolts, then?'

Up to now he'd spared his hosts' feelings and deferred to their respect, but Theophilus had seen too much of brother Blades begging for piastres in Capri to ever properly join in the awe.

'Well . . . no,' came the broken-reed reply. 'Such is not my way. I . . .'

'Or you, missy?' Oglethorpe loomed more considerately over Bathie. 'Any chance of a wedge of wonderful witchery?'

Theophilus had taken magecraft in his stride, along with all the other marvels and horrors of this world. He suspected it was latent and waiting in his own homeland and recalled a wise old grannie who knew more than she ought.

Bathie raised her right arm. It was as pale as print and failed to sparkle.

'All gone,' she answered, wanly. 'For now . . .'

'For good then.' Oglethorpe indicated the Null breathing down their neck.

He saw that Guy concurred. The Ambassador was stock-taking: so many bullets left . . . a seax knife for afterwards – unless God or an angel intervened. He, like Oglethorpe, knew it would end soon in a tangle of carriage and felled horses, Null streaking underneath to hamstring them. A sliver beyond the range of Dieppe's wall-guns, any survivors would emerge from the crash and have to show what they were made of. Then the Null would dine on it.

So there it was. All the tedious calculation business was taken out of Oglethorpe's hands and there was a sort of blessing in that. Never mind Blades and bogus deities: Theophilus felt god-like himself. He wondered about that. Perhaps it was something in the air here.

Alas, its primary constituents were now cloves and hatred. He could make out individual purple faces. Since he was the one they could see they *spoke* to him.

'Yes, yes, *yes* . . .' he answered. 'All right, all right. Patience.'

Oglethorpe handed Guy a letter. It was accepted and stowed and understood.

'It's all in there, Mr Ambassador. Now, slow down, shaggy-man, or Hunter or whatever your name is. Slow right down, please.'

That was a joke, for they were nigh down to walking pace now, but Theophilus wanted to alight with all dignity. They could regain the few sacrificed yards once he had lightened the load and was gone.

'No,' pleaded Hunter, looking back and neglecting his duties. 'There's no point. One man can't make a difference!'

Oglethorpe drew his revolver and levelled it at the driver.

'Do it, Mr Shaggy – or we'll see how our transport goes with two men short . . .'

He plainly meant it and Hunter obliged.

Oglethorpe baled out with two rifles he'd retained, a brace of pistols and Guy's beloved gift.

'Are you sure you don't have any more shells for it?' he asked. 'Last chance: confession's good for the soul and all that . . .'

Guy shook his head. 'If I had them they'd be yours, believe me.'

'Oh well, never mind. Cheerio then.'

'See you later . . .' said Guy – which made Theophilus laugh; a nice final present.

The two men shook hands. The turf was also shaking now.

Oglethorpe leant back over the carriage side.

'One man *can* make a difference,' he told Hunter, and probably them all. 'Or at least they should try. It depends on the man as much as moment – and now's the perfect match. Don't you worry about me. This is *my* time. It fits me better than Joanna; better than a glove. I mean, how often do you get this chance? You should be so lucky!'

Agreement wasn't that evident. Bathie mustered a smile and waved. Blades looked at Oglethorpe as if at a strange new species.

Then he was gone, advancing towards the Null, straggly wig streaming back, and firing from the hip.

Hunter flicked the reins and spoilt the moment. They lurched forward, slightly the faster for their loss and little rest.

Guy wasn't going to look, according the man a little privacy, but then he realised this was *tell-your-grandchildren* sort of stuff and once-a-lifetime. He shuffled round, casting an arm over the carriage edge to secure his view.

Bathie meanwhile settled to doze and Blades stared straight ahead, content with just the music of rifle fire and the extra seconds it might bring. The symphony itself sufficed, and he wished it long life. There was no need for him to actually see the musicians labouring away. Dieppe looked a shade more defined to him now. He was going to say a prayer of recommendation for his former host, in thanks for this and all his previous generosities, but then stalled at the brink. Here was a theological grey area, a field full of cowpats and the path unclear. He skirted round its edge and moved on without comment.

So, only Guy witnessed Oglethorpe's salvoes, and their bringing down a swathe of Null, who then tripped those who came after. Then, when one rifle had said its all, he flipped over its twin-brother, slung across his back, and obligingly repeated the lesson.

The monsters' advance was bopped on the nose and the furious face and head behind had second thoughts – if only for a second. The headlong pace blanded out for a vital while and, bowing to wisdom if not their ideals, those directly before the venom-spitting *meat* parted slightly, Red Sea style, just a shade to either side.

Rightly refusing to be ignored or by-passed on this, his special day, Oglethorpe punished those in particular, concentrating fire to bring them down in their rudeness. That stern policy's one – but important – downside was that the more intrepid Null spirits in front could draw near.

The second rifle was extracted from his hands, but he relinquished it gladly, having that moment just drained it of fun. The Null who'd thus obligingly pre-occupied both its claws, was then dubbed the gun's perpetual custodian by Oglethorpe's sword and curled down by his feet like a faithful hound. Oglethorpe almost went too, unable to extract his blade from an Excalibur type predicament, where Null-skull served instead of stone.

The brace of pistols were soon spent, with one hundred percent return but loss of all capital. He threw them at the mob and so learnt that even Null said 'ouch'.

Guy didn't hear it; he was now too far away, but he witnessed the play's closing scenes and would have applauded, had he a hand free.

He saw Oglethorpe reap a patch of privacy with the emptying of the revolver. One, two, three, Null went down, unmissable at that distance, close enough, Guy felt sure, to leave powder burns on each. In falling, the trio clogged the Null riposte and bequeathed Theophilus a final free second.

Left armed only with teeth and nails, Oglethorpe wouldn't demean himself or the moment. He spent it on a smile and wave at Guy. Then purple swallowed him up.

Even that melee seemed to go on longer than you'd predict, but Guy had said his last goodbye and didn't delay to watch. All too soon enough, the pursuit would be resumed in earnest.

Weaving unsteadily as they bumped along, he joined Hunter on the driver's bench.

'It was a fine sight.'

Hunter raised an eyebrow and cracked the reins.

'If you say so. Anyhow, he gained us a breather.'

Guy valued it higher than that but recognised some coarser souls dealt in different currency. There was no point evangelising the finer things of life – or death. On grounds of kindness he decided not even to hint at poor Hunter's blindness. Blades – or God – said it was wicked to mock or mark the afflicted.

'Well,' Guy said instead, 'whatever the case, if it was 'don't spare the horses' before, you should now proceed to murder them.'

'Poor souls,' said Hunter, even he urged them on, showing he was, after all, human and of some limited sensitivity.

The rhythmic breath of the Null, as coordinated as their loping steps, was practically striking the carriage now. Blades and Bathie happened to clench their shoulders at the same moment – and then denied it to each other with shamefaced smiles. She turned to Guy, for guidance or a final glance, and formed the awful suspicion he was preparing to jump. His hands were applying a death-grip to the carriage sides, far firmer than present turbulence would dictate, whilst his mouth moved over silent prayers. Her husband's eyes were focused . . . elsewhere.

That unacceptable prospect applied a boot to Bathie's lazy powers of invention. She *ordered* Guy not to and then swung around.

It oughtn't to have been any surprise but the sheer, love-making, *closeness* of the Null was a real bowel-clencher. The foremost were already extending their claws.

'Remember me?' she asked them.

If they didn't then here was the end. The powers of Null long-term memory and their facility for distinguishing individual *meat*, were moot points amongst those who made study of such things. Now Bathie had the ideal experiment to establish the answer once and for all. Her detachment from the result was truly scientific. Either way she'd be content. It was *Fruntierfolke* to go facing the enemy and despiting them, and she and Guy would go together. On the other hand, if she proved to be a *face*, then the climax might be postponed awhile; maybe for all the remaining years of life.

She made the wire-creating sign as before, drawing an imaginary hawser to slash their hurtling throats. Also, though her thaumaturgic sense had never seemed so drained, she smiled at them as if the High Mage of Yarmouth himself had guaranteed success.

They did recall. They'd run into her before – or else had heard. It did the trick. Most skidded to a halt, the rear ranks cannoning endlessly into those in front, till all order was lost and a Null sleeping pile recreated in broad day.

Guy saw and laughed and they embraced in the back of the carriage like newlyweds.

'Well done!' added Blades, who now almost believed in Dieppe as a concrete reality. 'So what next? Shall we walk?'

They might as well, for the team were now travelling little better than a two-leg's promenading gait. Their conveyance wasn't much more than convenience.

Hunter indicated the spent horses and then the town, spelling it out.

'If these two'd open up, we might make the gates,' he explained, a dispassionate assessment of odds about something of academic interest only. 'If them inside open up, then we might make it through the gates.'

The wall-guns of the foot-hold port could now be seen, together with a hint of agitated individuals along the walls. That they or their fan-club had been spotted was not in doubt, but what was required was a way to ensure the scene was interpreted aright.

Guy guessed that Dieppe's guns had been life-long mutes, their home purely a concessionary enclave rather than something owned as of right. They were there for bravado rather than earnest defence and thus were loathe to clear their throats and sing. The silence had lasted so long it now passed for normality

Yet sing – and shoot and bellow – they had to if the New-Wessex party were to bear their important tidings home. The Null, miming like clowns, had by now perceived the non-existence of the barrier or shimmied 'under' or 'round' it with their fury renewed.

They came on like a flash-tide, careless of formation or poise or anything save getting to grips. Nothing the party had left in their repertoire would daunt them any more. Only an uncompromising Mankind-militant response from the achingly close walls would do.

Unbeknownst to each other, all the carriage occupants were simultaneously wondering what a *please shoot over my head* gesture looked like. A mimicked slit throat? A hugely exaggerated taking aim and the hope of a perspective-glass up on the walls? All were possibles which Bathie ventured, whilst Guy supplemented her efforts with what he reckoned to be more practical action.

'If you don't mind me saying so, Lord,' he whispered to Blades, 'now might be a good time to lift aside just a portion of the concealing veil.'

Blades had to chew on that one before it revealed its meaning. Meanwhile, instinct forged a holding reply.

'I suppose I *could* summon legions of angels . . .'

Guy's brow furrowed. 'Well . . . that might n–'

"But what I *will* do is this . . .'

Actually, Blades hadn't the slightest idea, save for some desperate notion of setting fire to the horses' tails, and was relying on his facile tongue to weave a way round the problem. He done it for decades in his previous stint as god-king and now relied on the knack returning. The secret was to keep talking until something occurred to you.

That willingness to rely on a sword of straw was *the* defining difference between a true Emperor and the merely ambitious. That the Null might not cooperate with his bluff simply didn't occur to Blades. As the old role returned, his thoughts were solely of the passing moment. He owed not a bean to futurity and caution was strictly for lower ranks.

Fortunately, at the very same moment, Dieppe burnt its bridges and a fair few Null as well, by blasting their front ranks away.

Vindicated and de-molested by the couldn't-possibly-miss wall-guns, Blades in his carriage bowled past the outer earthworks and through the gaping gates.

To whom it may concern.

I, Theophilus Oglethorpe (junior), Englishman of the County of Surrey, Gentleman, and being of sound mind and lusty parts, feel that I owe some *explanation*. And, being ever one to pay my debts, of coin no less than honour, I hereby set pen to paper to tell all.

. . . and then I recalled our Lord and Saviour's prophetic words that '*Greater love hath no man than this, that a man lay down his life for his friends*'. I checked, and read – and rejoiced. *Here* were answered prayers: *here* the answer. My destiny and Christian duty might slide between the sheets and intertwine like lovers. I could do the right thing – as I see it – and *still* slip into Paradise!

... with your kind indulgence, unknown reader, I do have one last request and if it be fulfilled, hope to meet you, most merrily, in Heaven. It is this ...

. . . .
I remain sir, albeit beyond the grave, your obedient servant

Theo. Oglethorpe. Gent.

Oglethorpe rose again – wonderful to see at a distance, if no longer quite so wonderful in person. The advancing Null bore his broken corpse before them, fastened to a cross.

That insult or honour followed the parade of Null mothers, borne on palanquins lavishly fashioned from fresh white bone. Most of the bloated things were dead or as good as, and were brought forth so that the *meat* should see the terrible thing they had done. They were paraded round Dieppe with every display of bereavement.

Alas, the demonstration failed to provoke remorse and once the initial shock was gone, with nothing to lose, the garrison amused itself by trying to fell crucial bearers under each load and thus deprive the departed of even dignity in death.

That only distressed and angered the Null all the more, and was wasteful as well as unkind. Dieppe's Castellan swiftly forbade such indulgent use of shot. Like a full day's work ahead when all you wanted was bed, Sir Samuel Musket greeted the torrid prospects with caution rather than zest.

The Null didn't care if the *meat* were careful or profligate. As the land between sea and horizon gradually filled with purple they were of one thought only, as focused and implacable as the tide they came to meet. Null frolicked in the waves like gross nymphs and surrounded the Castle on all sides, mocking its deadliest efforts.

Then, when they'd displayed their commitment and the show was over, they flowed against the walls and shook them.

'They come. They come!'

Guy let the man pass without reproach; him and his few companions, carrying their wounds and confusion on into the castle courtyard. Then he waited for more to return in rout but none came. The outer earthworks, an innovation born of Sir Samuel's boredom, must have gone down as sudden as a broken-backed ship, vessel and crew together. The second line atop the walls were holding their fire in the interest of survivors who would never come.

Guy could now hear, could almost *feel* through his boots, the rapid pad-pad-pad of feet possessed of inhuman determination. Above his head on the ramparts, a festival of musketry broke out

'Secure!'

His team hurled themselves at the postern gate to lock and bolt and bar it. Then stout timbers were jammed between the entrance and the earth as though an uninvited giant was expected. Guy tested their work with grunting push and shove until he was sure it was good. Then all stood back.

The calm chime and gentle knock that came from the far side was an unnerving anti-climax. The soldiers looked to one another, undecided whether to laugh or cry.

Then one, a black-bearded ruffian, incongruously nimble, threaded through to the door.

'So good of you to call,' he shouted to the unseen visitor. 'How's your mum?'

A localised storm hit the wood as the presence went wild, hurling itself at the barrier, kneading in pure-hate with blows and claws.

Guy had temporarily closed down that part of him which was charmed by drama or gestures. For the moment he must be as dry as a loveless lawyer. The door shook but it would hold. What would be the epicentre of attention in normal circumstances could now be ignored.

Meanwhile, indications from above and the soldiers on the wall suggested there were other things to think about. Guy gathered all his charges to him and hurried aloft. Lieutenants and gabble-mouths rushed over but the story didn't require much telling. It was as he'd thought: unless the day-time pennants and nightly beacons did the trick and provoked rescue, then they were done for.

When the Null arrived they'd come forearmed and now concealed their intentions behind a screen of trees. They had little use for greenery in the usual course of events, save maybe to loll in on hot days or fall on their prey from. The risen Null also knew of the *meat* predisposition to sylvan charms. Therefore they must have found especial pleasure in uprooting fine specimens as they ran to Dieppe, bearing them on teams of strong shoulders to be transplanted along the siege lines. Digging furiously with the strong arms once used to extract humans from burrows, they soon had them bedded in. Now an incongruous, dying, ribbon forest leaned crazily around Dieppe, shielding what went on beyond from prying eyes.

Men were dispatched to the highest towers and from there they could at least see the further distance right to the horizon, and the unvarying tale of reinforcement it told. Nevertheless, the immediate enemy were shrouded in green obscurity and every attack was a surprise one.

In the first hours, Dieppe's few cannon had ventured knocking gaps in that concealing fringe but there proved to be no shortage of replacement trunks. Soon enough, what ammunition they had was husbanded for felling more active foes.

Thus the cages came as a shock, trundling through the

browning leaves. What the Null had spared from instant revenge, they'd thoughtfully parcelled up for their kith and kin to deal with. Wailing and far from reconciled, the remnant slave population of Paris came on to visit Dieppe in wheeled pens of wood.

It was a dilemma, but only for a moment. The Null sheltered behind them and it was *they* who were the inescapable fact. Sir Samuel gave the order.

Alas, shot and shell makes no distinction, and passed through one to get to the other. Some pink bodies, surviving all, were liberated from captivity by the hand of fate and crawled out to mix with the predominant purple. Their confusion was painful to behold. Guy saw some huscarls target those especially, to put them out of their misery. Well, that was a noble gesture, true, but also a bit of a waste. Should they see out this attack he resolved to have a few gentle words . . .

Dieppe's fire was thin; pitifully thin. Its garrison had only ever been a gesture and required either huscarl-level loyalty or conscription to keep in place. Sir Samuel was given just enough men to ensure he needn't open the gates himself or cook his own breakfast, but insufficient even for a crazed optimist's siege requirements. The ornate walls of Dieppe were just for show, sprouting cannon that were silent for lack of men to fire them.

Those outer earthworks, in whose complex modernity much faith had reposed, were casually brushed aside: their deceased defenders shockingly squandered. Now it was not the cannoneers or good shots amongst those left who were the lynch-pin of hope, but the old servant who raised the distress flag at dawn or the burly, stripped to the waist, sailors who fed the beacon by night. In brutal truth, Sir Samuel and Guy's coordination of the defence was only a waving of another sort of flag: the banner of human honour. Stuck between the devil (or his spawn) and the deep blue sea, it was the only valid role left for them to play.

Hunter was beside Guy now, wielding his beloved bow. He liked to select his targets and fell them with more expenditure

373

of effort than a mere tug upon a trigger. Somehow that made it personal and less like a sin. His shafts struck through and through and no one arose from a hit. The Null *saw* and hated him especially.

Bathie was with Blades in the Keep's Great Hall, secluded from everyone's great expectations. And that was the other fly in the ointment, beside the vast writhing bug of the Null. Sir Samuel had made obeisance when Guy told him the news and Blades confirmed it, but it was all done with a beady eye. Later, the Castellan was observed sneaking covert, comparing glances at the depiction which prefaced his *Blades-Bible*. Musket was not yet willing to divorce from false Blades XXIII in favour of the real thing, and still debated in his heart whether Guy had set the world afire on a whim. Granted, Ambassadors were hardly known for recklessness, but this one was Fruntierfolke-tainted. 'It seemed like a good idea at the time', was *their* second creed.

Guy saw the same reservations in the soldiers' faces. They awaited some more dramatic proof than mere assertion before they honestly bowed the knee. Most continued to hope as much of Bathie's magecraft as divine intervention. It was not the firm foundation one might hope for when all the Null in the world were going for your throat.

When their cage ploy had achieved all it was going to, the enemy swarmed over the ruined structures, reforming in neat lines drawn by captains on the far side – their machine-like discipline being not the least feature of their overall disgustingness. The human-soldiers had, for instance, learned not to fire in volley. At the bidding of perfectly timed commands, the beasts would fall prone and duck under the lead, leaping up to gain unharmed yards before you could reload. Then they would hit the walls in unison so as to spread the defence, or else held back and probed only where resistance was thinnest. Their orders were subtle and obeyed without question, almost by instinct. Guy himself observed a exquisitely choreographed assault on an out-of-the-way bastion that was brought in with barely a chime. He'd had cause to wonder if they could communicate by thought, whereas he had to bawl and *emphasise* to bring up the cauldrons of red-hot sand that had washed them away.

Now, the fashion was for anarchic fire that the Null couldn't anticipate and decline to accept. The skinny line on the walls picked their targets with discretion, looking for captains or inventive Null, or those whose falling might fell others. Particularly annoying specimens, the tallest or most agile, rendered themselves high-risk as well. As such, the few defenders of Dieppe were operating a sort of cull-in-reverse, which maybe galled the Null, but was small compensation when the infinitely more numerous only-average monsters rolled in unimpeded.

Further murdered trees had been carried forward to incorporate the captured outer line until they too were absorbed into the zone of obscurity. An attack could then issue out from short, surprise, distance – and soon enough did so.

All unknowing, Oglethorpe led the charge and Guy had to keep his eye on him – for their association had gained new legs, just like the deceased. As usual, life never let you *focus* on one thing, however important, but introduced distractions at every bloody moment. So, whilst coordinating the lead and edged welcome to the oncoming purple, he had at the same time to home in on his dead friend to renew their acquaintance.

The dry moat delayed the visitors barely at all, other than for a fluid, in unison, down-and-up-and-out motion. Then their claws were in the crevices of the walls and hauling themselves up. No call for ladders for the Null – the talons they lusted to employ were also the means of getting aloft and cracking this tortoise-shell of *meat*.

Portions of boiling sand and water all delivered, the thin huscarl line dealt with the residual purple stain. That task took them to the outer fringes of both parapet and exertion – and to beyond and death for some, hooked over the edge by a questing Null arm. Guy meanwhile patrolled up and down with a word here, a reminder there, and point-blank discharges from a double-powdered pistol here, there and everywhere. He also managed to be in the right place when the now grisly Oglethorpe, crucified like a collected butterfly or distasteful Christian effigy, showed his pale face over the wall. Guy ensured the Null mascot was allowed atop and then blasted its custodians away, leaving the husk high and dry.

He averted his eyes, preferring to remember the out-worlder as he'd been when he was bluff, not bleached. Some Castle servants on bullet-bearing duties were ordered to remove the object into safe storage in the Keep. Only then was there a chance to look around and reflect on the fact that the ramparts now seemed to be Null-free. They had prevailed!

Then the next wave arrived, just when the humans were congratulating themselves on survival and 'victory' – and this time the Null were royally enriched. The King of Null-Paris was with them in all his glory, armed with a weighted human-skull club and preceded by choirs and fan-bearers. He bounded in with the attack and led by example – both his own and by making one of any who lagged.

Naturally, every human eye with a free moment was upon his Majesty, and every spare barrel likewise. Even Guy, with his not-a-hope, over-loaded, gun had a go, augmented by prayer.

Closeted with Bathie in the Keep, Blades obviously wasn't listening right then, for Guy's shot went wild. There again, he was in good company in his lack of success. Along with all the other froth and flunkies, plus an honour guard to strike down those he decreed under-committed, the regal presence was shrouded and shielded by nimble aides with panels of hardwood or purloined metal. In the last resort, their own bodies served to save the great one from penetration. Guy saw a couple of willing martyrs peeled away and recognised the feeble prospects for joy. He ordered his men's priorities elsewhere.

Like the murdered Null-mothers, the King was a diversion: most probably a subtle and deliberate one. Even if he did suffer misfortune and acquire extra head ventilation, doubtless an heir apparent would straightaway rise to replace him. His bereaved subjects would then only attack with more vigour. Thus, what the humans possessed in the way of lethality was better directed at the *hoi polloi* coming on – and coming on they were, scorning Dieppe's very best reaction.

When that merely second wave broke on stone, its impetus was even less diminished than the first's, rising to lap right over the walls, nibbling away at the defenders in each place it touched. The Null swarmed over the edge like spiders pursued by hot water, and once aboard they snapped and snatched at everything; too swift even for protest.

Guns were being cast aside now, or else shoved into Null faces for them to take care of. The huscarl element drew their highly favoured *great axes* and contrived to be glad then, for *here* was their moment, even if it should be a last one.

A wedge of Sussex-Wealden steel, swung on a six-foot shaft by those bred to the pleasure, could put a serious dent in Null plans. Carving out huge, overhead, figures-of-eight with them, an intricate ballet cleared some space. Guy used it to make his exit.

For he'd foreseen the next few minutes with sorcerous clarity. It only took one blunted blow, one thwarted sweep and a Null willing to occupy the axe-blade with its own body, and the clever dance then started to unravel. The Null could nip in and join in. They soon became the dominant partners and called a new tune.

Guy clattered down the stairway, risking a broken neck by reloading as he went. Fiddling with the single-shot weapon, he repented of giving away his revolver in Capri, but then suffered a stab of guilt. It had gone along the weave of *wyrd* to its predestined owner and been put to good use. Such was God's will and he should be content.

A Null who'd missed out on the whole parapet adventure by vaulting right over, loomed in the way. Guy ran in fast and low in the manner he'd been taught and so just escaped the taken-by-surprise sweep of claws. The Null were unused to up-for-it *meat*, expecting a lot more deference. Guy's sword preceded his rush and wonderfully emphasised the point he was making. The Null sat down to think about it, holding back the freedom-dash of a boisterous coil of insides.

Granted a moment to consider, Guy studied the scene and found the courtyard already dotted with purple. He scanned the wall circuit too. His colleagues there had gone ahead – to safety or the next world. A body trail signalled their path. Of Sir Samuel Musket there was no sign.

The booted footsteps on the stairs behind Guy were few and hurried. Thus, with the war on the walls lost and the inner court already conceded, there was no impediment to the path of sense and the straightest route to the Keep. Guy took it and any who could keep up with him were welcome. Hunter and a few dozen or so huscarls, plus some lucky miscellany, tagged along on the trip.

Some Null felt strongly that there *should* be cowpats in the way, metaphorically speaking, and interposed themselves between the fugitives and the door of all-their-desires. Guy shot the first full in the face, hurtling him back against another. A third was partitioned by a surprise – if tremendously welcome – axe descending from just behind Guy's line of vision.

The rest, since he was now disarmed and puny, Guy had to dodge. Less sprightly humans received their attentions instead and the Ambassador weaved a path round troubles in the same way his clan were said to be able to dodge raindrops. He emerged, safe and dry, at the further end, not alone, but hardly spoilt for company either.

At the base of the Keep there was a drawbridge over a dry ditch and maybe the dramatic thing to do was try a last stand, whilst behind him axemen hacked at the planks beneath their feet. Fortunately, Guy knew better than that, though he was as much a one for epic scenes as the next man. Even if the bridge was downed, the Null would scorn a mere ditch and scale the walls as though they were thoughtfully ready laddered. Siege architecture designed with mere men in mind, failed to take account of enemies who could heave themselves up blank walls and arrive still full-winded and raring to go.

A more practical policy was to let the huscarls hold off pursuit whilst he knocked on the door. Since it was – in present circumstances – inconveniently thick and iron-studded he was obliged to use his sword pommel.

There came no clear answer, only babble and then confused dissension. Guy looked back. All around, the Null were coming over the outer walls in a constant stream, like boiled milk scaling the lip of a pan. And now that the invaders had discovered a remaining knot of opposition they were starting to pay it attention. In ones and twos Null were moving in their direction to join the skirmish on the bridge. Coming ever nearer, the music of chimes and men's grunts mixed was close enough to raise Guy's neck hairs.

'J-j-just open the door, if you'd be so kind . . .'

'Locked!'

A clear-enough one word response, cloaked in an humble accent; not one up to making such decisions.

Guy cleared his throat and composed himself. The end was not to be feared *as such*; certainly not for a believer. However, insofar as its earthly preface was a play put on for posterity, then an undignified exit was a horror beyond all dreading – something that might negate in memory all the hard work put in before. *Oh yes , he may well have been a brave warrior till then, but the executioner had to chase him all round the scaffold!* That sort of thing could last centuries and blight the life of a clan.

Bearing it in mind, Guy *stamped* on his stutter.

'Open-the-door-or-you-will-be-even-sorrier-than-me!'

He pressed one ear to the wood. It served to muffle the losing struggle right behind him and might make him better informed as to the unseen debate.

Guy thought he heard Sir Samuel's voice; distant, unraised; insufficiently involved.

Guy's defenders were being pushed right back, to the point of cramping his style. Within seconds he'd have to beware of an accidental axe backswing to the brain. Null were under and around the bridge, tearing at its beams in their zeal,

379

trampling each other down into the ditch in all-against-all fury for prime position.

Then came Bathie's voice, he was convinced of it: first protesting, then curtailed.

Hunter, by contrast, was all too crystal clear, right beside him.

'Now might be a *really* good time to go in . . .' he said, redundantly. People were bumping into Guy's back.

From beyond the wood came two retorts in quick succession: the first gunfire, the second a shooting of bolts. The door swung inward like the gates of Paradise.

Guy and co. fell through with little time to note the scene. There were familiar faces there, not all in familiar condition. More pressingly, Null entered in with them. They had priority even over hello's and thank-you's.

Guy turned back to the situation-of-little-relish and jab-jab-jabbed with his sword like a schoolgirl at a hated sampler. He got scratched but also struck home. One purple gate-crasher went down to him, another was felled by someone else's pistol discharged right up its nose. People perished under flailing claws but, for once, there were more of them and Man had the whip hand. Eventually, the last Null intruder was crushed as the door was closed on him and in his friends' faces, heaved unanswerably back into the socket by many willing hands. The bolts were hammered home, the bar lowered and suddenly the Null were 'just' an impotent symphony on the far side.

Bathie was tearing cloth from a dead man, doubtless to dab Guy's minor wounds. Extrapolating that sight back, from position and expression, he also met the shamefaced huscarl who'd been pinioning her right until the door opened.

Blades was there as well and Sir Samuel at his feet, unmoving. The god-king nodded to Guy and smiled, raising a pistol aloft. He scented it like a finger returned from intimacy.

'I'd forgotten,' he told the company, 'how *sweet* is the smell of powder in a cause that is righteous.' He thought on. 'In fact, I had forgotten many things that are good . . .'

380

'*He* brought you in,' Bathie whispered to Guy as she worked on him. 'Sir Samuel refused.'

His tandem gift and withdrawal of life ought to have caused a tricky moment, for Musket was the garrison's long-standing master and Blades merely just returned and dubious. Yet right now he looked so lordly and like the *Blades-Bible* picture, that no one spoke the vital first word which might unleash dissent. One commander was gone, the new one stood over him. The succession was so swift and seamless that it was easier just to concur.

Guy quickly added his own few stitches to the join.

'Whatever's loose,' he ordered to all, 'jam against the door. Including *that*.' He indicated the late Sir Samuel, whose sturdy frame could still make one last contribution. 'And bring that.' One long finger flicked at the ammunition box-cum-coffin containing Oglethorpe. 'Then come aloft.'

He recalled himself and bowed at Blades.

'That is,' he said, 'with your indulgence, Lord . . .'

The settling nicely into his role god-king waved a permissive hand.

'Day-to-day stuff, dear Ambassador. We shall be guided by you.'

Then the hammering on the door definitively drowned out all hope of non-shouted conversation and Guy had to bow his gratitude and wave-convey his directions to ascend.

In the Great Hall there were a few extra men, a cannon and some developments. The place looked just as it had when Guy and Bathie had dined there a lifetime and much good and misfortune before. All the banners hung limp in the drowsy air, even though the far windows were flung open. Guy joined the incongruous but welcome cannon there and looked out over the glittering English Channel.

On this day of non-stop surprises the Null now revealed themselves as apprentices in the boat-making trade. Paddling with what looked like scapula-blades, they had manoeuvred a flotilla of canoes and rafts round to deprive the castle of all hope and empty perspectives. Some of them saw Guy and

381

waved hello – or something.

'So, Ambassador, what now then?'

It was news that Hunter had silently dogged their heels. The question should have given Guy pause: there'd been mere seconds in which to consider all options – but in the present dilemma that sufficed.

'Well,' Guy blithely turned to tell, 'three endings, really. Either God,' he respectfully indicated Blades, 'or rescue,' he flung a thumb back at the sea, 'or glory. More than enough, in fact.'

Hunter thought and concurred.

'Number two I can't influence; the third will do me. I'll go see to it.'

And with that he took himself and his bow away down the stairs and out of sight: an archetypal *don't worry about him till you see him again* safe pair of hands.

'What I suggest we do . . .' said Guy, hoping inspiration would strike before he finished speaking, 'is . . .'

'Sail. Sail!' said a call from above, when Guy had clean forgotten there was anyone higher than them save birds and the Deity. A second of alarm preceded recollection they'd left a lookout up in the eyrie.

There was an undisciplined rush to the gaping windows and unhelpful babble. Guy had to still it to order up a perspective glass. By the time he'd acquired one, everyone had already glimpsed their salvation.

'The *Lady Bridget*. She comes!'

Guy gave up with extending the tube of brass. Following the forest of arms he could plain see the distant ship. Closer inspection would add nothing to the identification.

'Is she due?' He directed his question to the most restrained and sensible seeming. Unconfined joy was massively premature just yet.

'No' said a huscarl, who spoke calmly and thus with authority. 'Not for weeks. She must have seen.'

The alternating flag-signal and flames had presumably done the trick – or at least the easiest half of it.

'Whose eyes are keenest? Is she incoming?'

All peered and the answer was silently spoon-fed them in the perceptible nearing of those blowsy sails. Under the benison of the noonday sun they looked silken, or so Guy's pleased eyes were willing to interpret.

'If she's coming, she'll be here soon,' said someone.

'*If.*' The douse of cold water was Bathie's.

'*A?*' A multiple exclamation; mostly from the lower, less controlled, non-huscarl elements. They couldn't bear to have hope raised and then butted back down.

She had no mercy. 'I'll tell you. What they'll see is a castle festooned with Null. They'll assume us fallen, save maybe a last survivor on the roof. Nothing worth the risk of setting ashore for anyway.'

Guy saw her point and was glad for its airing. He had some ideas for a remedy but they were somewhat . . . bold. A pessimistic assessment of staying put was grist to his mill, serving to inspire waverers to quit this safe-seeming shell of stone.

'Also, they won't be the first to arrive.'

That was Mrs Ambassador again, rather over-egging it to her husband's mind. The opus for claws-and-wood from downstairs and the wild chimes all around didn't require interpretation. They were secure for the moment. The roof was sealed save for the eyrie's stairs, and they could expel any strays spidering up as far as the windows. This wasn't what Guy was looking for. Desperate men, yes, but despairing ones, no. He creased his brow at her.

She replied in kind.

'No, not *them*,' came explanation. '*Him!*'

Guy span on his heels, reproaching himself for the under-estimation.

Blades was backed against a wall by the great fireplace, clutching at his chest in an attack of the horrors. He found Guy's eyes with his own widened versions.

'Something,' he stuttered out, 'is seeking me!'

Bathie straightened her back, quizzing the hall's upper air.

'Help?' suggested Guy.

'Harm,' she corrected. '*Harm* has found him.'

As much in the interests of keeping them occupied and coherent as correct perceptions, Guy ordered the window cannon reversed and readied. Some boggled but enough obeyed: the Ambassador had sword to hand and swords in his eyes.

Then the *something* arrived. The angel was preceded by the scent of roses, pleasant to start with but rapidly cloying. The displacement of her actual presence pressed that sickly smell to the outermost limits of the room and many of those present to their knees.

'*Dear*-ly beloved . . .' she/it said to Blades.

'No, no. Please . . .'

He shrank further against the voluptuous plasterwork and then, worse still, to Guy's disbelieving disgust, crossed himself. Once again, the Ambassador felt the foundations shift, prey to yet more contradictory signals: another ice dagger to his heart.

The angelic smile seemed wider than the visage strictly should have room for. It wrapped around and invaded adjacent spaces. She loomed and beamed over the little people.

'We seek you. Seek seek seek you. We wish you joy and the sharing of love.' A slight furtiveness intruded on the angel face. Golden eyes flicked nervously side to side. 'No, *no*. The mad woman misleads. We intend no "*harm*"!'

Unlike Guy Ambassador. He did. He applied a glowing match to the cannon's touchhole and all the world seemed superseded by noise and smoke.

When the air and his ears and head had cleared a little, Guy looked to see. The cannon had recoiled against the exterior wall and bulged it outward, expelling jagged spears of window glass. In front, the shot had ruined Palette-Jenkins' pictorial masterpiece hanging at the further end. A blackened hole now made the face of the painted *Blades-in-glory* properly and piously invisible. All the objects in-between had suffered far worse.

384

Guy had winged an unlucky huscarl, for which he was truly sorry, since the limit of his malice had been the angel in the way. Otherwise, he'd had his way. Of course, it was too much to hope for that the visitor had been killed, but the violent dispersal of its atoms might take a while in reversing.

The angel remains, though fragmentary and messy, were still all of her. She sighed from each separated part as they began to inch together.

The molten voice was from everywhere and nowhere. It had the stage to itself amidst everyone else's state of shock.

'I should have *thought*,' screamed her voice – if a scream can also be omnipresent whisper, 'an insect time-dweller would have been . . . wiser than *that*.'

Guy's reply was as stout as his stance. He could afford it. He had his theory to test and little to lose.

'This *t-time-dweller* tires of caution and of you. He has few enough days and wants them free of your k-k-kind!'

Perhaps it was because the angel was still fragmentary in this specific set of nodes that Guy was not simply swept away. Or possibly he was still around in order to chase some correct conclusions.

'This creature is yours,' the angel told Blades. 'Rebuke it.'

Suddenly the rebellion was doubled in strength. Blades stiffened.

'No. He did well.'

'He did. My oath, he did!' Bathie's inconsequential support was added. Even some huscarls murmured.

'Rebuke him. Or be punished!'

'*I* think,' said Guy, his sword levelled at the angelic pieces, 'That you *can't* h-h-harm our Lord Blades . . .'

A second and pristine angel arrived and replied.

'Why should they wish to? His path is their path. The wrong path.'

'The right one,' she was corrected by her identical – in better moments – sister.

'And what of *our* path?' asked Guy. 'Doesn't that bear any mention?'

Apparently not. His question was crushingly ignored. But neither was *he* crushed, for all he fumed.

'Curate Blades once again flees from the Holy Spirit.' The latest arrival spoke on, honey-toned, as though nothing had been said. Her fingers illustrated, mimicking panic-stricken little steps. 'A poor and sorry man . . .'

Blades turned on her too.

'That's just what I'm *not*. No longer. I *repent* of repenting!'

'Beware,' said both angels, with one voice. 'Our indulgence is not infinite.'

'Oh . . .' That disconcerted him. Two steps forward, one step back.

'And ours?' asked Guy. 'How long do you reckon you can grind your heel on us?'

He didn't wait for an answer. Guy hit the second angel with his sword and it traversed less than nothing to carve off an arm and a great sliver of stellar-scintillating shoulder besides. The spectators couldn't countermand their eyes from glimpsing an infinite star-scape within.

The angel gave a great shudder and studied its loss – and flared, raising its remaining arm to chastise Guy. The dwarfed human couldn't help but flinch – only to cringe beneath an aborted blow.

The angels, both part and – comparatively – whole, looked at one another; each negating the other's desire. Despite the threat, it seemed that when acting in concert, both Guy and Blades could dare and win.

They dared some more, advancing.

'*Sinner!*' warned the arm-less one. 'Wretch. It was I who whispered your name to the Wessex-king. We put you on the path!'

'Ahhh . . .' said the piecemeal angel, learning something new.

'I didn't ask for it,' replied Guy. 'Or any other twitches on the puppet strings.'

'I . . .'

'I . . .'

386

'*We* – we watched over you!'

'For long enough, peeping toms!' Blades ordered. 'So now begone!' He pointed the way, any way.

The angels looked on with disdain – but also recoiled before him. In some ineffable way, they had become less than this shaven monkey.

'We must . . . consider this.' Their tone was magisterial but false. 'Your protection is withdrawn,' they added in petulant conclusion – and withdrew.

So there it was. In the end all that was needed was to step boldly across the line and have *faith*. The existence of miracle-working mages should have taught Man that long ago. With faith he could move mountains – and angels.

Silence fell in a hall filled to capacity with thinking. Even the Null clamour outside seemed remote. It was a while before any mortal moved. Eventually, Guy cleared his throat.

After liberating humanity, both the chosen ones had a rapt audience for whatever they cared to say. It was mere anticlimax for Guy to expound his wild proposals. Then everyone trooped out to charge straight into the heart of the Null.

They couldn't find Hunter and so had to leave him; which was both a shame and just as well.

He saw them go, a little group plunging down the walkway to the quay and would have cheered them on, save that that would give the game away. For the time being he was snug and smug and tucked away alone. A barricade of furniture would deter any nosey conquering Null poking about in the Castle's obscurer rooms. Solitude was ensured long enough for his needs.

For the time being Hunter had some peace and quiet in which to pray. He also had a roof over his head and a nice view and a purpose. Right at the very end of it, he'd gotten all he'd ever asked of life.

'*If* you don't mind.'

Guy both did and didn't. On the one hand it was wonderful god-king type behaviour to issue first into danger. On the other, Guy knew what was on the far side of the door.

Blades's fingertips were light upon his chest but implacable. Guy gave way. They all did.

Blades studied the wood in his way.

'We have a door problem . . .' he announced, as imperious as you like, and huscarls jumped to shoot the final bolt.

Glorious day was a shock to their eyes, just as much as their issuing out was to the enemy. These Null thought all the action was round the front at the splintering gate. The Null-King himself was waiting there, poised to enter in like a conquering hero and then *dine*.

Thus, only a token scattering of monsterdom lolled on the quay, basking in the light and amusing themselves in their inimitable way. That amusement faltered for a while to see the postern gate swing open, and they froze in mid-step or thrust.

The expected caustic hail of *fire-stick* spit didn't come. Instead stepped out a mere *meat*: old stringy *meat* at that, albeit draped in cloth-of-gold. The Null smiled.

Blades stepped out of the shadows alone. His meeters and greeters drew closer.

'Good morning, *crow-bait*. Now, *ut*. Ut. Out of my road!'

One of the Null-elders present, the designated calming influence on the troop, stopped in his tracks. All the breath in him was expelled through razor teeth. He pointed with trembling hand. He *recognised* – as much by bearing as description.

Amongst the *perfect-breed* there were sagas: tales of the misty time before the hearer was born and all became clear. Common amongst them were stories of the *Great Foe*; he who had ripped perfection and ravished the lovely days of innocence. The fun of the hunt had drained away through him. Worst of *meat*: evil influence and enemy of Mother-Sky. Now he had stepped out of the sagas and was here, and back, and real!

The old Null pointed and hissed and spoke – and fell back. The others heard and copied.

Blades advanced, lip curled; merely disgusted to see them. Here were slugs in his path and he would be obliged to tread on them to pass. It was a chore, a touch demeaning perhaps, but in no way a *problem*.

The ancient enemy of the Null walked amongst them and froze their bowels. They stood like statues, wrestling with their eyes but unable to *force* them round to meet his gaze. He passed safely under arms that might have pulped his skull and they were as nothing to him. *Blades Null-Bane* had a ship to catch and that was that.

It was long enough for Guy's purpose. He could push men through the narrow door and get bullets into those frozen guts. He'd always found musketry to be a marvellous lubricant and, true to form, the gold and purple tableaux now became a shade more animated.

Now that angels *wouldn't*, Guy was the one obliged to rescue Blades from any danger. He piled in like a whirligig of swords and Bathie assisted by shooting Null who dared to near the oblivious god-king. Meanwhile, the huscarls did their stuff, chopping a track through the mauve jungle.

When they saw they were – after hesitation, for there was no precise word for it in their tongue – *losing*, the Null called out their distress. Those who could, before axe fell or gun spoke, chimed of the great misfortune that had come back to haunt them. No longer a tale around the feast-circle, *he* was here.

The Null in the blockading boats woke and rose and took up the song. Guy heard echoes of it travelling around the siege line. In a spasm of pique he shot the loudest singer audible to him, even though there were other Null who were more pressing problems. Fate smiled on him however, and huscarls

389

were on hand to deal with those.

Then, for a little space, they had the sunny quay, still reassuringly fish-and-boat rather than Null perfumed, to themselves. Using the Castellan's great round of keys (Sir Samuel no longer having need of it) Guy locked the postern gate from the outside. That would puzzle the pounding feet he could hear even now, heading along the Castle corridors towards them.

So, New-Dieppe was fallen, and with it half of humanity's overseas possessions. A sad little foothold it had been, true, but also all they could claim in continental Europe. Now Guy was leading its whipped survivors home to an 'Empire' comprising just Wessex and the brimstone-fields of Sicily, with only a toy Emperor to rule over it. The Null had booted them out with contemptuous ease and all the wounds he'd inflicted on them, though wept over, were only pinpricks in the greater scheme of things. Once they'd devised the means, the infuriated Null would be across the sea to deal with the last *meat* enclave and finish the war he'd started.

That was one perspective. Another made Guy seize the *Long Man* banner of New-Wessex from its huscarl guardian, and wave it in an exuberance of glee. Either the *Lady Bridget* would see their little demonstration or she wouldn't. Whichever way, they were going out with flying colours.

They – no, why not say it? – *he* had done what he should and risked much to fetch back the true faith. Its epitome was beside him now and, should they ever return, no mere *Blades XXIII* could oppose the first and best and truest of that name. Guy had served his people. Though they didn't know it yet and slept in their beds or ploughed their fields unaware, he, Guy Ambassador, had given New-Wessex back its soul.

He'd also had Bathie and met Oglethorpe and burnt Paris and smiled over more dead Null mothers than any man before. Just when it might seem like the sea of humanity was at low ebb, Guy sensed the tide was turning. He could feel its storm-level strength at his back, forcing him forward.

As if to prove it, the *Lady Bridget* showed she'd seen the flag

– or something. Her fore-gun fired and blew one of the Null craft to matchwood. Its previous occupants failed to surface, save as colouring.

She was hard in and oncoming, committed beyond any doubt now. Some of the soldiers cheered, only to be drowned out by Null rage.

Part of the blockade paddled for the quay, though whether told to or in the grip of their own powerful emotions, wasn't clear. Another portion steered for the *Bridget*, like ants round a scorpion, whilst the rest maintained the line. With reinforcements imminent from inside the fallen *meat*-nest, the master-race thought they had all approaches covered.

Strangely enough and most unlike them, the *meat* seemed just as determined and committed. They came forward to greet the Null with every sign of enthusiasm. This wasn't playing the game at all: some paddle strokes were missed.

One row-boat had been left tied to the quay, surplus to Null requirements or shunned as *meat*-work, but a gorgeous vision to fellow *meat*. They took and filled it and heaved off with zeal, heading not for rescue but the thick of the Null. Here was a new spirit – and Blades stood at the boat's prow, brandishing the Long Man banner he'd liberated from Guy, to personify it.

Those Null craft which hoved in to the quay were met with equal conviction. Not a few were boarded and borrowed and turned against their own side. Sometimes one side prevailed, sometimes the other. Several huscarls' final act was to bury their great axe through the bottom of a boat they could not steal, and even that was a victory of sorts. There'd be no pursuit with *that* vessel and its Null crew were marooned ashore.

The monsters also proved to have misjudged the *Lady Bridget*, for she was in the hands of an expert. No longer the slow old supply-dropper of past contemptuous observance, she now offered voluptuous broadside views like a young and lively lady. Her wyvern-headed cannon, run out from under painted ports, raked the waves free of life. The spray filled with wreckage and purple parts.

As the *scop*-bards' songs would later tell it:
'*at the battle of New-Di-eppe, the Brid-get cleared the way!*'

Guy was still on land, with Bathie and a huscarl ring, awaiting a Null boat to be kindly provided him. There were several promising candidates heading his way and he was just *dying* to meet them. However, it turned out to be his turn to freeze, just as Null bowels had frozen when Blades promenaded the quay.

The postern door fell: fell outward and to bits. His Gracious Majesty, the King of Null-Paris strode out and Guy was surprised by his great height, never having seen him not throne-lolling before.

The King raised his skull-club to either accuse or greet Guy, and issued a sound of thrice-distilled hatred that none present had ever heard from Null lips before. Guy twigged that his demise was not likely to be quick or pretty.

His Royal Highness brushed back those who would have taken his place. He strode out like the champion of his species and his shadow, even far off, entirely covered Guy.

The Ambassador squared up to him, the arriving boats, alas and needs be, forgotten. His sword appeared puny, less even than the Null-King's risen prick, unequal to matching the distance between them.

The King strolled slowly, making this a considered pleasure, screened from harm by a honour guard to front and side. All the while his head tilted as though he sought a new angle on this . . . *meat*, this mere *dinner*, who, out of some white jelly in its skull and misplaced fire in its heart, had wrought so much evil. He looked and looked and still could not quite fathom it.

At last he stood before Guy. Then the King knelt and paid him homage, abasing himself upon the ground.

That wasn't through choice but because of the arrow Hunter had put in him. His bow was made of interleaving layers of twangy wood and sinew, tamed to suppleness through long *Wild* use. When pulled to the ear with passion, it could send a powerful message.

This particular missive, a yard long and iron-tipped,

penetrated the back of the regal skull, spent a short while within and then poked its head into the light once more. His Majesty probably didn't even register the transition between life and whatever lay beyond. He sprawled his great length at Guy's feet, slowly subsiding down the length of the arrow's shaft.

Hunter then added insult to injury by depriving him even of the respectful silence which ensued. The *Wild*-man leapt from his high eyrie into the sea below, an involuntary scream escaping the inexperienced diver.

He'd do more than scream if the Null caught him. Many dived into the sea in hot pursuit. The rest gave way to unprecedented lamentation.

It was a choir Guy was well up to coping with at that moment. They could sing their full repertoire ten times over and pain human ears to their heart's content, so long as they didn't bar his way. He turned about and jumped down into the Null ship which had just moored.

Bathie followed, which was as well, for her husband had little save courage left in him. She, by contrast, was positively overflowing with late-arriving potential. A coat of blue sparkling light was cast over the aghast Null crew, imbuing each with a burning ambition to be in the water. Even there though, they weren't saved, for the crackling force only gained in vigour and remained with them till they were crisped.

The few she'd missed, Bathie likewise dealt with, employing an invisible flail. Unseen filaments extended from her fingertips, lacerating those she berated, right down to the white bone. So they left too.

Guy covered her with an empty but hopefully intimidating pistol. Meanwhile, some huscarls joined them – complete with the boxed Oglethorpe, after Guy's reminder – and, inheriting some oars, they soon set to sea. A final diving swipe from a land-stranded Null just missed them. Guy and co.were the last away.

The *Bridget* had come in as close as she dared. Between her and the efforts of the commandeered flotilla which had gone ahead – the good ship Blades not least amongst them – a way was made free. The Ambassador and his wife took it, rejoicing, and collected Hunter along the way. The Null about to nibble at his toe-nails were musketed beneath the waves to put a pleasing seal on the story they'd jointly written. It proved the final close-to phase of the Battle of Dieppe: if also only an interval in an age old war.

On board, Viscount Sea-captain XII, wedded and wyrd-interweaved commander of the sixth successive *Lady Bridget*, was there to welcome them. Legend said that his first known ancestor had been brought to this world by Blades himself and so he all of all people ought to have been able to recognise *the* face. In fact, Guy learnt he'd fairly raced to make the knee and swear allegiance. All things were fitting into place: all – or nearly all – was well.

'Word percolates about,' Sea-captain told the Ambassadorial couple as they climbed the rail, 'like the fishes of the sea. You see shadows and hear things, then you put out your net in hope.' He looked at Blades who was accepting the worship of the crew. 'And just sometimes there's a mighty harvest. Just sometimes . . .'

The guns below were continuing to speak, peppering Dieppe. Great gouts of powdered stone erupted and whole dressed blocks abandoned the cause of the walls. Null went up and then down with them.

Sea-captain, a rascally old salt, mock-jolly but your nemesis if need be, leant close to confide.

'The angels are become a fresh terror in Wessex, you know – and the old god-king falls to silence. The people are dismayed and haven't anyone to turn to. There's riots, the Null trying it on; everything. Me though, I'm made of stubborn stuff. I couldn't credit we'd be left bereft. There's the *promises*, isn't there? So, when I heard of your signals I wondered if it was just more tribulation or something else. I prayed – first time in years. Something said I should go see for myself. Good job I *did*, eh? I mean, answered prayers –

whatever next?'

He turned again to study Blades, not yet quite master of the enormity of it all. Events were moving faster than the tides he was used to.

For his part, Guy's eyes were drawn back to the lost coast. The Null were everywhere, even atop the eyrie, tearing down the flag. They were all over it, like insects overrunning a rival colony. The place, the whole continent was defiled. For the moment at least, it was no place for humans, neither it or the lands beyond. They didn't belong there – for the moment . . .

'*Next?*' he belatedly answered the Captain, with laughter in his voice. 'Why, *home*, of course. Where else? And in t-t-triumph!'

Blades heard and he laughed too, confirming the order.

Then as Sea-captain silenced the guns and turned the *Lady Bridget* about, Blades summoned Guy and Bathie to join him at the prow, right behind the buxom figurehead.

He directed their eye-of-faith attention to the distant Wessex coastline.

'Your Lord thanks you,' he said. 'As does all mankind. Believe that we shall never *cease* to thank you. There will be great days again: and great things. That much I promise.'

And they believed him.

Guy and Bathie and Blades all stood up *straight*, stiffened by the breeze admittedly, but mostly through their own effort: the first of their race to really do so for centuries.

The wind, both southerly and historical, was behind them. The *Lady Bridget* sped on. England – *United England* to-be – became a dark ribbon on the horizon.

The vanguard of the species was now ready. Their thoughts and spirits had been refined in the fire. All was prepared. Soon they would be home, each in their own way to inherit the kingdom.

AN EPILOGUE – AND NEW BEGINNING

It was surprisingly long after that King Guy I found the time and inclination to fulfil his vow. In all fairness, there'd been a lot of distractions in the intervening years, along with some remarkable changes of mind.

By now, Oglethorpe's bones were suitably sparkling white and, tied with a black bow, handily portable in a rucksack. They'd been a reproach to Guy, sitting there with all the other objects on a 'pending' table, every time he passed them outside New-Godalming's Council Chamber.

Bathie had said nothing, although that also *meant* nothing, for she was increasingly quiet of late, what with all the problems, inside and out. Guy liked to delude himself such reticence might be a measure of her contentment but, either way, he could still sense even a unspoken embryo of criticism from that quarter. He'd caught her looking at the skull one day and then *almost*, before she restrained herself, turning round to look at *him*.

That did it, and Oglethorpe's homecoming soared up the priority list. Guy made enquiries: of rustics and apothecaries and coiners alike.

The pink portal was still there, according to the happy and prosperous yeomanry settled thereabouts. It appeared only fitfully they said, but when it did, his Majesty might be assured they were there to pay respects and leave flowers and first-fruits. They were properly grateful folk.

Guy didn't doubt it or their word: staunch mortar of society that they were. He likewise was confident it would come again in the cause of righteousness. It was that kind of portal: not one opened by the dark angel faction for their tormenting amusement, but more likely by the other variety: just as meddling but more tolerable. Alternatively, it was the thought construct of a infinitely more acceptable source. If that were so he need have no fear.

And so it proved. When King Guy went to keep his word, kept company by a glittering entourage, the pink portal was there waiting for him.

Guy found himself rather fancying a reunion and now wondered what had detained him so long. The answer to that, of course, was rooted in the glee with which he greeted any diversion. After all the traumas and (dear, departed, Nicolo's favourite word) *dramas* of the angel wars, he deserved a little holiday – even if it were a mystery tour.

Straightaway, Guy perceived it as a *good* place. Indeed, save for the glow of pink, it was barely recognisable. The *Wild* was tamed, the land restored to stone-cold sobriety. All the titan-butterflies were shot down or flown away; the Tomfools humanely housed. If a tree should brush against you it was through ill-fortune rather than ill-intent. Guy felt justifiably proud of that. Here served as an epitome of his achievement.

It was through here mankind had snatched back some or other salvation. Here, he and Bathie had come together. The gateway felt like his now, his by possession – just as it had been the occasion of possession. He trusted it more than the sister portal he now knew resided in New-Godalming Cathedral's Holy of Holies. That was Blades- and angel-tainted and might lead only to perdition. Here, Guy the betting-man felt able to try his luck backed up by cautious optimism.

Just in case though, he paused and kneeled and crossed himself, commending his soul to the one-and-Christian God that seemed increasingly inescapable. Though Guy never ran nowadays, he was pursued. Everywhere he went, and in all his thoughts, he heard a certain pair of footsteps patiently keeping pace. He needed only to turn and . . .

Guy plunged in. The scene had changed, the sunshine moderated from last time. He came through a wall in a street as before, but here was more brick and tile and long-peace and thus money. The street was even cobbled.

He'd dressed down for the trip, leaving off his habitual green and gold glory, but even so the passers-by noted him. He saw that his hat was more . . . ambitious than theirs, his shoes more exuberantly pointed. Still, it was a happy sign that several people doffed their headgear at him and said 'good morning' in almost-English. Unbeknownst to them, they received a royal bow in return.

Suddenly, two thoughts occurred to Guy. One: that he might be here a lot less longer than envisaged, and secondly: that his mission had approval from on high. Back in Imperial New-Godalming, he'd pondered on how he was to get from *Capri* to the Godalming Oglethorpe referred to. There were sketchy instructions in his farewell letter but Guy saw no way round hiring an intelligible guide, chartering or stealing a ship and then braving unknown oceans to find this *England*. He'd accordingly brought a deal of treasure with him; unstamped *Gold Guy* blanks, as well as the more . . . tampered-with coinage Oglethorpe had specified. Now Guy strongly suspected the portal's further end had moved on in accordance with someone whose wishes were law.

Even so, it still required a wealth of faith to make the fact stay down. This humble place and the metropolis Guy ruled might share a name but there seemed precious little other connection. He looked and looked but scepticism's song remained stronger. Those enfolding wooded hills, those timbered dwellings, could *they* be the originals for the pleasure palaces and marble he knew? He had Blades's word on it – but that didn't necessarily conclude things nowadays. Oglethorpe's seconding of the motion was required to clinch it. At length, Guy accepted the implausible gift-horse and walked the homely streets in wonder.

King Guy looked at the passers-by, assessing whether they might *bite* him if he tried to converse. He had a revolver to hand, naturally, but something in these broad, knobbly, faces told him it would not be required. He chose one, more or less at random, even though his selection was visibly armed.

'Excuse me – yes, you. Could you tell me something, please?'

His stuttering days were over – like many other things.

The old man stowed saw and hammer underarm. He

puzzled over what had been said before finally deciphering it.

'Depends what it is, friend. And what accent is that when it's at home?'

'I-am-from-America.' Oglethorpe had told him to say that. It granted, he said in his instructions, a magic password to excuse all kinds of outlandishness.

'Oh . . . Well then, welcome, I suppose. What is you want to know?'

Guy didn't want to be too pedestrian after being offered the huge shortcut. He went for the jugular.

'Could you please confirm that this is Godalming – in the land of Eng-land?'

The old man expelled the air out of his nose and, looking from one end of the High Street to the other, from Market Hall to River Wey, serially clubbed down all the smart remarks that occurred to him. This stranger couldn't help it. He came from a land of log-houses, bears and scalpers. All this civilisation was probably a bit of a shock.

So he settled for a simple '*yes*.'

'I am obliged. And could you now please direct me to the office of a Mr Fry?'

That got a frown. 'Him – *that* land-pirate? What d'you want a lawyer for? The law's only for Normans and lickspittles!'

Guy was both wary of enthusiasms and a stranger in a strange land besides. He wasn't clear on the usage but had plainly struck a sore point. He lazily selected just any old backing-off excuse.

'I have bedded his wife and now go to apologise to him.'

'Oh. . . . right. I see. Well, he's down that lane there. There's a sign.'

Guy bowed his thanks and moved on, blissfully unaware he'd just met the Great Blades's brother Silas. Likewise, Silas, troubled, puzzled and amused in his heart, watched Guy go, spared awareness he'd brushed by chance of news of his long-lost brother. Life is like that. We stride past the miraculous every day.

The lane was short and the sign plain. Guy put on his gloves before entering in; brushed aside a clerk and soon found his objective.

'Hello. I-am-an-American. Are you Fry-the-lawyer?'

'I have that honour, sir,' said Fry; a large, meaty, man with a plum-pudding rich voice he employed and enjoyed. For some reason though, his imposing bulk failed to impose. Guy, a practised eye in such matters, saw runny weakness within – and went for it.

'Then you can do this.'

He gave him Oglethorpe's letter detailing the required obsequies and headstone.

'It must be . . .' Guy recited meaningless things from rote-memory, 'a *1662 Common Prayer* service. The mourners and bearers must all be poor men who shall dine at the vicarage afterwards – and have a new suit of clothes apiece. The headstone must show this verse.'

Guy handed over a second sheet.

The lawyer read – and snorted. 'By no means. It's pure *treason*, sir!'

Guy showed forth the glint of gold. Its rays dissolved all objections.

'But *well-intentioned*, nevertheless,' added Fry, hurriedly. 'I feel sure I could resolve any prob . . .'

'You will do everything. I must return to . . . America. I shall depend on you that all is performed right.'

'Dear sir,' oiled the lawyer, '*depend* away . . .'

Guy gave him the special gold in its bulging purse.

'And thus you may *depend* on this.'

He could indeed. Though transient and only good for one handling, the poison in which it was dusted would, if well handled, see the man off in a month. And that would be quite long enough – especially at the latter, painful, end.

Guy saw he could rely on man and coin alike. Fry was already counting away, giving the booty a good mauling, the light of love shining in his eyes. Fingers made trips to moist lips to facilitate the task. He didn't even lift his eyes to speak.

'One other thing, Mr . . .?'

'Null.'

'Just one further tiny question, Mr Null. Where *is* the dear deceased?'

Guy landed the knapsack on his desk. The rattle from within told all – or nearly all.

Fry looked from sack to gold and back again till any misgivings shut up.

'I see . . . Um . . . so, Mr Oglethorpe died in foreign climes, did he?'

'To him, yes.'

'In America?'

'The same place as I come from, yes.'

'And please do excuse me asking, but the Justices and Rector will want to know. How did he die?'

Lost in dribbling lust over the root of all evil, Fry hadn't noticed his visitor was almost to the door. For that specific question though, Guy was willing to return and reply.

He slapped his hands flat on the lawyer's desk.

The stranger's eyes were inspired. The puny giant shrank back.

'Well!' Guy told him.

In the brief time left to him, Fry did all that he was asked, and exactly as he was asked – although he was too ill to attend the burial in person.

Thus, a stripped-down Oglethorpe was laid to rest in the land of his fathers. And over him, in due course but ready in time for Fry's few mourners to read and tut-tut at, a stone was laid which read:

Theo. Oglethorpe. Gent.
1682 – it matters not.

LISTEN

To my true king I offered free from stain
Courage and faith; vain faith, and courage vain.
For him, I threw lands, honours, wealth, life, away.
And one dear hope, that was more prized than they.
For him I languished in a foreign clime,
Grey-haired with sorrow in my manhood's prime;
Heard Capri's sirens whisper 'stay . . .'
And pined by the Tiber for my lovelier Wey;
and beholding each night my home in sleep,
Each morning I left that dream to weep;
Till G*d who saw me tried too sorely gave
The resting place I asked: an early grave.
Oh thou, whom chance leads to this poor stone,
From that proud country which was once mine own,
By those cliffs I never more must see,
By that dear language which I spake like thee,
Forget all feuds, and shed one English tear
O'er English dust. A broken heart lies here.

Years later, Thomas Babington Macaulay (1800 – 1859), poet, Whig-historian and Jacobite-bane, found and liked – and copied – it whilst strolling amongst the leaning graves on an idle afternoon. Now that particular family squabble was resolved once and for all, its every passion spent, he thought it permissible to let the vanquished cry a valediction.

After a few civilising amendments, the poet deemed it worthy of a wider audience – and yet was slightly troubled by the matter of attribution. His quill hovered to sign the page many a time but just as frequently found excuse not to. Quite understandably, he couldn't recall its inspirer's odd name, nor, as a busy man with War Office duties to perform and a definitive (if savagely *Whig*) five-volume history of England to complete, could he spare the time for another trip to back-of-beyond Godalming. Some days he thought: '*to hell with it!*' and almost signed. What was done was done, as the verse itself suggested, and it was no use arguing the toss with Madame History. Other times though, his heart was touched and he-happily passed on to other projects. And then, in 1859, he passed on himself.

Hamstrung by honour, his *Epitaph on a Jacobite* had languished in literary limbo until the Grim Reaper called, hotly followed by literary executors. Less aware and less scrupulous than the testator, they read and pounced and published, in the posthumous *Macaulay's Miscellanies* of 1860.

So, through no real fault of Macaulay's own, English literature remembers the verse as *his* work and once the tombstone weathered and fell, there was no way left to correct that. Its manuscript original lay buried for centuries, even deeper than its author, in Fry's archives. Then along came a Land Registry Act to make those redundant and his solicitor-successors had a glorious clear-out and bonfire of ancient deeds. Historians made frenzied appeal to the Law Society's chilly heart and the holocaust was finally curtailed when merely half of England's history had gone up in smoke – alongside Oglethorpe's/Macaulay's poem.

It didn't really matter – as so very little does. For a long while those words were taught in schools. Palgrave printed – and reprinted – them in his *Golden Treasury*. Oglethorpe's spirit lived on.

Meanwhile, the real he looked down and laughed.